GRIMS' TRUTH

BOOK 1: THE SPINNER'S WEB

ARC 1: THE TAINTED

ISU YIN & FAE YANG

THE SPINNER'S WEB
[Grims' Truth – Book 1]
*Copyright © 2017/2020 by Isu Yin & Fae Yang

*SECOND EDITION SOFTCOVER
ISBN: 1622538773
ISBN-13: 978-1-62253-877-5

Editor: Lane Diamond
Cover Artist: Cindy Fan
Interior Designer: Lane Diamond (w/Image Masters by Briana Hertzog)

*Originally released in October 2017 as *Rota Fortunae*, this book has been significantly rewritten, re-edited, and re-released in 2020 under the new title of *The Spinner's Web*.

EVOLVED PUBLISHING™

www.EvolvedPub.com
Evolved Publishing LLC
Butler, Wisconsin, USA

Printed in Book Antiqua font.

For the unusual, the undesired, the unheard, and the unaccepted. Within every soul is a message waiting to be told. Within every world we may hope to find a glimmer of ourselves, and we hope you find the representation you deserve in ours.

TABLE OF CONTENTS

BACK-OF-THE-BOOK EXTRAS:

Reference Guide

Book Club Guide

Interview with the Authors

What's Next from Yin & Yang?

Acknowledgements

About the Authors

More from Evolved Publishing

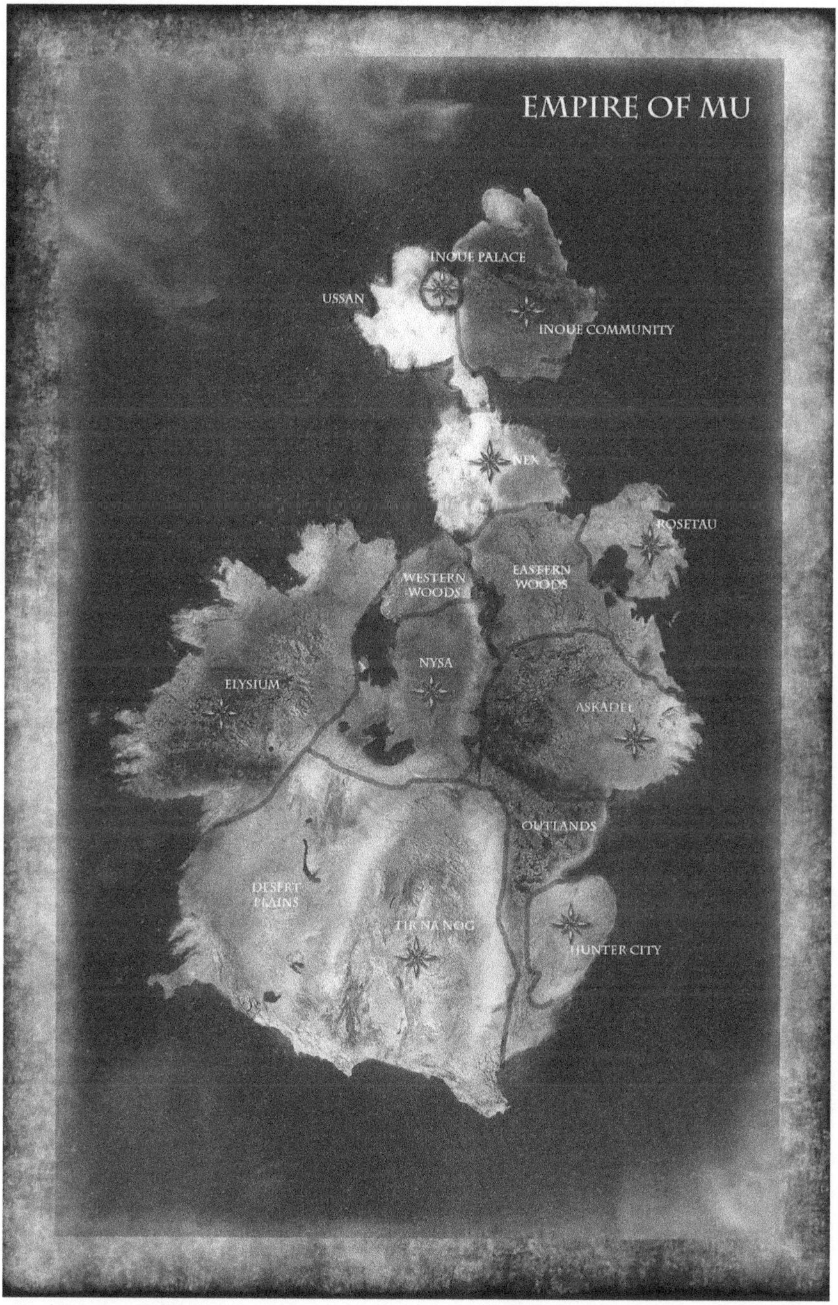

EMPIRE OF MU

INOUE PALACE

USSAN

INOUE COMMUNITY

NEN

ROSETAU

WESTERN WOODS

EASTERN WOODS

ELYSIUM

NYSA

ASKADEL

OUTLANDS

DESERT PLAINS

TIR NA NOG

HUNTER CITY

PROLOGUE

THE SEALING OF THE SPINNER

"Doom often surfaces in the most unlikely places."
The Teachings of Grim, Tablet IV, Line XIII

The faint glow of a candle flickered among the dense shadows, illuminating twelve creaking wooden pillars with dozens of symbols burned into their surface. Each pillar nestled deep between the rock slabs that made up the altar room floor. Up the steps rested a massive stone box, built into the platform. The weighted lid lay askew across the top, revealing the cold, somber cavity below.

A soft crinkling, like that of aged paper, traveled through the darkness. The smell of incense filled the air and mingled with the faint scent of flowers and decay. A slow, frigid chill caught the smoke from the metal censer and carried it over the smooth stones until it crept up to the altar.

Fati lay on the icy floor. Her eyes canvassed the blackened symbols engraved on the pillars and walls, but she failed to comprehend their jagged inscriptions. Disoriented, she attempted to identify the strange, stale room, taking long deep breaths to rouse her clarity. The curious room differed from any place in her recollection, and the tingle in her chest forewarned danger.

Although the shadows masked them, she sensed numerous eyes upon her. Low hums emanated from unseen figures—

chants or incantations. In her confused state, she found it difficult to tell the difference.

Fati attempted to lift her arm and, with the clang of a chain, realized her predicament. She tried again to raise her body, but her muscles complained and fell weak against the restraints. The clank of metal against stone affirmed her imprisonment.

She lay still for a moment, trying to remember how she had come to this place. Images flooded her mind... visions of a field blanketed in white flowers, and a crystal throne against a backdrop of a million stars. These memories led back to a vivid image of golden light strewn across her fingertips — anima, the blood of the Ancients — glowing like starlight; her own blood, no less. The newfound lucidity evoked questions: *How did I get here? What happened to me?* Even with her head adrift in a haze, she quickly grasped the answers. Someone had betrayed her.

She made a moue, unable to form words, for the metal pin forced through her tongue and lower jaw kept her silent. The tag prevented her from calling upon her strength. She felt the sting of the pin piercing through the bottom of her jaw, and the sensations of her aching teeth and of dried blood on her neck. Her throat emitted naught but a furious grunt as she choked on the thick fluid. She directed all of her energy on gaining her freedom, and the connecting chain under her chin rattled. The attached tag pulled at her tongue, tearing at her flesh and muffling her gagging while it drained her life-force. She clenched both fists and resisted the chains, which shook vigorously until her anima waned, her strength depleted, and her body lay limp against the cold stone. The tag stole what little vigor she mustered.

The candle's flame swelled, reflecting in the eyes of an onlooker. She surmised it to be the person responsible for her imprisonment, but lamented their familiarity. Now that she understood who held her captive, her anger grew. Tears stung her cheeks as she painted the image of her captor in her mind. Even if she wished to speak this perpetrator's name, the tag in her mouth prevented it.

A figure in a white robe stepped into the light, extending a long prong with an affixed mask, melded from gold. The metal curved around the bridge of the nose, its grooves forming patterns of flowers that held tiny, red jewels. On the outside, this mask appeared elegant and impressionable, a fallacy she knew better than to believe. On the inside, long metal stakes stuck out from the eyes to blind the wearer in mortal form and, more importantly, in the ethereal realm.

As the robed figure turned the stakes towards Fati, she writhed in protest, but another forced her head still.

Her muffled cries fell upon uncaring ears. In her efforts to avoid watching the approaching stakes, she met the gaze of her captor, who watched on, unfazed.

The chains rattled as she resisted, searing the moment deep into her memory. As the stakes pierced the soft tissue of her eyes, she screeched, her throat burning with the sound of betrayal, and her eyes filled with blood and throbbing beyond compare. The shackles around her wrists dug into her flesh and the tag tore at her jaw as she thrashed. The robed figures removed her bindings, and she clutched the metal forced into her sockets, letting out a garbled moan as she vomited from the agony.

They pried her hands free of the mask, took her by the arms, and dragged her toward the altar.

She staggered after them, tripping up the steps and kicking against her aggressors, but they ignored her screams. They picked her up and tossed her inside the stone box, and her body rocked from the impact, sending a wave of sharp pangs to her extremities. For a moment, she struggled to find her bearings, and felt around the stone walls until she understood where they had put her.

The lid of the box grated, stone against stone, above her. In a final attempt to escape, she reached out and grabbed the edge, pulling against it as she pleaded. Even if they didn't understand her words, she knew they must understand the sound of her pleas.

The robed figures pressed harder against her grip, and the lid continued sliding closed.

Fati cried out to them, her words incomprehensible but desperate for forgiveness — anything to earn her freedom. She wished to fix whatever she had done to deserve this suffering. Her hands trembled as she clung to the edge, hearing stone scrape against stone. Her captors forced the lid shut on her fingers, splitting the skin and crushing the bone. Pain shot down her arms in a furious bolt as she attempted to withdraw her torn and bloodied fingertips. Only then, she realized that her hands were trapped, smashed into the crevice between the dense slabs of stone, and she expelled a deafening howl. Yet even with her bleeding, stabbing fingertips, her heart ached most of all.

She had done nothing but what her master asked of her, to watch over the fate of the Mortal Realms. Her cries brought no comfort, though, and only served to quicken her descent into darkness. Thoughts and questions riddled her mind, slowly spiraling her into oblivion as she waited for an answer that never came. Alone, she waited in the pitch-black prison, knowing only the agonizing pain of her mortal form and the icy embrace of the darkness.

No sound penetrated the walls of her prison. No sign of life reached into her from the outside. It left her alone to wallow in her thoughts and condemn her imprisoner. She fell into despair as she feared for her Bound, her one true friend. Her soul warped and crumbled with her pain, and she slowly lost what former glory and grace she once held.

In time, the world seemed as dark as her prison and became twisted with resentment—not even the wrenching agony in her stomach from starvation, the steady pounding in her skull from lack of water, her bloodied and blinded eyes, or her mangled and dying fingers, compared to the fury she felt. Her captor may attempt to escape judgment, but, eventually, all things circled back. The harrowing wail in her soul grew deafening, and she swore the greatest of all calamities to befall her tormentor. Alone, she wept, overcome by pain, fear, and hatred.

I will escape from my cage... and when I do, you will suffer divine retribution for your crimes.

As time dragged on, Fati immersed herself in the darkness. She rocked back and forth inside her box, tugging against her rigid arms and decaying fingers, humming to herself until the words of an incantation echoed in her thoughts.

> *Spinning, spinning wheel of fate,*
> *Which one shall you choose?*
> *A sinner from the shadows,*
> *Shall you win or shall you lose?*
> *Turning, turning wheel of fate,*
> *The spokes are slowing down.*
> *Hush, the demon's dance is ending,*
> *Don't you make a sound.*
> *Stopping, stopping wheel of fate,*
> *She tiptoes through the crowd.*
> *If you hear her whisper,*
> *You are Fated now.*

1

KINGDOM COME

Fate sat at the wide balcony of the palace, her burdens making her feel much heavier than her petite stature. She peered through the balusters at the marketplace, long tresses of her black hair dancing in the draft from below. Her red gown swirled about her legs, ebbing and flowing with the breeze. Everything but the fabric appeared grey and lifeless. Even the setting sun strained against the ashen clouds and sank towards the horizon in defeat. She gazed down at the once-united kingdom, now divided by a massive stone wall. It reminded her of a broken clock — all of the cogs were accounted for but one, rendering it useless. She tried many times to find her place within the kingdom, but ultimately resigned herself to the same spot to contemplate the riddle. Though she doubted it, her father told her daily that she carried more beauty and charm than any other, and that neither he nor the people expected any more of a princess. Yet, deep down, she yearned to serve a greater purpose.

It called to her. She wanted to be a shining light amongst the bleak surroundings. Her soul contained more power than her small form seemed capable of accommodating. She gritted her teeth desperate to prove it, but it all seemed so far away.

Everything in Macellarius appeared disheveled to her from that height — from the clustered columns and pointed arches, to the dirty streets below, and even the looming haze that constantly cloaked their city. It appeared to her that the kingdom had fallen victim to apathy — each person caring only for their own well-being or advancement—and all the while they forced her to witness their continued self-destruction from the confines of her drab cage. A small pit formed in her stomach, as it often did when she stood at her perch taking in the tragic view.

The same as every morning, she observed while scruffy vendors with tattered carts tried selling expired wares to the poor. The kingdom suffered from a fatal sickness as she watched on, helpless. Try as she might, a child, even an Ancient one, held no weight of authority.

In spite of her tender age of seven, Fate already understood the struggles of her people and suffered quietly for them. Most Ancients like her took little time to contemplate the lesser beings, but Fate's overwhelming impulse to aid them consumed most of her thoughts. Something about the Rahma made her sad. Perhaps it was how much shorter their life spans were compared to that of the Ancients. For every twenty-five tahrun of their lives, the Ancients aged only one turn. Thus, the seven-turn-old, who had only lived in the palace for two of her turns, had spent fifty Rahma summers and winters viewing the endless and deteriorating predicament unfolding outside her Macellarius Palace.

She took little comfort that their proximity to the Ancients extended their meager lives. A Rahma in her presence may earn an extra few hundred turns of life but.... *To what end?* She sighed. If their lives meant nothing but hardship and struggle, the extra turns seemed more of a punishment than a reward. In many ways, she identified with the Rahma, for they too lived lives over which they had little control.

She studied her pale fingers, feeling detached from her own form. Her existence in the palace had left her with two odd, glaring questions: *What happened during the first five turns of my life? Where did those memories go?*

She asked herself the same questions every day without fail, feeling an odd compulsion to solve the riddle, because she feared the answers held more than ends to her menial questions.

The only clues lay with her oldest memories of a glowing white forest. The chiming sound the trees made still echoed in her ears. She felt certain that the trees sang to her, and even heard them speak, but the specifics beyond that had vanished like a whisper in the wind. All it told her had dissipated long ago, leaving her mind with little to grasp, her soul empty, and a burning curiosity about whether or not the experience had even been real.

She watched her subjects from afar until the sun hung low in the sky, and then heaved herself from the balcony. Upon entering the sunroom, she ran her finger across the dusty doorframe and glanced around with a pout. It seemed silly to refer to such a drab and murky place as a "sunroom." Macellarius held no light save her dear brother.

She saw no point in lingering any longer to wallow in confusion and despair.

Fate meandered through the palace hallways, dodging bustling servants as they decorated for her birthday party. They strung tiny white lights through each room to cast away shadows.

She observed them as they worked, wondering why the Rahma feared darkness so completely. Whenever given the opportunity, they added lights. Many of them kept a lamp on throughout the night. It troubled her that she found comfort in what they feared. With a heavy sigh, she resigned to the possibility that she may never find common ground with them.

A hand brushed against hers, and after the momentary surprise, her soul eased and a familiar sensation of peace washed over her. She turned her head and gazed into her brother's violet eyes, so alike her own and yet so much livelier.

She smacked him with her free hand. "Abyssus!"

He commemorated her. "Happy birthday." Despite the fact that they were twins, he towered over her. Beyond that, his spirit shined far brighter, on both the outside and the inside, a fact that often distressed her.

"You scared me."

He scratched the back of his neck with a guilty grin. "Means you were thinking something you shouldn't be."

Fate rolled her eyes. She adored her brother but not his implications. "I was watching them set up the lights."

"You should see the garden. It's extraordinary, really. Come with me."

Her brother brought joy to the void inside of her. His smile comforted her unlike anything or anyone else. She'd questioned herself many times on the matter. In the end, she decided it *didn't* matter. Abyssus alone kept her grounded, and she felt eternally thankful for the peace he provided. "Okay."

He tugged her by the hand and led her through the hallway, past the flat grey walls and lackluster portraits of the Cruentus Family. The paintings themselves required some skill, with their adept detailing and strokes of the hair, skin, and eyes, but something about the dull paint and the vacant expressions unsettled her every time she walked by.

Abyssus glanced at the paintings as if sensing her brooding. "We should put a painting of me and you up there to brighten up this hallway."

She shook her head with a smile. No amount of dreary surroundings seemed to dim the light within him. He radiated life and energy, a quality she found curious.

He trudged on, undaunted by the gloom that held them captive. With a quick flick of his hand, a small burst of darkness spun before her. It whirled about in his palm like ink in water, releasing tiny wisps of black smoke. The slightest hint of blue light wove through the tendrils and swam about, giving the dark ball a life as it reflected off his hand.

She waved it away, drawing her mouth to one side. "You'd better stop that or someone will see you."

"Come on," he said with a slight smirk and shoulder shrug. "Cheer up. It's fun. You know you like it."

She smirked back. "True, but... if someone sees you, they'll report it. You are too reckless, brother. Do you want to be erased?"

He frowned, and his face hung heavy with disappointment. For a moment, his gaze showed a hint of something buried, like someone caught in a trance, but he broke free of it and answered. "We are what we are."

Their debate ceased, as neither wished to dampen the other's mood, and they exited the palace's back doors to the garden. There, the lights took center stage. Every tree and shrub glowed with tiny white bulbs. The yard burst with flowers and ribbons. A huge table full of savories, including pastries, sun-dried fruits, and colorful punches stretched along the length of the palace wall.

Fate admired their father's incredible display. She held no fancy for her birthday but enjoyed the liveliness the celebration seemed to stir.

The servants moved around with improved vigor and genuine smiles. Aromas of sweets and delicacies filled the air and mixed with the gentle fragrance of the honeysuckle flowers.

The surrounding splendor helped Fate relax and enjoy what may be the perfect evening.

Abyssus released her hand, dashed into the garden, and across the main lawn, his sights set on a tall, lean young man carrying two hefty tables. He chattered wildly as the man set the tables down.

Fate watched on, checking her abandoned hand, and then folded her arms as the pair talked. Finally, she relented and crossed the garden to her brother's side.

The man stopped his work, leaving one table on its side, and slightly bowed his head to her with a shy smile and a flicker in his amber eyes. "Lady Fate, happy birthday."

She studied the striking young man with scrutiny. He dressed like any other noble on a common day, something she deemed completely inappropriate for a party. She considered him attractive, as most Ignis were, but the simple pants and slightly oversized knit sweater did nothing for his general appearance, and appeared thoroughly opposite of everything she knew about the clan, albeit slight. Somewhere beneath his trodden attire hid a godlike physique and the fiery Ignis charm laced with unmistakable sexuality. She questioned whether he intended the result, to keep him from standing out, perhaps because he lacked confidence. Regardless, the Ignis kept her brother's interest, so she did her best to be kind.

She mustered a cheerful, practiced smile. "Thank you, Firmus. It's good to see you. How is your family?"

With one fluid movement, Firmus swung the table into an upright position and scanned the yard, appearing to search each nook and cranny for something. "Good, I guess." The way the man observed things reminded her much of a prowling cat. He may sometimes look lethargic but when he moved, he moved decisively and with immense strength and speed.

Fate studied the Ignis, examining the clan's distinctive ember-like eyes, dark wavy hair, and tan, freckled skin. A part of her riddled over why other clans avoided such a magnificent clan, so rich of anima. She knew that the answer to her question must be related to the family's buried history. As much as she wished to learn, the documentation lay within the lost Hall of Records, ages old. Now, only the Elders and Igni themselves may ever tell the history. Whatever records remained, the Council kept locked up in the new Hall.

Firmus seemed to be her best chance of finding out some morsel of truth, but his refusal to speak more than a couple words at a time made him difficult to probe.

Abyssus nagged. "Fate, can you just enjoy the day?"

Fate defended. "I didn't say anything."

He gesticulated around his own head. "I can feel your thoughts radiating. They're so intense."

Firmus lowered his head, pretending to adjust the tables.

Fate returned her attention to her brother, crossing her arms with a sour face. "It doesn't bother you that the Council has sealed all records?"

Abyssus placed his hands on his forehead and laughed. "I'll take that as a no."

Firmus twitched uncomfortably as he surveyed the garden. "Honestly, you should keep such curiosities private, Lady."

Fate leaned towards the significantly taller Ignis. "One day, you'll tell me what really happened."

He nodded. "One day, but not today and not here."

She gave a single nod of affirmation before a din of excitement rose, overriding her curiosity.

The servants scattered, picking up any odd job that made them seem busy, leaving only the three youths at the center of the lawn.

Fate knew instantly the reason for the mass departure. The Royal elites arrived before the masses, as per their privilege. Even so, the commotion seemed extreme for such a common occurrence.

At first, a small group exited the palace into the garden. They swarmed and fawned the two people at the center of the cluster — a female wearing a gold hooded cloak that obscured her face, and a kind-looking man, an Iu, as best she could tell by his long black hair and violet eyes. His pale skin appeared to glow against his dark clothing. The fawning around him came as no surprise, considering the Iu clan still held most of the power in Euphoria. They led the two major empires of Euphoria, Mu and Thule. Then, with a parting of the crowd, the frenzy became clear. Both individuals wore Council robes and the emblem of Thule. These two were the elite of the elites, the most powerful in Mu and Thule alike.

Fate watched as they made their way across the lawn, seemingly unaware of her presence. Then, the man turned and made eye contact, and her hands sweated. He represented the

Royal Council—one wrong move on her part and her father would pay the price.

The man shooed his admirers away with a gentle wave, and crossed the lawn with his Council robes flowing behind him. He stopped before her and leaned forward, making a polite bow. "The Council wishes you a happy birthday, Lady."

Fate curtsied with a smile. "Thank you...."

He chuckled. "Yes, I am sorry. That was rude of me. We get so used to everyone just knowing who we are. I am Navarriel."

She pressed her hands together and nervously shook her head. "Oh, no, it's rude for me not to know. Pleasure to meet you."

He smiled with a slight nod, raising his hand to his chest. "No need to apologize, especially on your birthday. I have only come to wish you well."

"Thank you, kindly. I hope your trip was comfortable."

He winked. "It always is. My travel companion, Sisera, can form portals. It is a most convenient way to travel."

Fate ogled the hooded woman. "That's extraordinary."

Sisera turned her head by an inch, revealing long brown locks and honey-colored eyes. With the slightest frown, she studied Fate in a most tentative manner. Her aura differed from Navarriel, pushing others away rather than drawing them in.

Navarriel adjusted his posture, standing even taller and straighter than before. "It is. You are a royal, Lady, and if you wish, one day you may accompany us and travel one yourself. You may even come to see how the Council operates and join our cause."

Her heart fluttered. Receiving acknowledgment from someone so regarded made her feel as though she'd float away. "Really?"

"Truly. Remember, we are here to help should you need it, Lady. I know the people of Mu are not fond of our rules, but I hope that you will learn that we have them in place for a reason."

She looked out at the garden, imagining how her kingdom might differ if under full Council rule. These days, the Rahma gathered around the remaining Ancients like insects around their queen. The disheartening Macellarius proved to her how much the Empire relied on the Ancient people to maintain balance and prosperity within the land. She considered that, perhaps, the Teachings of Thule held some weight.

She said, "I will keep that in mind."

Navarriel bowed once more with a pleasant smile. "I can ask for no more. I bid you a good evening. I am afraid I shall take my leave before the masses arrive. You see, I have never been one for crowds."

Fate curtsied. "I wish you well and thank you for your visit. We will meet again someday, I'm certain."

"As am I." Navarriel turned and made his exit as promised, with his entourage returning to trail behind him.

Firmus huffed once the group left earshot.

Abyssus warily looked at the indignant Ignis. "Shh! Someone will hear you."

Firmus eyed Abyssus with disdain. "Doesn't really matter if they do. The Council does as they please, whether or not we resist."

Fate frowned, trying to understand Firmus's outward disgust. "He seemed agreeable to me."

It surprised her to see Firmus so vocal. Even the temperature rose by a few degrees.

Firmus crossed his arms with a scowl. "Things are often not as they appear, Lady. You should get out of the palace while you can."

Fate shifted, uncomfortable with his unwarranted rage. She wanted to fill the evening with music and laughter.

A sudden ruckus among the crowd informed all present of the Rahma King's arrival. Neco entered the gardens from a side door of the palace. He waved and smiled at his adoring crowd.

Fate waited patiently as her father greeted guests and gradually inspected the preparations.

He moved from the shelter of the palace veranda and walked the length of the dessert table with a crumpled brow. Only when he saw Fate did his expression finally lighten. "My dearest daughter, look at you. You are a vision."

Her father brought an immediate smile to her face. Abyssus's attentions may wane, but her father always treated her as though she was the most important person in the Universe. "Thank you."

Neco approached her with open arms and hugged her.

Abyssus shifted uneasily with a grimace, stuffing his hands into his pockets.

Fate beamed. "It's all so lovely, Father. Thank you."

"Of course, my beautiful girl, this is a momentous occasion for both of us. I would have it no other way."

She looked back at the locked gates, finding the thick iron still barred and heavily guarded. "And the people will be able to join us?"

Neco squinted at the gate, his words delayed. "Oh, of course. It was your birthday wish, after all."

Fate hugged her father again, much to his delight. "I'm so happy."

"Me too. Now, I'm not suggesting you start the festivities, but you may want to start on that table before the rest of the guests arrive." He kissed her forehead and took his leave.

Abyssus glared at his back as he walked away. "Something's not right."

Fate took her brother's hand. "You just say that because you never got along."

The blood left his cheeks as he met her gaze. "Listen to me, there is something wrong. I can feel it. First, the Council comes to your birthday and Father seems happy about it. We both know he should be terrified right now, but he's calm—chipper even. No, this is all unnatural. You don't find it odd that our father is Rahma when we are Ancients?"

Fate felt the pressure rise in her chest. "We've been through this... several times. Why are you doing this again, today of all days? You're the one who told me to enjoy myself."

Abyssus's gaze drifted with his thoughts. "Because it *is* today."

Firmus spoke in a low voice. "He's right. It isn't possible for him to be your father. You are a pure blood, and he is Rahma. He would have only been a boy when you came to be."

The truth hit her like a slap to the face. She knew Neco wasn't her father, but he treated her with the delicate care and adoration of any loving father. "I'm not an idiot. I know he's not our father, but he cared for us as his own. Isn't that enough?"

A look of revulsion flashed across Abyssus's face. "He cared for you—you alone. He didn't even greet me just now. He watches you when you sleep. If you trust me at all, believe what I say."

Fate felt confused by her father's special attention. He had done nothing to betray her trust, so she couldn't understand Abyssus's cryptic warning, but it still resonated inside her.

Several guards entered the garden and opened the gates, allowing a flood of nobles to enter.

Fate moved around the surging crowd, looking for signs of the commoners.

Firmus set a hand on her shoulder as he leaned down and whispered, "If you are looking for your subjects, he lied to you. They were not invited."

Fate pressed a hand over her heart, suffering a pang of betrayal. "He promised...."

Abyssus looked at her, his face full of dread. "When will you wake up? We are in danger here. We need to leave."

Her pulse quickened as the panic rose within her. "And go where?"

Firmus asserted. "Tir Na Nog. We can protect you. Our army rivals that of the Council's."

The world drifted away from Fate and all sound faded, leaving only a hollow ringing in her ears. She sensed their father's scheming but refused to accept it. She wanted to believe that she and Abyssus were safe in Macellarius but, in reality, she knew that no one was. Worse, it hurt her to know that Abyssus had been secretly planning with Firmus instead of speaking with her.

I have only myself to blame.

In the past, she'd resisted his advice, and chose instead to be what she considered the perfect daughter. Her eyes stung as they filled with tears.

The surrounding Royals laughed and conversed without a care in the world, while her subjects starved and suffered just outside the gates. In her dismay, she glimpsed a small girl peering in through the bars. They locked eyes for an instant before the guards chased her away. She unintentionally aided in the prolonged misery of her people.

She hung her head for a moment, then raised it and said, "All right."

Abyssus held his breath with wide eyes. "What?"

A new resolve filled her thoughts. They must escape Macellarius if they wished to uncover the truth. "Let's leave."

A slight smile crossed Firmus's lips, and just as quickly faded as he lightly squeezed Abyssus's arm. "Give me a moment. I'll get you both out of here. Try not to worry. We've been planning for such an occasion for some time now."

"We?"

He hesitated before confiding in her. "Yes. There are quite a few people concerned about your well-being, Lady. We've been working on various ways to get you and Abyssus out safely. Unfortunately, it's been more difficult than we initially thought."

"I see. I will wait for your return. Perhaps, then you'll explain more."

Firmus gave a slight nod. "Of course. Let's just get you both out of here first."

Abyssus glanced around the garden. "I'll collect our things. Fate, stay here. They'll notice if you're gone."

She accepted her brother's proposal even though she felt trapped among the visiting Royals. "I'll wait here for you both."

Fate stood alone in the garden, running her hand up and down her arm as she evaded the gazes of curious nobles. She hoped her brother and Firmus hurried, as it seemed to be an especially bad time for their escape. On this day, she held the most interest for their visitors and her father alike. The guest of honor may be ignored but not unnoticed.

2

A GREAT ESCAPE

Fate's heart pounded heavily in her chest as the wait stretched into eternity. Just as she thought her frayed nerves might snap, another Ignis joined the party, firmly holding both her feet and her attention.

The voluptuous woman captivated the crowd with her gold gown, each bead glittering in the light as she glided through the gates. The guards offered to collect her fur coat and faced pleasant refusal.

In a smoky voice, the woman replied with a gentle caressing of the guard's cheek. "No, thank you. I'd simply perish in this chill."

Fate examined the other nobles, who strutted about in thin silks, before returning her attention to the dazzling woman. When she looked forward again, she found the woman's amber gaze upon her, and it sent a shock through her. It seemed like more than simple curiosity.

The curvaceous young woman sauntered across the lawn with a trail of lusty nobles rambling after her. She briefly flirted and then sent off her admirers to celebrate.

Firmus returned to Fate's side. "We've cleared a way. We just need to...."

Fate followed his line of sight back the other Ignis.

As she approached, she cast a glance at Firmus, her eyes glowing like embers and her crystal earrings gleaming in the lights. Her gaze moved over him slowly as she drifted closer and adjusted his sweater. "Why so rugged? Honestly, what have they done to you? You look like you haven't properly eaten since you left. Isn't that boy taking care of you?"

Firmus shifted, carefully removing her hand from his sweater. "What are you doing here?"

The woman leaned down to take a closer look at Fate, intoxicating her with lusty perfume and exposing a great deal of her ample bosom. "You must be Fate."

Her flaunting astonished Fate, who knew of the Ignis appeal but had never seen such a seductress in person. "Who are you?"

Firmus interjected. "This is my sister, Fortuna."

Fate glanced from one sibling to the other, astounded by the difference in their personalities but accepting the resemblance. "Sister?"

She knew at least the minimum about pure breeds like the Ignis. Those born in pairs typically shared a natural spiritual binding. For this reason, most referred to twins with this special union as Bound—two souls intertwined in every possible way, from their thoughts and feelings, to their pain and death—but these two appeared more different than the sun from the moon.

She hesitated before finally asking, "Are you twins?"

Fortuna patted Firmus on the cheek with a coy sneer. "Triplets, actually."

Fate staggered at the thought. "Is that possible?"

A man's boisterous greeting rang out over the din of the crowd. "Oh, what a surprise!"

The sudden outburst drew Fate's attention, as well as that of the Ignis siblings.

He jumped up and down, forcing his way through the crowd.

Fortuna groaned. "Oh, here he comes."

Firmus explained. "*That* is our brother, Fortis."

The young man finally approached the group, panting and pouncing wildly at Fortuna and Firmus.

Fate struggled to get a good look at him due to his erratic dodging and behavior. When he finally settled down, and she managed to examine him, the similarity was undeniable. She puzzled over her findings aloud. "I've never heard of three before."

Fortis let out a loud chortle with a flip of his hair. "Three of me? Praise be, whatever would the world do?"

He looked so much like Firmus, Fate felt the need to check them twice.

Fortuna elbowed her lively brother in the ribs. She then scanned him from head to toe and pursed her lips. "Look at this fool, so dandy. Firmus, please take some of this bliss for yourself. He has more than enough as it is."

Fate pondered the puzzle before her, trying to fathom what effect triplets might have on their clan, and on the future of Ancients as a whole. The Council always stressed the importance of natural bindings, which seemed impossible for these triplets.

Before she even opened her mouth to ask, a loud crack echoed throughout the garden.

Fortuna turned sharply at the sound, staring long and hard at the old woman who'd made it.

The old woman cracked her cane against the border tiles at the gate, and allowed the clang to echo throughout the garden again.

People stopped their conversations to stare and whisper.

Fate peeked around the triplets to catch a glimpse of the bitter-looking old woman. She dressed in Ancient noble fineries but appeared to be a Rahma, and a haggard one at that.

Fortuna gave a partial curtsy, her voice terse as she dismissed herself. "Excuse me. I have some business to attend to. If you have any of your own, I suggest you attend to it quickly."

Firmus leaned over to Fortis and whispered in his ear.

Fortis's eyes bulged as he looked down at Fate.

Firmus crossed his hand over his chest and bowed. "Lady Fate, I'll leave you in my brother's care while I find out what is keeping yours."

She understood the transaction that had taken place, and her body trembled as she thought of running away. The Ignis triplets seemed trustworthy, but she didn't really know them.

Fortis offered his hand to her. "Lady Fate, if you wish, I would be honored to have your company during this important occasion."

She took his hand and allowed him to lead her to the dessert table. "I'm not particularly hungry."

He looked out over the crowd of nobles while tampering with the bottles of alcohol. "Understandable. It's hard to accept that we are all merely pawns in someone else's game."

She fought her tears. "Is that what you are?"

He looked down at her with a heaviness she felt in her soul. "I am your uncle's personal guard."

She failed to make the connection with his solemn expression. "A noble profession, I would think."

He folded her small hand over his arm and lightly patted it. "I am also a prince of Tir Na Nog."

Her mind reeled as she fit the pieces together. It made no sense for an Ancient, particularly a Royal, to serve mere Rahma, especially not under Council law. *What is happening?* She swallowed hard, unable to comprehend Mu's disarray. "I'm sorry."

"For what?"

"I did not know."

Fortis led her alongside the table, slowly making his way towards the gate. "Do not concern yourself with trivial things. My siblings and I serve a higher purpose. Know that we will always protect you."

Her heart raced as they drew closer and closer to the gate. She traced the faces of the guests, each seemingly unaware of the escape in progress. Her tiny fingers clung to Fortis, fearful of the impact their departure might cause.

Ruddy-faced strangers laughed and ate as they consumed vast quantities of alcohol. They chattered mindlessly while conning and wooing one another.

Fate looked up at Fortis. "Where's my brother?"

He smiled and patted her hand. "Stay focused and trust us."

She scanned the guests with disgust and confusion, until an unusual boy her size crossed her line of vision.

He slipped through the crowd as overlooked as she, his stark white hair glaring in stark contrast to that of the guests. In a flicker, his radiant mint-colored eyes caught hers, and then he disappeared into the shadows.

Her mouth hung open as she craned her neck in search of him.

Fortis stopped so fast that she walked into him in her stupor.

Neco frowned at the young Ignis and removed Fate's hand from his arm. "What are you doing with my daughter?"

Fortis smiled. "We were walking. It seemed a shame to find her alone on her birthday. I have a gift for her."

Neco looked over Fortis's empty hands. "Is that so?"

Fortis protested, wearing a pleasant smile. "It's from your brother."

Neco grumbled. "Niteo is here?"

"He wouldn't miss his niece's party."

Neco pulled Fate by the arm and pressed her against his side. "You're his guard—guard him. I'll take my daughter from here."

Fate checked the gate and then gazed up at her father. "He was just—"

"Fate," Neco snapped. "Where is your brother?"

She chewed the inside of her cheek. "I'm not sure. I can find him if you wish."

Neco smiled down at her and patted her arm. "That won't be necessary, dearest. I'd like you to spend some time with me."

Haunted, she glanced once more at the gate, sensing the danger her brother warned of. Turns of training and expected politeness led her down an ambiguous road. "Yes, Father."

Fortis watched, glowering, as Neco took Fate. His hand twitched as Neco pulled her away from him.

Neco kept her close and paraded her around the garden for all of his guests, introducing her to countless Royals. Each fawned and pawed at her, praising her beauty.

Fate suddenly felt dirty having so many strangers touch her in a familiar way. "Father, I'd like to get some punch, if it's all right."

He jerked her arm. "You can get some in a moment. There are some very important people I need you to meet first."

He tugged her over to a group of revelers.

One of the women wore a jeweled necklace that matched her vibrant gown. She hummed with delight the moment she regarded Fate. "Aren't you lovely?"

Another woman leaned forward, drenching Fate in the stench of alcohol. She reached out and stroked Fate's chest. "Not much to play with but I like the look in her eyes."

Fate recoiled, appalled by the drunken woman's behavior, and the fact that her father seemed to laugh it off. Her lungs constricted, making it difficult to breathe. "Father...."

He glanced down at her and, for the first time, the hunger inside him showed itself. The way he held her in his gaze, and ran his tongue across his teeth as his grip increased, he revealed the hidden monster her brother had seen.

A tremor wracked her entire body. Never before had her father behaved in such a callous manner, yanking her around and flaunting her before his guests like a trophy. She frantically searched for Abyssus, while praying the triplets would intervene and take them far away from Macellarius.

Neco spun Fate around to face one of the Rahma nobles. The man's foul breath struck her nose before her head fully settled from the spin.

The man reached out and took her by the arm with his dry, aging fingers.

Fate tried to retreat but Neco blocked her escape. Her head reeled as she tried to process his sudden change. She missed the man's name in her whirlwind of thoughts and emotions; instead, she fixated on her father's face.

The cold, calculating eyes he used as he looked at her seemed ominous to her now, just as Abyssus had cautioned. The air felt thick against her skin, making it increasingly more difficult to breathe.

Neco continued the introduction. "....he is one of our most respected leaders. Be polite and give him a kiss on the cheek, will you?"

Horrified, she searched his face for humor but found only a stern expression and his persistence in the matter. A lump formed in her throat as she turned back to the vulgar man.

Everything about the shabby Rahma repulsed her, from his smell, his scraggly beard and wrinkled skin, to his yellowing teeth and grabby hands. He repeatedly shifted the growing bulge in his pants as he advanced.

The man urged her to obey, with his fingers clawing at her relentlessly. "Yes, come give me a kiss."

Fate shivered, attempting to resist until her father firmly grabbed the back of her neck and forced her to kiss the man, who groaned in ecstasy and drank in her anima with his dry lips, as tears streamed down her cheeks.

The repulsive man rubbed against her. "Oh yes, Neco, you have my support."

He proceeded to ogle and grope her as he half-listened to Neco's response.

Neco boomed. "Excellent. I look forward to our partnership."

She defended her body as best she could, but the man forced his hands over her tiny form like a hungry animal. Bile rose from her gut into her throat as the man's breath lingered in her nostrils, and as Neco dragged her by the arm through the crowd, the sound of the chatter and laughter blurred into a mindless din in her ears.

Abyssus's warning rang in repetition.

Abyssus, where are you?

She wondered why no one came to her aid. Everything happened in plain sight, and not a soul stopped it.

The party continued as the guests watched on, seemingly thrilled by the experience.

Neco kept a tight hold on her as he led her back to the palace.

Random guests pawed at her, seizing any chance to fondle her as they passed, tearing at her dress, body, and hair.

Neco flung her inside the palace doors like a wet sack, and bowed to his adoring crowd with a broad smile, slamming the door shut with his foot.

Once inside, he turned on her like a viper as he pushed her down the hall. "Are you trying to embarrass me? I really expect more from you."

She scoured the halls for a possible escape and scrambled for the foyer, only to be snapped back by his grasp on her neck. She cried from the pain of his grip, and of his betrayal.

He forced her farther down the hall, away from the party. "Come now, I need you to dry it up. You can't be a mess. No one wants to see an ugly face."

When they reached the end of the hallway, Neco flung open the door to the downstairs study and shoved Fate inside. She caught her footing as she slid into the center of the room. Terrified, she searched for another exit, glimpsing a shadowy figure watching from the balcony upstairs, but the other figures standing before her quickly drew her attention.

The old woman and Fortuna had apparently been waiting for their arrival with a handful of guards.

Fate gasped as she fixated on the sensuous Ignis. For a fleeting instant, her heart clung onto hope. Firmus had promised to help them escape; certainly his sister held the same intent.

The old woman stepped forward and lifted Fate's dress to peek underneath.

Fate thrashed until Neco applied more pressure to her neck, sending a bolt of blinding pain throughout her body, allowing the old woman to slip beneath her undergarments and complete her probe of Fate's goods.

The old woman withdrew from under the gown and rested against her cane. "We're going to change that attitude of yours. There is proper etiquette for a girl like yourself when someone wants to see your wares. At least she is fresh."

Neco released Fate, pushing her forward into the arms of the old woman. "You must raise her well. I expect that she return with proper training."

Fortuna answered. "We will raise her with all of the proper etiquette. She will have the grace and charm of only the most elite Royals."

Neco squinted hard with disdain. "You know what I mean. If she is to become my wife, she'll need to be able to fulfill the needs of her King, and I will have many needs. If I'm expected to wait, I want her well-versed and just as fresh as I'm sending her."

Fortuna's voice grew strained and her expression darkened. "I raise all of my girls well."

The old woman gripped Fate by the hair and drew her close. "She may yet be a girl but, once we are done with her, she will certainly be your queen. She will learn the art of pleasure and she'll like it."

Neco countered. "I don't want her training on men. Is that understood?"

Fortuna bowed her head, keeping her fiery eyes on Fate. "Perfectly."

"Good, I won't accept a soiled wife."

"Very well. We will discuss the terms of purchase on her sixteenth birthday. Until then, she'll remain unsullied."

Fate's skin turned cold with sweat, and she wrestled against her captor. Her breathing quickened as the terror of the words reached into her reality.

Abyssus's shout rang out from the balcony. "Your wife?"

Fate cried out at the sight of her brother and darted for him, but the old woman yanked her back by the hair. She gripped at her roots, trying to ease the pain, while searching for any hope.

Abyssus raced down the stairs in leaps and bounds as Firmus bolted onto the balcony in pursuit.

Neco sighed with irritation and waved his hand. "Guards, collect him."

Firmus hollered, "Wait," but the guards followed the King's orders.

No sooner had the guards reached for Abyssus than the banister burst into blue flames.

Firmus leapt between the advancing spears and Abyssus, shielding him.

The side door slammed open and with a flurry of Council robes, the hooded representative halted the commotion with her mere presence. In a flash, the flames retreated and the room fell silent.

Neco gasped with a respectful bow. "Sisera."

From beneath her hood, she shot him a blistering gaze before turning to Firmus and demanding, "Stand down. You oppose Council law by interfering in this matter."

Firmus held his position and countered. "Abyssus is a Royal, as is the Lady Fate. Therefore, they are under your protection."

Sisera narrowed her eyes and removed her hood. "Yes, and if they were Bound to each other as proper Ancients should be, we would not be in a debate. This matter has already been settled in accordance with Council law. Should you choose to continue your defiance, we, the Council, will take great offense."

Firmus snarled. "You should take offense at a Royal child being sold into prostitution. I thought such matters were settled during the Verna Conflict."

Sisera nodded as a crease formed between her brows. "It is regrettable, but she is being trained for her position in this kingdom as per her father's request."

Abyssus blurted, "Father or husband?"

Sisera rubbed her forehead with a sigh. "He is legally the King of the region. Therefore, your complaint has little bearing on the result. We do not take pride in these situations, but we must take action."

Firmus gripped the banister. "But this is wrong! It's unnatural."

"Agreed. The Council has warned of consequences much like this throughout the ages, and yet many, such as your clan, have turned a blind eye and allowed the Rahma and the Tainted to continue on unchecked. When things turn out less fortunate than you would prefer, you blame us for your decisions."

Abyssus balled his hand into a fist. "But he's a Rahma. For their kind, this behavior is repulsive."

"The Lady Fate, however, is a Royal, so this makes perfect sense for her upbringing. We are, after all, considering the well-being of the region first, no?"

Fate's knees gave out and she dropped to the floor, sobbing.

Fortuna stepped forward with a cold hard stare and forced the old woman to release Fate's hair. "This is not productive to her training."

The old woman raised her cane. "How dare you." With a swift drop, she brought it down.

Fortuna caught it in her palm, her amber eyes glowing like flames, and growled. "My brothel, my rules."

Sisera glared, pointing a finger at the old woman. "Do not dare speak so freely to your superior."

The old woman turned her silvery eyes away and huffed, withdrawing her cane.

Fortuna turned to Neco. "Release my brother, and he will help your son find his way out."

Neco remained steadfast, arms crossed. "Firmus, deal with that child. Sisera, is it safe to say this incident is resolved?"

Sisera looked at Firmus, who reluctantly conceded.

The guards lowered their weapons, allowing Firmus to collect Abyssus.

Abyssus screamed, laboring against Firmus's hold as he retreated up the stairs. "You can't take her! Fate, fight back!"

Sisera turned to Fortuna. "So we have an accord?"

Fortuna inhaled sharply. "We do."

Fate shouted, releasing a bolt of electricity that spilled out onto the floor, forcing everyone to step back. In the commotion, she saw an opportunity to break for the door. She scrambled to her feet, stumbling on the length of her dress. As she reached for her escape, a strong arm grasped her by the shoulder and a stinging sensation coursed her neck. Slowly and unsteadily, she staggered one foot in front of the other as dark shadows swirled around the room.

The sound of her brother's cries became garbled and incomprehensible as she stretched her hand out for the doorknob. Her body finally relented, and she collapsed, unable to move. The room spun around and around as Neco leaned into her last small, clear tunnel of vision.

Tears spilled down her cheeks, but her body lay limp and useless. "No."

The swirling room grew darker until the tunnel closed.

3

MY GUIDING LIGHT

Fate's eyes shot open, and she gasped for air. Her body throbbed as an unfamiliar ceiling spun overhead. She regained her bearings to the best of her ability and gradually sat up.

From a distance, the old woman's voice crackled. "I hope you know what you're doing. This will bring chaos."

Fate wrestled with her grogginess as she listened to the conversation, trying to determine the subject of the old woman's accusations. While listening, she took in her surroundings, noting a large round window and a lattice gate connecting her room to the rest of the brothel. With rickety movements, she crept to the gate to check if she could see anyone, but the structure of the building prevented any view beyond the hallway.

Fortuna replied with blatant annoyance. "Stop treating her like a monster. She's a little girl, and it's my duty to protect her, even if it's from you."

The old woman flew into a rage. "You don't care about what you've done! She'll kill us all!"

"It's you that doesn't care. You only think of yourself. These girls deserve better."

The two women continued to bicker as Fate searched for a way out.

Fine silks stylishly decorated a bed that rested on the floor beside a cherry wood tea table and dresser. Delicate rugs lay scattered about the floor, and ornamental umbrellas and fans lined the ceiling and walls. Unfortunately, the room provided little in the way of self-protection.

Fate turned her sights to the window and thought of Abyssus. His cries, even now, rang in her ears. She wanted to tell him that he was right, that she should have listened sooner. Her violet eyes traced the window for a latch as she crawled closer—she *would* get back to him. She found the latch, unhooked it, and swung the window open, allowing a gust of frosty air inside.

A thick white blanket covered the brothel courtyard. Trees, which no doubt boasted their vibrant flowers in the spring, now lay dormant, appearing little more than sticks. Harsh snowfall buried whatever beauty the courtyard may have to offer. The biting air combated the warm room, dropping tiny flakes of snow onto the ledge and floor.

Her soul withered as she analyzed her surroundings. After the shock faded, she breathed in the chilled air, bringing clarity to her drugged mind as she clambered out the window to the frozen courtyard. She gripped her arms, shielding her skin from the icy wind and falling snow. A dense stream of vapor left her lips as she scouted the area in search of her route back to Macellarius— back to Abyssus.

The frost in the air mingled with her fear to choke her. Even her tears refused to leave her stinging eyes as she slunk through the courtyard behind the brothel. Thoughts of Abyssus, trapped and alone, flooded her mind, and the guilt that crept in urged her onward. She desperately needed to leave this place. She no longer saw Nex as their home, but as a prison and torture chamber.

She eased her way along the outside wall, and stopped when she spied another young girl tending to the brothel pond. Curiously, both the pond and the girl remained free of the chill. The drug made Fate's head swim, blurring the lines of reality as she struggled to stay focused. Were the girl and the pond real or a hallucination? Her priority remained on escape, so she crouched low and did her best to sneak despite her imbalance.

The dark-haired girl at the pond began walking towards the brothel. She stopped and turned her head to survey the area. Her cobalt-blue eyes searched as though she sensed a presence.

Fate halted, covering her mouth, certain this girl somehow detected her.

The peculiar girl remained quiet and concentrated for a moment before turning back to the brothel and entering through a sliding door.

Fate slipped through the last few paces of the courtyard and across a snowy path towards the brothel's teahouse. Her shoes slid over the smooth icy stones, breaking her stride and forcing her to regain her balance. Her fingers and toes grew more numb with every instant she remained exposed to the snow, and though shaking uncontrollably, she persisted, determined to flee. Once she steadied herself, she snuck beneath the teahouse veranda, knowing that the light growing with each passing moment brought her closer to discovery.

Steam rose from the roof of the teahouse. Laughter and music emanated from the windows. The smell of perfume permeated the air and invaded her senses, seemingly screaming *this is your future* at her.

On her hands and knees, the pain to her nearly frozen limbs made the gravel unbearable, and all the emotions from her dreadful experience surfaced. Overwhelmed, she covered her face with the hem of her dress and bawled. Her body shook and she fought for air between stifled cries and the urge to vomit.

Her head and lungs ached, and she coughed away the last of her self-pity. The bitter cold helped her to finally clear her thoughts. She raised her head, wiped her tears, and focused on the task ahead — the next step. She would get past the border and return for her brother.

She crawled out from her hiding place and examined her options.

The wall between Macellarius and Nitor towered above her, an impossible obstacle to climb, especially when the guards watched so carefully. This left the gate as the only option, but if she attempted to travel any farther, she'd freeze. As time dwindled, so did her options.

Two guards inspected everyone that passed without fail. Getting through undetected presented a nearly impossible obstruction in her plan.

Then she noticed a group of nobles approaching the gate on foot. Being a noble herself, she might be able to blend in with a group without notice. Half crazed, she looked down at her party dress and straightened it, as well as her hair.

As she started for the group, a deep voice called out from behind her. "Hey, little girl."

A hand brushed against her arm, triggering her instinct to thrash and fight against whoever may stop her journey.

"By all that is." A fair-haired man protected his face from her assault while kneeling down before her.

She stopped and stared at the calm gentleman. The fact that he remained so poised helped her regain a sliver of rational thought.

Every part of him displayed his nobility—his polished, well-made coat and vest, his kempt hair and fingernails, and his polite behavior. He rested his hand against the wooden pillar of the teahouse's outside corridor, and steadied himself in the slippery snow. "Are you all right?"

She shivered as she stared into his verdant eyes, uncertain of what to do or say. His gaze alone relayed a comforting air of concern.

A small frown formed on his lips as he mulled over their interaction. He looked at her and then toward the gate. "Are you trying to get past the guards?"

Her eyes pored over him, searching carefully for signs of deception.

"I can help you," he said.

She clenched her jaw, afraid to reveal anything that might send her back.

He removed his coat and wrapped it around her as she trembled. "You are from the brothel, no?"

Fate pulled away from him.

"I will take you to Macellarius, if that is what you wish, but I cannot guarantee your safety. It is best if you leave this place altogether."

She hesitated, taking the subtleties of his expression. Her brother remained a prisoner, and she refused to leave without him.

The man offered his hand, beckoning kindly. "Please, I wish you no harm."

She demanded, "Who are you?"

He sighed, took a quick look around, and then flashed a pained smile. "My name is Nigel. I am Lady Fortuna's... accomplice. I assist in helping girls just like you escape from the brothel."

She buried her cold face into the warmth of his coat and thought about her options. Her gaze traveled from the gate to the teahouse and finally back to Nigel, who patiently awaited her response. "I need to get to my brother."

He grimaced, glancing over at the gate. "I will not force you to leave Nex, but I wish you would reconsider. There are pieces in play that you do not yet understand."

She clenched her fists. "I don't care about any of that. I need to get to my brother."

Although reluctant, he conceded to her wishes. "Very well. Follow me and I will return you to Macellarius."

Nigel led her to a sleek black carriage covered by specks of white, melting ice. It stood in stark comparison to the snowy landscape. He opened the door by a curved handle and checked around to see if anyone watched.

She glanced at the two gray horses waiting impatiently in the snow before peeking inside. Uncertain of what she expected, she felt relief at finding nothing out of the ordinary, just the rich velvet fabric that ran across the seats and floor of the cart.

He leaned in and lifted the seat, revealing a hidden compartment. "It's not fancy or even clever, but no one will even know you are there. Silly, I know, but it works — no one questions the nobles around here. I will let you decide if you want to trust me or not. I am going inside to get my coachman. If you choose to cross the border, climb inside before I return." He gestured to his coat. "Sorry, but I'll need that if I'm not to stir curiosity."

With that, Nigel took his coat from Fate, and left her alone as he reentered the teahouse.

Her heart climbed into her throat, making her teeth tingle and her mouth dry. The cold bit her skin, leaving her face mostly numb. She clenched and opened her fists several times as she watched the shadows move through the screens on the teahouse. A hollow moan emanated from her throat while she wrestled with her decision.

Finally, she scurried into the carriage and closed the door behind her. As soon as she climbed into the hidden compartment, she shut the lid. In the dark, she waited for what seemed an eternity with nothing but the sound of her breathing to quell her anxiety.

Nigel's voice eased her nerves as he exited the teahouse with his coachman and neared the carriage. "Yes, I need to make a quick stop in Macellarius, if you do not mind."

The coachman responded. "Are you sure you want to go there, Sir? It is not safe at night. I hear that people have been going missing."

"I am certain. It will be brief, I assure you."

"As you wish, Sir."

The carriage door creaked open, feet shuffled above her, and finally, the snap of the reigns resounded. Her heart lulled to a steady beat as the carriage began to move. Nigel appeared trustworthy for now, but she would wait to solidify her conclusion until they passed through the gate.

The carriage paused intermittently as they passed through the community towards the gates. At the border, the guards chatted with Nigel briefly and the carriage started moving again.

The warmth of the compartment held her in secrecy and, for that, she remained thankful. Her head sloshed with each bump, due to the lingering effects of the drug, but she forced herself to remain focused on retrieving Abyssus.

At last, the coach rolled to a stop and the door opened. Nigel invited the coachman for a drink, and their voices drifted into the distance.

Fate cautiously lifted the lid, crept out into the carriage, and peered through the window.

Although it sat a quick jot from the brothel, Macellarius seemed locked in perpetual springtime.

Thankful to be out of the biting cold, she rubbed her still icy hands together, freeing herself from the last of her discomfort.

Guards patrolled the grounds as always.

They paid little mind to the carriage, alerting Fate to the fact that her father must have had many visitors from the brothel without her knowledge. She remained still and watched the routines of the guards many times, until she felt confident in reaching Abyssus's room without incident.

With more stealth than speed, she slipped from the carriage and around the palace to the servants' entrance. She cracked the door opened and snuck in, all the while keeping a watchful eye out for anyone who might spot her. The familiar palace now seemed like foreign territory—the enemy's lair. She scurried through the lower level to the stairway, slunk up to the second floor, made her way down the hall, and entered her brother's room.

"Abyssus," she said in little more than a whisper.

A light turned on, and Fate stood before Neco and a team of armed guards. One of the men held a blade to Abyssus's throat.

Neco crossed the room and wrapped his arms around Fate.

She dared not struggle for fear that her brother might be harmed.

Neco looked down at her. "I thought something like this might happen. My dear, you have training to complete, and I can't have you distracted."

Her body grew rigid and her gaze locked onto Abyssus.

Neco knelt before her and kissed her lips. "You can return when it's time."

Tears streamed down her cheeks and her words caught in her throat. She remained focused on her brother, whose gaze reflected the same pain she felt.

Neco pressed his finger to her lips. "Shh... I know... it's difficult to be separated." He wiped her tears and kissed her cheek.

Fate shuddered as she watched Abyssus strain against the guard. Her brother wore guilt like she wore her disgust for their so-called father.

Neco ran his finger down her chin and over her chest with glee. "Soon... soon we can consummate our bond and rule the kingdom together. Until then, I'll keep your brother safe, not to worry."

She knew exactly the threat he made, and swallowed the bile rising in her throat. The harder she worked to hold back her tears, the more it ached, but she formed a smile with quivering lips. "Very well. I needed to make sure he was well without me."

Abyssus's eyes widened as she relented to Neco's will.

Neco took her hand into his and sucked on one of her fingers before responding. "As you can see, he is as well as your word." He leaned forward, drawing close to her ear. "You know what I want in return."

Fate's lip trembled but she forced out her answer. "Then, we have an accord. May I please be excused to return to my training?"

Abyssus screamed through the guard's hands.

Neco bowed his head. "As you wish. Get my Lady a carriage, please."

One of the guards replied, "There is one waiting."

"Very good. I will miss you terribly," Neco said, taking Fate's face into his hands and kissing her once more on the lips.

She withdrew the moment he released her, and ran out into the hall and down the stairs without looking back. The lump in her throat choked her and the pain stormed through her body. Even so, she continued racing out of the palace, dismissing the muffled sound of her brother's cries. She ran and ran, until she reached the courtyard and faced Nigel.

He looked down at her, his face full of regret despite the soft smile. "They said you needed a ride, Lady."

Fate ran to his side. Her body shivered, unable to withhold the pain any longer. She held Nigel's coat and bawled, her face hot with tears.

Nigel drew his arms around her and ushered her back into his carriage, where she curled up on a corner of the seat to cry. First, he signaled to the coachman. As the carriage rolled forward, he removed his coat and draped it over Fate's shivering body, then stroked her head, holding her close to his side. "There is still hope yet, little one. Not all is what it seems, I promise you this."

Fate said nothing to him. His words seemed like mere drivel and lies, and it felt as though her entire world had collapsed and all had been lost.

When they arrived at the brothel, she jerked her head up with a gasp. Cold air rushed in as Nigel opened the door and revealed Fortuna waiting outside before the brothel entrance.

Fortuna leaned forward and let out her arms to Fate without comment. She patiently waited for her new pupil to come closer, and then shielded Fate from the bitter wind with her thick fur coat.

Nigel stepped down last, closed the carriage door behind him, and the two of them led Fate inside and quietly down the hall to her new room.

For a moment, Fate stood in the hall and stared at the room with a warm tear streaming down her cheek. She cared not about the fineries of the palace, but about the loneliness of being without her twin, and knowing the danger he faced every day. Seeing her room forced her to connect with reality. She too faced a new danger — that of predators who sought to sully her.

Nigel hovered in the doorway as Fortuna let Fate sit on the edge of the bed.

The pair exchanged a concerned glance before Fortuna rested her hands on Fate's knees and said, "This may be hard for you to believe right now, but I will do my best to protect you. Try to rest. It will get easier, I promise."

Fortuna stood, leaving Fate to her thoughts, and retreated into Nigel's arms as they exited the room.

Fate observed the wooden planks of the floor as the door slid shut. Everything felt numb, and with her fingers still cold, she grasped the edge of the bed as her soul sank deep inside. She lay back on the bed feeling the surge of emotions well up inside her again. The storm still brewed. Her heart ached so tremendously that she curled into a ball and cried herself to sleep.

THE REBELLION

The sun rested low along the edge of Nitor Community's snowy rooftops. Steam rose from the ice-covered vendor stands in the market place as the kingdom slowly began its day. Sluggish clouds grazed the tallest buildings as they moved past the brothel, dropping tiny flakes of snow that instantly vanished as they touched the ground. Macellarius Palace loomed over the sleeping city, dark and gloomy in the distance, warning those that set eyes upon it that something was terribly wrong.

The moon hung through the high window in the brothel hallway, resisting the morning light. Decorative screens caught the morning light and reflected their elaborate patterns in a display of luminosity amongst the shadows still lingering from the night.

The faint sound of clanging pots and pans reminded Fate that daylight crept in silently. The smell of meat buns wafted through the halls, stirring all who still slept. Little by little, the brothel roused from its deep slumber.

Fate's room lay at the farthest end of the brothel and still basked in the last persistent grip of nightfall. She rolled from the silk sheets out into the brisk morning air, collecting the satin printed robe that hung on the wall hook. She turned with her bare feet against the cold wooden floor, and sleepily made her way to the round window to gaze wistfully at the fading white haze that rose from the courtyard.

She knew better than to delay too long. She left the darkened room and trudged down the long hallway to the sunken hearth room, to face her future.

A large, square fireplace rested at the center of the room, casting orange light onto the nearby folding screens that led out to the gardens. A small cast-iron kettle, which hung from a bar over the fire, released the faint scent of tea. Two short tables rested at each side of the room, containing a variety of curious bobbles and trinkets. Daylight slipped passed the screens and trickled into the room, where it mingled with the flame's glow.

Fortuna sat on the floor nearest to the gardens with her red koi silk robe, which barely contained her ample bosom before spilling out onto the floor around her. She'd swept her hair up into a loose tussled bun atop her head, and a pipe rested firmly between her teeth as she analyzed the contents of a leather journal with an emblem made from amber gemstone. Whatever the book contained, it held her captivated until she glimpsed Fate entering the room. She closed the journal with a slight sigh, rose from the floor, emptied her pipe into the fireplace, and stashed it between her breasts.

"Good morning, Fate," she said.

Fate stepped farther into the room, her eyes still swollen from crying herself to sleep. It seemed that after the recent events, her now upside-down world would never turn upright again. She hugged herself and moved closer to the warmth of the fire. As she watched the dancing flames, she wondered if she should just fling herself in.

Fortuna crossed the room and set the journal down on one of the small shelves. "We will begin your lessons today."

Fate only managed to mutter out a response. 'Yes, Madam."

"First," Fortuna continued with her back still turned. "You are never to use your element—not against me, your sisters, or our clientele. Is that understood?"

Fate sniffed, thankful she unleashed electricity instead of darkness. "Yes, Madam."

Fortuna turned back to Fate. "Next, all girls under the age of twelve work in rotations from dawn to midnight. They assist by cleaning and organizing the teahouse and theatre during dinner, and they also provide entertainment. This is the category you fall into. While you are here, you will train in a variety of lessons I've chosen for you, including music, dance, reading and writing, time management, and etiquette." She walked back to the sunken fire and warmed her hands. "Older girls work from mid-day to early morning, so you will do your best to keep all of your activities quiet in the morning to allow them time to rest."

Fate's violet eyes shifted to the floor as she hung her head low—hiding behind her heavy bangs—and attempted to contain her surfacing emotions. "Yes, Madam."

Fortuna approached and gently lifted Fate's face by the chin. "Now, I must tell you something of extreme importance. Please listen carefully. When our girls are sixteen, they must be bid off to our clients. We do not celebrate the coming of age. Every day is a struggle, but we can get through this trial together."

Tears streamed down Fate's face as she withdrew and shielded her grief with her arm.

Fortuna wrapped her arms around her, offering a warm place to cry. "We do our best to keep you from the ills that plague our world."

Fate wiped her tears with her sleeve and withdrew from Fortuna's arms. "That man, Nigel, told me you help the girls. Is that true?"

Fortuna frowned. "We do what we can, but your case is not like others. You will need the help of your sisters if we are to free you."

"Sisters?"

"Yes, you should think of the other girls here as your sisters. Not one among you finds herself in a desirable position. Individually, each would fall prey to unworthy predators, but together, you can persevere. You should grow as a family by encouraging, assisting, and protecting each other in this challenging environment."

The word *protect* echoed in Fate's ears. She feared what her time in the brothel may bring, and the thought of having others like herself brought a minor sense of relief. "Where are they?"

Fortuna offered a tender smile.

Fate focused on the glimmer in Fortuna's eyes, which seemed to reflect some inner pain, and perhaps the hope she used to quell it. Fate wondered if the madam might be grappling with a moment of vulnerability.

Fortuna finally answered in a more resolute tone. "They have gathered together in the dining hall for breakfast. Would you like to meet them?"

Fate squeezed her arm, wrestling with her building anxiety. Her mind darted from the moment of her father's betrayal to her current predicament. As the heat rose in her cheeks once more, she fought the tears that wished to surface. She wanted to leave and go far away. The madam's own brother had promised Fate protection, and now her only security lie with other girls her age, caught in the same awful circumstances. The image and smell of the grizzled old man and her father repeated over and over, causing her stomach to writhe in protest.

Fortuna waited patiently for Fate's answer.

Fate's voice shook. "I want to leave. I want to go to Tir Na Nog."

The madam pressed her lips together and averted her gaze, glancing to the garden as her words caught in her throat. "That time has passed. We, unfortunately, cannot undo the decisions we've made. I can assure you that we will do our best to prepare you for whatever may come, and get you out before the day of your auction."

A flood of tears filled Fate's eyes. Although she saw and felt them brimming, along with the lump in her throat that grew to an ache, she clenched two tiny fists and held it in. Her nose burned, and she sniffled, daring not to blink lest the tears pour down her cheeks again. The moment they prepared to fall, it struck her that it did her no good to mourn. No amount of crying would change her circumstances.

Fortuna raised her hands as if she wanted to reach out and comfort Fate, her expression full of remorse and empathy. Surely, she also knew how much it hurt and simply kept moving forward to ease Fate's suffering.

The more that Fate realized this, the more respect she held for her new mentor. She wiped her eyes and pushed down her sorrow. Small hiccups overtook her but she held them in as best she could and straightened her posture.

Emotion surged through the madam, heating the room by several degrees. She knelt down and met Fate's gaze. "I don't know what the future brings for us, but I can promise that we will face it together."

Fate nodded and briskly wiped her face of the few relentless tears. "Okay."

"Are you ready to meet your sisters?"

"I am."

Fortuna stood tall and guided Fate through the building, past sliding doors covered by shiny art of flowers and long grasses. Together, they walked to the end of the long portico and entered through one pair of doors into the dining hall, a vast space with a stone kitchen inserted at the far end and large tables spread across the floor. Lanterns hung from the ceiling, casting a cozy orange glow around the room, which made it seem more inviting.

A group of nearly twenty girls Fate's age sat around the tables, eating and talking.

Fortuna ushered Fate into the room and announced, "Girls, I'd like you to meet Fate. Please do your best to help her adjust."

All at once, every girl in the room stopped and stared at their new sister. A wave of silence passed over them and then, everyone clambered from their seats and swarmed Fate, chattering excitedly.

"Where is she from?"

"How old are you?"

"Your hair is so pretty."

"We'll take care of you, don't worry."

Fortuna patted the air with a smile. "Girls, girls, slowly... she is still adjusting. Remember your first day, please. Back to your seats."

The girls bellyached but returned to their seats.

Fortuna draped her hands over Fate's shoulders as she addressed two girls, who sat shoulder to shoulder at a table across the room. "Tori, Myrna, the two of you will be responsible for teaching Fate how things work."

The girls replied in unison. "Yes, Madam."

"Thank you, girls. Why don't you two come up here and introduce yourselves."

The madam's invitation caused a ruckus amongst the other girls.

Fortuna shook her head and brought the room to silence again. "There is no need to hurry. There will be plenty of time for you all to get to know each other. Fate is a sister now, so I'm certain you will all take care of her as you do each other."

By the time Fortuna finished her statement, one girl stood before Fate, with the other just over her back shoulder.

"I'm Myrna," the close one said, shifting her weight to one side. Her long, dark, tight curls caressed her sculpted cheekbones and plump lips. Golden eyes seemingly glowed against her smooth dark skin. She flashed a bright smile of pearly teeth that matched her silky voice.

Fate awed over the girl, whose coloring differed from anyone she had ever seen. Unintentionally, she reached out and touched Myrna's face. "You're so pretty."

The other one, clearly Tori, snarled and crossed her arms. "By all that is."

Fate took in the second girl before her, one equally as striking, with a small willowy frame more graceful than a dancer's, and her voice as mild as a mouse. She remembered Tori from the night before as the girl who stood beside the pond. The girl's unmistakably blue eyes appeared a stark contrast to her lustrous skin and dark hair.

Before Fate realized, she'd reached out with her free hand to touch Tori's cheek. "Is everyone here so attractive?"

The girls laughed and whispered to one another.

Tori's scowl faded as she raised a brow. She seemed more at ease knowing that Myrna was not Fate's sole fixation.

Fate quickly withdrew her hands with burning cheeks. "I'm sorry. I was rude."

Myrna rebuffed. "How? You've done us no disservice."

Tori leaned forward and rested her chin on Myrna's shoulder. "In fact, you paid us a compliment. You're a little creepy but that's okay."

Fate fidgeted with the ends of her hair as she looked around the room of agreeing girls. "I haven't been around many girls my age."

Fortuna stroked Fate's hair. "You'll adjust. Make sure you eat. Girls, finish eating and start your chores. Tori, Myrna, I'm counting on you."

All of the sisters answered in harmony. "Yes, Madam."

Fortuna turned and exited, leaving the girls to their routine.

Myrna led Fate to a chair while Tori made her a bowl of rice and eggs.

No sooner did Fate sit in her chair than the swarm of girls gathered again.

A small girl with bright eyes and golden hair asked, "Where are you from?" Looking at her in close proximity made Fate aware of the abundance of Ancient traits around the room. Each girl... each *sister*... who surrounded her also appeared to be of Ancient blood—If not all, then most. It alarmed her to see so many without Bound, save Myrna and Tori, whom she suspected may have a binding by their uniform behavior.

The girls hummed in agreement.

Fate took a spoonful of food and looked from one curious face to the next. "Macellarius."

Another girl leaned forward, her gaze dark and concerned. "Is it true you're a princess?"

Tori smacked the girl's arm. "You know Madam doesn't allow that."

Fate spoke clearly. "Yes, my father sent me here."

The girls gasped and a din of disapproval and mistrust stirred around the hall.

Myrna rubbed Fate's back. "We're all here for different reasons. We're your sisters now."

Fate took a bite and swallowed hard. The flavor of the food brought joy but the thought of her father wanting to use her made it sour again. With her tongue, she rolled the ball of sticky rice to the side of her cheek. Her mouth grew dry, and the food stale, as she remembered her birthday party.

"I had to leave my brother," she said. "I don't know what'll happen to him."

The girl with the golden hair stood and raised her spoon into the air. "I vote we help."

The girls quickly moved through a count.

Tori confirmed. "We'll find out about him. Don't worry, we can get information about anything. That's what sisters are for."

Fate felt the first real gratitude since her arrival. She exhaled slowly as she forced down another bite of food.

Myrna looked out at their riotous sisters. "It'll get easier. We all work together—you'll see. We're getting out of here. *All* of us."

All the girls hummed in affirmation.

Tori and Myrna sat with Fate as she ate. They kept the other girls from interrupting. After the group gave up their need to probe, they returned to their tables to finish their breakfasts and move on to their duties.

Myrna headed to the kitchen and started washing dishes. She kept the younger sisters on their toes as they tidied up from their meal.

Tori stayed beside Fate, watching her carefully. "Fate, may I ask you a question?"

Fate nodded, fearing the endless possibilities of Tori's curiosity.

"Are you angry with your father?"

Blood rushed to Fate's cheeks. The pressure made her head ache. "I hate him."

Tori nodded, a small frown forming on her lips. "Understandable. What do you want to do about it?"

Fate considered the question. She wondered what she *could* do under the circumstances. Her eyes lost focus and she stared into some endless and unseen void, wallowing in despair and frustration. Something dark stirred within her chest. It urged her to thrash and scream violently in protest, but she remained limp and hollow, feeling as though something had broken inside of her.

She bit her lips as she considered the question. Her heart raced at the thoughts that crossed her mind. Finally, she turned to meet Tori's deep blue eyes, which seemed to peer into her soul. "If possible, I'd kill him in the most painful way imaginable."

Myrna turned away from the sink and rested a wet hand on her hip. "Then you and your brother could rule Macellarius. You are an Ancient, after all."

Tori listened to both girls and stared at the ceiling. "True. The Council wouldn't place the life of a Rahma above that of an Ancient, especially if it enforced their laws. The lesser Breeds may be on an uptick here in Mu, but they have yet to tread ground in Thule."

Fate gaped at her bowl, questioning her current environment. She tried hard to comprehend how casually both girls contemplated murder. She was no longer alone. Her sisters thought of the world as she did. "Is that possible?"

Tori flashed a big smile. "With enough time, anything is possible."

Myrna wiped her hands on a towel and approached the table. "We'll teach you about the Rebellion."

Fate shook her head. "Rebellion?"

Tori smirked. "You may find that you were more of a prisoner before you came here."

Fate reveled in the fleeting elation of hope, but soon forcibly suppressed any foolish notion that might stop her from making her desires a reality. "Perhaps."

Myrna twisted her mouth to one side, casting a sideways glance at Tori. "She's still young and, right now, we need to teach her the rules. If we finish quickly, there will be time to introduce her to what's possible."

Fate set her spoon down and sharply inhaled through her nose. "Does Madam know about your Rebellion?"

Tori's eyes glimmered with confidence. "It's not our Rebellion— it's hers."

The air left Fate's lungs and, when she drew breath again, she felt as though she breathed in new life. "Teach me everything."

Tori and Myrna glanced at each other again.

Myrna shrugged. "We'll show you what we can, but it really depends on you."

Fate rose from her chair as her new-found determination brewed. "What do I need to do?"

Tori laughed. "Right now, you need to do dishes."

Fate didn't take the statement lightly. They may be playing some kind of joke but she decided to follow instructions anyway. If there was the slightest chance for her to create a path to freedom, she would.

She walked to the sink, rolled up the sleeves of her robe, climbed atop a stool, and started scrubbing away at the soapy dishes.

Tori approached her, leaned against the counter, and signaled to Myrna to watch the door. "This place is more stained than the Void. We'll watch your back, and you'll watch ours."

Fate continued scrubbing. "Agreed."

Tori moved her mouth from side to side in a poorly concealed smile. "Madam will insist we keep up all of our lessons and chores but, after that, we gather and work on new ways to get all of our sisters out of here. Work hard and be of some help, and you can join the Rebellion."

Fate set another dish out on the rack and shifted her eyes to the ceiling. The vibe of the brothel made her feel as if she'd stepped into another world rather than across the kingdom. It already struck her as familiar to view the screens, lattice, and fine wood rather than the dark and dismal stones of Macellarius Palace. "If all of the girls get out, who is working at night?"

Tori tapped her slipper against the cold stone floor. "Older girls who either didn't want to leave or couldn't. Believe it or not, this life is better than some."

"I see." She thought of the starving people in Macellarius and understood what Tori meant.

"That is not all that we do. We also help repel the advancement of the Council."

She stopped checking Tori's expression for humor. "Repel? Mu is under Council rule. Why do you wish to change that?"

Tori smirked. "Someone has been told what to believe, Myrna."

Myrna turned away from the door to shake her head at Fate. "How has their rule worked out for you?"

Fate considered their words carefully. Crossing the Council meant changing forever. It meant they must defy the law itself and face the consequences.

Tori drew close to Fate's shoulder. "Ever thought of becoming a rebel?"

She watched the tiny bubbles that stuck to her fingers. Happiness seemed as fleeting as a bubble and just as easy to destroy. By herself, she stood no chance of understanding their grand Euphoria, let alone Mu or the forces that kept her and Abyssus apart. At least, if she joined the Rebellion, she may yet succeed in doing far more. She may even change the Empire altogether.

Fate clenched her tiny fists. "My brother always said, '*If you find yourself at your worst, you can only get better.*'"

Tori and Myrna kept their gazes fixed on her, waiting for the rest of the thought.

Fate smirked. "As sisters, we'll stand together... for better or worse."

The lovely pair leaned against each other, wearing the same soft smile, as they answered. "For the Balance, we stand."

5
ON THE PRECIPICE

Fate picked up the decorative comb from her bedroom vanity and ran her fingers over the intricately formed crystals placed along the spine. On her bureau rested expensive gifts from her many patrons. It often surprised her, the lengths patrons went to in an attempt to woo her. She belonged to the brothel, and yet they persisted on showering her with trinkets and bobbles. Each of her sisters bore the blood of the Ancients, and yet she alone received the lavished attention. In spite of giving many pieces away to her sisters, she still wallowed in an abundance of self-loathing reminders. No matter how she tried, every gift screamed that she meant little more than a prized painting to a fickle noble, something to be won, briefly admired, used, and then left to collect dust. Although she must accept all of their gifts, she only truly cared about this one comb, a gift from Abyssus.

In the reflection of her mirror, she spotted the nine fake roses pinned to her wall. Each girl chose a way to count her days in the brothel and she chose this to count her turns. It amazed her how quickly two turns had passed. Every rose she pinned to the wall led her closer to the day of the auction, and every one reminded her of how little time remained to escape from Neco's grasp.

A knock at the door pulled her from her thoughts, and Tori stuck her head in and held out a letter with a small smile. "The usual."

Fate hurried to take the letter, tracing her brother's seal with her fingertips as Tori exited and slid the door shut once more. The arrival of the letters proved that her sisters held some power or ability to attain information and sneak about undetected, though knowing *how* they managed unsettled her.

She took a seat at her vanity and considered her current position as she opened the letter. Although she worked hard towards earning a respectable place in the Rebellion, she still felt the tinge of suspicion. Madam definitely kept secrets. It appeared that everyone kept secrets — even she coveted a few of her own.

> *Dearest Fate,*
> *Neco has finally relented to your visit in Macellarius, though I do not understand the reason why. It worries me when he suddenly changes his mind about something... makes me think he has ulterior motives. When you arrive, I'll be here to protect you.*
> *I look forward to your visit.*
> *Abyssus*

She set the letter down on the vanity and let her own determination swell inside her chest. Her rage for Neco burned so brightly that her cheeks glowed pink. As she gazed at her reflection in the mirror, she patted them with her cool hands to ease the anger, albeit to no avail. Her fury was hers and hers alone. She sought the means of her revenge privately.

With delicate hands, she collected a tube of red lipstick, applied it, and pressed her lips together to spread the color evenly. Even at the age of nine, she felt old and jaded beyond her turns. "You are Cruentus Fate, are you not?"

She stared at the reflection before her as she might the painting of a meadow. It may seem pleasing and well-constructed but, in reality, she looked at a blank canvas covered in bright flashy colors.

The entire brothel represented fallaciousness. The building and all the girls inside performed in a sleek show, promising sultry nights of passion, but instead delivering freedom to the helpless, and unexpected justice for the wicked from the Rebellion. She prided herself on her small role in freeing her sisters from the clutches of filthy Rahma and greedy Ancients. It often enlivened her hardened heart to watch the girls as they left, hoping that, one day, it would be her turn.

She stood and collected her lavish red coat, a one-of-a-kind garment designed especially for her by Nigel, which held more joy than any of the foolish bobbles thrust upon her by thirsty admirers. It hung patiently on its hook, waiting for this special day—just like her. She exited her room with a backwards glance, amazed that such a place concealed the heart of the Rebellion. With a tiny smirk, she threw her coat over her arm and began her trip to Macellarius.

The two kingdoms rested so close together that it seemed silly to take a carriage, so Fate waved off the coachman and started for the gate on foot. The brisk air filled her lungs with the freshness of a spring day. She took the time to enjoy it before heading into the Macellarius gloom. As she moved, the chill broke and the warmth of the day embraced her.

She arrived at the gate feeling refreshed, and flashed the guards a bright smile with her red painted lips.

Both men swooned and bowed, allowing her entrance without query. She marveled at how easily sensuality moved them. As she walked away, they raved about her beauty and discussed when they might visit the brothel again. Little did they know... she'd be long gone before their chance of touching her ever came.

Macellarius Palace hung over the rooftops as hollow and dark as she remembered. She meandered through the short stretch of city streets, taking note of the horrific conditions in which her people lived.

The roads fell apart under debris and garbage, and rats scurried along the buildings in search of their next meal or nest. Signs of the Plague revealed itself in the citizens' insatiable and empty gazes. A thick shroud covered the community, ailing all those within. The rotting stench of corpses saturated Fate's senses but she refrained from blocking the smell with her hand, out of respect for their loved ones.

She walked the long dirty roadway to the palace stairs and stood outside the entrance. Although she lived in a brothel, she much preferred the company of her sisters, Madam, and Nigel to that of dreary Macellarius. If not for Abyssus being captive, she might never have returned to the palace, except perhaps to save the future of her people.

After collecting her thoughts, she pulled the long, dulled golden cord to ring the bell. Footsteps echoed from inside as she waited, tapping her foot and wrenching her hands. Her desperation to see her brother had grown in her time apart from him, and the feeling only deepened as she stood at the entrance.

At last, the door opened and a huge man towered above her, his form filling the entire frame. His brilliant green eyes pierced through her with an unnatural emptiness.

Her mouth fell open and she gaped at the massive person before her. After a brief analysis, she noticed his bright red hair. *An Aska?* Her heart dropped, knowing the clan's direct link to the Council.

A familiar voice called out from behind the gigantic man. "Fate, come in. I have so much to tell you."

Fate squeezed by the unmoving Aska as her brother rushed across the entryway floor towards the stairs. She peeked over her shoulder at the immense man, who stared back expressionless, and swallowed hard to push down her unease. Even as she followed Abyssus up the stairs, she felt the man's eyes boring into the back of her skull.

Once she caught up to her brother, she drew close, glimpsing the frightful man once more from over her shoulder. "Not very friendly, is he?"

Abyssus looked down at the entryway with a pout. "Who cares? You're not here for his company." He took her hand, hurried down the hall, and pulled her into his room. The door swung hard from the forceful entry, bounced back, and slammed shut behind them.

Fate put the matters of the massive man behind her as best she could, and took comfort in the familiar surroundings. Her brother's small bedroom seemed crowded by the desk, bed, and dresser... a stark difference to her grand bedroom chamber at the palace. Guilt settled in deep as she realized she had not noticed the difference before.

Even after all this time, it looked the same—just as meticulous as always, with hordes of alphabetized books stuffed into built-in shelves. Black curtains blocked most of the light from the window, letting in only a small ray where a book lay open on the bed.

As Abyssus released her, she ran her finger across the edge of his desk, spotless as usual and possessing the faint scent of concentrated cleansers. It reminded her of the brothel halls that she cleaned every morning with her sisters. These days, everything led her thoughts back to her new home, a place closer to her now than Macellarius.

He darted across the room and collected a blue journal from one of the shelves. "Whew, we made it. I didn't want you to have to see that man."

She knew to whom he referred, and her skin crawled at the mere mention of the king. With a quick inhale, she pressed her lips together and forced a practiced smile. "Let's not talk about him. What do you have there?" Eventually, she would have to face the king to fulfill the bargain she'd made to visit the palace, one she kept secret from both Abyssus and Fortuna.

Abyssus pulled back one of the curtains, opened the glass doors, and walked out onto the balcony. "Let's talk out here."

She removed her coat and tossed it onto his bed, disappointed the weather prohibited such fineries. "Out there? Do you think it's safe?"

He turned back with a raised brow. "Safe?"

Images of the Aska returned, invading her mind. He seemed to be made of nightmares, and she feared she might wake one night with him standing over her. "That Aska is scary."

"Mortis?"

She grimaced with a shiver. "Is that his name? I don't remember him. I think I would have—he's enormous. When did he come here?"

"Hmm... I think it's been seven suns. Anyway, I found something interesting, and I wanted to show you."

His nonchalance made her nervous. She wanted to believe in Firmus's ability to protect Abyssus, but remembered how poorly he'd managed to protect her on the night of her seventh birthday.

She stepped out onto the balcony as Abyssus leaned against the guardrail. "What did you want to show me?"

A devious grin stretched across his face as he pointed to the long hedges across the garden lawn. "It's over there. I made notes about it in my journal."

Fate squinted hard at him, drew her mouth into a tight, twisted pucker before accepting the journal he extended to her, and briefly skimmed the handwritten notes. For as long as she could remember, she always associated the scent of paper with her brother. The crinkling of the pages brought back memories of the time he spent reading beside her. A smile formed on her lips as she examined his drawings of the hedge. His jotted notations described a hole that led to the other side.

After contemplating his notes, she pressed her hand to her chin. "So, there's a secret way into Nitor?"

Abyssus folded his arms and rocked heel to toe and back again. "That's right. I've been taking notes. You know, just in case."

She stopped reading and turned to her fidgeting brother. "In case of what?"

He often got his way by being endearing, but Fate saw through his amiable disguise. She disliked that he even tried what she called *rabbiting*, a term she found suiting for Abyssus because he used quickness and intellect to escape.

His mischievous smile proved her suspicions. "You never know. I mean, anything can happen, and I want something tangible to safekeep my knowledge, and hopefully to be kept safe. I could fall down and hit my head. Then what?"

She put a hand up to cease the prattle. "How about you just stay out of trouble?"

"I can't spend my time hiding from Neco and Mortis. I have to prove my worth."

His words rattled her, and a deep pit formed in her gut at the thought of her brother angering Neco's henchman. "If this is about worth, then you're worth more than the world to me."

He fumbled for a retort but gave into a failed attempt of hiding behind his collar.

The action only made him more endearing to her. She recognized that he lacked confidence, but she admired his inventive mind. The trouble was his boundless curiosity, which she feared would one day bring him misfortune.

He threw his leg over the side of the guardrail and climbed down the pillar to the ground below, once again proving her concerns about him correct. "Come on!"

Fate followed as quickly as a gown and heels allowed. She reached the bottom and hardly caught her breath as he dashed across the garden lawn towards the massive hedge that separated the two kingdoms.

Abyssus reached the hedge, crouched down, and waded through the mess of leaves and branches.

She scanned the garden to make certain no one could see their palace escape, and then followed him into the hedge. A tangle of twigs blocked the hole, but she pushed through them, revealing a well-worn tunnel through the hedge. The branches snapped back as Abyssus released them, each one smacking her in the face. Startled, she jolted forward and caught her dress in the undergrowth. She tugged against the knotted mess as she crawled out of the tunnel, but the branches clung mercilessly to her dress. Finally, the twigs cracked, releasing her against her own force, and she toppled into Abyssus, knocking them both onto the soft dirt.

The impact sent his journal flying from his hands. He raised his head and leaned against his elbows, sounding exasperated. "Fate."

She buried her face against his back. "I'm sorry. I was stuck."

Once she sat up, he crawled out and collected his journal, dusted it off, and stood to observe the garden.

She followed him out to the bright yard, full of flourishing white roses and a dewy green lawn. The sunlight glared off the equally white marble of the nearby palace. Everything about this place appeared the opposite of Macellarius, namely the brightness and the grandness of its design. Long columns ran outside the patio exterior towards doors and windows made with colored glass.

Abyssus opened his journal and began sketching the immense structure. "Wow. Nitor Palace looks amazing in this light."

Fate drew closer to his side, concerned that guards might catch them, and whispered, "We should go."

He eyed the palace with a puzzled look and pointed at a balcony, which overlooked the yard. "Hey, I know that guy."

She followed his gesture, hoping to put an end to the distraction, but ended up staring just like her brother. She also recognized *that guy* as the boy she saw on her seventh birthday.

His white skin and hair made it impossible to confuse him for another. As casually as a stroll on a spring day, he climbed up onto the guardrail of the third-floor balcony and dangled his foot over the edge. He then took two unprotected steps before slipping and catching himself.

A rush of adrenaline coursed through Fate's body and she instinctively lurched forward. "Don't jump."

The white-haired boy tilted his head and stared down at them, his apathy noticeable even at a distance.

An armor-clad woman bolted from the far side of the yard and then suddenly stopped at the patio to admonish him. She kept her composure, calmly sweeping her blonde hair away from her face, despite the distinct trace of concern in her expression and voice. "Hero, what are you doing? Get down from there."

He gazed at her with the same indifference as he did the siblings, only now, a subtle smirk formed on his lips before he took another step.

The woman vanished in a flash of golden spindly light and reappeared in the palace doorway, shouting for the guards.

Fate tugged at her brother's arm. "We have to hide."

Abyssus crawled back into the safety of the tunnel, but continued to watch the scene unfold. "Did you see that? She used flash step."

Fate retreated into the shadows and sat beside her brother. "Abyssus."

"That was the Prince of Nitor."

She wrenched her skirt, trying to ease her instinct to get involved. "What does it matter? He's about to kill himself!"

He casually returned to scribbling in his journal. "Nah, he won't jump."

"How do you know?"

"He's a Caeles. If you had studied like me, then you would know better."

She growled as she pushed against the branches poking into her back. "Can you stop being sarcastic? You know I study. If I had your free time, I could investigate my interests as well." She wanted to ask how well he'd study if he lived in a brothel, but refrained from starting an argument. In reality, the prince didn't jump, which made her choice not to spark a debate doubly wise.

Abyssus pulled a piece of candy from his pocket and slipped it into his mouth as the guards pulled Hero back to safety under the armored woman's watch. He stared long and hard at the empty balcony before closing his journal. "He's one of the last ice elementals in existence. He can't die, or, more accurately, the Council won't let him. If he did, they'd have a fit. The woman that was shouting... she's here to guard him. Someone will lose their job tonight for sure. Nope, he's stuck here. They won't let him go—in *any* way. Believe me when I say, we have a higher chance of seeing the sky fall."

Fate considered the situation. "If that's true, how did he end up on the balcony with no one watching him?"

He shrugged. "Like I said, someone is getting fired."

She shifted her jaw to one side and picked stray branches from her hair. "Is this what you've been doing since I left? Spying on the neighboring kingdom?"

His voice dropped and intensity washed over him. "You didn't leave. They took you away. Don't ever confuse that."

She felt her own face grow stiff as a board. "I won't."

He maneuvered a small circle on his hands and knees, then started crawling towards home. "I'm studying for the greater good."

Fate trailed behind him. "What's that?"

He glanced back at her. "I threw away the Cruentus family name. I will never serve Neco, nor will you. I will fight until the day I die. Who am I kidding... long after that."

He crawled out into the Macellarius garden.

She hurried after him and grabbed him by the arm. Her body shook with fear and frustration. "Abyssus, don't say such things so flippantly. If you test your will against the Universe, you're really going to be killed."

He sucked air into his cheeks, puffing them up, and then exhaled glibly. "He can't kill me without losing his hold on you."

A dark omen fell over the siblings in the form of a shadow.

Fate traced the darkness to its source and gasped at the sight of the gargantuan Aska. *Mortis.*

Mortis reached out his enormous hand and gripped Abyssus by the head, the cold dead look in his stare warning against any heroic ideas.

She froze, terrified that a single blink might cause Mortis to crush her brother's skull.

The grip applied so much pressure that the veins in Abyssus's face bulged. He clawed at Mortis's hand, trying to get the beast to release him.

Mortis's presence chased away the natural flow of air. His spirit polluted everything in proximity with his menacing intent, to near asphyxiation.

Neco meandered haphazardly out into the garden, taking in the ordeal with bewilderment.

Fate stood open-mouthed, surprised to see the once strong, proud ruler looking much older and frailer in the passing turns. The difference in their breed had finally worked in her favor.

When he noticed Fate, he stood aghast before snapping back into his senses. "Unhand him immediately. I told you, he is not to be harmed."

Mortis turned to Neco with hollow eyes, ignoring the Rahma king's demand. He clutched Abyssus tighter, and added a sneer.

Neco halted his stride and stood with his hands out as though attempting to soothe a wild dog.

Finally, Mortis dropped Abyssus and returned to his patrol without uttering a word.

Abyssus fell to the ground, reeling in pain and holding his injured head.

Neco heaved a sigh of relief and took one last solemn look at Fate before returning to the palace. It appeared that the drive he'd once felt had left him, and he seemed smaller for it. Although he left without confrontation, she knew he expected her to uphold her end of their bargain.

Fate shook off her own fears and briefly puzzled over the power struggle she'd witnessed. Then her attention turned to Abyssus, fueling a forceful rage. She swung her hand and cracked him against his already wounded head. "Are you stupid? Why are you testing your luck? There is something wrong with that man. Stay away from him. I mean it."

Abyssus ignored her strike and ranting, quickly scrambled for his journal, and jotted down notes. "Something *is* wrong with him, more so than I imagined."

She stamped her foot. "Seriously? What are you doing? This isn't the time to take notes. He almost killed you."

He inhaled long and slow, pressing his fingers against his brow bones. "I know you don't understand — you couldn't — but one day you'll thank me."

His tone shook her to her core. "What's going on? Why won't you tell me?"

He crawled to a spot near the hedges to continue making his notes. After finishing another paragraph, he looked up at Fate and patted the lawn, beckoning her to sit beside him.

She settled in next to him, hoping to hear words that alleviated her concerns.

"Something bad is happening in the Empire. I've been taking notes for some time now, actually, since we first started studying together. I know you lost interest, but I couldn't let it go. After some research—well, a *ton* of research—I discovered that the Capital has a problem."

"Which is?"

"They don't have an heir."

She twisted her head. "They have two princes. What are you talking about?"

"First, they are not a Bound pair. Second, Iunu Ryou has not been seen for some time, and lastly, Iunu Kyou is a philanderer and doesn't seem willing to settle down to rule."

She waited for him to enlighten her, but he stared as though she should already understand. "Okay, what does that have to do with us?"

He blinked hard at her and then finally flipped through his journal to a page titled *Dolls*. "Tate, you know that we aren't Neco's children, don't you?"

"Of course, we're Ancients, and he's Rahma."

He hesitated. "I believe we're Dolls."

She turned her head and chuckled. "That's absurd."

He remained steadfast, his gaze fixed upon her, more still and calculating than she'd ever seen him. "Think about it. Two Dolls were stolen from the Capital several turns ago. One of them was meant for the Capital Heir, Iunu Kyou, but she vanished before they could be Bound."

Her anxiety grew with each new possibility. She felt like a sea creature stranded on land, desperately hoping for the tide to sweep back in and rescue her. "We can't be Dolls, we're Iu."

He shook his head. "Dolls can be made to look like any clan. Besides, you're much too small to be Iu. You're more likely modeled after the Feh. It would explain why we can't remember anything before that day in the Capital. It may sound crazy, but I've been tracking this for some time now. It all makes sense."

She hugged her knees. "You sound excited, but you're just jumping to conclusions on your own. Do you know what people say about Dolls? Nothing good, that's for certain. You should be praying that we're not like them. Dolls bring chaos."

He chuckled. "Chaos is already here, you can trust me on that one."

She took the journal from his hands and read it through more carefully. One paragraph logged an account of the Grim visiting the Capital at the High King's request. It confirmed that they intended for a Doll to be the Bound of the Future High King, Iunu Kyou. She felt short of breath as she continued down the page to see his record of the Doll's theft.

He allowed her to read until he finally interrupted. "I think *you* are the missing heiress."

She took in his words and stared at the journal, which appeared as little more than scribbles to her in her emotional state.

"I found the information buried in a weird book," he said.

"What was so weird about it?"

"It appeared out of nowhere, like magic."

Her body felt heavy. She lacked the patience for children's fantasies. "There's no such thing as magic."

He pulled out a note from the back of the journal, which read:

I hear you like secrets. Shall I tell you one?

"That's creepy," Fate said with a scowl. "They have a phrase for this: *playing with fire*."

He sneered. "Are you suggesting something?"

She realized that her words made it sound like she'd referred to his affections for Firmus, and rolled her eyes. Although thankful someone cared for her brother in her stead, she felt ill at ease with the trouble Abyssus seemed to procure without guidance.

"Books don't just appear out of thin air," she said. "This isn't magic. Someone left it for you, someone who knows you well enough to know when and where they should leave it. Someone who is watching you closely."

"I know that, but if they wanted to hurt me, they would have done so already. They wouldn't have given me a book." To quell her doubts, he pulled the book out and handed it to her.

She gaped at both his determination and his general flippantness. Mystified by the journal and its author, she accepted it and examined the patterned black and silver cover before leafing through the pages.

The events outlined in the book certainly aligned with their arrival in Macellarius. It covered a wide array of topics from the High Queen to the Grim, all of which indicated a complex scheme to hide the power struggle occurring in the Capital and the theft of two Dolls.

She searched the pages, then closed the book and carefully examined the cover and binding again. "Who in the world wrote this?"

He shrugged and gazed up at the clouds passing overhead. "I don't know. It doesn't say."

She shook her head. "It's too weird. How can you believe anything written in here?"

He groaned. "Don't you think I investigated?"

She pressed a cool hand to her warm cheek and pondered.

Abyssus reinforced his question. "Firmus helped."

She considered her role in aiding the Rebellion. The Ignis triplets headed the efforts of her precious group, and she chose to put her faith in their efforts, hoping they, in turn, might put their trust in her once she was old enough. "Firmus did?"

"Yeah, he did, so believe it."

She rested her eyes on her brother once more, trying to decipher the truth from his misleading charms. "If this is true, we're children of Grim."

A smile stretched across his face. "I know. I always knew we were no good. Plus, it explains the darkness."

Her body tingled. Madam had trained her to maintain a calm demeanor under pressure, but she felt as though she might explode. If the book contained the truth, everyone, including Madam, had kept it from them. Fate drifted away in her mind. She became an island apart from all of Mu. She looked at the murky palace and realized the only thing keeping her prisoner was herself.

"If that's true," she said, "why didn't anyone come for us? To be made by the High King, the Council, and the Grim... it doesn't make sense. It's all too far-fetched."

Abyssus ruffled his hair and then straightened it again. "I don't know, but I want to find out. I'll keep searching until I can explain it all to you. Next time we meet, I'll update you on what I've learned."

She shifted onto her hip, placed her hands on his arm, and forced him to look her in the eyes. She needed their connection to convince him of what she felt in her chest. "Abyssus, even if we aren't Dolls, we don't belong here. This is all wrong. Everything about this feels wrong."

She'd lived the first turns of her life without knowing fear, but ever since she lived in the brothel, she feared many things.

She feared Mortis, and her future, but more than anything, she feared her brother's hunger for the truth would lead to his death. She grimaced as the bruises from Mortis's grip on her brother's forehead became visible.

She cared little about King Neco's plans. One way or another, she intended to put an end to him and his tyrannical rule in order to free Abyssus. She may not know how, but she held no fear of Neco because, in the end, he was only a Rahma.

The only part of Neco's involvement that seized her thoroughly was Mortis, an Ancient unlike many others. His size, strength, and energy raised a terror in her like no other. She sensed something entirely unnatural about the man. He polluted anything he touched. His mere presence radiated death, like puss oozing from an infected wound. The image of him standing over her hung just behind her eyes, warning that he already once had Abyssus in his grip. The next time might result in her brother's death.

She searched the darkness of her mind for a ray of light, and suddenly, the Prince of Nitor flickered brightly in her mind, sparking a new question. "Abyssus, that boy from earlier was Hero, no?"

"Hmm."

"He's the Prince of Nitor. His father is our Uncle, Cruentus Niteo, no?"

Abyssus rested his chin on his knees. "What are you really asking?"

"That would make him a Half-Breed."

"Obviously."

She put a finger into the air as though conducting a symphony.

He puzzled at her behavior. "What are you doing?"

She stopped clasping her fingers together. "Do you think—"

"A Doll? Is that what you're thinking?"

"No, something else...." Fate pressed on her temples, trying to ease the frustration her brother inflamed.

She closed her eyes and played through Hero's scenario again. He stood on the balcony dangling a foot over the edge, the armor-clad woman shouting and calling for the guards and, finally, the guards—growing as clear as crystal in her memory— she found the image of Ignis Fortis, with another guard, pulling Hero from the guardrail.

She gasped. "The Rebellion."

"What rebellion?"

"I think I just figured something out. Madam is the head of the Rebellion... and don't you dare act like you don't know what I'm talking about. You have been far too nosy not to know who they are."

He put his hands up in defense. "I won't."

"It may be the real reason Madam took me to the brothel."

Abyssus snapped, "To protect the missing heiress." He opened his journal and scratched out new notes. "Tell me everything, and I'll research it and see what we can come up with."

She bit down on her thumbnail, enthralled by the excitement of discovering the possible truth of their existence. "So, the Ignis Triplets are part of the Rebellion against the Council. They likely believe we're the missing Dolls that were taken before a new heir could be established."

"Right."

She twisted her head to one side, hoping the new perspective might trigger a sudden epiphany. "Hero... Hero...."

He tried to encourage her train of thought. "He's one of the last Caeles and ice elementals."

She tipped her head to the other side. "Power... if he's the youngest living heir to his clan, both sides would want to claim him. I'm not fully sure I understand how that would help them, but it makes a kind of sense, no?"

He wrote fanatically without looking up. "It does. Continue."

"If Mortis came from the Council — I hear the Aska are closely tied to them — then it would make sense that he was here to keep an eye on all of us, possibly even remove us if we were to become a problem."

"I'll ask Firmus about him. Maybe Hero knows something. I can sneak into Nitor and see what he knows."

She snapped from her thoughts. "Didn't you hear me? I think Mortis might be here to kill us if we step out of line."

"Just because it's difficult, doesn't mean we shouldn't try."

"Hero's always guarded. You said so yourself."

Abyssus leaned his elbow on his knees and rested his head against his hand. "If we're to get to the truth, we need to follow up on our information."

She shout-whispered, "The truth is that we don't know anything yet. This could all be wild fantasies."

He swayed forward and gazed at her, his expression alone telling the story of his determination. "We know quite a bit, actually. What we have yet to learn are the key players of the Game."

Fate embraced him tightly. "This is not a sport. I'm so scared right now. You mean the world to me, and I won't risk you for anyone."

Abyssus pressed his lips together, briefly forming a tight line, and then blew air out, releasing the full pout Fate knew so well.

She urged him, "Listen to me. Just this once, keep your distance from Mortis, and be careful in reaching out to Prince Hero. We may be formally related to him and his father, but we don't really know them."

"I promise, no matter what it takes, you will be free of the brothel."

She lifted the hair from her neck, allowing the cool breeze to run over her torrid skin. "Focus on finding the truth. I'll get *myself* out of the brothel."

"Fate," Abyssus started.

With a hard shrug, she feigned a smile. "Try not to do anything reckless."

He floundered for words, pulling springs of grass up from the ground.

She stood and dusted the debris from her gown. "I better get going or I won't be able to visit for some time."

He stared up at her as though she were the sun itself, but whatever thoughts rattled around in his mind, he kept them to himself.

Reluctantly, she waved and trotted across the lawn towards the side of the palace. Neco would be waiting for her, and she needed to distance herself from Abyssus before he discovered the details of their bargain.

6

FAIR BARGAINS

Dread filled her soul as she rounded the palace to the front lawn. Already, Neco loomed like a shadow at the front doors, knowing she'd pass by before returning home, and catching sight of him caused her muscles to seize. She slowed to a walk.

As she approached, the wear of turns showed clearer on the man. Time proved bitter and cruel to him, and she barely recognized the once vibrant king. A lump formed in her throat and she swallowed hard, pushing it down.

His eager, calculating eyes devoured every inch of her as she came to rest before him. "I wasn't sure if you intended to flee our deal."

Fate clasped her trembling hands in a miserable attempt to steady herself. "I keep my word."

The hunger in his eyes grew and a smile formed upon his lips. He stepped back and opened the door. "Then right this way, my Lady. I'll show you to my room."

Fate stepped inside the palace, fighting her instinct to flee. Everything in her warned of how wrong a union with Neco would be. She already felt his mortality all over her, lapping at her energy.

He followed her in, closed the door behind them, and ushered her upstairs. His eyes clung to her as they strolled down the hallway.

Her heart sank deeper into her chest with each step.

Neco reached out and ran his fingertips over her cheek. "Do you see what your absence has done to me?"

As she took a closer look at the man she once saw as a father, she noticed the deep lines in his skin and the way his color waned. Her skin crawled under his ravenous gaze as he slowed to a stop and pushed open the door to his bed chambers. Thoughts flew from her mind as she peered inside at her future—give up her body and anima, or give up her brother. Without thinking, she stepped inside and crossed the room to the glass doors on the opposite side.

Neco closed the door, straggled along behind her, and stroked her hair, allowing his hands to pass over her backside. "It so nice to have you home. I can't tell you how bleak it's been without you. You are the only light in this kingdom."

She faced him, taking note of how the life had returned to his eyes, and how the folds in his skin eased, after spending that brief moment in her presence. A part of her pitied him, but before that feeling could take hold, he lurched forward and grabbed her, rubbing his face over her neck and chest as he panted heavily.

Fate leaned away but did not flee. She knew better than to endanger her brother further. Her small form gave under the pressure of Neco's desires, and they fell to the floor. She turned her head, forcing her attention on the passing clouds as he fumbled with her gown.

A loud knock at the door drew his attention, but he started to strip anyway, first removing his jacket. "Not now."

Fortuna's voice carried through the dense wooden door. "If you have Fate in there with you, now is the only time you have."

Neco sat back on his heels as he unbuttoned his shirt. "Go away. She and I have a deal that does not involve you."

A loud bang resounded as the doors flew open. Fortuna stood in the hallway with her fiery aura and heat bleeding into the room. She set dark, enraged eyes upon Neco, and spoke so softly it made it difficult to hear. "We have a legal and binding contract, Highness. If you refuse to comply, I will be forced to petition the Council for your erasure, and put Fate on the throne earlier than intended. The only thing this will change for them is how it works out for you."

Perspiration formed on Neco's brow as his eyes darted around in their sockets. He recoiled against the glass doors as he deliberated.

Fortuna's eyes met with Fate's, and she made a quick motion with her hand for Fate to come with her.

Fate glanced at Neco and quickly made haste to her madam's side.

Neco shook his head furiously. "You can't just barge in here and take her. Our deal was clear."

Fortuna pushed Fate behind her. "We still have a deal. If you still want her as your wife, you will purchase her as per our agreement. By law, Fate is mine until she comes of age, and as you so clearly stated the night you handed her over, 'She is not to practice on men.' You are male, no?"

Neco slapped the ground and shouted, "You damn well know what I meant!"

Fortuna narrowed her eyes. "Do you wish to end our bargain?"

Neco growled and pointed a finger at the madam. "She *is* mine."

Fortuna took a step backward, easing Fate out of the room. "Yes, my king, and one day, she'll return to you as a woman. Then you will reap all that your bargain is worth."

The tone of Fortuna's voice caused goosebumps to rise on Fate's skin, even amid the increasing temperature.

Neco crawled to his feet and crossed the room. "This isn't right."

Fortuna tipped her head and whispered over her shoulder to Fate, "There is a carriage waiting for you downstairs. Go now. I'll speak with you when I return."

Neco shouted as Fate darted down the hall. "Wait! You swindled me! This is criminal."

Fortuna remained behind and spoke with her honey-drip voice, the one she used to appease angry clients. "It's only a crime if you don't get what you need. You do *need* something, no?"

Fate raced away from the room with Fortuna's voice drifting in her ears. She hurried down the stairs and into the carriage.

The driver tried to close the door but Fate stuck out her arm and leg, blocking it. "Wait, Madam is still up there."

The driver looked up at her with purposeful eyes. "Yes, she said to return for her after I take you home."

All sensation left Fate's extremities as the door to the carriage closed. She gaped up at the palace doors to Neco's room as her mind spun itself in circles, and her pulse quickened as the driver pulled away from the palace, and a feeling of helplessness settled in.

Guilt struck her as the carriage stopped outside the brothel. Her actions had put Madam in a difficult position, and Fate nearly collapsed under the burden of knowing that Fortuna would be expected to fulfill the bargain she'd made.

She jumped when the door opened, and for a fleeting moment, she stared at the driver as she tried to wrap her mind around the turn of events.

Tori approached the carriage looking glum. "I'm sorry. I couldn't let you go through with it."

Fate slipped out of the carriage as the pressure mounted in her chest. "Why? Do you know what she has to do?"

Tori looked toward Macellarius with glossy eyes. "I do... and so did Madam." When her gaze returned to Fate, there rested a hint of agelessness. "You cannot make choices like that without conferring with us first. There are things you do not yet understand."

"Then explain them to me!" Her emotions bubbled over. A mixture of anger, betrayal, sadness and relief all toiled about inside her, finally giving way to a new kind of anxiety. She rubbed her head. "I can't take all this secrecy. Why won't anyone just explain what is going on?"

Tori turned to the brothel and walked away without a response.

Fate stamped her foot. "Tori?"

Tori stole a glimpse of Fate from over her shoulder. "You're acting like a spoiled child. Wait for Madam in the hearth room."

"Tori? Tori!"

Fate's anxiety increased as the carriage rolled away. She walked in a circle, swinging her hands in the air, before finally doing as instructed.

She sat by the fire pit and waited in the hearth room, feeling as though eternity had come and gone. The pressure in her head built until squeezing it became a surreal experience.

Fortuna finally entered from the screen doors to the garden, appearing as neat and well-kempt as always.

Fate stood and rushed to her. "I—"

Before the words left her mouth, a loud crack rang out and she felt the flaming sting of her cheek. It was only when she saw

Fortuna's extended arm that she realized her beloved Madam had struck her. She gripped her face and stared up at Fortuna without uttering a word.

Madam's gaze spoke volumes in the simple lack of fire in them. She held only love and fear for her pupil. "You are never to do something that foolish ever again. Do you understand me?"

Fate's voice shook. "Yes, Madam."

Fortuna threw her arms around Fate and held her tight. "Never."

Fate buried her face into Fortuna's silks. "Yes, Madam."

Fortuna released her and strode across the room, collected her pipe from her cleavage, and lit it. "I think you understand. You may go."

Fate gripped the skirt of her dress as she eyed the madam. "May I ask you something?"

Fortuna turned her amber eyes to Fate, but did not reply or move a muscle.

Fate ran her tongue over her teeth, hoping she wasn't about to tread into unwelcome territory, and swallowed hard. "The old woman... what happened to her?"

Fortuna squinted hard, then her eyes widened. "You mean from when you first arrived?"

"Hmm."

With a grating throaty sound, Fortuna exhaled with a slight laugh. "Like many people these days, she needed time to consider her position."

Fate took a couple of steps to see the madam's face more clearly. "What do you mean?"

Fire burned in Fortuna's eyes as they remained fixed on a memory. "She forgot the girls were people deserving of respect, so I sent her somewhere to learn respect for life."

"Where is that?"

Fortuna turned to face Fate with a soft but wicked smile. "The Abyss."

Fate shuddered. "You should not make such jokes, Madam."

Fortuna exhaled a long stream of smoke, clenching the tip of her pipe in her teeth. "It's not a joke. I know someone who can open the way. It seemed a fitting end to her miserable existence."

Fate took a step back, her body trembling with disbelief. In her eyes, Fortuna had exuded a mother's gentle love. To see her act so coldly shattered that image of her beloved madam.

Fortuna took another drag off her pipe. "Don't look so surprised. She was evil to her core. A few turns down there and she'll understand the value of life."

She exhaled another plume of smoke and took the journal atop the nearest shelf, crossed the room once more, and sat by the fire pit.

Fate followed, still curious about a great many things.

Fortuna eyed the journal as she sucked on her pipe, then snapped it shut. "You still wish to talk, no?"

"Hmm." Fate bit her lip, twisting the ends of her hair.

Fortuna scanned her pupil carefully. "You want to know about my clan."

Fate fidgeted with her robe. "I do."

"Sit," Fortuna said with a heavy sigh.

Fate scurried to her side, eager to hear what the madam would say.

Long streams of smoke left Fortuna's lips as she gazed at the ceiling. "We are a clan of degenerates and criminals. Not so long ago, we sought to rule the empire, and our kingdom was consumed by the Plague."

"But you survived."

Fortuna pressed her front teeth together behind her thick lips in something akin to a smile, but the pain in her eyes made it clear that Fate's comment stung. "Sure, we still live. We even have a kingdom."

"A strong one at that."

"True. We are very powerful." Her eyes reflected the flames of the fire pit.

"Then why do you and your siblings always seem so sad?"

Fortuna cast her solemn eyes to Fate. "There is no cure for the Plague. We are a dying kingdom in a forsaken empire."

"Is that why you came here?"

"I came here to see if I could do some good. Our world is full of corruption, and every turn that goes by, more fall from grace into depravity. If I can save even one of you girls from that future, I'd gladly give my life."

Fate watched Fortuna as she dwindled into thought. She knew that there was much of the story that Madam had kept to herself, but found peace in being allowed to know more than most.

Madam still kept her secrets, but at that moment, Fate lost the desire to learn them. She trusted Fortuna in spite of the lies she spun, because she understood that they were meant to keep the girls safe. She hugged Fortuna as tight as her small arms allowed, and accepted the truth of Tori's words. From that day forward, she needed to become a protector and give up her childish actions. Her sisters depended on her, as they all depended on Fortuna and one another. Their rebellion was still young but she felt deep in her soul that in time, they could be a force of reckoning.

7

YOURS TRULY

Fate sat in her room watching the way the morning light poured across the twelve fake roses pinned to the wall. She reflected on her days spent with Madam and her sisters. She now held a firm position in the Rebellion and worked towards gaining her own freedom. Sometimes she wondered what life might have been like, had she not been forced into the brothel. Hero crossed her mind, and she debated whether her life may have been similar to his, trapped in a palace.

She allowed herself to pore over Abyssus's newest notes once more. Although brilliantly detailed and accurate, they lacked the critical information to explain why, in the unstable balance of Mu, the Council, the Rebellion, and the Grim had not only allowed two illegal life forms to be created, but stolen and misused, and more importantly, if she and Abyssus were those very Dolls.

She brooded over the information, trying to fit the pieces together. The truth lay in plain sight, but it seemed that nearly everyone in Mu had attempted to bury it.

Fortuna poked her head through the doorway. "Fate, you have a package. Come to the door."

Fate stashed the notes in her dresser, hurried out of her room and down the long hallway, to the entrance where Fortis waited with his usual charm and smile.

The cheerful Ignis radiated a euphoric air. "Good day, my lovely Lady. I come bearing gifts."

She beamed, glad to see the most entertaining of the triplets. "Gifts? From you? Sir, someone will get the wrong idea."

Fortis smirked, clearly pleased with the game. "My dear Lady, it is impossible to get the wrong idea about me unless I intended it so. I am *quite* open about my endeavors... as everyone knows. I am simply the bearer of the gift, not the giver."

She laughed aloud and beckoned him inside, fearing what harm may come from leaving a fire elemental outside in the cold. "Please, come inside before you catch your death."

He hid his discomfort of the temperature behind a melodic response and a wave of the silver-wrapped package.

Fate took the gift as he extended it. "And who do I have to thank for such a lovely gift?"

He bowed his head ever so slightly with a coy grin. "Prince Hero."

Fate turned to Fortuna, who stared back at her with full skepticism.

Fortuna pulled her pipe from her ample cleavage and lit it with a spark from her fingertips, her amber eyes flickering as hot as the flame itself. "Is it explosive?"

What?" Fortis laughed heartily. "It's not. At least, I hope it isn't."

Fate inspected the package with ceaseless curiosity. "I'm not usually on his list of priorities."

Fortis scratched his head. "I don't blame you for being suspicious, but he put a great deal of effort into this gift. He even asked Queen Heqet for help."

Fortuna flung her hands into the air. "The High Queen! Is it expensive? Oh, it must be something special. Fate, girls here don't get gifts like this. This is meant for a princess."

Fate held the gift in her hands, suddenly concerned about the prince's unexpected interest in her.

Fortis teased his sister. "What do you think it means? Could this be the start of young love?"

Fate muttered, "I seriously doubt that."

Fortuna countered her brother's question. "Seriously, do you truly believe that all women do is sit around waiting for someone to woo them?"

Fortis refuted, "I know *I* do. You don't?"

The madam's fiery Ignis temper flared, and she scoffed with a throaty sound. "Don't project onto me, Brother."

He cooed. "Oh, that's right. Where is that lovely Tau you've been stashing under your robes?"

Fate slipped away as the siblings bickered, and strolled down the long hall, avoiding the watchful eyes of her sisters. Once in the safety of her room, she closed the door and settled on the bend in the round window.

She first noticed a small envelope with her name — her *full* name — which no one except Abyssus knew:

Cruentus Stella Atra Fate

Hero's practiced penmanship lined up so perfectly, she thought the letters might have fit stencils, but the subtle incongruity suggested otherwise. He seemed too meticulous in nature, which gave her cause to question his state of mind.

She opened the letter without further thought, and read silently to herself.

> *Lady Fate,*
> *I'm sorry that I'm unable to give you this note directly. I received notice that your birthday passed recently.*
> *To be blunt, this has nothing to do with your brother. He told me that you're studying away from home to become an entertainer, which I find highly improbable.*
> *Since I don't know the truth, I can only speculate that these matters are beyond my understanding. I've never been very sympathetic. I believe that the others would prefer if I remain an outsider.*
> *I'm uncertain of how I should introduce myself, as I rarely have the opportunity to meet with others outside of my father's work.*
> *When I asked Lady Heqet what I should buy for you, she told me to send something I like. It's a book I saw while visiting the Capital, and I thought you might like it.*
> *Happy belated birthday,*
> *Hero*

Fate debated with herself, not sure whether to laugh or frown at the opportunity within her grasp. Her brother clearly had ignored her warning, but at least created a way for them to get to know Hero. For the first time, she thought she could see the wheel of fate spinning.

She carefully unwrapped the silver paper and revealed a novella, *Sands of Time*.

The deep bronze cover with the gold lettering reminded her about stories of the mirrors from the age of the First Thirteen. Madam insisted that all the girls study history. Although she believed it to be in spite of the Council law, she felt grateful for the knowledge now. The book rang of folklore, and yet the title and the author remained a mystery.

She ran her hand over the rough surface, opened the book, and escaped into the story.

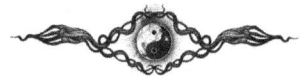

The god Solaris loved *Chaos* above all else that resided in the Light. No matter what trials came, he kept *Chaos* close and cherished it with all of his being. As a manipulator of time and space, he never aged, so he and *Chaos* remained in *Harmony* and basked in the Light.

Solaris sat in the Halls of *Time*, duty-bound to the hourglasses that measured mortal life. He watched the grains as they passed through the hourglass and fell lifeless to the bottom. From over his shoulder, *Chaos* made suggestions on how they might make the time pass more quickly, or slowly, for certain grains to provide a sliver of entertainment. So, the Mortal Realms grew with times of *Harmony* and *Chaos* as the hourglass was shaken, and then the gentle hand of Solaris passed over to calm it again.

Eons slipped through the stream of the Universe, and Solaris's attentions waned. Watching the hourglass only made him sad, and he wished to fill his never-ending life with something more. Weary, he walked to the edge of Light and peered out at the field of white flowers. There, he found himself drawn into Darkness.

In the Eternal Realm of Night, the Goddess of Destruction, Ulnaire, resided amongst the stars. Her hair hung so long and dark that it created the night sky, and her skin was made of moonlight—no other existed like her in all the Universe. She sang her world into existence, bringing light and beauty into Darkness, only to then shed her skin and return it into Darkness once more.

Fate spun her wheel and wrapped Solaris in the web of devotion. Each strand allowed him to hear Ulnaire's song, until her voice lured the young god away from the Light, leaving *Chaos* behind.

Swathed in *Fate*'s silver-spun threads, Solaris was so captivated by Ulnaire's beauty that nothing else existed in his world but her. The sound of her voice brought *Order* into his once chaotic world. He ventured through the gates of their realms and watched her for ages. As he watched, his love grew, until he could no longer keep his attraction to himself, and he wooed Ulnaire.

Their love grew, as did *Chaos*'s jealousy, for the god discovered the meaning of *Time*, and found he only contained enough for two. He must choose between *Chaos*, Ulnaire, and his duty.

Torn between his duty and his loves, he made his choice and snuck down from the Light to steal away with her behind the watchful eyes of the Light. Together, in *Harmony*, they created the Balance, a cycle for which the mortals could base their concepts of *Time* and *Order*. Solaris reveled in his newfound world and the embrace of truest passion.

Before the mortal sun rose each day, Solaris climbed back to the Beyond and cast his grand illusion, hiding his truest love, shielding her from those who would destroy her, for the only crime of Light was to love Darkness. Without fail, he completed his duty in the Halls of *Time*, ensuring both the safety of the Mortal Realms and hiding his affection for Darkness, before returning to Ulnaire's bed when the sun set.

The God rested under her protection and adoration, listening to her songs as he drifted off to sleep in her arms. In return, he snuck her into the heavens and showed her the majesty of the light among the clouds, winning her undying love and binding the pair for eternity. Together, they created life in the many forms of their love and spread it across the Mortal Realms.

Chaos, left alone, did what came most natural: he vowed to shake the world of Solaris and Ulnaire until both realms lay in ruin.

The day came to pass when *Chaos*'s vow came to fruition and the Watchers rested an uncertain eye upon Solaris, and they closed the gates to Darkness. They warned the love-stricken God to focus on his task, or he would be erased to create room for a new god, a god that understood the responsibility bestowed upon him.

Fearful, he worked endlessly in the Halls of *Time* as to not endanger Ulnaire, but *Chaos*, who had grown so jealous of their love, would not be ignored, and he stirred the Watchers' *Wrath* until it grew, shaking the Realms of Light and the Darkness alike.

Heartbroken, Ulnaire's song rose up from the Darkness, rocking the heavens, and shattered the hourglass.

Solaris cast himself into Darkness, and returned to Ulnaire's side.

Collapsed and frail, she caressed his face and, in her final moments, with what little strength she had left, sang, "Blessed are ye, Solaris. I'm afraid the *Time* has come. Though our Bond is severed, it cannot be undone."

The God wept tears of gold, unable to stop her passing, and held his love as she sang.

"Do not mourn my passing, my love. There's no need to weep. My voice will carry on with *Time* and find you when you sleep."

Her song symbolized her ceaseless love for him. The pure strength of their union, and the Balance they created, maintained their existence. Without this Balance, without Ulnaire, Solaris could not live.

Stricken with grief, he held the dying Ulnaire in his arms and used his remaining time to give her a new life—a life he hoped to live once more by her side.

Fate pressed her hand over her mouth as she considered the plot. It appeared to be about Bound and their eternal bond in spite of universal circumstance. Without their mate, a Bound died quickly and often painfully, just as Ulnaire and Solaris. She considered the quick death a mercy, knowing that if they did not follow immediately, they could spend eons in agonizing pain, searching for their lost half until they could once more reunite. For this reason, Bound were born together, as twins... at least until recently.

She stretched her stiff neck and sighed, trying to piece together Hero's intent when sending it to her. "Surprisingly romantic."

Stories like *Sands of Time* often appeared in old literature, reminding the Ancients of this union of spirit and soul. Many of the scriptures taught that Bound experienced echoes of each other's pain. Every tale about them depicted this shared pain and infinite devotion.

Fate closed the book and inspected the cover once more, reflecting on her history lessons. She'd read a few of the old tales, but Abyssus knew them better and always spoke highly of them. Any heart-wrenching story captivated her because it made her contemplate love, life, and the meaning of it all.

In this case, the book came from Hero, so her thoughts traced directly back to him, and his intentions when choosing it. She lay back on her pillow, thinking of how she should respond and what to tell Abyssus.

Suddenly, her mind spun and she sat forward with a gasp. "It's a riddle." She opened the book again and quickly scanned the words. "You clever devil. That's why they're italicized—it's the Lords of Light and Shadow."

Before she could relax her mind, the lattice gate scratched against the mats as it opened.

Tori popped her head in and spoke in a low voice. "Fate, that looker is here to see you again."

Fate chuckled. "Good grief, call him by his name."

Tori scrunched her nose and whispered. "And spark that heavenly flame? Praise be, what do you think I'm made of?"

Firmus leaned in, brushing against Tori as he moved. "Is this a bad time?"

Tori shrieked, flapped her hands, and ran away in a fluster.

He glanced back at her. "Did I do something?"

Fate smirked, covering her laugh with her hand. It amused her that Tori was so flustered by the Ignis anima. "That's just Tori. She's a touch flighty. Don't mind it. So, what brings you?"

"Oh." He held out a letter. "Abyssus sent me."

She took it gleefully. "I feel loved today."

He sat down at her table and crossed his ankles. "Did something happen?"

She genuinely smiled, thankful for their banter. It had taken her several turns to get the quiet Ignis to open up to her. "My brother's beloved Prince Hero sent me a letter."

He rubbed his nose with a sniff. "Beloved, huh? He does stick to Hero like paste. He says they're like brothers, but I hardly see the resemblance."

Fate winced with a practiced smile. "I think he meant brothers in spirit. Perhaps this union is based on their interests."

Firmus raised a brow and pulled his mouth to one side. "Lady, do you intend to mock me? I was referring to their spirit. Even a Rahma can see they are unrelated. They are just so different—like fire and ice."

She felt silly for thinking he meant it in a sexual way, yet still found it impossible not to note the pun. "Fire and ice? Rather ironic coming from you, no?"

He chuckled. "Indeed." He was the only person she'd ever met who, through his mere presence, could make the darkness within her retreat. Although their contact remained minimal, she greatly enjoyed his company when she was able.

She opened the letter, thankful for her brother's continued safety.

> *Loveliest Sister,*
>
> *I'm sorry I haven't written in a while. I've found it difficult to meet with Firmus when Mortis is watching. It's infuriating, really. How can we maintain a line of communication with that man waiting around every bend? You'd think he was fond of me by how closely he watches, but alas, I shan't prattle a moment longer.*
>
> *I've got some news for you. Hero will be participating in the Astor Tournament at the turn of the season. He shall compete against the other potential successors to become High King of Mu. I will not be joining the competition, of course. I have no interest in ruling Mu, or Nex for that matter. Wild, isn't it? If not for his father, he wouldn't mind a bit about it.*
>
> *Speaking of bits, I've discovered that the Lady Heqet is involved with the Rebellion. That's right. The High Queen herself is close with your Madam, and has turned against her spouse! There is apparently some kind of conflict over the Tainted. It has both the Rebellion and the Council up in arms. And that's not all.... You'll never guess who I met— Hero's aunt, Caeles Chi. She serves directly under the High Queen as the Head of the Elite Guard, though I suppose I should call it the Queen's Guard, knowing how close they are.*

*I say we watch and see how the Astor Tournament
goes before making our next move.
I wish you the best,
Abyssus*

Fate folded the letter and smiled at Firmus. "Sorry, I didn't mean to take so long. I was just taken aback."

"He said you would be." Silence around Firmus seemed normal due to his quiet nature. He never took offense and always appeared contented to wait.

Everything about him comforted her, but she struggled to understand why. "You are so good to Abyssus."

He noted her words without comment.

She decided to trust the Ignis. "I need your help. I'm really worried about him. He acts like he's free to do as he pleases. I beg of you to stop his meddling before something terrible happens to him."

Firmus stroked his chin and neck uncomfortably. "I thank you for placing your trust in me. However, I must be honest and tell you that your brother has his own mind, and he wields it like a weapon. It will not be easy for me to deter him from his path, but I will try."

"You are patient, perhaps too patient. Even I know how difficult he can be."

His eyes glowed like embers. Something about him differed from his siblings. Sometimes his eyes appeared to flicker like flames, even without cause.

Fate tucked a piece of hair behind her ear, feeling awkward, and sat down at her table to write a response. "I'll admit I've envied your bond with Abyssus. It's made me wish to be more like you, so I can be stronger and protect him."

Firmus pressed his pouty lips together and formed the slightest smile. "You have a wonderful heart."

"Flatter me anymore and I'll transform into Fortis."

He laughed silently and waited for her to finish her letter.

She concentrated for a moment before folding it and placing it into an envelope. "Here you are. I suppose I should write Hero as well."

"If you'd like. I am more than happy to deliver it for you."

"Would you be so kind?" She pulled another stationary from a box on her dresser, and set it down on the table, pausing only an instant until the words came to her.

Dear Hero,

I have received your package. Thank you for the book. I found it thought-provoking. In my home, we do not celebrate birthdays, we dread them, so you have brought a hint of unexpected joy into my routine. If possible, I'd like to know more about your life — about you.

Tell me, is the grass really greener on the other side?

She signed and sealed the second letter and handed it to Firmus. "My thoughts are with you."

"I shall deliver them safely." He stood in one swift movement. "Please excuse me, I must return to Abyssus now."

She gazed up at the strapping Ignis. "Be well, Firmus."

His face softened and he bowed his head. "Be strong, Lady Fate."

She watched as Firmus exited, questioning herself. She needed to work harder if she truly intended to become his equal. In her current state, even protecting herself often proved difficult. She sighed, frustrated.

Tori entered, still watching Firmus walk down the hall. "I know how you feel. That man makes me tingle all over."

Fate rolled her eyes. "It's not that."

Tori flopped on the floor across from her. "What's wrong? Bad news?"

"Actually, the news was quite good."

Tori stared at her with a raised brow. "Then, why so gloomy?"

"I see people like Firmus, and I realize how far I am from becoming stronger."

Tori scowled. "You know, physical strength isn't the only thing that matters, Fate."

"I know. You tell me all the time."

Tori poked Fate's forehead. "You have a wonderful brain. Use it. And... you have us."

A smile crept across Fate's lips. "I know. You all mean the world to me. I don't know where I'd be without you."

With one hand raised above her head, Tori proclaimed, "I could be this big and still not be smart enough to win a battle. Trust me, my eyes see much."

"I do trust you. I just want to work on every aspect of my being. I can't shake the feeling that there's something I'm not seeing."

A knock at the door interrupted their conversation.

Fortuna entered, appearing pleased to see the two girls together. "Who would have guessed that you two would become so close? I am sorry to intrude but the teahouse needs cleaning before tonight."

Tori frowned. "Where's Elana?"

Fortuna folded her arms with a coy smile and a wink. "I'm afraid our dear Elana has left our brothel for a new home, but something tells me she'll write."

Tori and Fate clapped their hands together in excitement.

Fate clamored to her feet and ran to the madam. "Really? Where, in Mu?"

Fortuna laughed and gave in to the excitement. "She has been placed in Nysa. The King is very influential, so she'll be safer there than anywhere in Mu."

The girls celebrated the liberation of their sister.

Fortuna paused and regained her composure. "I really do need the teahouse tidied before the guests arrive. If you could handle that immediately, there isn't much time before we open, and I don't want you two in there when the guests arrive."

Fate and Tori scurried out of the room, down the hall, and out to the courtyard still riding the high they felt for their sister.

As they passed through the courtyard, Fate cast a worried glance towards the back end of the brothel, at the double doors to the auction room. Their intricate design and the way they caught the sunlight disguised the morbid truth of what they concealed. She could almost hear a clock ticking every time she set eyes upon them.

Tori took Fate's hand as they entered the teahouse. "It'll be your turn soon, Fate."

The elation surged through her body at Tori's words. She wanted nothing more than freedom. It seemed ages since she knew what true joy felt like. For now, she'd live vicariously. Not even the mess in the teahouse dulled her spirits.

Both girls happily cleaned and scrubbed. They collected trash and forgotten items, and prepared the lavish room for the evening's business.

Fate bent over the chair to pick up a piece of jewelry, and suddenly felt hands gripping her hips. When someone thrust against her backside, she shouted and tried to crawl away.

Tori charged the man and lashed at him with her small cloth. "Get off her!"

He repeatedly rubbed himself against Fate, clawing at her dress and trying to lift it.

Madam burst into the room, causing the temperature to rise. She seized the man and flung him out the open door into the snow. "We're not open yet."

He floundered on the ground with a red face. "This is how you treat your clients?"

Fortuna stared down at him with her full Ignis fury. "You are only a client during business hours, and if you want one of these girls, I suggest you bid on them properly. No money—no business." She slammed the screen shut and turned to Fate with a warm embrace.

Tori cracked the door and peeked out to make certain the man had left.

Fortuna took Fate's face into her hands. "Did he hurt you?"

Fate shook her head. Once again, she felt helpless. She needed to learn to fight. "Madam, would it be possible to take fencing lessons?"

Fortuna stepped back and studied Fate. "We've been through this. We are performers, and ladies, not brutes of battle."

Fate protested. "Wouldn't it be best for us to be able to defend ourselves in situations like these? What would have happened if you were away?"

Fortuna puffed out as if smoking. "I will consider it. It is nearly time for your auction. Perhaps it would be best if you learn some sort of defense."

Fate hugged Fortuna tightly around the waist. "Thank you."

Fortuna forced a pained smile. "Be responsible with all of your training, girls. As you have so eloquently pointed out, I may not always be with you. Now, off with the two of you. I don't want you here when we open. Go out the back. I don't even want them to see you."

"Yes, Madam," Tori responded for both of them, taking Fate by the hand.

They hurried out the hidden panel in the teahouse, ran into the brothel, and down the hall to the sunken hearth room.

There, a group of their sisters waited and immediately greeted the pair with open arms.

Fate sat down next to the fire as Tori made her way to Myrna's side.

Fate warmed her hands. "Sorry we're late."

Tori complained, "We had another one."

The girls groaned in unison, and it didn't take long for the chatter to begin. The sisters had grown close in their turns together, and reveled in the quiet moments when they could catch up, share news, and push forward their agenda to change Mu. Their conversation carried well into the night, until Fate finally stood.

"Sorry," she said, "but I've been really tired, so I'm going to get some rest."

The girls taunted, trying to get her to stay longer, but Fate needed to make her retreat if she intended to get the answers she sought.

She made her escape, walked farther down the hall to her room, and closed the door behind her. She pressed her ear against it, making certain no one followed her—no footsteps, just the distant sound of laughter. She crossed the room, took the red cape hanging from the wall hook, gathered it around her shoulders, and placed the hood over her head.

A shadow passed through the light at the end of the hall, causing her to pause. Again, no sounds except the distant chatter and a door closing as someone exited the brothel.

Fate turned off the light, took the gold scarf resting on her dresser, and placed it around her neck. After a final inspection, she opened the round window and climbed out, quickly sneaking her way along the brothel wall through the courtyard and past the teahouse.

8

HEART OF THE STORM

Fate kept her head down, avoiding eye contact with the amorous nobles that entered the brothel grounds. She'd grown accustomed to their client's numerous reactions, and knew better than to engage in any sort of interaction.

As she moved farther from the brothel, the air grew colder and the snow fell in a flurry.

Fortunately, the gates to Nitor were only a short walk. She left the barrage of leering eyes and approached the two gate guards with a curtsy. "Good evening."

One of the men smiled with burning red cheeks. "Lady."

When away from the brothel, people viewed her as a Royal rather than a girl from the brothel. It somewhat surprised her that more did not recognize her, but then again, her father had kept her secluded so a select few knew the truth. For now, she still held her royal title, but her time in the brothel made that fact seem small and untrue. Nevertheless, people made her out to be whatever suited their fancy the most, a circumstance she'd learned to use to her advantage.

She suspected the young guard saw her with the same eyes as most thirsting Rahma. "It's a lovely night, no?"

He fidgeted, rubbing the back of his neck. "You think? You headed into Nitor?"

She flashed him a bright smile and gently placed her hand upon his arm. "How did you know? You are so clever."

"I wish. You seem quite well out here. Don't you ever get tired of the snow, Lady?"

Fate spun in a small circle, allowing her dress to flare around her. "No, I find it peaceful."

The guard adjusted his gear, appearing even more flustered than before. "Be careful. If the King hears you, he'll try to marry you off to the Prince."

She feigned naivety, playing the guard for confirmation on rumors circulating about Hero. "What would make you think that?"

The guard relished, feeling like her intellectual superior in at least one aspect, oblivious to both her knowledge and his own shortcomings. "Well, you know, the Caeles are ice elementals."

"Hmm."

He drew close to her. "But the prince is different. When he's in a bad mood, we get heavy snow like this and, when he's feeling foul, we get blizzards. Look around—he's in one of his moods. It's his fault we can't stop the snow. I'll bet he enjoys watching us suffer."

"That's dreadful." She removed the scarf from her neck and put it around his.

He blushed so profusely, his ears turned red. "I couldn't."

She caressed his cheek. "You must, I insist. I can't stand the thought of you out here in the cold when I'm on my way to a warm palace."

"Thank you, Lady."

She bid him well and crossed the gate without incident. A part of her felt guilty for how little effort it took to persuade him.

As she moved toward the palace, she scouted the path of least resistance. She wanted to find Hero before she froze. The guard's warnings proved true, as the winds increased and the temperature dropped.

It only took a moment before her direction became clear. Once she breached the main gate, she avoided the guards and servants, and hurried up the side stairs. No one wanted to risk slipping on the ice at night. Fortunately, her dance lessons had made her agile, so scaling the slippery incline proved easier than expected. "Thank you, Madam."

Once on the second floor, she walked the perimeter and peeked through windows from the shadows. Finally, in the glow of a candle, she found Prince Hero leaning against one of the windows and jotting notes onto a piece of paper.

She craned her neck to see what he wrote. To her surprise, she uncovered staff paper filled with music notes. *A musician?*

Her eyes left the paper and returned to the prince, only to meet his gaze. She gasped and fell back into a heap of snow. Something about his gaze rattled her, and she pressed her hand to her chest, shocked to find her heart racing.

She looked up at him and took in his pale skin, white hair, and brilliant mint eyes. Despite his striking features, his face lacked expression, and his aura suggested she proceed with caution, as though dealing with a wild animal. Even more unusual to her, he donned a pair of black gloves while indoors.

Hero stood, opened the window, and gazed down at her. "What are you doing?"

Her heart danced around in her chest, giving rise to both butterflies and concern. In all her turns, she'd never met another whose aura disarmed her... until now. She rose to her feet again, dusted the snow from her dress, and quickly regrouped, searching her mind and soul for the reason he left her feeling breathless.

The obvious spiritual disruption disconcerted her, and her need to learn more about him grew. "What did you mean when you sent that book?"

He smiled and opened the window wider. "Why don't you come in before you freeze?"

She glanced around, not sure if she should check for guards or backup. Even though his smile was clearly intended to offer her ease, it left her feeling more startled. The young man before her stood as lovely as the most coveted art in Mu, but the energy he exuded, and the predatory look in his eyes, hinted at something unpredictable and unruly—something *chaotic*. Her mind flashed to the story he'd sent her and ignited her curiosity to burn brighter than her fears.

The warmth of the room engulfed her as she stepped inside, removed her hood, and rubbed her hands together vigorously.

Hero closed the window and stared at her for a pause before extending his hand. "Let me."

She put her hands out and he took them into his own, blowing hot breath onto them and gently rubbing them until the warmth returned to her.

Before Fate knew to control it, she blushed, feeling the heat move over her skin and through her veins.

He stopped and looked up at her. "I'm sorry, did I embarrass you?"

She shook her head. "No, I turn pink when going from cold to hot, that's all."

He raised a brow to her obvious lie. "Very good. Now, why are you here?"

She hesitated, realizing she lacked all reason and memory of why she came. "Huh...." Then reality snapped her back with a vengeance. "The book.... Why did you choose that one?"

"Oh, I particularly like *Sands of Time*. Although it's not proper folklore, and there are too many flaws to count, still, it's an excellent representation of Bound, no?"

She chewed her lip, deliberating her response. "Is it?"

"Pardon?" He leaned to the side, studying her.

"I thought so at first, but after reading it a second time, I came to see it as a riddle about the Lords of Light and Shadow."

His eyes sparked with fascination and he stood upright, moving closer to her, watching her every move. "*Nolai.*"

Fate questioned, "I'm sorry, what?"

"Seems you've learned a bit about folklore from somewhere, no?"

"Right." She caught herself trailing off.

He lowered his brows. "Is something wrong?"

"You're very strange," she said without thinking.

He laughed. "And you're very rude."

She pressed her hand to her head, willing her mind to return to her. "Uh, that's not what I meant. Caeles... Caeles are rare, are they not?"

He squinted and faintly pulled his head to one side. "True, though I'm not sure I understand what you're trying to ask."

Her clarity wavered, and she wondered if it would have been wiser to wait for the letter. Her impatience made her look a fool. "Sorry, I'm a touch scattered."

"It happens."

"Are you responsible for the snow?"

He shrugged and glanced out the window at the falling snow. "It's hard to tell. It always snows here." His eyes ventured back to her, paired with a newfound frown. "Are you displeased with the book?"

"No. It was fascinating. I wrote you a letter telling you so."

He covered his mouth with the back of his hand, presumably hiding a laugh. "Yet, here you are."

"Yes, and you don't seem the slightest bit surprised to see me."

His eyes gleamed in the low light. "It seems to me that you're the sort to do as you please, much like Ulnaire, so I have no reason to be surprised by anything you do."

She started to speak but her words caught at his comparison. She then considered his statement and replied, "You really think so?"

"What?"

"That I'm like Ulnaire."

He turned and reconsidered before finally nodding. "I do. I think you are passionate, compulsive, and, most likely, if given the chance, destructive."

She crossed her arms. "You don't even know me."

He smirked. "But you don't deny it."

Her mouth fell open.

"So, my guess is that you're really here to see if I had nefarious reasons for giving you a gift, or if my intentions were genuine."

Fate bit her tongue, wishing she could think of a superior retort. "I wouldn't say that."

"They were genuine. I thought you might want a friend."

She felt both flattered and slighted. "I have many friends. I hear you're the one that has difficulty getting along with others."

"That's not untrue. It's one of the reasons I thought we might get along."

"Oh."

Hero kept unusually still compared to Abyssus's description of his clan. At most, he shifted his weight from one side to the other after standing in one place for a while. "I spend most of my time reading and, as you saw, writing music. There are few people I wish to associate with, but your brother has become my dearest friend, so I thought... your brother... my friend — we must at least have something in common."

Fate pondered the manner in which Hero spoke. Everything sounded perfectly reasonable to her, just lacking the depth of sincerity. She found his energy infectious but cautioned herself not to lose sight of her goal. "You make a valid point. I would very much like to continue our interactions."

He nodded. "Agreed."

She pulled her hood back over her head and gazed at Hero. "I'm glad we had this chance to meet."

He simpered. "You broke into the palace illegally. I wouldn't exactly call that chance."

She shrugged. "We are technically related."

He stared at her with a dry expression. "No, not really."

"Close enough. I'd better get back before someone notices."

He moved to the window and opened it. "Please take care in the chill."

She beamed. "I don't mind. I've always loved the cold."

For the first time, she saw authenticity in his response when he opened his mouth as if to respond, closed it again, and then shone a gentle smile before finally answering. "Then we should get along nicely."

Her cheeks burned hot once more as she stepped out of the window to her escape.

He studied her. "The hot and cold thing?"

She pressed her hands to her enflamed cheeks. "Yup." After giving a short wave, she hurried away into the shadows, and didn't turn back until she reached the stairs.

He stood at the window and pointed to the banister at her right.

She inspected the snow that had gathered there, atop of which rested an intricate ice crystal flower. Carefully, she plucked the flower from its resting place and returned her gaze to Hero.

He still stood at the window, and this time held up a piece of paper to the glass:

Keep it. Goodnight.

She waved to him before climbing down the stairs, ice flower in hand, and into the darkened gardens below. The snow eased to a stop, and a clear night sky opened above her.

Hero, are you feeling better now?

She returned to the brothel as quickly as she'd left, warily avoiding the drunken patrons that roamed the property in search of their next escapade. They disgusted her.

She kept to the shadows and hugged the brothel wall all the way back to her room, and slipped in through the round window.

The instant the lock clicked, Fortuna spoke from her seat on Fate's bed. "That was both foolish and dangerous. If those men had gotten ahold of you, how would you defend yourself?"

Fate spun, her heart pounding. "I'm sorry, Madam."

Fortuna rushed to Fate and took her into her usual warm embrace. "I'm just thankful you're safe. You girls are going to kill me one day."

Fate swallowed hard. She knew she was in trouble but felt more guilty than punished.

Fortuna released her and stared down at her with a frown. "What could you possibly find so important that you left the safety of your room at this hour?"

"I went to see Prince Hero."

A spark ignited in Fortuna's eyes. "You actually spoke with him?"

Fate smirked and pressed a hand to her cheek, still questioning her reaction to him. "Yes, and he's not at all what I expected."

Fortuna held Fate's arms and leaned down, looking her eye to eye. "You know, it's not a poor match. He may be your best chance out of here."

Fate felt herself drifting. "What?"

"I'm serious. He's a potential heir to the High King. That gives him great power. Not to mention what it would mean for the Rebellion. It makes perfect sense."

Hero flustered her but she still didn't know why. Fortuna's words held their own logic, but she felt strange about aggressively engaging someone she hardly knew. Her mind raced through her options, knowing that the day of her auction drew closer. "It does."

Fortuna flapped her hand in the air. "If we pull this off, you could actually be High Queen. I will make you a promise: train hard with your dance, and we will put on the show that will bring every eligible Ancient to your feet. In return, I will allow you to practice fencing as you requested. Fate, this is everything you need. It will free you from this place, your father, and it will raise your status within the Rebellion and all of Mu. You can be a leader of the free people."

Fate shrank within herself. Her curiosity about Hero lingered, but not enough to see herself married to him. She knew nothing about him, and the energy that resonated between them gave way more to concern than to hope. Given her limited options, she knew Fortuna spoke the truth, yet her soul swelled with doubt.

Fortuna kissed Fate's forehead. "Get some rest. We can talk about this more tomorrow."

Fate nodded as the madam hurried back to her nightly duties.

Once the room fell silent, she removed her cloak and flopped onto her bed with an agonized sigh. The mess she'd created with her simple desire for knowledge had turned into a tidal wave of dread that swallowed her. Her eyes traced the ceiling as though the answer to her challenge hid between the decorative fans and umbrellas.

She rolled onto her side and stared out the window into the cold night, and something even colder and darker stirred within her. This darkness called out to her, pleading for release with the promise of fulfillment. She struggled with the turmoil brewing, and tried to calm herself. "You are Cruentus Fate, are you not?"

In spite of her fear and anxiety, she drifted to sleep.

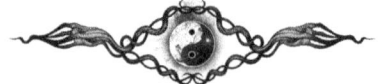

When Fate woke in the morning, the weight of the previous night's conversation had diminished. She sat up and stretched, looking down at the gown she should have removed.

A light tap at the door alerted her, and Tori poked her head in. "It's really late. Madam has been asking for you."

Fate crawled to her feet. "Sorry."

Tori entered the room and closed the door behind her. "Were you out all night?"

Fate shook her head and yawned. "No, I'm just tired."

Tori lifted her chin and pouted. "Did you come in contact with a lot of anima?"

"I don't think so. I saw Prince Hero of Nitor."

Tori's eyes bulged. "He's Tainted."

"What?"

She hurried to Fate's side. "It's true. Everyone in Nex knows about it. That's why they keep him locked up."

Fate tucked a loose hair behind her ear. "Madam didn't tell me." She spoke against Fortuna, but her real concern came from why her brother had hidden it from her. These days, he kept close company with Hero, so he must have noticed.

Tori pulled a new gown from the armoire and helped Fate change. "I'm not surprised. King Niteo doesn't like people to discuss it. The Council protects them because Hero is one of the last Caeles."

Fate turned to Tori once her gown was zipped. "How did he become Tainted?"

Tori looked around the room uncomfortably. "Well, there's a debate on that."

Fate leaned in with fascination.

"His mother was murdered. They think he was Tainted by the murderer, or that he murdered her because he is Tainted."

Fate puzzled. "When did she die? I don't remember her at all."

"When he was about three."

She shook her head with a snarl. "How could he commit that kind of crime at three?"

Tori shrugged. "With the Tainted, it's hard to tell. That's why the Council fears them."

Fate thought about the possibility that Hero may be a killer. She needed to get closer to him if she intended to escape the brothel and take back her kingdom.

Tori quickly combed Fate's hair with her fingers. "We need to get over to the teahouse. They made a huge mess last night."

"Did something happen?"

Tori exited the room and strolled down the hallway with Fate in tow. "I'll say. That same guy who bothered you got really out of hand last night, and Madam roughed him up some more."

Fate glanced into the sunken hearth room as they passed, caught a glimpse of the girls cleaning, and waved. They shouted and waved back.

At the teahouse, as expected, they discovered the unruly man had trashed the place. Broken glass lay across the floor, and tables sat askew beside tea stains and strewn rice crackers. A clay tea kettle sat half-collapsed, surrounded by bits of colorful porcelain.

Fate sighed while looking at the horrendous mess. "She needs to ban him."

Tori moved to the first pile of broken plates. "I think he's some kind of Noble."

Fate started clearing the debris scattered across the table. "Another Rahma. Doesn't anyone else find it strange that so many Rahma are becoming Nobles?"

"Oh, I know exactly what you mean. They aren't all bad, but those aren't the ones being elevated. It's always creeps."

Fate crossed the room, dragged the garbage basket closer to the table, and started tossing in anything broken or disposable. "Look at the disarray Neco and Niteo have brought to Nex. I'm not really sure what it was like before, but I can't imagine Ancients letting it get to the state it's in. Ancients as prostitutes and Rahma as nobles — the world is out of balance if you ask me."

Tori sat on the floor and scraped an unknown sticky substance from the floor. "I can say for certain that you wouldn't see it in Thule."

Fate snickered. "But I wouldn't want to live there either—too uptight."

Tori chuckled until they heard a knock at the screen door.

Both turned to see Hero holding hands with a small, ragged girl in a filthy dress.

Tori jumped from the floor and hurried to the child. "Honestly, Hero, you couldn't have cleaned her up?"

Hero shifted, wearing a firm pout and the hiss of irritation. "I was more concerned with feeding her and finding her a home."

Fate pointed first to Tori, and then to Hero. "Do you two know each other?"

Tori fumbled for words. "No... I mean... not really."

Hero sneered at her. "We've met. but I wouldn't say we are comfortable enough to be using informalities."

Tori glared at Hero. "He's absolutely correct. I also wouldn't say we are comfortable enough to cover up atrocities committed by the other—say like child abuse."

Fate stood agape, unsure of how to handle the heated debate.

Tori burst into laughter. "We're just teasing you. We met earlier today."

Fate checked Hero's face for confirmation, and his smile proved Tori's statement true.

Hero explained. "Tori came to speak with me earlier today, after I contacted Fortuna about Yuzu here."

"Oh," Fate said, taking in the whirlwind of confusing humor.

Yuzu clung to Hero's leg and peered at Fate. She shared Tori's brown hair and vivid blue eyes, but her skin appeared darker than most in Nex, yet not quite dark enough to be a member of the Si.

"You're pretty," the girl said.

Fate knelt down in front of her. "So are you... Yuzu, is it?"

The girl nodded.

"I'm Fate. It's a pleasure to meet you."

Yuzu buried her face into Hero's leg.

Tori patted Yuzu's head. "Hero met Yuzu in the shops this morning."

Hero nodded as he agreed, his voice smooth and pleasant, albeit aloof. "I did, and we had a lovely conversation. Did you know that Yuzu is six turns old?"

Fate feigned surprise. "I didn't but that's amazing. You're such a big girl."

Yuzu beamed.

Tori grimaced. "She's been taking care of herself now for almost a turn, just like a big girl."

Fate covered her mouth. "So long? Wow, you are amazing. I can barely do that now."

Hero rubbed Yuzu's back and let out a hand to his side as he spoke. "I told her she could have a real home with a bed, food, and sisters."

Fate nodded. "I see. Madam knows?"

Hero nodded. "She said it would be fine, but only if I would teach the girls how to fence. She was quite persistent on the matter."

Fate stood. "We'll take good care of her."

Hero glanced out at the pond. "I know."

Tori took Yuzu's hand. "Let's go see Madam. She is very excited to meet you."

Yuzu checked with Hero, who winked at her and said, "Go ahead. You're going to like it here. The girls are all really nice."

She squeezed his legs with all her might before leaving with Tori.

Fate realized how much her heart ached for the young girl. "Children shouldn't have to pay the price for adults."

Hero hesitated for a long moment, his lips parted but silent. Finally, he returned from his deep thoughts and said, "I couldn't agree more."

"Thank you."

He kicked the ground with his foot, turned and started down the stairs. As he walked, he glanced back. "I'll see you for your lessons after the tournament."

Fate remembered Abyssus's letter on the subject. "That's right... the Astor Tournament... I heard it can be rather dangerous. I hope you'll be careful."

He stopped at the bottom of the stairs and gazed at the pond. "It should be fine. We just need to collect seals from the great houses and take them to the Capital. I guess you could say it's more of a race."

She leaned against the doorframe. "Be well just the same."

He stuffed his hands in his pockets. "Thanks. I'll see you."

"Hmm."

As he walked away, she experienced the same dread she'd felt when her brother promised everything would be fine. She knew the best she could do was wait, and returned inside the brothel, leaving naught but a prayer for the wind to carry.

9

THE PRINCE AND THE PROSTITUTE

Fate sat up in her bed, shivering as snow piled up outside her window. The glass rattled from the powerful gusts blowing outside. At her side, her newest little sister slumbered as she hugged a dog plush kept together by Nigel's patchwork. She rubbed Yuzu's back and pulled the blankets up around the small child.

Her door clattered and Tori entered to hand Fate a letter marked by Abyssus's seal. After delivering the letter, Tori left the room again, providing Fate the privacy to read.

> *Dearest Sister,*
> *The storms are worse than ever before. I'm afraid there's little I can do to quell Hero's sadness. Even his visits with the High Prince seem to be of little help. I wish there was something more, something that could get his mind off the Astor Tournament, once and for all.*
> *Any ideas?*
> *Abyssus*

Fate closed the letter and observed the blizzard, her mind on the events that stirred this storm. It had already been two seasons since the Astor Tournament ended, leaving Hero the new successor of the High Throne. Instead of feeling victorious, he seemed to be in such a dismal mood that it had stormed every day since his success. For two people living so close, Fate felt farther away than ever.

She slipped out from under the covers. After placing the letter on her desk, she snatched the red and black flower-patterned robe from the hook beside the window, and sat down at the vanity to comb her hair.

While staring at her reflection, she asked, "You are Cruentus Fate, are you not?" Every day, this seemed less a question and more a habit. She felt hollower than before, or at least accustomed to her life as a courtesan.

The door opened in the reflection of her mirror, urging her to turn and look.

Fortuna leaned against the doorframe, stifling the smoke from her pipe as she noticed the sleeping girl under the covers of Fate's bed. "Yuzu has really taken to you."

"The sound of the wind frightens her at night. She says it sounds like someone howling."

Fortuna also watched the snowfall. "You said you wanted to learn fencing."

Fate placed down her comb. "Yes."

"Don't you think you should talk to him about it?"

"In his current condition?"

Fortuna blew smoke towards the hallway. Despite her calm expression, something had triggered her smoking addiction so early in the day, and whatever it was clearly weighed on her mind. "Especially so. Perhaps it would do some good for him to get out of that stuffy palace."

"Would King Niteo allow it?"

"He's visiting the Capital," Fortuna said, pressing her tongue to her teeth. "My darling brother is on watch at the moment."

Fate mouthed, "*Oh,*" without uttering a word aloud. This seemed like a good time to begin training, as well as an opportunity to calm the storms. The lack of clientele both hurt and aided their cause. Even with Fortuna being heir to the Tir Na Nog throne, they required many funds to continue their secret work for the Rebellion.

"Not to mention...." Fortuna smirked. "...it certainly wouldn't hurt to have the Future High King in your good graces. If you can win his affections, you could truly gain your independence. You're already fourteen. What better way to free yourself from Neco's clutches than to involve the Nitor Royals? Maybe even become High Queen yourself."

Fate spent so much time focusing on the impending auction that she gave herself little time to contemplate such things. If Fortuna really considered it a possibility, she would act immediately and bring it up again soon enough. Council law forbade interference of one Royal family with another. The Council held everyone to these laws by penalty of erasure. This path ensured the safety of herself and her brother.

"I'm not certain he sees me in such a light, but I will do my best."

"Nothing would make me happier than seeing Neco's face if you became High Queen." Fortuna walked closer, returned the pipe to her cleavage, and took Fate by the shoulders. "You've trained in the arts of beauty, charm, and seduction since you were a little girl. You can do this."

Fate gazed into Fortuna's eyes, recognizing the source of her stress as her own ambiguous future. Time passed so quickly in the Rahma's world. Any Ancient may already see her as a woman, if not for the count of the turns. They desired the mind of a woman, but the body of a child, a fact that often filled her with disgust.

Only two turns remained, leaving Fortuna with the weight of the world on her shoulders. Every day, their struggle to defend themselves against the Plague grew more tremendous.

When Fate saw her mentor's pain, she nodded. "Yes, okay, I can do it."

The corners of Fortuna's mouth turned down, but she did her best to keep her practiced smile. "Good. Get ready. I'll send for Hero."

Will he even come?

Fortuna kissed the top of Fate's head and left the room, closing the screen behind her.

Fate returned to her vanity and finished combing her hair. Upon finishing, she went to her dresser to find attire for this supposed visit, but found nothing suitable for training. She exited her bedroom and traveled through the hallways towards the outside corridor by the front courtyard. The snow covered so much of the beautiful yard that she saw little aside from the steam and the ice.

In spite of the cold, she found Nigel in Fortuna's room with the windows wide open and fire blazing, as he worked on an extravagant white beaded gown. He sat on a little wooden stool before the clothed dress form, with a needle sticking from the corner of his mouth as he gathered the fabric in one hand.

Fate leaned forward and whispered, "Nigel."

Nigel jerked back, pressed a hand to his chest, and laughed. "Oh, Fate! You gave me a fright." He took the needle from his mouth and embedded it into the cuff of his black dress shirt. "Is something the matter?"

"I'm sorry to disturb you. I know you're busy."

He leaned forward on his knee, his eyes twinkling amiably. "Not to worry. I'm always busy with something. What can I do for you?"

"Madam asked me to dress for fencing lessons, but I only have gowns. The shops are closed because of the snow. I hate to ask, but could I use your assistance."

He waved her closer, and as soon as she followed his directive, he took a measuring tape from beside the gown and measured her waist, hips, shoulders, arms, and legs, then sat down again and jotted down the numbers. "You have grown, Lady Fate."

She smiled as she checked the numbers over his shoulder. "Really?"

He smiled back. "Yes. If you intend to practice today, your clothes may not be ready by the time you start, but they shall be ready for you by the end of the night."

"Thank you!"

"Of course. I am only sorry I did not plan for this sooner."

"Don't be. The fault is mine. You always make us the most wonderful garments in all of Mu. We could only be so lucky. I look forward to training in my new attire." She scurried off in delight. She always loved Nigel's handiwork, as he considered the person and the design carefully whenever he made any piece.

As she approached the entrance, she slowed her gait and let out her hand. A few snowflakes drifted through the air, much fewer than before. *Hero?* When she raised her gaze, she froze, as within the sea of white, a pair of mint-colored eyes watched from beyond the courtyard gate. Then her eyes fell upon the fitted black gloves, which she intended to ask him about once they grew more comfortable with one another.

Hero stroked his neighing horse, which shared in the stark whiteness of their surroundings, his attire, and Hero himself. To add to the contrast, he wore a bright red scarf and a single drop earring with a ruby jewel.

Fate lifted the front of her robes, just enough to not trip, and stepped down to the courtyard, sifting her way through the snow to greet him. The gate creaked as she opened it. "Good morning."

Hero leaned his head against his horse's nose, keeping the reins tight in his hands. Although he watched, he said nothing.

Fate grinned at the horse. "Who's this?"

He finally spoke. "Holly."

"She's beautiful. Do you like horses, Hero?"

"I do. I wanted a puppy, but she's almost as cuddly." One corner of his mouth quirked back, as though to express his approval. "You can pet her, if you'd like."

Fate allowed him to draw her hand towards Holly. The horse exhaled hot breath into the cold air, hesitated, then relaxed and allowed Fate to stroke her. "Let's take her around to the back and cover her up so she's not too cold." She gestured for Hero to follow around the side of the building and into the back courtyard to a heated stable.

Hero studied the stable, seeming awed. "You even have stables here."

"We get many visitors, after all. She should be more comfortable in here."

He removed a blanket from a satchel on the saddle. He then unbelted the saddle, set it aside, and covered Holly with loving delicacy. After giving her a final nuzzle, and a kiss on the nose, he allowed Fate to guide him inside through the back screens.

Fortuna greeted them at the door. "Thank you for coming on short notice. Before we begin any form of training, I'd like to be certain that this arrangement will be suitable for both parties."

Hero patted the snow off his shoulders and head, then blurted his thoughts without any form of expression or intonation to suggest his motives. "So, why the sudden desire to fence?"

Fortuna withheld her response and glanced at Fate. "Would you like to answer?"

Fate answered respectfully. "Prince Hero, I'm underage. I will not become a full-fledged prostitute until I turn sixteen. Until then, I hope to be fully equipped to defend my assets."

Hero kept a fixed expression, making it unclear what he thought during his pause. Soon, he cracked a coy smile. "Assets... right. Fair enough."

Fortuna silently exhaled. "I would like to reach out to your father and make an exchange. This exchange would allow you to leave Nitor Palace and come here to be Fate's mentor. From that point, how you two spend your time is entirely up to you, though I do hope for each sister to learn self-defense."

His smile faded, and he dropped his head and thought to himself for a time. "Surely, by now you know the results of the tournament. My condition isn't—"

"Are you going to let it control you?"

He raised his head and stared back at Fortuna with dark eyes.

She kept her gaze fixed and challenged him. "Are you? Not every bad thing must be a result of the Taint. Whether you remain sealed up in the palace or you come out here, the Plague will continue. It would do you well to find a way to stop your miasma from spreading, rather than remain cooped up and let it fester."

Fate listened on, gathering that Hero's presence in the brothel may very well bring the Plague into their home. Each of her sisters may contract the disease from being in the presence of this ailed energy. She knew not the cause of his ailment, only that he posed a danger to everyone in proximity.

But how or why?

He faced a palm upward and stared at his gloved hand with a wistful expression. "What about your girls? If they become ill, what will you do? Worse yet, what if something else happens to them? Shall I take responsibility for it?"

Fortuna shook her head. "No. Everyone here is fighting for the Balance. We all know what's at stake. If your being here to train them brings us any closer to success, it's a risk we're willing to take."

Fate understood the underlying meaning behind this, but supposed Hero might find it nonsensical. After all, for them, it meant the future of the Empire. For him, it just meant extra work in order to get out of the palace.

Hero shut his hand and scanned Fate from head to toe. "Must be quite an asset to take such a high risk." With his flat expression, he met her gaze. "Are you certain this is what you want?"

Fate scrunched her brow. The way he gazed at her seemed to be so full of wisdom, as if he meant to forewarn her of something. The sounds and colors of her surroundings faded, making her feel as if she stood in a black and white painting. Her ears filled with the crackling of static, and the room pulled away from her.

This moment persisted until she finally answered. "Yes. We stand a better chance if we know how to fight."

The colors and sounds returned, leaving her to question the meaning behind the weird moment where time seemed to stop.

"Very well," he said.

Fortuna smiled as she looked between Hero and Fate, most likely seeing an opportunity for them to deepen their bond and the potential for Fate to win his affections. She gracefully bowed out to give them time to talk privately. "I shall prepare a contract and send it to your father. For now, enjoy your stay in the brothel."

Rather than dwell on her weird experience, Fate followed Fortuna's cues and redirected her attention to Hero. "I didn't take you to be the type to accessorize."

Hero appeared distracted by his study of the architecture. His gaze wandered even after he responded to her comment. "Hmm?"

She pointed to the earring.

When he noticed her movement, he touched the red jewel. "Oh, this? It's a family heirloom. I got it from my mother."

She touched her chin. "It's pretty."

"Do you want it?"

"No, no," she said, waving her hands in refusal. "I thought you said it's a family heirloom. How can you give it away so easily?"

He smirked. "I simply asked if you wanted it. I didn't say I would give it to you. It's always good to know how greedy a person can be."

How insolent. She shifted her mouth side to side in an attempt to hide her distaste. "You said you got it from your mother.... Was it before her death?"

"No. My aunt, Chi, lives in Inoue Capital. I wasn't able to visit her until long after my mother's death, but she'd kept many things that my mother intended to give me. In that regard, I suppose you could say that I didn't receive it from her directly, but her thoughts reached me."

"That's nice," she said, smiling. "You must be tired of standing in the portico. Come with me. I'll make you some tea so we can continue talking."

As she led the way to her room, she thought about Hero's statement. It made little sense for someone who murdered his mother to wear something he considered a gift, even after her death, unless he kept it as a trophy.

Something is wrong here.

Fate entered her room and ushered Hero inside.

He glanced at the ice rose on her dresser. "You kept it."

She looked back at the rose with a smile. "Of course. It's a gift from someone special." Although the rose seemed to be made of ice, it remained at room temperature and behaved more like a glass or crystal figurine, something she considered peculiar. She lowered to her knees, placed her hands against the panels on the floor, and took out the tea table stashed within a hidden compartment.

Hero leaned forward to look inside. "Abyssus?"

"You know how he is. He insisted on installing it just in case I needed somewhere to hide."

"Clever." He cleared his throat and placed a hand against his chest. "*Efficiency and order are the way of all things.*"

Fate smiled, hearing her brother's voice as clear as a bell. She imagined him standing beside them and felt at peace. She closed the compartment and set up the table, then gestured for Hero to sit.

As he knelt down, a sound drew their attention to the bed.

Fate gasped. *I forgot about Yuzu.*

Yuzu rubbed her eyes as she stirred from sleep.

Hero remained frozen, mid-motion, most likely mimicking Fate's sudden stiffness.

As Yuzu fully awakened and noticed Hero, she also gasped.

Hero smiled. "Hello again."

Yuzu jumped from the bed and ran to Hero, throwing her arms around him. "You're here! Hey, aren't you sick?"

Hero frowned at her, appearing a lot like a pouting child. "That's not very nice. Do I look sick?"

Yuzu shook her head. "No. I'm sorry. I didn't mean it like that."

His smile renewed. "Don't worry. I'll come to visit more often."

Her stomach growled, and she pressed a hand over it to muffle the sound.

Fate stood and brought Yuzu to her feet. "Up now, and so much for tea. Let's get you some breakfast." She motioned for Hero to follow them out of the room.

They walked to the dining hall, which lay vacant at the time since most girls were already hard at work. Yuzu sat down at one of the low tables while Fate went to the cupboards to pull out the raw rice and fish they cooled, using blocks of ice. She also took the kettle to the hearth room across the hall, set the kettle, and returned to prepare the food.

"Let me help," Hero said.

Fate tied up her sleeves and rinsed the rice in a metal bowl. "You can cook? But you're a prince."

"You're the Princess of Macellarius, and yet you're in a brothel."

She pressed her lips together.

He removed his gloves, stared at his hands for a long moment, and then rolled up his sleeves.

Fate leaned over and picked up one of the gloves from the counter. "I'm surprised you took them off."

He exhaled in an uncomfortable laugh. "Yes, they're difficult in water."

"You must be fond of them." She left room for him to explain.

He twisted his mouth, disappointing her. "Something like that."

As soon as he finished prepping the fish, he opened the cupboard by his leg and pulled out the cutting board. After he set it up, he scooted Fate to the side, opened the cupboard above her, and pulled out several decorative plates.

Fate's mouth fell open. "How did you know where to find those things? Have you been here before?"

He drew a knife from the butcher block in front of him, inspecting the sharpness by running his finger over the edge. "Nope."

She scrutinized him. If she continued to accuse him without evidence, she figured she would just sound crazy, and he didn't show any indication that he had lied. "Right."

With two people at work, Yuzu shortly sat before her breakfast, each food separated onto its own bowl or plate, as Hero had insisted.

Fate placed a cup of tea in front of him as he leaned against the counter. Most men showed some reaction to her by now, either lust or admiration. She tried brushing her hand against his arm, but missed because he moved to pick up his teacup.

Did he just dodge me?

She drew closer to his side and shone a fond smile. "So, you write your own music. Have you finished any pieces?"

He placed his teacup on the counter. "Almost. My goal is to compose a symphony... so four movements."

"That's incredible! Do you play any instruments?"

"A few, but I prefer piano and violin."

She took the corner of his sleeve and pulled him along. "Then come with me! I'll show you something wonderful." As she ran by Yuzu, she told her sister, "We're going to the theatre. Eat your breakfast and join the others, okay?"

Yuzu agreed with her cheeks full of rice.

In order to reach the theatre, Fate left the brothel through the back screens and ran along the rocky path to the outside corridor of the teahouse, taking the long way in order to avoid the auction room. She half-ran to the end, and motioned for Hero to follow down the right connecting portico. At the end of this hall, they entered a door to the side of the theatre. Of all the places in the brothel, she loved this place the most.

A simple raised stage faced the auditorium of empty seats covered by red velvet. Long, plush curtains of the same deep red hung open, displaying a sleek black piano that rested between handcrafted dividing screens, a walkway, and a stage for the brothel's performers. Delicately carved flowers embellished the wood and filled the room, from the chairs and the pillars to the stage itself.

Fate ran up the small steps at the side of the stage and straight to the piano. "Isn't the theatre magnificent?"

Hero walked after her, scanning the theatre while nodding. "Indeed." Once he reached the piano, he swept his fingers across the key lid.

She leaned towards him and flashed her best smile. "Will you play something for me?"

He thought to himself, then sat down and bared the shiny keys. "It's not yet complete, so I hope you won't judge me too harshly."

"Never."

He positioned his hands so carefully, it appeared as if he thought the keys might break. After a brief pause, the soft clinks of the piano filled the air.

She meandered to the edge of the stage and sat down, closed her eyes, and swayed to the sound of the music. The song began tenderly, the sounds light and played in higher keys. As it developed, he played the deeper registers, adding a melancholy to the blithe airs from the beginning.

She hummed along to the tune, and then added nonsensical words that matched how she felt inside—first hopeful, then full of yearning and sorrow. With her eyes closed, she slipped into a daze and a story unfolded before her. She dreamt that she stood in a field brimful of glowing white flowers that swayed in the breeze. Although she sensed that someone stood ahead, she saw only the lavender sky and the storm of petals caused by the wind. She began to step forward and... nothing.

Fate stirred from the trance, realizing that Hero had stopped playing. She turned to look at him as he studied her.

"So, you can sing," he said.

"I like to think I can."

He stood, tossed the back of his coat over the bench, and stepped away from the piano. "I'm saying you can."

Her cheeks flushed. "Thank you."

He joined her in sitting on the edge of the stage. "The Mortals think that the Gift of Song was created by the one they call the Mother of the Watchers. What do you think?"

"But Hero... *you're* mortal too."

He leaned towards her wearing a frightening grin. "Am I?"

She winced, choosing to take his question for play. "I don't know what I believe. Those are Council teachings, aren't they?"

He shrugged while nodding. "You're not wrong. They're much older than the Royal Council, though. I find those tales fascinating." His gaze trailed off as he babbled. "Sometimes I wonder, if I commit a large enough crime, would the Watchers heed me any mind? Or perhaps, if their mother is the creator of song, would my symphony bring them down to the Mortal Realm?"

Fate sat open-mouthed and at a loss for words. *Is he some kind of fanatic? Maybe being cooped up in the palace has made him stir-crazy.*

She exhaled heavily. At least, if he held this deep a fascination for mythology and history, she may use it as a way to grow closer to him. "Is that why you like music, or is this just a fleeting thought?"

He snickered. "Who can compose a symphony grand enough to call the Watchers down to our meager realm? If I ever succeeded in such a feat, I'd take the Throne of the Universe for myself."

"I say go ahead and try. A universe run by Caeles Hero? Fascinating, indeed. At the very least, I'd like to see what kind of world you conceived."

He leapt down from the stage, crossed arm across his chest, and bowed. "Very well. I do not disappoint. I strive for perfection in all that I do."

Fate laughed to herself. Out of all the people she'd met, he said the most curious things.

He might have been eccentric, but it provided her an opening.

She spied an opportunity to swindle his affections. "Maestro, I realize that your taste is refined, but I shall perform sometime before my auction. If it interests you, I would hope to see you that night."

Hero returned to his usual leaning stance and tilted his head. "Are you inviting me to watch you perform?"

She carefully pressed the matter. "I can promise that it will be unlike anything you've ever seen."

A smile grew on his lips. "I accept your challenge."

He's easier to bait than I thought.

He turned towards the row between the theatre seats. "Well, I should get back to study."

As soon as she heard the declaration, she stood. "Already?"

"Yes. If I don't complete my work, it'll cause problems later." He met her gaze a final time, exposing a faint smirk. "Prepare yourself. We begin training tomorrow."

"Next time, bring your studies!"

He walked away, tossing his hand up in a sort of wave without looking back.

She waited for him to exit through the doors, then slunk down the stage steps and out the other door, which led to the corridor. Vapor escaped her lips as she stepped into the brisk air. A pair of her younger sisters ran around her, shrieking as they chased each other. "Girls, remember to complete your chores before this evening."

The two girls bowed. "Yes, Miss Fate."

She smiled and patted their heads, realizing she sounded more like Fortuna with every passing day. "Good."

The girls ran back down the hall to continue their cleaning.

It relieved her to know they could still laugh and play, that they remained hopeful about leaving the brothel and leading a better life outside the servitude of others.

She ventured back down the hall to the brothel courtyard, breathing into her hands to warm them as she entered in the back doors. The Madam's smoke led her into the sunken hearth room. After checking for her sisters, Fate joined Fortuna. "I invited Hero to my performance."

Fortuna lowered her pipe. "And?"

"He accepted. Today, I learned that he has an interest in mythology and history. Next time, I will try and learn which stories interest him. The only one I know is *Sands of Time*. I feel like I can use my performance to win him over."

"That's wonderful news. Inform me as soon as you know of his particular tastes. We'll need time to prepare."

Fate bowed her head. "Yes, Madam." She rose to her feet and turned towards her room.

"Fate."

She faced Fortuna again.

"Remember always: do what you must to survive."

10

A STATE OF WAKENING

Fate lay in bed, feeling the morning sun on her face and the icy embrace of the chill creeping in from outside. She flinched as her cheeks turned cold.

Why is it so cold?

A voice called out to her. "Mistress, wake up."

She gasped, startled by the sound of the voice so close. She shot up and caught a glimpse of something reflecting in her mirror. The bedroom door snapped open, but no one entered or exited. She took a shallow breath, then stood and peered into the hallway, left and right. Still nothing.

Weird.

She rubbed the back of her head as she wandered back towards her bed, but stopped fast as she almost tripped over a small boy standing in her path.

The boy wore a dark mask with only a slit for a mouth and no space for his eyes. His white hair resembled that of Hero, but he appeared no more than four or five turns.

He grasped Fate's robes with one hand, tugged, and repeated, "Mistress, please wake up."

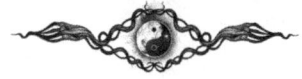

Fate inhaled sharply. Again—or perhaps for the first time—she sat up in her bed. This time, she found Hero staring down at her, his expression blank as usual. She questioned her sanity and the genuineness of his presence.

"Hero?"

"Yes. At least I'd like to think so." He grinned. "I would think it rather uncomfortable to wake in the morning as someone other than yourself, no?"

If not for the disorientation, she might have laughed. "What are you doing in my room?"

He gestured a jabbing motion. "Fencing. Remember? Lady Fortuna said to wake you and that she doesn't recall raising a bear."

She squinted, and raised the heavy hair from the back of her neck to ease the tension. "I'm not hibernating. I just had a strange dream."

Hero pulled back the sheets, offered his hand, and helped her to her feet. "A dream? Do you often dream?"

"No, not usually. It started just recently."

"They say dreams are the first sign of lunacy."

She stared at him for a long time, again lacking an acceptable counter response. "Thanks, Hero." Even if she'd slept late, she still took the time to brush her hair, as her reputation relied on maintaining her appearance. "It's not like I dream all the time. Don't make me out to be ill."

"Dreaming at all is odd. You're not a Rahma. Though, I've also read that if an Ancient dreams, it can be a sign of an Awakening. Maybe you have a past life that you don't know about."

The words of the small masked boy, though simple, echoed in her mind and sent chills up her spine. She set down her comb so hard it clanked against her vanity. "What kind of books are you reading? Are those Council approved?"

He snapped his fingers and pointed. "The same books your brother reads."

Damn it, Abyssus.

Fate shooed Hero out of her room, hoping for the chance to collect her rapidly scattering thoughts. "I need to get dressed. Why don't you go and greet Yuzu before we begin our training? The girls are just dying to see you."

"What about you?"

"Huh?"

He appeared to her like a whipped puppy. "Were you dying to see me too?"

She puzzled over her answer, unsure if she should play along and try to seduce him, or deny it. His questions always seemed to catch her so off-guard, she kept failing in her plan to entice him. He made it impossible for her to read his intentions. She felt as though he were playing some kind of game at her expense.

He scanned her from head to toe, cracked a smile, and left without further commentary.

Fate closed her door, mumbling under her breath as she lovingly took the clothes that Nigel had made for her. He'd spent much of the previous day designing and sewing her new garbs, all fitted attire suited for fighting. His designs always stood out with luxurious patterns. She first put on the navy-colored long-sleeve shirt, and buttoned up the high collar. Shiny gold thread glimmered in the light, showing the faint patterns of leaves over the base color. Lastly, she put on her grey pants, her boots, and tied her hair.

The process took longer than expected, especially since she took the time to appreciate Nigel's work. Shortly, she finished her examination and stepped into the hallway to search for Hero—not terribly difficult given the giggling from the dining hall.

Her sisters gathered around him, clinging to his arms and legs. He shook them around playfully.

Fate clapped her hands. "Okay, now it's time for us to train, so let Prince Hero go."

The girls let out a concurrent whine.

"You can play with him later."

He shot her a look of surprise.

They finally relented and returned to their tables, albeit complaining.

Fate shook her head as Hero approached. "You're rather popular around here."

"A popular toy, but popular won't make you a better fighter, nor will getting dressed up."

His comment irked her. Every time she thought they might move forward, he pushed them back again, so consistently that she deemed it intentional.

He looked around the dining hall. "Where's the best place to fence?"

"The stage? It's the most open area. We won't have to worry about hitting any paintings."

He opened his hands to each side, gesturing to things as he added, "...or furniture... or walls!"

"Okay, okay! I know this isn't the best place to train but we're here."

"We should be *not* here next time, if there isn't a place to train properly."

It took everything in her power not to roll her eyes. "I'll get right on that."

Hero took a detour in the sunken hearth room to collect the fencing foils he'd brought, then walked towards the theatre while smiling back at Fate. "Well, odds aren't always favorable in battle."

They entered the theatre through the front doors and used the center aisle to get to the stage.

Fate went behind the curtain and backstage to the light switch, to illuminate their training area. Her heart beat fiercely with the promise of growth, but also from the anxiety of realizing that Hero wanted to fight her without training gear.

"Should I put on safety gear?" she asked.

He stared at her for an uncomfortable few seconds. "I never fought with safety gear."

She rubbed her arm, questioning both *his* upbringing and *her* well-being.

Once she returned to the open part of the stage, he passed one of the foils to her.

She lifted the coil and swung it two times, testing the weight.

"It's not a toy."

She pointed the foil towards the ground like a reprimanded child.

He crossed the stage and faced her. "Today, we'll start simply. You'll need to work with your foil and whichever element you wield."

"All right."

He stared at her long and hard. "Which element do you wield?"

She hesitated, fearful of the consequences that clung to her every word. Even now, she dared not tell a soul of her darkness. "Electricity."

His head bobbed a little as he processed the information. "Really? Explains why you're so petite."

"How so?"

"Electricity is the element of the Feh. Compare that to your diminished stature and—"

"I'll have you know, I'm still growing." She hated hearing about her height.

He lowered his chin and squinted. "Hmm... your name must have been a mistake."

She felt the blood rush to her face. "Excuse me?"

"Like all Feh, your name should have been a representation of the clan, so it's fair to say your name should have been F-E-H-Y-T, since all traditional Feh names start with F-E-H, but to the Rahma it sounds like Fate, which they associate with the three fates, namely the Spinner. Who knows, perhaps I'm wrong and Neco really *is* your father."

Fate felt sick to her stomach. The glimmer in Hero's eyes suggested that he meant every word he said, and yet it all made her out to be no more than a pawn in someone else's game.

He waved it off. "We need to focus, though, or we'll never get you trained, and Fortuna will be furious."

Baffled by his apathy on the subject, she fell to a habitual response. "Right, sorry."

He frowned and his expression shrank. "Ready?"

"But I still don't—"

He charged her with alarming speed.

She thrashed with the foil, attempting to defend, but he quickly deflected her swings and froze the floor. Her feet slipped out from beneath her, and she landed hard with a thud, banging her elbow on the ground.

Before she could pull the foil up, he held the point of his to her neck. "You're dead."

She slapped the floor and shouted, "I don't even know what I'm doing yet!"

Hero removed his blade and extended his hand. "True, but now I see how you react under duress. You're too relaxed for someone in your circumstance."

She got back to her feet and straightened her clothes with a wounded ego.

He turned and crossed the stage to his original position. "Let's try it again, now that you have an idea of what to expect. Center your balance and remember what your skills are. This time, do try to protect your assets."

Fate growled. Not only was he unimpressed, but he was making fun of her.

"Ready?"

She concentrated on her foil and on Hero. He bolted again, and this time, knowing that thrashing would be of little use, she held the foil still and formed a ball of electricity in her free hand.

In an instant, he crossed the stage and launched his assault.

His blade moved too fast for her to keep track of, and again the ice formed beneath her feet. She used the foil to stabilize, and released the electricity with a pop as Hero drew near.

She smelled the singe of burnt cloth. *Got him!*

He retreated across the room, un-singed, with a smirk. "I know this is difficult, but try not to set yourself on fire."

"What?" Fate looked down at the burnt shirt and hem of her pants.

Hero moved again, denying her time to mourn Nigel's garment. He struck, and she defended, causing the foils to sing. Her feet slid on the ice, forcing her to one knee.

He stopped and put his foil down. "You're dead."

"What? How?" She looked down again, this time finding her leg and hand frozen to the ice. Long spikes extended towards her.

He released her from his trap. "You must pay attention if you want to live."

"This is the first time I've ever fenced. You're supposed to be teaching me, not bullying me."

The corners of Hero's mouth turned down, and he folded his arms behind his back. "Your enemies will not offer you more."

Fate struggled to understand him, but found his methods nearly unbearable. "Try explaining."

"I have been. If you really want to learn, you'll stop complaining and start listening and utilizing our interactions. Not everything is tea and dancing, Lady. There are serious issues in the Universe that do not involve your assets."

Fate fell silent. She wanted their interaction to bring them together, not push them apart. The lessons were not going as expected. For a moment, she thought she might cry, but she shook free of the feeling and pressed on, deepening her commitment. "You're right."

A curious expression washed over Hero's face. He clearly had bigger things on his mind than their training. "Very good."

She wanted to talk with him and learn more about what made him tick, but he guarded himself too closely. She needed to persevere and earn his trust, so she sighed, shook off the rest of her waning self-pity, and readied herself for the next assault.

Her eyes traced his actions, noticing for the first time how elegantly he moved. He kept himself surprisingly still while he advanced, not a single step or swing wasted. He used his element and the foil together.

Fate dropped a ball of electricity, allowing it to spill out on the floor between them. It danced and crackled, which delightfully brought Hero to a stop.

The glee faded quickly as he adjusted his approach. Ice rushed under the lightning, forcing Fate to back away from it. No sooner had she done so than he darted around the lightning and closed in from behind.

She moved too slowly to stop the attack.

He held the foil to her neck. "You're dead."

She sighed as he released her. If it always resulted in death, she saw little point in training.

He patted her on the shoulder. "But much better this time. There was real thought behind your choices."

A tiny spark of hope ignited. "Really?"

"Hmm. Rest a bit. You'll be sorer than you'd expect." He gestured to the stage. "We'll meet again—elsewhere—to start your real training."

"So, that's it?"

"For today, yes. Remember, you're not the only person I agreed to train."

She felt foolish. Once again, she wasted her chance to woo Hero, and came out looking vain and irrational. "Of course. I'll get Myrna for you, unless you would like a moment to rest."

"I'm fine. I'll wait here."

She set the foil down and turned to leave.

"Fate?"

"Yes?"

"Remember, not here next time."

Defeated, she merely nodded and exited the theatre. In a daze, she strolled through the halls until she found Myrna.

Myrna saw her face and frowned. "What's wrong? What happened?"

"I don't think Hero finds me appealing... at all."

Myrna chuckled. "I wouldn't know about that. I think he's just eccentric. His interest in you may lie somewhere unexpected."

"I'm serious."

Myrna placed her hands on her hips. "I think he just keeps things to himself. I was like that for the longest time, but it changed with Tori. I can't explain it, it just... changed."

The aches slowly crept into Fate's body. "Perhaps."

"Give it time. Don't be so uptight."

Fate nodded. "He's waiting for you."

Myrna shouted back as she hurried down the hall towards the theatre. "Talk with Madam. I'm sure she'll have an idea of what to do."

Fate made her way to the sunken hearth room feeling low. Everything she tried failed when it came to Hero.

Madam sat in her usual place by the fire, reading as always. She stopped, looked up at Fate, and arched her eyebrows. "Did something happen?"

Fate flopped on the floor beside her and bellyached. "Nothing is working."

Madam set her book down and gave Fate her undivided attention.

Fate stuck her leg out, showing Fortuna the burnt part of her hem. "I even ruined Nigel's hard work. What's wrong with me?"

"He's Tainted." Fortuna reached into her cleavage to withdraw her pipe, then lit it with a snap, took a slow drag, and exhaled. "You'll have to work your way through it. He will unnerve you, and remove all sense of grace and reason, without even realizing it."

Fate leaned forward, resting her elbows on the ground and her chin against her hands. "I'm at a loss. People have always been drawn to me, but he just evaluates me like one of his books. There's no desire, very little amusement, and whatever amusement I do cause is usually at my expense."

"What you're experiencing is normal. Being around someone Tainted gives way to dark thoughts and feelings. The more you're around him, the harder it will be for you to control it. So, I recommend you start meditating until you can get it under control."

Fate sat upright again. "All right."

"You know, we might be able to use this to our advantage."

"How?"

Fortuna smiled. "You said he treats you like a book."

Fate crossed her arms. Hearing the words from someone else made it sting all the more.

"It may be a good thing. He seems to treat everyone the same, but he treats you like one of his beloved books. Try making the connection there. It's the only thing he seems passionate about."

"So, should I study more folklore?"

The madam winked. "I have just the thing." She stood and exited the sunken hearth room, leaving Fate to wonder what her mentor intended. When Fortuna returned, she held a book in her hands. "Why don't you deliver this to Hero? Tell him it's a thank you from me, but wait until he's left the brothel."

"You want me to deliver it to the palace?"

"Hmm. Meet him where he is most comfortable."

"But he hates it there."

Fortuna silently chuckled. "We all hate the idea of the brothel, and yet it is our home. Comfort and enjoyment are often not one and the same. You would be surprised by some of the things people find comfort in."

"Thank you," Fate said, taking the book. The gold-embellished title gleamed in the light: *The God Who Cried Rainbow Tears*. It shocked her that Madam kept illegal books on the premises.

Fortuna hugged her and ran a gentle hand over her head. "We'll figure this out. You are too precious to waste away here."

Fate sighed in relief. Fortuna had a way of picking her up when she felt the worst. "I'm going to the bathhouse, if you don't mind."

"Sore already? That boy will make a warrior out of you. Just don't let him ruin your skin. I'll take his if he does... and do mind the book."

Fate laughed at the needlessly shallow and false comment as she hobbled towards the door with the book tucked under her arm. It amazed her how tight her skin felt. The muscles screamed before she made her way out of the room.

Fortuna called out. "Take the rest of the day to rest and deliver my package. I'll let your sisters know."

Fate waved her hand over her head as she exited to let Fortuna know she heard the instructions. She limped to the baths, growing stiffer with every step, and griped as she removed her clothes by one of the large sunken tubs. "What did you do to me?"

She stuck a toe into the steaming water. The prickle of heat eased, and she stepped into the tub, gradually slinking deeper into the hot water. Her tension and pain melted away as she lay in the tub's warm embrace and shut her eyes.

She slipped beneath the surface, and her thoughts and worries drifted away in the dark watery silence. All sounds grew hollow and muffled, and she sank to the bottom, relaxed and clear-headed — like floating in space, passing by distant stars adrift in a sea of endless night.

A soft voice called out to her. "Wake up, Mistress."

She opened her eyes and, realizing she needed air, pushed off the bottom of the bath and rushed to the surface, gasping. Frantic, she looked around the empty bathhouse, expecting to find someone there with her.

The experience sent a chill down her spine and a spark of pure longing through her soul. She gripped her chest, surprised to feel anything so intensely. For as long as she could remember, her feelings seemed dim and muted, but this ran deep and vivid, unlike anything she'd felt before.

She gazed at the steam that rose from the water and her skin, wondering if Hero's condition had driven her mad. Her muscles eased, and her skin grew pink and wrinkled, and she finally pulled herself from the tub. She wrapped herself in one of the bathhouse robes, gathered her clothes and the book, and left.

Upon stepping outside, she breathed in the brisk air to clear her senses, and gazed upward into the sky. The snowfall had stopped, allowing the sky to flaunt its most brilliant array of stars. She smiled, knowing this meant Hero had found some relief from his recent depression. Her hair often took so long to dry, that it relieved her to feel the warmth on her skin. She climbed through her bedroom window and flopped onto her bed to ponder the book Fortuna had given her, and her encounter with the Prince of Nitor.

After lying on her bed and staring at the ceiling for a time, she heaved herself up and massaged her returning aches and pains. She went to her wardrobe, chose an outfit worthy of the palace, and sat down at her vanity. Every time she saw her reflection, it seemed somehow wrong.

"You are Cruentus Fate, are you not?" She reached out and touched the mirror, unable to find the missing piece or even identify what she lacked.

Color faded from the room, and static filled her ears as a sudden pulse emanated from the glass and rippled through her room. She jumped from her seat, clutching her robe, but the pulse vanished just as quickly as it had come. Terrified, she turned in a small circle to see if anything had changed, but it appeared the same as always.

She shook it off, but grew more concerned about her state of mind. This fear drove her to move quickly, so she combed her hair, breezed through her makeup, and dressed in a flash. The moment she finished, she escaped the room to the safety of the hallway, and hurried past the empty sunken hearth room towards the kitchen.

The kitchen also lay empty. "Where is everyone?" She continued her search of the brothel, but every room she checked came up empty.

The sound of garbled screaming rang throughout the darkened hallway.

Fate's heart thumped until she thought it might burst, and she lurched forward, grabbing her torso in a full panic. A tremor ran through her body and jolted her from the vision.

As she lifted her head, she found herself sitting at the edge of her bed in her room, covered in sweat.

A nightmare.

Her sisters' laughter carried down the hall, confirming that the empty brothel had been nothing more than a dream.

She stood and rubbed her face vigorously. After standing deep in thought for a moment, she smacked her cheeks, hurried to her wardrobe, opened it, and pulled the outfit she'd worn in her dream. She felt sick with déjà vu.

Her decision to dress before sitting at the vanity was little more than an attempt to prevent the loss of her sisters. She laughed at her own ridiculous thoughts. "Where would they go?" She shook her head, combed her hair, and applied a touch of makeup.

Once her nerves settled, she picked up the book, checked herself one last time, and exited the room. She walked down the hall to the sunken hearth room and presented herself to Fortuna.

Fortuna glanced out the window and then back at Fate. "What are you doing?"

Fate faltered. "Uh, taking the book to Hero like you asked."

Clearly puzzled, the madam closed her book and stood. "Are you feeling unwell?"

Fate pressed her hand to her forehead. "I think I'm all right."

Fortuna rounded the fire and checked Fate herself.

Fate stared up at her. "Why? What's wrong?"

"You only just left here. Hero is still training your sisters. I thought you were going to the bathhouse."

Fate wallowed in confusion. She vividly remembered being in the bathhouse for hours.

Chimes filled the air and particles of white dust fluttered down from the ceiling.

Fate sat up at the edge of her bed yet again, and grabbed her head, feeling her world would tear apart at the seams if she repeated the moment. She feared Hero had affected her too much. When she looked down, she wore the outfit from her dream, and the wet ends of her hair proved that she had been to the bathhouse.

She lifted the ends of her hair to study them. "But they dry first. What's going on?" Her attention turned to the window as she remembered what Fortuna had told her in the dream, but she saw that the sun sat low in the sky.

Daylight?

The vision of stars shone in her memory, and she wondered how long she had or had not been in the bathhouse.

She stood, crossed the room, and exited into the hall.

Tori and Myrna walked towards the bathhouse with towels and robes in hand.

Fate called out to them. "Sisters, where are you off to?"

They turned to her, their faces full of bewilderment.

Tori stepped towards Fate. "Are you all right?"

Fate rubbed her forehead. "I'm not sure."

Myrna explained, holding up her robe and towel. "We're going to the bathhouse like we told you only a moment ago."

"You did?"

Both girls nodded, still looking distressed.

Fate laughed. "Of course. Where is my head? Sorry! I'm just nervous about going to the palace. Go on. I'll tell you about it later."

Myrna hesitated. "Are you sure you're all right?"

Fate waved her hands in front of her. "Other than making a complete fool of myself? Yes, I'm fine. I'll see you both later. Have a wonderful soak. The water is amazing."

Reluctantly, her sisters continued down the hall.

She returned to her room, closed the door, and leaned on it as her mind slowly slipped away. She needed to follow Madam's advice and meditate, but she also needed to get to the palace before it got much later. Hero's taint had made a mess of her thoughts.

She picked up the book and took a solid look at herself in the mirror. "You can do this. Don't lose your mind."

She exited through the round window, walked along the back of the property, passed the teahouse, and lumbered up the street to the palace gate.

The guards greeted her with their usual cheer, with one of them asking, "On your way to the palace?"

"I am."

The other pointed to the book in her hands. "Good choice. He loves his books."

Fate beamed as she strolled past them, carefully concealing the title. "Good to hear. He can be a bit hard to please."

Both guards laughed and waved her on, then continued whatever conversation they'd been sharing before she arrived.

She walked up the long path and arrived at the front doors. Before she could knock, the doors opened and a servant girl glowered at her, eyeballing her from head to toe.

Fate smiled, hoping to counter the girl's seemingly foul mood. "Oh, hello."

The girl tossed one of her long braids over her shoulder and ran her hands over the front of her apron. "Yes?"

Fate pulled her chin back and bit her lower lip before responding to the rude servant. "I'm here to deliver a gift to Prince Hero."

The girl leaned against the door jam, folded her arms tightly across her midsection, and narrowed her eyes. "Is that what you're calling it?"

"Excuse me?"

"You're one of those brothel girls, no?"

Rage burned inside Fate. The insult extended to her sisters and Madam. "Do you treat all guests with such disrespect? As Princess of Macellarius, I will have to speak to my uncle about you."

The girl stood upright and stepped towards Fate, forcing her to move a few steps down the stairs. "I know who you are, and I know what you're trying to do. Prince Hero is special, and he doesn't need filth like you messing with his head."

Fate's anger burst. "Messing with him? Do you even know him?"

"We've been friends for ages, which is more than I can say for you."

Fate shoved the book against the girl's chest with as much force as possible. "This is a gift from her Highness Fortuna of Tir Na Nog. I will be checking to make certain he has received it unharmed. You would do well to learn some manners." With that, she spun on her heels and stormed down the stairs.

The girl shouted after her. "And you would do well to keep your legs closed, if you were able."

Fate clenched her fists—fighting the palace's servants would reflect poorly on her and the brothel. She did her best to quell her fury as she returned home, but it burned her up that the pestilent girl had gotten the last word.

One of the guards called out to her as she passed. "That was a quick trip. I thought you'd be there longer. I've heard that the Prince is fond of you."

Fate ceased her fuming and perked up. "What would make you think that?"

The man shrugged. "It's common knowledge. Why else would he train the entire brothel staff when he wouldn't train his own guard?"

Fate looked back at the palace. "I would expect that he thought they should be trained already."

Both guards laughed, and the second guard explained. "Training for a Rahma and training for an Ancient are completely different. Most of the King's Guard isn't qualified to protect him. It was in his best interest to train them, but he refused. Have us all for a party and a dance, but not training—not even those of us who are Ancients."

"Interesting... I know it's a touch far, but did you happen to see the girl I was talking to?"

The first guard shook his head. "Sorry, I didn't. Describe her."

"Angry face. Rahma. Long brown hair in braids."

The guards looked at each other, and one finally said. "Maybe Lara. She wears braids, but I wouldn't call her angry. She's a quiet girl."

The other guard added, "She keeps to herself mostly, or the prince. She's been here since childhood. Why?"

Fate shook her head, not wanting to divulge their interaction until she had more information and confirmed that *Lara* was the girl to whom she'd spoken. "No reason. She just mentioned that she knew Hero well, and I hadn't met her before."

"Not to worry, she's just shy. Sweet girl, really. I'm sure she'll warm up to you."

"Hmm." Fate waved goodbye. As she walked, her anger returned.

That sneaky bitch.

She needed a better plan, and to discuss her newest issue with Fortuna.

11

GRAVE REMINDERS

Fate entered the brothel in a flurry, slamming the screen behind her and causing several of her sisters to stop in their tracks. She waved them on and stomped down to the sunken hearth room, interrupting Fortuna yet again.

The madam closed her book. "You're back sooner than I expected."

Fate erupted. "There was this awful girl."

Fortuna raised a brow but said nothing.

Fate continued to boil over. "She was a servant—rude, haughty even. She actually mocked me and told me to keep my legs shut!"

Fortuna's expression grew dark, and the room temperature rose. "Describe her. I'll find out what I can."

Fate tried to restrain herself but her rant persisted. "I just want to rip the braids right off of her smug little head! It's tiny by the way—freakishly so."

"What?"

"Her head. She's unattractive... even for a Rahma."

Fortuna set her book down and stood. Her anger subsided and concern surfaced. "Fate, that is unusually harsh for you to say. Are you feeling well?"

"Well? No. I'm furious." She paced the length of the room and back again.

Fortuna stepped in line with Fate's pacing and forced her to stop. "It's the miasma. You didn't meditate, did you?"

"There wasn't time."

Fortuna reached her hand out and touched Fate's forehead, releasing a glowing golden ball of anima that quickly absorbed into Fate's skin.

Fate's rage diminished and her body grew heavy and sluggish. After a moment in the soothing effects, she gasped, covered her mouth, and gaped at Fortuna in terror. "I was completely inappropriate. I forgot all of my training. I wanted to fight her."

"I know, and rip her braids off. This is why I told you to meditate. You need to find your center. Not many can accomplish such a feat but you can. Honestly, I'm surprised it has affected you this much."

Fate shook her head and covered her eyes, hoping all of her problems would disappear with her vision. "She said they were close. Ugh, the guards said they were close. What if she tells him?"

Fortuna pulled out her pipe. "Deny it. He won't know. All that's important is that you win his affections and a way out of here. Remember: *we do what we must to survive.*"

Fate kept her response to herself and nodded. She didn't want to lie to Hero. They'd already built up too many hurdles to overcome, but she wanted to try in any way possible to reach him without causing him harm.

"We just need to come up with a draw too great for him to resist. Hopefully, the book will give us an opening."

"If he gets it. That girl was so nasty, she may throw it away."

Fortuna's fires reignited. "Did you tell her it was a gift from me?"

"I did. She didn't care."

The madam pressed one hand to her forehead and landed the other on her hip. "That little imp. I'll find out who she is and deal with her. She'd better not harm that book or I'll have her hide."

Fate clasped her hands together. "Maybe I should just focus on the folklore."

"Good point." Fortuna sucked on her pipe, walked to the screens leading outside, and gazed at the courtyard. "*Sands of Time... Sands of Time.*"

Fate crept up beside her and leaned in to see if her expression gave any clue as to her thoughts.

Fortuna's eyes appeared glazed as she simply whispered the title of the novella over and over. Unexpectedly, she too clasped her hands together and suddenly shouted, startling Fate. "I've got it! We'll use the Spinner's Tale."

The colors faded from the room and all sound grew distant.

Fate experienced a suffocating sense of repetition and an eerie chill of being haunted. "The Spinner?"

"What?" Fortuna stared, clenching her pipe between her teeth. "Oh, you don't know it? Well, I guess it's not exactly the Spinner's Tale as much as it is the Sealing of Lady Fati."

Fate gaped at her, not understanding anything she spoke of, and yet still reeled in a sense of déjà vu as the color and sound slowly returned.

"Lady Fati was a Farseer, present in the Caeles Village during the rise of the Crystal Empire."

Fate shook her head, wondering if Fortuna intended to give her a lesson in folklore or tell her the plan.

Fortuna exhaled, billowing a plume of smoke into the air. "In short, she was sealed, quite dramatically I might add, and forced to spend the rest of her days as a prisoner in the temple."

Fate stood abruptly, horrified by the madam's suggestion. "That sounds terrible. He would have to be really twisted to find that romantic."

Fortuna made a throaty sound. "Not all passion is romantic. Sometimes people are moved by other things. I am willing to bet that Hero is such a person."

Fate thought about it. "All right, I'll study her story. I'm assuming you have a plan."

The spark in Fortuna's eye grew with her grin. "I do. Your sisters and I will get to work on it. For now, just learn the story — understand the nuances. He'll notice that sort of thing. Oh, and you might want to start learning the Language of Ages."

Fate froze. "Huh?"

"I'm serious. It'll impress him far more than shallow flirting. You have much to do, so I suggest you start immediately. I need to find out about this servant girl."

Fate hummed in agreement and headed for the door with a clear focus.

Fortuna added one last thing for her to consider. "Fate, when you train, do your best to heed his advice. I get the impression he lacks patience."

"I will." Fate took her leave.

She felt much better after talking with Fortuna. The weight bearing down on her finally lifted, and she considered Fortuna's warning about Hero's condition. She needed to be more cautious while around him. If she truly intended to win his affections, she would have to find a way to counter the miasma.

She stopped by the study room to find a book on Fati. Madam had collected many books for the girls to study, and she hoped at least one contained the information she sought.

When she entered, one of her sisters sat at a desk reading. The girl looked up surprised. "Fate, what brings you here? It's been ages since we last saw you in here."

Fate smiled, pulled up a wooden chair, and sat across from her sister. "I know. It seems that I graduated an eternity ago."

Her sister laughed aloud. "I know what you mean. I remember being a student and, now, I'm the teacher. It makes me feel old, and I'm only twenty-two."

"I'm looking for a book on the scaling of Lady Fati."

Her sister's eyes widened. "Oh, wow, that's a tough one. Let me think." She sat staring at the wall of packed bookshelves, eventually raising a finger in the air. "I think, maybe...." She crossed the room and ran her finger over the dusted titles.

The musty scent of old books brought Abyssus to mind. While Fate labored in her studies of entertainment and a life of pleasing others, he ventured Mu searching for answers. She saw the difficulty of uncovering these buried stories and facts, and wondered how and where her brother had managed to collect such a plethora of information. The more she thought about it, the more distant she felt from him.

Her elder sister drew a massive book from the shelf, her movements sluggish as she returned to the table and opened it. "If I'm correct... yes, here it is." She spun the open book around and pointed to a section.

Fate peered inside and then looked back up at her sister. "I need it, to give me the whole experience. Madam said it was rather dramatic."

Her sister affirmed. "Then this is definitely the one. It's tragic, really. I researched it for a while and found the whole thing so unfair. It made me sick."

Fate held up a scrap of paper left on the desk. "Can I take this?"

Her sister nodded.

"Great. I'll start on this right away." She slid the scrap into the book, shut it, then stood and picked it up while reading the cover—*Teachings of Grim,* another banned book. Some would call it history, and others mythology.

"Glad I could be of some assistance."

Fate waved and headed for the door. "You're outstanding. We're lucky to have someone so knowledgeable here. Hopefully, I'll be back more often. I need to take a few lessons from you."

"I would love that."

"See you soon." She exited with the book and a feeling of elation. It always made her happy to connect with her sisters. None of them felt true freedom. The threat of being sold or violated always hung over their heads, but it strengthened their bond because, at the end of the day, they all faced the same dangers together.

She hurried back to her room and immediately delved into the world of Lady Fati. Before long, she burst into tears, overwhelmed with frustration and helplessness, unable to save the character. She wiped her eyes so she could finish the story.

A knock at the door interrupted her read. She wiped her cheeks one last time and quickly fanned her face before checking the hall.

Yuzu looked up at her from the doorway with big eyes and a tiny frown. "Big sister, are you crying?"

Fate stood from her bed and laughed, still fanning herself. "I was reading a really sad story. I'm all right, Yuzu. Thank you."

Yuzu rushed to her and hugged Fate's legs. "I don't want you to be sad."

Fate crouched and wrapped her arms around the small girl. "Don't worry, it was just a story, I promise. Now, what brings you here?"

"Prince Hero."

"He's here?"

"Yup. He wants to talk with you but Madam told him it's late."

Fate glanced over her shoulder to see that the sun had already set, then lowered her gaze to a pale face in the window... and let out a shout.

Yuzu shouted too. "What?"

Fate turned away from Hero and made up an excuse. "I just realized I forgot something."

"Oh."

"If Madam sent him away, why are you here?"

Yuzu lifted her hands to her mouth and smiled. "I just thought you should know since you like him."

The heat rushed to Fate's cheeks. She hoped Hero couldn't hear their conversation. "Got it. Thank you. I'm sure he'll come again if it's important. Otherwise, I'll see him this week for lessons, but I really appreciate you telling me."

Yuzu rocked back and forth. "Can I sleep with you tonight?"

Fate checked over her shoulder again to see if Hero still stood at the window.

He crossed his arms.

She stammered. "Uh, Madam has me up late with studies, so I think it's best if you sleep in your own room tonight. Maybe tomorrow."

Yuzu pouted. "All right. Goodnight."

Fate kissed her on the head. "Sleep well. I'll see you in the morning." After Yuzu left, she shut the door and turned back to her room.

As Yuzu's footsteps trailed away with quick little pats, Fate ran to the window, unlatched her lock, and pushed open the panel. "What are you doing here?"

Hero kept his usual composure, seeming somehow perplexed by her reaction. "I wanted to thank you for the book."

She sucked air into her cheeks and exhaled slow and hard, unable to process his vacillating behavior. "It seemed like something you might enjoy, so Madam sent it."

His brow dropped and his mouth tightened. "Oh, I'm sorry for bothering you then. Lara said you gave it to me."

A chime rang in Fate's ears as she heard the girl's name, and she felt even more confused by Lara's actions than Hero's. "Strange. I mean, I did drop it off, but I clearly told her it was a gift from Madam for teaching the girls."

He bit his lip and shoved his hands into his pockets. "Thank her for me, will you? Actually, I'll do it the next time I'm here. She might roast me if she finds out I broke policy."

"Good point."

He took a couple of steps back from the window but still faced her. "Have you been crying?"

Fate sighed. "I was reading a really sad story."

One side of his mouth curled into an awkward smile. "It's nice to know someone else still reads."

His simple pleasure brought her tremendous joy, so much so that it struck her as strange. She played with a tuft of hair that swept over her shoulder. "I'll see you for lessons."

He simpered. "Practice, because I won't go easy on you, even if Madam sends me gifts."

Fate shook her head as he sauntered away, and tried to rectify the feelings he'd stirred in her—something akin to love, but not at all the same.

Once he disappeared into the darkness, she shut the window and locked it. Thanks to their brief interaction, the wind blew softer than before. She fell onto her bed reflecting on the seemingly positive interaction, and reminded herself that his moods changed as often as the weather in Nex... or, more accurately, the weather in Nex changed as often as his moods.

After pointless pondering, she gave up, changed, and went to bed. Sleep took her quickly after the strange, frustrating emotional swings of the day.

A couple weeks passed without incident, and the world felt more at ease after Fate and Hero's simple interaction. Fate managed her chores, her studies, and her fencing without difficulty. She determined the cause of her bizarre dreams and occasional volatile fluxes were due to her direct contact with Hero.

As usual, she entered the hearth room and flopped on the floor next to Fortuna as she read over the mysterious journal. "I always see you reading that book. What is it about?"

"It's a journal," Fortuna replied without looking away from it.

Fate examined the cover. "Whose?"

Fortuna closed the journal and scrutinized Fate with a sideways glance. "The one true heir of the Ignis Family, Fenix."

Fate opened her mouth wide and reached out, nearly touching the journal, but quickly retracted her fingers before

Madam burned them off. "Fenix, like the myth? I read about him in one of the books while I was studying."

"Fenix is not a myth, nor is Fenix a *he*, per se. Like all ethereal beings, Fenix chooses whatever form suits Fenix from day to day."

"Really? It's strange how all of the books portray so many of the important characters in folklore as he, and occasionally she, when so many are neither."

"Very wise, but you should take care when referring to another's history as *folklore*."

Fate tucked a stray hair behind her ear. "Of course, Madam. I'm sorry. Your clan fascinates me, that's all."

Fortuna took a deep breath. "What brought you?"

"I wanted to update you."

The madam retrieved her pipe and lit it. "Excellent, what news do you have?"

"Well, he is detached, isolated, and obsessed with—"

"Folklore. Yes, Fate, these things I already know. That will not help you."

Fate bobbed her head, noting Fortuna's unusually short fuse. "He's more focused on the truth than the folklore itself. It seems that he craves the emotion behind it."

"Hmm... that makes sense. He lives apart from emotion, but desires it nonetheless. Go on."

"That servant girl, Lara..."

Madam turned fiery eyes to Fate, and leaned forward to hear the report.

"...Tori said she's not a servant girl at all."

"Praise be, who is she?"

Fate sighed and twisted the ends of her hair. "The King's ward."

Fortuna reacted as if slapped in the face. "Of course! How could I be so stupid? I heard about her. It's an awful story, really. This is bad. I never dreamed she'd live this long. Curious."

"Madam?"

Fortuna waved her hand. "It's nothing, just something for me to ponder, like the rest of the news. Not to worry, we'll have a solid plan soon."

Fate reflected on her interaction with Lara. The girl may have spoken rotten words, but they held an element of truth that unsettled Fate. As Lara stated, she truly intended to seduce Prince

Hero to escape the brothel. She chose to see it as a mutual benefit—a pact of sorts.

Fortuna stood with a sense of purpose. "First, I must alienate the prince."

Fate twisted her head to the side as though the words made more sense when turned. "I'm sorry?"

Fortuna winked. "He's hungry already. Let's starve him."

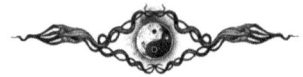

Surprisingly, the more often Madam turned Hero away, the more often he came. He even brought Fate a book on Lady Fati to help with her studies.

She delighted in the fact that he seemed genuinely invested in helping her with the very tool she'd used to lure him.

Without fail, another sparring day arrived, and Fate worked hard to prove herself. She reached the clearing behind the brothel, which Madam had set aside for training, with her spirits flying.

Hero stood at the center of the clearing, stoic as usual. "You look chipper."

She answered merrily. "I've been training."

"Good. You're going to need it today."

Fate glanced around to see multiple foils stuck into the ground in seemingly random places.

He appeared relaxed as always, with a slight sway in his hip as he stood observing. This unguarded stance gave clarity to how little strength she wielded by comparison. "We start new training today."

She approached one of the gleaming silver foils and plucked it from the damp soil.

Hero shifted just once, sprang to another one of the foils, plucked it from the ground, and hurled it at her.

A rush of ice shot across the field as she dodged the flying blade, and pain shot through her chest before she'd even noticed that he'd landed a kick to her sternum.

She crashed to the ground and tumbled, the foil flying from her hand. After training with Hero for so long, she heard his voice in her head whenever she failed: *You're dead.* Rather than lament or suffer from the blow, she scrambled to her feet and grasped another foil from the dirt in just enough time to block.

In a flash and a crackle, she shot a ball of electricity out, charged his foil, and gave him a shock.

The foil clanked to the ground as he withdrew with a singed hand. His expression darkened with concentration, and he then spun in a low circle, collected a foil in each hand, and advanced on Fate.

She brought her foil up as he struck, but ice flashed over the length of his foil, freezing hers to his. With his other hand, he brought the second foil to her side. "You're dead."

Fate released her foil, letting the frozen pair fall to the ground.

Hero dispelled the ice, collected the loose foils, stuck them back into the ground, and returned to his starting position.

Fate returned to her position as well, and cleared her head of any needless thoughts. She slowed her breathing and focused on Hero's aura, which glowed with a sheer haze of multi-colored light. Even if her eyes didn't actually see it, her mind clearly observed.

Hero's aura never faltered before her, nor did he exert any extra energy during her training. It remained constant and unaffected, something she wished to change.

She readied her electricity and prepared for the battle of her life. *I must win.*

She wanted a victory so badly that she breathed it in like air, stirring the darkness in her soul. She desperately needed it, if for no other reason than to prove that she was worthy of being taken seriously.

A flicker of deviance flashed through her mind. *I'm ready.*

She threw herself forward, moving as fast as her feet allowed.

Hero countered with equal speed.

All at once, she released her electricity, charging all the foils and leaving Hero with only his speed and ice to fight with.

He dodged the sparks, leapt over the electrified foils, and landed beside her.

She turned, palm open, electricity flaring, and swung, but he caught her hand and threw her onto her back.

With his hand around her throat, he looked calmly down at her. "You're dead."

Fate slapped the ground. "Yes, yes, I'm always dead."

Hero helped her up by the hand, his aura maintaining its unfaltering shape and energy. "You surprised me for an instant there. Good work."

She took solace in what little he gave her. "Thank you."

"I mean it. You've really improved."

Applause rose from the brothel veranda, stopping their conversation.

Fate's focus trailed to the edge of the courtyard. "Abyssus!" She charged him and embraced him tightly.

Hero smirked and said, "If only you could move that quickly during training."

Abyssus teased as he returned her hug. "Look at you, all serious and trying to kill my friend."

Fate stepped back, unable to contain her happiness. "I still die every time."

Abyssus chuckled. "With Hero, everyone dies every time. Don't let him fool you. You looked amazing."

Hero bowed slightly. "I told her she did well."

Abyssus held his hands to his face. "How about me? Did you tell me I'm beautiful?"

Hero threw his arm around Abyssus. "You always look beautiful."

Fate beamed. Having her brother close always made her happy, but seeing Hero chatter normally added to her glee. "You must be hungry. Would you like me to make something?"

Abyssus looked startled. "You're in the middle of practice."

Fate glanced at Hero, realizing her mistake.

Hero smiled and replied, "Don't be ridiculous. You hardly get out these days, and I know what they feed you."

Fate took her brother's hand and started walking toward the brothel, while Hero followed behind and engaged in child-like bantering with Abyssus.

Several of her sisters saw the pair of princes, and swarmed and fawned, showering them with compliments.

Fate laughed. "I'll see you both in the dining hall."

She left them to deal with their fans, and entered the kitchen to scour the shelves for food. As she prepared pastries for Abyssus and a carefully separated meal for Hero, Neco crossed her mind; he likely treated Abyssus like a prisoner rather than a guest or prince, let alone his son. A part of her wished for her brother to take matters into his own hands, and go to trial with Thule over this ridiculous Rahma rule, but it occurred to her that he might have a good reason for avoiding it.

By the time the boys freed themselves, she'd prepared the food, set the table, and served. She nearly burst into laughter as they entered looking worn, leaving behind the crowd of swooning girls. "I was starting to think I'd eat alone."

Hero slipped in first with a chuckle.

Abyssus pointed to the girls in the hallway as he closed the door behind him. "They're relentless."

Fate sat down and eyed her brother. "Should I tell them you prefer the company of men?"

Abyssus sat across from her and pointed at her now. "That's not untrue."

Fate chuckled, recognizing the phrase as one of Hero's. She looked between the two of them, happy that they at least had one another to confide in.

Hero sat beside Abyssus, his eyes widening as he inspected the small plates of food. "You even separated it."

Fate responded with pride. "Yes, I read somewhere that Caeles don't like to mix their food groups."

Abyssus nodded. "Also not untrue. You seem to have gotten smarter since I last saw you."

She took a slice of apple from one of the plates. "I've been studying."

Abyssus reached across the table and patted her head, then turned to Hero. "Good job. I've been trying to get her to study for turns."

Hero started on one particular section of his food while laughing at the sibling's interaction.

Fate mused, "Easy for you to laugh, huh?"

Hero remained silent and continued eating, an unapologetic smirk lighting his face.

Abyssus patted Hero's head and scratched under his chin. "He's so cute too."

Remarkably, Hero simply laughed and continued to enjoy himself.

Fate wondered if he, like her brother, preferred the company of men, thus explaining his lack of interest in her advances. She studied the pair as they interacted, but discovered nothing more than what appeared to be brotherly banter.

Abyssus stopped eating his pastry and asked her, "Why are you staring like that?"

"I'm just enjoying the moment."

Hero slid his plate to one side. "I have to go. Thank you for the meal."

Fate nodded, feeling pleased that he ate her cooking. He seemed to have tunnel vision when it regarded his studies and training. She doubted he ate when he should. "Oh, that's right, you still have more training to do."

Abyssus whined. "Really? I just got here. I never see you anymore."

Hero stroked Abyssus's head. "I know. I'm sorry. I'm just more important than you. It can't be helped." He strode towards the door, scrunching his face with a pleased smile.

Abyssus's jaw dropped. He picked up a piece of pastry and threw it at Hero, who effortlessly dodged it. "Never! I'm far prettier than you'll ever be."

Fate leaned forward on the table as Hero opened the door, revealing a half dozen waiting girls. "Ooh," she said loud enough for all to hear. "We should dress you both as girls and see if that's true."

Abyssus grimaced, Hero shrugged, and the girls shrieked with delight.

Abyssus hissed, "You're evil."

Hero exited into the growing crowd of excited girls. "So, you would all like to see that, huh?"

The girls shrieked their approvals as Hero leered back at Abyssus with a victory grin and a wink. "See you around, pretty Lady."

Abyssus shouted at him, "You too! You're evil!"

Hero closed the door, leaving Abyssus to wallow in his pastries while Fate laughed at him.

After a pause and some sulking, Abyssus looked up. "It seems to be going well with you two."

Fate leaned against her hands. "Does it? I can never tell where I stand with him."

Abyssus picked up a slice of apple. "He's comfortable around you, which is more than I can say for anyone other than me."

Fate gazed at the door, still picturing Hero with the clinging girls. "Everyone here adores him. It's hard to find times when we can actually speak. He does stop by from time to time, though."

Abyssus nodded. "See, you're making progress. Your fencing was impressive. I'm sure he noticed. He can be a bit of a stickler when it comes to things like that."

"By *that* you mean everything."

He laughed. "Exactly."

She spun a spoon in circles on the table. "Have you found out anything about the missing Dolls?"

He lowered his voice to nearly a whisper. "I did. It appears they were created by a Puppeteer named Bethshan. More fascinating than that is the fact that they disappeared the same night our mutual white-haired friend was accused of murdering his mother."

The world expanded away from her, leaving her feeling suddenly small and isolated. "The very night? Do you think it could have been orchestrated by the same people?"

In truth, she still questioned Hero's innocence, as all facts led back to him in some way. No one would believe a small child could be capable of such things, and yet the Council had some reason for suspecting him.

Abyssus shrugged. "We'd have to ask the High Queen herself. Seems she was there that night, as was Hero's aunt, Chi."

"Is there any way for us to speak with them?"

"You mean with you trapped here in the brothel and me being stalked by a tall, red-haired, homicidal beast?"

"How did you get away from him, by the way?"

"His sister came to visit, so he doesn't have the free time to harass me. Hence, I'm here for a visit."

"Hmm... his sister, huh?"

"Yeah, she's the Head of Artillery for Nitor. You remember that night we saw Hero hanging off the balcony?"

"Hmm."

"The woman that got him down... that's Mortis's sister."

Fate thought back to the night, but her memory of the woman was hazy at best. "Well, I'm thankful for her visit and sorry to her for being related to such a creep." She pinched Abyssus's cheek. "I guess not everyone can be so blessed to have such a charming twin."

"Right?"

The siblings laughed and continued their conversation for as long as possible, but as time wore on, his discomfort grew.

She finally said. "You need to get back, don't you?"

He frowned. "I'm afraid so. I'm sure Firmus will be out of his mind by now. Mortis will be looking for me, and I'd prefer my lovely head uncrushed."

She stood, and he followed her movements. Every time she saw him, he looked a little less like a boy and more like a man. Even his voice sounded deeper than before. She forced herself to smile as she linked arms with him and walked through the brothel towards the entrance. "Today has been wonderful. I've missed you so much."

"Me too." He hugged her tight and reached for the door. "Tell Hero to stop by if he has the time. I feel we were cut short today."

Fate hesitated but found the courage to ask, "Are you two lovers?"

Abyssus appeared stricken. A weird, high-pitched sound escaped his throat, and then a guttural laugh burst out. "Funny, but no. Is that what you were calculating earlier?"

"It's just a question."

He shook his head with deep chuckles and waved. "I'll see you later."

She watched him go, feeling a mixture of peace for having seen him, and sorrow for not knowing when it would happen again.

Be well, Brother.

12

MIRROR IMAGE

Days in the brothel continued, each the same as the last, cleaning, and studying with the occasional letter from Abyssus. At least with the addition of Hero's visits, the brothel seemed livelier.

The chill in the air gradually subsided as the suns came and went. Time slipped by so fast that Fate feared the day of the auction may arrive without any change to her current lifestyle. It made her more desperate to keep Hero's attention, by *any* means necessary.

After practicing fencing with Hero one morning, Fate set him up in one of their private lounges to read. "I thought it might be a nice change from the palace."

He examined the room briefly. "This is very considerate of you."

She went in and out of the room, first leaving him with a variety of books Fortuna had collected, and then she rushed back to the dining hall and prepared him some refreshments.

She returned to the lounge, opened the screen door, and carried in a tray with tea and rice crackers, which she placed on the table in front of his open books. "Here, have these while you study. I'll go and complete my chores so you can focus."

He touched her hand to stop her from leaving.

Their gazes locked.

The look in his eyes always made her wonder if he knew his influence over her, and her predicament. He exuded confidence and amusement, like a large animal playing with its prey.

The warmth from his hand caused her skin to tingle, reminding her that beneath his glove, miasma seeped from the Taint. No matter how light the touch, she needed to be wary of the Plague he carried.

He soon withdrew and returned his attention to his studies. "Thank you."

Fate reminded herself to breathe. "You're welcome."

She pressed the tray to her chest as she stepped out of the room. Her lungs felt heavy whenever she spent too much time around him, causing her to question what she really understood about the Tainted.

Hero didn't appear as the Council described — shrouded in the spiritual blood they called *miasma*, unruly, and constantly spreading the Plague. If anything, he appeared little more than a socially awkward, eccentric recluse. Besides, none of her sisters exhibited a single sign of ailment. In stark contrast, they showed only an improvement in both skill and intelligence, which warranted their admiration for him.

She cracked open the doors again to check if he really was studying, and sure enough, Hero focused on his books, making notes as he went. If she succeeded in her plan to seduce him, they might marry someday, so better to understand the circumstances now rather than die of the Plague later.

She returned the tray to a cabinet in the dining hall and, as she exited, stopped to investigate a sound from the front door.

An aged and haggard King Neco entered one of the side doors with Mortis and Abyssus following close behind. The three men spotted Fate the moment they arrived.

She strained to contain her hatred. By the look of it, Mortis kept her brother closer than he used to. The way they stood made it appear as though the colossal man intentionally blocked her brother from moving anywhere unless he or Neco advanced.

Neco sneered at her from a distance. "Fate, we thought we should pay you a visit. It has been some time since I last saw you. Would you be a dear and prepare a room?"

She clenched her jaw and held her breath. Both she and Neco knew that she'd do anything to ensure her brother's safety, even if it meant serving a man she abhorred. She desperately wished she could throw policy in his face, but Royals held a different standard and, therefore, abided by a different set of rules.

Neco had visited her many times throughout the turns, and each time her skin crawled as though it were the first.

Abyssus looked at her, his face riddled with apologies, though he could do little without endangering himself.

"Come this way," she said with practiced diplomacy, and led the group towards the back doors. All their clients knew to visit the teahouse, not the brothel lodging. It just proved that Neco intentionally broke policy, and specifically sought her out to quench his thirst for her anima.

As she passed the first few lounges, she glanced at the door of the room she'd prepared earlier and thought of Hero. All of her father's nonsense reminded her of why she sought to seduce Hero in the first place.

But am I any better than my father if I trick and seduce the Prince of Nitor?

The time she'd spent with Hero helped her develop a sort of fondness for him. At some point, she began to consider him a friend, one she needed in her life... for selfish reasons.

Unable to bring herself to put the two so close together, she decided to lead the group out to a room in the teahouse. Not only did it keep her interactions with Hero unscathed by her father's corruption, but it also forced Neco to follow rules he felt entitled to break. She threw open the back screen doors and stepped down to the stone path, which led towards the teahouse corridor. Her father's presence always engendered negative thoughts, reminding her of the approaching auction, and her backup plan to murder him if he managed to buy her back.

Am I really considering murder? I've lost my mind.

Hero's miasma must have passed through her thoughts again. The Council always said the miasma evoked negativity in all things, the Universe and people alike. Miasma or no, she considered it possible that if anyone found themselves in her predicament, it would lead them to negative thoughts.

Is it even miasma, or are we all so far gone that we'll blame anything to save ourselves? In truth, I've wanted him dead from the beginning.

Shadows fell over the teahouse hall as she walked towards one of the rooms. In her most welcoming voice, she ushered her father and his guests inside. "Please, take a seat. I shall return shortly with your drinks."

As soon as Neco sat, he grasped her by the waist, pulled her onto his lap, and kissed her cheek. "You don't greet me properly anymore. What are they teaching you here? I should speak to Madam Fortuna about our arrangement."

She forced herself to turn, hug him, and plant a kiss on his cheek. Her skin crawled as his warm breath saturated her senses and he nuzzled his lips against her face. From the corner of her eye, she could see her brother scowling, his eyes as hardened and calculating as *she* felt. His aura swelled so exponentially that she worried he may draw Hero to the teahouse, or Mortis to lash out at him. They shared a moment of immense revulsion, but Neco caught Abyssus glaring and forced Mortis to take him out of the small, enclosed area, and out into the larger community room of the teahouse.

She maintained her act while quickly slipping from his clutches. "I shall prepare refreshments and return shortly."

"Very good, I am quite parched. It would be good of you to relieve my discomfort," Neco said.

She exited the room and closed the doors smiling, but the moment they closed, she wiped her cheek and lips so hard that her flesh stung from the friction caused by her robes. More than fencing, she wished she knew how to unleash the darkness that writhed around inside her.

For now, she crossed the main room of the teahouse, exchanged concerned glances with her brother, and exited out onto the outdoor hallway to the separate teahouse kitchen area. She considered spitting in Neco's tea, but the thought that he may like it disturbed her too much.

What if I poison him? No one will miss him anyway.

If anyone caught her for the crime, her hopes of freedom and becoming High Queen would forever be lost. Not to mention, Mortis.... She worried so much for Abyssus that she dared not challenge Neco. A Rahma posed no threat, but his looming guard and Council law stopped her.

In her anger, she tossed some rice crackers into a bowl, but took more precaution scooping out some of the hot water contained in a pot over the stove. She breathed deeply, urging herself to a state of calm before placing the kettle, teacups, and bowl of crackers onto a tray.

She shook her legs and arms, freeing herself of any unwanted tension, then collected the tray and marched back to the teahouse.

She entered and carried the tray to the table where Abyssus and Mortis sat. "I've brought you something to make your wait more enjoyable."

As she set the cups down and poured, she noticed the strange way Mortis stared into empty space. His general appearance and aura unsettled her.

Aside from his staring, his skin seemed to lack the luster of the Aska clan. He bore the red hair, but even that appeared deficient in color. Everything about him held an unnatural air.

Abyssus reached out and took the teacup. "Thank you."

Fate slid the crackers towards her brother while keeping a cautious eye on the immense Aska. She expected some kind of reaction but received none.

The colossal man sat on his chair and hunched over the table, staring into empty space with his lifeless eyes as if in a trance. His aura dimmed and faded quickly.

With each new interaction, she feared him more, but she continued her work, picked up the tray, and walked back to the private room where Neco waited.

She looked at her former father. The man made her squeamish. A part of her writhed just seeing him, let alone feeding into his disgusting fetishes and greed. Rather than walking, it felt as if she'd descended into the ocean, unable to swim her way back to the surface. She slid the door open with one hand and closed it behind her.

Neco grinned at her as far as his lips allowed, though it appeared more like a grimace to her.

Fortuna's words repeated in her mind—*you do what you must to survive*—as she went to the table and knelt down to set up the remaining refreshments.

He stroked her behind. "That looks good."

A sting of humiliation burned her cheeks and rocked her head. Her face hurt from the forced smile, and her stomach ached from the growing knot.

The door scratched against the mats and Fortuna stepped into the room, glowing and radiant. "Neco, so glad you could join us."

"I'm thrilled to be here," he said, easing his hands slowly between Fate's legs.

"I'll bring out some of our girls to accommodate your needs," Fortuna said through her smile.

Neco squeezed Fate's thigh. "I'm fine with my little princess here."

Fortuna folded her hands before her gown, each bead glimmering in the light. The dress itself seemed to know that it clothed a noble queen, and yet, despite all that glimmer, they still seemed dull compared to the fire in her eyes.

"That may be," she said, "but she is not yet of age and is not allowed to provide such accommodations. So, I'm afraid Fate will have to return to her approved schedule. Not to worry though, we have all that you require, as you well know."

The smile faded from Neco's face as Fate pulled away and hurried out of the teahouse. Once out of sight, she sprinted to her room, slammed the door, and slid to the floor, seething and cursing as she tore at her hair.

She reminded herself that Hero quietly studied close by, and that his visits grew longer and more consistent. Her brother's encouragement also echoed in her ears. Not all was lost. She still had time if she used it wisely.

Her head spun with fury as she sat, listless, on her bedroom floor. She lost track of time, and only snapped to when footsteps approached her door.

Hero knocked. "Lady Fate, may I come in?"

Fate forced herself to her feet and straightened her robes. "Yes."

He entered and closed the door. The way he looked at her seemed full of genuine concern, but he kept his commentary about whatever he noticed to himself. "I've finished my studies."

"That's good news."

He tucked his hands back, swaying slightly as he scanned his surroundings with a smile. "There's something pleasant about the brothel."

She retorted spitefully. "I think a lot of men would say so."

"Hmm... indeed. Perhaps it's harder to see the beauty in its design when you're so close. It's the Igni warmth and anima that makes this place so pleasing." He mulled over something while staring up at a wooden beam. "They do say it's important not to look too closely, as one must view the larger picture to fully understand the scope of any one thing."

Fate's head jerked by an inch, like a cog sticking in a mechanical doll. Her spite drifted away in lieu of this new consideration.

He continued. "There's ingenuity in fighting fire with fire."

She pressed. "What do you mean?"

"I mean Queen Fortuna's trafficking control plan."

She'd fixated so much on the surface of the brothel, and the terrible people who entered, that she felt distanced from the number of girls who'd escaped Nex. Hero's commentary showed that rather than admiring the architecture, as she'd always assumed he did, he really admired the hidden escape routes that the brothel concealed.

So many girls came and went through the brothel that no one had time to count them, and clients didn't care enough about the women they objectified to differentiate or grow an attachment to them.

Fate stopped to think about how this may pertain to other things. *Look at things too closely and you'll miss details. I have to look at the bigger picture.* She raised her gaze to analyze Hero. *Who is this person, really?*

Upon noticing her studying him, he grinned. "I suppose I should return home. It was nice to visit with you today. Until next time, Lady."

"Oh, yes... thank you for sharing your wisdom."

He watched her over his shoulder as he departed with the usual sway in his walk. The Prince exuded too much confidence to be a mere prisoner of Nitor Palace. He clearly hid a card up his sleeve, but she couldn't imagine what, how, or why.

Fate touched her chin as she deliberated, but pondering didn't help her situation. Only time would tell what Caeles Hero intended, and whether it would aid or conflict with her plans.

13

EN GARDE

Every new day mirrored every day before it in a dizzying repetition, with only the seasons changing. Fate rose in the morning, combed her hair at her vanity, repeated her mantra, and met her sisters in the dining hall to listen to the Madam's daily requests.

After a long winter, spring finally lifted its head.

Fate delighted in the rise in temperature and the blossoming garden. Not only did she appreciate the warmth, but it meant that Hero faced no further complications in his mood or life. These feelings made it difficult to remain focused as Madam shared her thoughts and complaints.

The teahouse needed cleaning and, once again, Madam asked Fate and Tori to handle it.

The pair entered the garden through the open screen and walked by the pond as they always did. Water trickled down the rocks of the pond, past the massive swarm of colorful fish and the moss that grew along each stone. The sun shone down, casting a soft light over the community and lending warmth to the normally chilly atmosphere.

Fate realized she'd drifted into a daze while admiring the view, and turned to follow Tori up the portico to the back of the teahouse. The golden doors of the auction room mocked her and, before she knew it, she stopped walking and gaped at the door, swearing she heard the ticking of a clock.

Tori continued up the stairs without fail, determined to complete her chores quickly.

Fate snapped from her stupor and rushed after her sister.

As she caught up, Myrna opened a pair of screen doors along the teahouse hall and took in the morning air, surely a much-needed reprieve after her Rebellion missions.

Tori stopped her usual prattle to steal a kiss from Myrna. "How did it go?"

Myrna ran her fingers through Tori's short hair. "It went well. I've missed you."

Tori glowed. "Hmm... not anymore. We're cleaning the teahouse, and then I'm done. We can actually spend some time together."

Fate hastened behind one of the nearby doors, not wanting to invade a personal moment. While she listened, she muttered under her breath. "I'll get started. Take your time."

She sighed to herself, partially out of happiness for them, and partially out of self-pity. As she strode through the tearoom, she reminded herself that if she sought to be the Future Queen of Mu, she must prepare herself to spend her life with someone who benefitted the kingdom, not just her own desires.

She walked down the right side of the hall and took cleaning supplies, a bucket, and a rag from the closet at the end. They kept all their extra hand towels, robes, and sheets here as well, something she learned at a young age.

For a moment, she paused and gazed down the long outside corridor. It had been some time since she experienced the hanging feeling of the nearby Auction Room. Even with the door hidden around the corner, she sensed it the same as she sensed her impending auction.

She brushed off the looming feeling.

Since Tori and Myrna needed time together, Fate started cleaning at the opposite side of the teahouse. She tied up the sleeves and the hem of her robes before carrying the bucket through the building and out the front to the bathhouse, where they received all their best water.

The plump older woman at the front desk tapped her pipe against an ashtray as she read from a worn book. Her grey hair looked nearly as drab as her clothing.

Fate supposed the woman had earned the right to live as she pleased after retiring from the brothel. Strangely, it brought Fate some measure of peace to know such people existed. The woman merely glanced at Fate as she hurried through the side opening, to take note of her use, the reason, and the date. After signing her name on the paper, she carried the bucket towards the baths.

At this time of the morning, either her elder sisters or the local mistresses occupied the baths, all of them familiar and friendly. Each girl she encountered greeted her as they soaked but let her continue her work. In all this cleaning and training, she built plenty of muscle and, if she applied this muscle to training, she might really have a chance at becoming a decent fighter.

A sliver of hope arose through her daily routine and brought a smile to her face.

She carried the bucket of steaming water back to the teahouse and entered the first room. Once again, the clients had left a mess of dishes, towels, and food products. For Fate, this reflected the state of the Rahma and of the Plague that frenzied the people of Mu. She started gathering the random dishes and glasses left behind, and set them at the far end of the massive table. Her time was running short—only two turns remained before the auction. If she failed to gain independence, she would have to entertain the unruly guests in the teahouse, or return to the arms of an old, withering Rahma.

Pressure built in her chest as she sensed her freedom dwindling away from her. It did her no good to question her motives towards Hero. There would be plenty of time to pay him back after winning his affections.

She leaned down and picked up an earring from the floor.

The scraping of the sliding door reached her ears, and Fate spun to look, spying an unwelcome client. Her darkness stirred, whirling around inside her and urging to be free. "We're closed."

The man stumbled forward, the thick stench of alcohol seeping from his pores from the night before. Vomit clung to the hair on his chest and scraggly beard as his shirt flapped in the breeze. "Maybe... you'll show me out before I go?"

Whenever her motivation waned, people like this very literally stumbled into her life, as if the Universe meant to remind of her of why she struggled. If she gave up at any point, she may find herself reduced to someone else's lusts and whims for the rest of her life—a mere tool at someone else's disposal.

The unkempt man ran his dispirited eyes up and down her figure and subtly smirked.

She stood, keeping a watchful eye on the intruder. "Unlikely. I have other duties to attend to. Please, show yourself out. You may return during the appropriate hours."

He sniggered, running one hand over his balding head and the other over his exposed belly as moved towards her. "You'll show me out now."

She plucked a stiff reed from the floral display and cracked the man on the hand. "I said we're closed."

He lunged at her and received another crack to the face, then stumbled backward, defending himself. "You bitch!"

She shuffled, advancing with precision, and struck him again, snapping his arm with the reed. It left a tiny slice and cracked his leg, as she continued to push him towards the door.

He slapped at the reed, trying to grab hold, but she moved too quickly for his hangover. Each step brought him closer to the door, until he finally tumbled down the stairs into the courtyard.

Fate withdrew her reed and glared down at him with cold, calculating eyes. "Thank you, come again."

Tori and Myrna hurried to the sound of the commotion and gawked at her with gaping mouths.

The man staggered to his feet, still fuming, and started back up the stairs.

Fate readied her reed once more. "I will ask you to respect our policies, sir."

A sudden gust of wind surged, and Fortuna appeared on the stairs between Fate and the angry man. "You heard the Lady. Return during the appropriate hours. We will not ask again. If you wish to continue our services, you will respect our policies."

The man growled, stumbled through the courtyard, and exited the gate.

Fortuna turned to Fate. "You did well. I suppose I have Prince Hero to thank for this solution."

Myrna rushed to the stairs. "That was incredible. Beaten with foliage!"

Tori chimed in. "Extraordinary."

Fortuna eyed Fate and pressed a finger to her lips. "Perhaps, but... Fate, he'll be horrible to deal with. Do you think it was worth it?"

Fate thought of her sisters that tended to the teahouse and its patrons. She didn't want to make things more difficult for them, but she also felt that they needed to keep control of growing abuses from clientele. It seemed unlikely that the effects of the Plague would fade any time soon. The people grew more ravenous for anima by the day.

She gasped almost inaudibly and snuck a glimpse of Fortuna as she remembered Hero's words: *It's the Ignis warmth and anima that makes this place so pleasing.* She looked around at her sisters, unaffected by the Plague and its tendency to make people ravenous, and her mouth fell open. The brothel's patrons always left better than when they arrived.

It's Fortuna. Her anima must be cleansing them.

Fortuna narrowed her eyes and made a small humming sound as she waited for Fate's response.

Fate shook her head fast and picked up where she left off. "Worth it? Certainly. They feel they can take liberties with us. Ultimately, they need to be checked before something terrible happens."

Fortuna shifted her eyes to the gate. "Agreed."

Fate fidgeted. "Hero can't possibly pick up more training."

Fortuna exhaled and ran her thumb over her fingertips, a sign she needed a smoke. "Agreed. I'll bring others in from home. It may also find the girls a proper spouse."

Fate hugged the madam, grateful to have such a wise protector.

Fortuna patted her head while delivering the rest of her directive. "Myrna, I know you've only just returned, but would you please notify your sisters that they will all defer one more of their subjects to train in combat? I fear times are changing, and their safety takes priority."

Myrna nodded with a wide smile, and as she started for the brothel, she shouted back, "Absolutely!"

Fate looked at Tori. "I'll clean the teahouse. Go with her."

"Thank you." Tori hurried after Myrna.

Fortuna pulled her pipe from her cleavage and lit it with a spark from her fingertips. "You have grown to understand your sisters and the real purpose of this brothel quite well."

"With your help."

Fortuna nodded, taking a long slow drag from her pipe. "True, but you wouldn't be where you are without your own efforts. It seems you have your own motivation."

Fate watched the passing clouds. "I do."

"How are your rehearsals going?"

"My ankles are sore but nothing I can't manage."

Fortuna entered the teahouse and started tidying with her pipe clutched in her teeth.

Fate followed her inside and assisted.

Fortuna stopped. "I want you to practice something new, since you seem able to withstand the outfit."

Fate agreed without knowing what might be expected. "Hmm."

Fortuna cooed. "Good."

Fate looked up from her duties, both curious and concerned by the tone. "What did you have in mind?"

Madam stood over her with a fiery glint in her eyes, exhaled smoke through her nostrils, and chuckled. "You just have to see it for yourself."

Fate cleaned faster, interested in what Madam's new performance concept might be. She was willing to make any effort if it aided her in getting out of the brothel unsoiled.

Fortuna slid her pipe from her teeth and lightly pressed her tongue to the inside of her cheek. Whenever she devised something sneaky, she used her smokiest intonation. "It's time to prepare for battle, Lady Fate." She stroked Fate's face. "...or should I say Mistress Fati?"

Fate smirked back at her mentor and bowed her head. "Certainly. It is my duty to perform. Whatever it takes to survive... whatever it takes to change the fate of the Empire."

"Very good," Fortuna said. "This shall be the most anticipated performance in the history of Mu. Follow closely. There's still much to learn."

14

SMOKE & MIRRORS

Time passed with more hard work, training, endless rehearsals, and studying. In the end, Fate questioned if her efforts were enough. Everything she'd done hinged upon the night of her performance. One wrong move and her world would fall to pieces.

She sat before her vanity and stared down at the comb. Her eyes traced the skillfully formed gold leaves and flowers down the chains to the tiny ruby beads dangling at the ends. Her heart ached with fear for the future, her decisions, and something else that seemed just out of reach. As she picked up the comb and pressed it into her thick dark hair, she stared at her reflection, feeling strangled by her own existence. The performance makeup nearly glowed white on her skin, giving her a ghostly appearance. The darkened eyeshadow shimmered in the light, as it should, but it made her seem skeletal in the low light. She needed only to apply a final touch of lipstick. Everything appeared perfect, yet something still nagged at her, something sleeping deep within her soul — it called to her, beckoned her to free it.

Her reflection betrayed her. She'd aged much since first arriving at the brothel, and the reflection in the mirror of the fifteen roses pinned on her wall taunted her.

As did time, Madam, and all the people who'd sworn to free her before her auction. She stared at the warped image before her and dwelled in sorrow and anxiety. Darkness churned in her chest, and she wanted nothing more than the freedom to bring it all down.

For a fleeting moment, she wanted everyone to suffer for their lies and broken promises, then the cold dark wave subsided and her hope returned. She reminded herself that her fight would end when she decided, and not a moment sooner.

She plucked the bright red lipstick from her dresser and applied it. With the façade finally complete, she stood to remove her robe, and dressed in the hand-beaded gown Nigel had made just for her. She lifted her arms and inspected the details in awe.

A light tap at the door marked the time. She carefully slid her petite feet into the platform performance sandals. It had taken her two turns to be able to move properly in them, and somehow being a head taller in her shoes gave her more strength and courage than the skill itself.

She walked a half-circle, careful not to trip on the train as she made her way to the lattice gate and slid it open.

Tori, Myrna, and Nigel stood in the hallway, admiring her form and grace.

Myrna tapped Nigel's chest with the back of her hand. "You outdid yourself."

"No, but I am about to." Nigel turned towards a box by his foot and removed an ornate headpiece, gold and beaded, with long jewels that hung down the sides. He placed it on Fate's head, completing her transformation.

Tori covered her mouth. "It's incredible. You are the spitting image of Lady Fati."

Fate pressed the headpiece down on her head until it met the comb she had placed there. "Not sure how you would know that, but perfect. If all goes well, people will talk about this day for turns to come."

Nigel shined. "Eons."

Myrna urged Fate onward. "You'd better get backstage before Madam sets it aflame."

"Right." Fate hurried down the hallway, leaving the trio behind, and went to the screens at the back of the theatre. She poked her head inside, alerting the Madam to her presence.

Fortuna threw her hands in the air. "Praise be! You know I can't smoke back here. Are you trying to kill me?"

"Sorry, Madam, I just wanted everything to be flawless."

Fortuna ushered her backstage. "With you, it will be. You have an enormous crowd. We can do a great deal of good with the profits alone, so no matter how tonight unfolds, Fate, you are a hero."

Fate laughed at the unintended pun. "Let's hope Hero is too."

Fortuna released a nervous and hollow laugh. At first glance, she looked as noble and stunning as should any proper queen, especially with Nigel's gorgeous beading on her gown. Everything from the gloss on her lips to the dazzle of the jewels on her body appeared regal and elegant. The woman emitted a presence of unwavering authority, but the quiver in her voice and her trembling hands indicated that far more was at stake than Fate cared to think about.

The stage twinkled in the low light, revealing two sets of rolling screens. The first rested forward, concealing the stage from the audience, and the second hid Fate and Fortuna.

Fate slipped by the second set of screens and peeked through the gap to get a look at the audience. Madam's assessment appeared modest as she scanned the massive crowd waiting and talking. It seemed every Royal and noble in Mu attended, but her eyes landed on the only person that mattered to her at this moment—Hero.

He sat front and center, looking apathetic, as usual.

She wondered if he felt no excitement, or if he merely lacked the proper facial muscles to show it. Her studies suggested his Caeles nature as the cause of his outward indifference, but she still debated over whether that explained the individual.

Fortuna loomed over her head. "What are you looking at?"

"Hero."

She withdrew from the screens. "Hmm. He's been bickering with Niteo all evening."

Fate turned to the madam. "Really?"

"Oh yes. They've given your sisters some trouble. Hero is polite and charming even to the point of fault."

Fate frowned. "What does that mean?"

Fortuna rolled her eyes. "I had to remove several of the girls for claims of true love. Damn miasma is a mess."

Fate laughed until she saw that Fortuna did not laugh with her. "Seriously? No, he's charming but not like that."

"Tell that to your sisters. I know this sounds strange after all we've worked for, but there is something off about him, no? And I don't just mean the miasma."

"Yes. I noticed it straight away. It's like he's there but not there."

Fortuna flapped her hands in the air. "Exactly!"

"What were they fighting about?"

The madam pulled her pipe from her cleavage and sucked on it without lighting it. "That's a good question. In reality, there isn't much that Niteo can do. Hero holds all the power. He'll be the next High King." She shrugged. "False hope, maybe."

"Maybe." Fate thought about the situation, and clung to the hope that she'd developed enough of a bond with Hero—and perhaps his attachment to her brother helped—to warrant her rescue.

Music played, signaling for the crowd to find their seats.

Fate prepared for the curtain call as Fortuna hurried to the center screens and motioned for her to hide.

Her sisters flooded the dark stage dressed and ready, praising her as they passed.

The lights dimmed over the audience, leaving only a few amber chain lights for ambiance. Everything she and Fortuna had planned would finally come to fruition.

The sound of a wind flute soared through the darkness, its low, heavy tones drawing the audience into Fati's web.

The first set of painted screens parted, and the stage illuminated with the intricate set Fortuna had designed.

Fate peered through the crack from her hiding place to see how the jeweled flower trees gleamed in the spotlight. The set turned out to be an immaculate reconstruction of the Verna shrine, each pillar perfectly carved around an altar that held a stone chamber, shaped like a box.

She slowly exhaled to alleviate her stress as her sisters readied themselves.

The orchestra joined the wind flute, bringing the robust tune alive as her sisters moved and swirled in intertwining circles, drawing the crowd further into their world. Each spun with purpose, creating a whirlwind of vibrantly colored fabric in a stunning display of shimmers and a flurry of delicate motion.

Their movements and the floating fabric made time appear to slow, and the stage seemed to float, suspended above the audience. Each girl put her heart into the final presentation.

Several onlookers gasped at the visual awe.

Colored lights shone down from carefully placed branches, lending a surreal effect to the foggy atmosphere below.

More sisters tenderly speckled glitter from above, allowing just a tiny bit to catch the light here and there, as the dance continued.

The music dropped low and soft as the story unfolded.

More of the young sisters hurried to the stage in long, white robes embellished by gold trim. They played the part of the priests that sealed the Lady Fati's powers away. Each displayed a flawless execution of Madam's choreography.

Fortuna stood behind the screen on the opposite side of the stage and released tiny orbs of golden anima, much to the crowd's delight. The orbs drifted across the stage until meeting the twirl of fabric that carried them high into the air, speckling the darkened theatre. The light reflected on the falling glitter like flecks of broken glass falling through the air.

The combination of all these elements left the audience dumbfounded.

Fate took a deep breath and exhaled. Her eyes fixed on Hero, who watched the display calmly, as though reading a book. She hoped her plea would reach him.

She moved to her mark and prepared herself for the physical exertion required to complete her dance, her small ankles locked in place, firmly holding her feet in the raised shoes. She thought about the many times she'd fallen, twisted her ankles, or injured herself to get to this moment. Gradually, calmness nested in her, allowing her natural grace to shine in the darkness.

As the orchestra continued and the dancers flowed across the stage, Fate remained hidden and sang out a long, well-rehearsed note. She followed it with another and, slowly, she sang until her melody blended with the orchestra.

The crowd murmured and hummed.

She cast a final glance at a tearing Fortuna before the second set of screens parted and revealed her. As she stood before the crowd, the beaded gown and golden headpiece twinkled in the lights.

Her sisters left their marks, taking their new places on each side of the stage.

Fate moved forward with the utmost caution in the platform shoes. She crept into the spotlight and sang, channeling the

Spinner's pain into a melodic wail. She poured her heart in the lyrics, reciting the Language of Ages to the best of her ability.

> *Iraneu meil, cwar raja,*
> Unknowing love, with red eyes upon you,
> *Nox cela eoh ge tera eid.*
> Moonlight flutters from the garden on the cliff.
> *Ara istar ge fata, fenne so nodia,*
> Silent are her pleas to bring balance and judgment,
> *Erul hatteo aimeu il sola crysta.*
> Before a traitor deaf to celestial tears.

A gust of air blew her long dark hair upwards, fully exposing the gown that framed her delicate form. She spun, sending her gown and all of it shimmering details into the air.

Another moment of suspense struck the audience, which gaped at her in silence.

She caught several people weeping quietly but, again, her gaze locked onto Hero, the only person who truly mattered here.

He sat center stage, in the first row, his eyes gleaming in the darkness, with the slightest smile upon his face.

The shift in the music cued, bringing them to a moment of pure darkness. In the time it took for the lights to ease back on, Fate's sisters had secured finely woven cords to the bands on her limbs and returned to their positions.

A minor murmur of curiosity rose from the audience, but she paid them no mind. The most difficult part of her performance began with another shift in the music.

The cord tugged at her wrist as her sisters pulled hard on it, lifting her tiny body into the air and then quickly setting her down. She moved in tandem, creating a flow of air through her gown, much to the delight of the crowd, but, more importantly, to remove it from her feet before she landed. She locked her ankles with practiced balance and landed carefully on the platforms.

Once again, she felt the tug, this time with her opposite leg and arm, sending her into a sideways spin that caused the audience to shout in concern and amazement. It took all her concentration to work her gown, so as not to interfere with her landing. All the while, she kept her voice strong and steady, continuing her vocal banter with the orchestra.

One by one, her sisters joined the movements, everyone impeccably graceful, keeping the balance of people on the stage flowing seamlessly together. They all spun round and round, lifting Fate into the air and then setting her down. The flurry of movement and the chaotic tune, combined with Fate's song, created an energy laced with agony and a sense of betrayal.

The music and the tension grew as the tale neared its end.

One of the sisters slunk out from backstage, holding something behind her back as she stepped out to the front of the stage. She presented a dark mask to the audience as the whirlwind of dancing continued behind her.

Fate landed on her platforms with careful precision, bringing the sound and motion to a halt.

The sister with the mask turned as the other performers grabbed Fate, laid her down across their arms, and lifted her. The one sister then placed the mask over Fate's face and locked it to the headpiece, releasing tufts of gold glitter into the air that shimmered and sparkled like dissipating anima.

As the music hit its peak, the sisters released Fate in a flurry of sound and motion... then all fell silent. They moved out of the light, leaving Fate suspended at the center of the stage. Slowly and softly, the wind flute started in and the cords pulled Fate into a standing position.

With a sudden burst from the orchestra and thrashing movements from Fate, Fati's struggle against the sealing mask began. Fate sang with all her power to project her voice beyond the mask, and her sisters pulled and released the cords, sending her careening face-first towards the stage.

The audience gasped.

The cords stopped her just before she hit the floor, and then pulled her backward, repeating the violent motions to replicate the struggle of the Spinner's tragic tale.

Finally, the music fell silent and Fate collapsed into the altar chamber, much like a broken doll, and the lights dimmed again.

She panted and pulled at the cords wrapped around her throbbing wrists. The theatre felt as though it spun in the darkness. Her ears rang and her body ached, but she was proud of her sisters for giving it their all. She sat in silence in the dark for an uncomfortably long time before the lights went up and divulged the results of their efforts.

The crowd stood and the theatre boomed with cheering, as Fate removed the mask and forced herself out of the chamber and to her feet in the most graceful way possible. They'd succeeded in creating a breathtaking performance, but she'd held only one intention, and her heart pounded in her chest as her eyes finally met Hero's.

He stood close enough to reach out and touch, clapping with the rest of the audience. His expression displayed more inquisitiveness than delight, but revealed that she'd caught his attention on at least some level.

She patted her neck, attempting to cool herself, and curtsied for her adoring fans.

Her sisters rushed in, hugging her and singing her praises as Fortuna entered the stage.

The Madam opened her hands to the audience, her gown and earrings glittering in the light. "Thank you all for attending our showing of *Rota Fortunae*, and for your generous contributions. Please stay for refreshments. You may remain here, or join us in the teahouse, as to your preference." She glanced back at Fate and winked before descending into the mass of chattering people.

Fate took in the affections of her sisters, and slowly they dispersed into the flood of admirers, drawing attention so that she could make her way to Hero.

He had moved farther away in the bustle of the crowd, but she managed to find him again. As the crowd pulled away, she saw that he spoke to someone. His overall expression differed from usual, seeming vexed.

She slowed her gait and watched, until the people cleared enough for her to spot Niteo engaging Hero in a heated conversation.

A hand reached out from the crowd and grasped her by the arm. Abyssus pulled her back, shushing her.

He came? She scanned the crowd for Neco and Mortis, or even a sign of Firmus.

He managed to forestall her admonition for sneaking about by leading her along the back wall and down an aisle of seats to eavesdrop on Hero and Niteo.

Niteo raised a hand towards Hero's face. "I will not hear another word of it. You think you can do whatever you want while I'm away. You've had your fun. It's time to stop."

What are they talking about?

Abyssus whispered, "Apparently, Niteo didn't know about Hero leaving the palace to mentor you."

Fate whispered back, "How? No one noticed Hero was gone? I thought Madam reached out to get his permission."

He shrugged. "Guess he didn't respond... or maybe he did."

She knew him better than to let it go. "If I find out that you're a part of this...."

"You'll what? Just be glad Hero's that eager to meet with you."

He's right. This isn't the time to be scolding him.

Hero leaned up close to Niteo's face, speaking too low to understand. Whatever he said made his father clam up tight, and the debate ended that instant.

Abyssus gestured for Fate to follow him out of the aisle. He made haste through the crowd to where Hero and Niteo stood.

Abyssus waved at Niteo. "Hi, Uncle!"

Niteo straightened his coat and cleared his throat, still noticeably shaken. "Abyssus, my lad, what a surprise."

Something brushed against Fate's hand. As she looked down, she gathered that her brother motioned for her to go and see Hero while he distracted Niteo.

She finally seized the opportunity after taking a last deep breath to steady herself.

Hero gave her his full attention, not allowing his gaze to wander the way it usually did.

She kept up her calm façade. "Did I deliver on my promise?"

He considered her comment, then twisted his mouth to one side and made a teetering gesture with his hand. "Hmm... I don't know. *Sau p'hi loa en...* meh."

She held her smile but her heart beat profusely. "Hmm?"

"I said your pronunciation in the Language of Ages was meh."

"Oh." The fact that she received criticism, from Hero of all people, hurt far more than expected. It had taken only moments for him to dash her hopes.

He glanced at his father then smiled at her. "Nevertheless, I enjoyed it." His smile faded again. "But what made you use that mask?"

She thought of the mask, the same one she'd seen in her dream of the young boy. At the time, it disturbed her because it looked like something used to blind someone. "Oh, well...

remember the dream I told you about? I saw someone who wore that mask. I found it unsettling. When I first began planning with Fortuna, she said it's a type of seal used to mark those who've committed heinous crimes. It seemed to me that whoever sealed Fati must have seen her in a similar manner."

"Well, you're not wrong. Still, it's strange to dream, let alone dream of something like that."

"I can't help my dreams."

Hero looked around again. "I wouldn't confess that too loudly."

Fate gently took his arm and nodded towards the door to the outside corridor. She expected him to refuse, but he just checked his father a final time and followed her out.

Hanging lanterns lit the hall and tinted the wood in a warm orange, making it seem warmer than the brisk air.

Hero removed his scarf and put it on her as she began to tremble. "Your performance was very memorable."

Both relief and anxiety stirred in her heart. Even so, she smiled at his praise, and buried her face into the warm yarn. "Thank you. I'm happy you enjoyed it. It's hard to perform knowing that I'll be auctioned off to a stranger. I feel more at ease when I see a friend in the crowd."

His face softened. "It strikes me as odd that no one has tried to take you away from this place. You're an Ancient and a Royal." After saying this, he feigned a smile. "Then again, I'm the youngest of a Lost Clan and an Ancient Royal, and that never stopped anyone from sealing me up inside the palace."

For the first time, she really felt a strong connection and relatability to him. He lived in a palace, but people had caged him just the same. At the very least, he understood her circumstances more than the brothel's usual clients. It seemed ironic that their parents were twins.

Hero distracted Fate from her thoughts. "Are you busy tomorrow?"

"No more than usual. Why?"

"Would you like to come to the palace?"

Fate's mouth fell open. *The performance may have worked after all.* "Wha—I mean, yes, of course. Would that be acceptable?"

He wore a fixed smile and averted his gaze. "My father will be busy tomorrow. Who would complain?"

She recalled the interaction between him and his father. *Is that really so, or did you threaten him?*

The nature of the Tainted perplexed her. If Hero was any indicator of their behavior, they appeared to find it normal to intimidate others for their own benefit or desires. However, she also knew that this might be indicative of Hero's personality, and not of the entire group.

At the moment, she pushed matters of the Tainted and of Hero's threat to the side. She needed to go to the palace and secure her future, at any cost. "When should I visit?"

He cocked his head to one side with a friendly grin. "I wouldn't want to interfere with your work. Come when it best suits your schedule. No matter if it's day or night, as there's always time for celebration in Nitor Palace."

"Celebration? What are we celebrating?"

"Your visit, of course."

Every now and then, he said things that rendered her speechless. His behavior confused her, vacillating between endearing and unsettling.

Which one is the real Caeles Hero? It's so hard to tell.

She smiled back at him to show her appreciation and approval. "Thank you. It's been a long time since I last celebrated anything."

"You don't celebrate in the brothel," he said, in reference to her letter.

The sheer fact that he remembered brought a genuine smile to her face. "Right." She finally saw a ray of hope, a possibility to attain her freedom. "Don't worry about my work. I'll be sure to visit you in the morning. Trust me when I say that everything else can wait."

"Very well, I'll return home now so I can prepare." He kissed her cheek, waved, and disappeared into the theatre.

Fate pressed a hand to her cheek, burning with embarrassment from head to toe. He always seemed so reserved, and the gesture, although a positive sign that the performance worked, had caught her off guard.

She pulled down the scarf to give herself breathing room... and gasped. "His scarf!"

By the time she stepped inside the theatre, both Hero and Niteo had departed.

Abyssus waved to Tori, with whom he briefly chatted before passing through one of the aisles to greet his sister. "Is that Hero's scarf?" He chortled and shook his head. "Silly me, of course it is. I bought it for him. What I meant to say is... wow, Hero lent you his scarf. Tell me the details."

She half-screamed, half-whispered, "He kissed my cheek! *And* he invited me to the palace."

He teased. "Ooh, Sis. Quite the seductress now, aren't we?"

"Stop that. You know how serious this is."

He rubbed her arms, something he often did to calm her down. "I'm teasing you *because* it's serious. You need to keep your head on straight. If it wasn't Hero, a greeting like that would be normal. It just means he's warmed up to you, so don't let your guard down."

She exhaled. "You're right. I can't let him fluster me like this. I don't know what it is about him that stuns me. I'm supposed to be the courtesan, not him."

Abyssus raised his brows. "I guess he's better at it. Begs the question, doesn't it?"

"Not funny."

"I was being serious." He patted her gently. "Hang in there. You're just one step closer to climbing out of the spider's web."

She nodded, exhausted from the performance and her rapid-firing nerves. The loud chatter around her seemed distant and unimportant compared to the immense stress caused by the upcoming auction. She closed her eyes and reminded herself not to lose focus.

Just for one night, she wanted to revel in her tiny victory.

15

THE SPIDER'S WEB

Fate woke in the morning as the light stretched across the floor from the round window. She rolled onto her side to watch as tiny snowflakes descended from the grey sky upon the courtyard, a vast improvement from the previous turns. She sat up with a smile, pleased by her positive response from Hero on the previous night.

She slid her feet into her slippers, wrapped herself in a silken robe, and sat at her vanity. Her reflection appeared more warped every day, and though the woman before her looked young without makeup, she felt old inside. It took every ounce of strength in her to not shatter the mirror. She hated her reflection, and only sat before it to prepare for her visit to Nitor Palace.

Out of habit, she applied simple, clean makeup and ran a brush through her hair. For a final touch, she added her comb with the tiny ruby beads, then dressed, took her red cloak from the wall hanger, and draped it over her shoulders. She turned back to the mirror for one last assessment, nodded her approval, and left the room.

She walked into the hall and pushed her door shut, taking in the soft glow of the morning light. The typical clang of pots and pans echoed through the building, the same as every day since she'd first arrived at the brothel. Even supposing that so much remained the same, she'd experienced a lot of change as well. Sisters had arrived and left, and Fate had learned countless lessons and grew into an important member of the Rebellion, as well as a leader to all of her sisters. These recollections brought her inner peace, as this once-lost girl had gained independence. She felt confident that she trod the path that led not only to freedom, but to control of her future... and possibly the futures of everyone in Mu.

If she ascended to the position of High Queen, she could accomplish even more. Her plans, hopes, and dreams depended on her winning Hero's affections. The only thing that caused her alarm was the fact that, in many ways, she saw herself as detached and as confusing as Hero. Perhaps she might be able to use that common thread to tie them together.

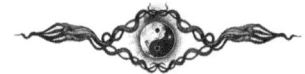

Fate walked passed the sunken hearth room, surprised to see it empty, and continued to the dining hall.

Her sisters looked up from their plates and conversations, and greeted her with chipper smiles and waves.

Tori scooted over to make room for Fate.

Fate shook her head. "I'm just grabbing a snack."

Myrna turned her attention from Tori to Fate, the look in her golden eyes casting a veil of suspicion. "Where are you off to?"

Fate smirked. "Nitor Palace."

The girls teased.

Yuzu stood on the bench. "To see Prince Hero?"

Fate nodded as she plucked a boiled egg from Tori's plate. "That's right."

Tori smacked her hand but allowed her to keep the egg.

Yuzu stretched her arms out as far as her body allowed. "Tell him I love him *this* much."

Several of the girls added their love for Hero into the mix.

Fate shook her head in wonder, amazed that such an awkward person managed to achieve such affections from girls he barely knew. Perhaps something in his anima caused it, or the stain affected them in such a manner. After taking a bite of the egg, she waved and started for the door as her sisters shouted their goodbyes.

She exited back into the hallway and strolled through the brothel in search of Fortuna, while eating the rest of the stolen egg. Eventually, she exited the brothel and walked into the garden.

She found the madam standing next to the pond with her pipe in hand. "There you are."

Fortuna turned and let out a long stream of smoke. "Are you heading out now?"

Fate spun in a circle for inspection. "I am. I will make the most of this visit, not to worry."

Fortuna's smile emitted the stress of a mother sending her child into battle. "I know you will. Fate, you are meant for this. I just wish I had more options for you. Sometimes I feel like I've let you down."

Fate drew close to her. "You have not. This is a chance for me — for all of us."

Fortuna nodded. "It is." She leaned forward and hugged Fate. "I worry."

Fate returned the regard. "I know. It's going to be all right."

Fortuna released her and flashed a smile. "I'm proud of you. I hope you know that."

Fate winked. "I do."

She waved and quickly made her exit. She'd already spent too much time dawdling, and needed to make up some of it, so she quickened her step and rushed to the gates, keeping her interaction with the guards to a minimum.

They understood her urgency and allowed her through without a fuss.

"Thank you," she called out to them as she ran up the road.

She jogged through the front garden and up the palace stairs, and arrived at the front doors panting. A couple of deep breaths and slow exhales brought her breathing back to normal. Once she felt collected enough, she knocked.

The doors opened and, to her surprise, Hero stood before her.

He stared back at her as she stood, dumbfounded. "Is something wrong?"

"I think I'm just surprised."

He lowered his brows and drew his mouth to one side. "By what?"

She fumbled for an explanation. "That you answered the door."

He crossed his arms and leaned back. "You're shocked I answered the door at my own home?"

She fiddled with the skirt of her gown, feeling silly for her astonishment after his question. "I just mean... you're a prince with servants.... Don't *they* normally answer the door?"

He unfolded his arms. "Oh." He took a step forward and leaned in close. "I don't trust them around such a beautiful guest."

Heat rushed to her cheeks. Again.

He squinted. "The hot-cold thing?"

Although the sun shone with warmth, she replied, "Exactly."

He stepped back from the doorway and extended his hand for her. "Let's join the party."

She followed his lead into the palace, excited to be a guest rather than a trespasser.

The layout of Nitor's palace interior mirrored that of Macellarius's, except everything in Nitor appeared brighter due to the natural white stone. The chandelier above her chimed a bit as the violet stones clinked together.

Hero motioned for her to follow him past the doorway, straight ahead and beneath the stairway, to a larger room where servants bustled about adding last-minute touches, like stringing lights and hanging flower ornamentations. They brought in more food and drinks to a long table set up against the wall. On the left side, musicians warmed up their instruments before a row of tall, curtained windows. Some of the chairs held just the instruments and not the musicians.

Hero cleared his throat.

Everyone stopped what they were doing and greeted Fate unanimously. "Welcome to Nitor Palace!"

A group of musicians gathered next to the hors d'oeuvres set their plates down, hurried to their chairs, picked up their instruments, and started playing.

The servants cheered and the festivities began. Some flooded the food tables, and many went straight to dancing.

Fate watched the festivities unfold before her. Her heart sang as she retraced the long lost wish of her seventh birthday — a simple dream of Rahma and Ancients celebrating her birthday together. She pressed her hand to her chest to quell the excitement; Hero had made her dream a reality.

She hesitated, speechless in witnessing the leniency Hero showed his servants. She thought Nitor to be the most joyous palace in all of Mu. Certainly, not all Royals treated their servants with such frivolity. Everyone's admiration of him finally started to make sense.

A pair of hands gripped her waist with force, and she spun fast, ready to defend herself.

Abyssus beamed with pride for his near-fatal fright.

She smacked his arm. "Abyssus!"

He chuckled while shielding himself, then gestured to the chaos of celebrating servants. "This is the Nitor treatment... or maybe, more accurately, the Hero treatment."

Fate looked at Hero, who patiently waited for her to say or do something. "I must admit, I am a touch amazed that they're allowed to behave this way."

Hero shrugged. "My father isn't here, so why not? I don't mind. They have more fun this way. They're the ones who did all of the work, so why shouldn't they enjoy their efforts?"

Fate tipped her head with a soft smile. "I'm impressed."

Lara entered the hall. In the palace, she wore an apron over her usual plain dress, a curious appearance for the King's Ward — intentionally misleading, perhaps. One of her braids fell over her shoulder as she slid into the Celebration Hall and spied Hero. Her natural grouchiness dissipated the moment he entered her line of sight.

She ran across the room. "Dance with me!"

"I have guests," he said.

Lara gripped him by the arms, pleading.

Abyssus sneered at her.

Fate watched her brother's expression grow sourer with each action Lara took. She studied Lara, trying to understand why he felt as strongly as his face suggested.

Hero slipped free of Lara's grasp. "How about we play a round of *Rota Fortunae*?"

Fate blinked in rapid succession. "*Rota Fortunae*?"

"It's a game from Undal."

Abyssus brimmed with excitement and partook in a familiar jig. "We'll need a blindfold!"

Hero glanced at the ribbon around the waist of Fate's dress. He reached out and took hold of it, twisting it around his finger until the bow came undone. He slipped the knot and pulled the ribbon free. "Can we borrow this?"

"Um, sure... it looks like you already have."

He smirked and said, "I knew you would say yes."

She considered arguing, but then he looked up at her with those mint eyes and his broad smile, and lightly pressed his tongue to his teeth. In that instant, all possible arguments fled with the blood in her face. His expression made it clear that he knew his tactics had worked.

The interaction alarmed her.

He seemed different from before. Sometimes, Hero appeared distracted and distant; other times, he was like a lost, gravely wounded puppy; and on days like this one, he carried himself cocksure and flirtatious.

In all of her studies on the Tainted, she'd seen no mention of such erratic behavior. Hero's condition seemed to be unique.

Hero turned to Lara and flippantly asked, "Are you joining?"

Her eyes sparkled at the suggestion. "Of course!"

Abyssus shook his hands in a façade of joyous celebration, but his tone fell flat and disenchanted. "*Ohh*, yay, Lara's playing."

She glowered at him from over Hero's shoulder.

Hero patted Abyssus on the cheek. "Play nicely. I always do."

Abyssus rolled his eyes, indicating the blatant lie.

Hero led everyone past the tables, across the room, through the revelers, and out the big embellished glass doors to the garden.

The air felt warmer than usual, lending to the blissful ambiance of the long stretches of lush grass, full trees, and white roses.

As Fate drew closer to inspect the flowers, it became apparent that they were white due to the thin layer of frost that coated their delicate petals. Her wonder deepened as she queried how the frost remained in such warm conditions.

She looked up from the ice roses to see Hero leading the group into a labyrinth at the edge of the garden lawn. Her distraction had caused her to fall behind, so she lifted the front of her dress from the ground and hurried to catch up.

When she arrived, she caught only the tail end of the playful banter between Hero and Abyssus.

Abyssus concealed a smirk with his hand. "So, who's going to be the Calamity?"

Fate asked, still trying to catch up, "What's the Calamity?"

Hero looked over his shoulder as he ventured farther into the labyrinth. "In history, the Calamity was a Goddess believed to be a Spirit Walker, capable of venturing into the Dreamscape and communicating the Spirits, best known as the Spinner, as in *The Spinner of Dreams*. She could Spirit Walk because she had the Eyes of the Abyss."

She scrunched up her eyebrows. "Eyes of the Abyss?"

Hero faced forward again, pressed his hand to his chin, and thought for a moment. "Think of it as a filter that allows you to see into an Ethereal Realm. It gives clarity to things the average eye can't see. For instance, they see more than an Ancient, as an Ancient can see more than a Rahma."

Abyssus interjected. "Except with the Eyes of the Abyss, you can't see the Mortal Realms."

She took in the lesson, still confused as to the rules that applied. "How does this pertain to the game?"

Hero explained. "One person is blindfolded—they can no longer see in the Mortal Realm. That person takes the role of the Calamity, whose job is to 'taint' other people who come close to them."

Abyssus added, "First, the Calamity is isolated, then we all clap and sing the Spinning song to allow the Calamity to try and find us."

She rubbed her head. "What's the Spinning song?"

Lara interjected, her comment laced with condescending disbelief. "You really don't know? The Spinning song comes from the folklore of *Rota Fortunae*, which is why it's the name of the game. You know of the *Book of Ages* at least?"

Fate locked her jaw, finding Lara's impudence barely tolerable. "I do."

Abyssus made a dramatized look of disgust behind Lara's back.

Fate forced down a laugh.

Lara continued her haughty explanation. "The tale, as well as the songs, were passed down until children finally turned it into a game. Pretty much *all* children in Mu know the game. It's amazing, really, that you don't know it."

Fate considered the historical content, as well as the game implications. "So, what is the song's purpose? Is it just to find the other players?"

Hero raised a finger into the air. "Ah, now that's a good question. It is suggested, historically speaking, that the song was a method mortals used to summon the Calamity and mark the next Fated."

She puzzled more so, since he ignored her question and responded with a history lesson, rather than the rules of the game. "Fated? This is surprisingly complex, not to mention disturbing, for a children's game."

He smiled. "Indeed. According to the Teachings of Grim, the Fated were people infected by the Tainted. Anyone who became Fated died of illness or unfortunate circumstances."

Fate chewed her lip, trying to understand Hero's reason for choosing a game based on his own illness.

Lara grumbled. "Back to the game. If she can't understand the rules, maybe she should just sit this one out and watch."

Hero disregarded the blatantly spiteful comment. "So, as I was saying, in the game, the Calamity has to touch people to taint them. Once someone is tainted, they can taint other people. The object of the game is to either taint all of the free players, or touch the Calamity without the Calamity touching you."

Abyssus chimed in. "The Calamity will start by the gazebo. We're almost there now."

Hero started walking with the group following. "Thanks. I hadn't even realized we stopped." Each wind in the labyrinth led deeper into the massive yard.

As Fate trailed behind Hero, it grew darker and darker. She watched his back and the way the sunlight cast shadows onto it. A rustling passed under their feet as they traveled. Finally, they stood at the edge of the gazebo within the center of the labyrinth.

Lara let out a low sigh. "I think Lady Fate should play the Calamity."

"I agree," Hero said, tying the ribbon around Fate's eyes.

Fate jolted. "What? Why me?"

"Because you are the least familiar with the rules and it somehow seems fitting. Don't worry, we can't leave the labyrinth, so you'll know we're in here somewhere. Plus, the shrubs are soft, so you won't get hurt."

The cold air stung her cheeks and sent a shiver down her spine. It had been warm just moments before, so she fretted as to the sudden change. "Is it just me, or is it colder in here?"

Hero replied, his voice carrying a hint of amusement. "It's darker too."

The sound of his voice relieved her. "To be honest, I have a really bad sense of direction, so I'm a little worried."

Abyssus shouted from somewhere in the maze. "You'll be fine. Now, when we start singing, you have to spin for twelve verses, so take it easy. We don't want you to pass out."

Fate put her hands on her hips, tiring of Abyssus's and Hero's jokes at her expense. "Is that truly a possibility?"

Lara answered, still somewhere in proximity. "It's happened a few times. People have been known to freak out while playing this game. They believe they've seen the Spinner herself and would swear by it."

Fate frowned; certain that Lara wanted to frighten her out of playing. "I'm not sure I would entirely mind that. She is folklore incarnate. Sounds interesting." Much to her delight, Lara offered no snappy retort.

Hero rested a hand on Fate's arm. "Once we complete the twelve verses, take the blindfold off. Like I said, the hedges are soft, so even if you spin into them, you'll be safe."

"All right."

His footsteps moved quickly away from her, and a sudden jolt of panic ran through her body. She stretched her arms out and felt for anyone or anything nearby.

A voice spoke softly to her. "Safe journeys, Mistress."

Her senses tingled with the energy in the air. She pressed her lips together and inhaled deeply, hoping to calm herself.

Abyssus's voice resounded from a distance. "Are you ready?"

Fate's heart beats slowed, each heavy and adding to her anxiety. She swallowed before answering in a raised but quivering voice. "Yes."

The clapping began and the Spinning Song echoed through the labyrinth as the three players sang:

> *Spinning, spinning wheel of fate,*
> *Which one will you choose?*
> *A sinner from the shadows,*
> *Shall you win or lose?*

Fate spun in circles as the game instructed. In the darkness of the blindfold, every sound around her grew dim, as if everything stretched far away from reach. She reasoned that the sensation derived from dizziness due to the blindfold and the spinning. It made sense that the game was designed to cause disorientation for whoever played the Calamity. No matter the reason, she quickly lost touch with her surroundings.

> *Turning, turning wheel of fate,*
> *The spokes are slowing down.*
> *Hush, the demon's dance is ending,*
> *Don't you make a sound.*

Her mind played tricks on her, as the unknown verses sounded familiar and echoed in the back of her mind. Her throat constricted but she continued to spin. Time lost meaning and, before she realized, she lost count of the verses.

The players continued to clap and sang:

> *Stopping, stopping wheel of fate,*
> *She tiptoes through the crowd.*
> *If you hear her whisper,*
> *You are Fated now.*

She spun two more times after the last verse, only stopping upon realizing they'd finished the song. Her head swam, making her feel as though she still spun well after she'd stopped.

The darkness beckoned to her from everywhere and nowhere, pulling her into a trance. It felt warm and inviting, calling to her like an old friend with whom she desperately wished to reunite. She drifted farther away from the labyrinth and the game, and into a world of endless black.

A woman's voice spoke low and soft, her words incomprehensible.

Fate reached up and removed the blindfold. She stood alone in the dark labyrinth, her only company being the chill and the occasional dancing leaves. The wind howled, a sound much like a wailing woman, and she spun again in a circle, looking for the owner of the voice.

Nothing. No one. Just Fate and the empty gazebo.

The nip in the air made her uneasy. Beyond that, it smelled old and musky, leaving her with a sense of dread.

A shadow had fallen over the labyrinth during the song, and it now appeared much as it would after nightfall. A low haze developed, clinging to the ground and easing ever closer to where she stood.

She stared at the disturbing changes, reminding herself that Lara had warned the game sometimes had this effect. She rubbed her eyes to see if the haze cleared, but it grew thicker. A hollow static filled her head as she took her first steps into the labyrinth. Her heart beat heavy and thumped against her chest, forcing her to breathe deep to calm it.

The chimes of a thousand tiny bells reached her ears, drawing more darkness into the world and draining the once vibrant colors of the labyrinth into a pantone of grey and dismal shadows.

She moved deeper into the maze, the cold urging her to move faster. The hedges all looked the same, each tall and as dense as the rolling fog. She rubbed her arms as panic set it. "Hero? Abyssus?"

At the end of the path lay an opening, where she turned and observed. A long, narrow passage, carved from the hedges, stretched out before her. She looked one way and then the other, not sure which direction to take. Both indicated a long walk into the unknown.

The clapping started again, but this time it ricocheted all around her, as though emanating from a vast, vacant cavern. The constant overlap of the empty claps and their echoes filled her mind with questions and concerns.

The song resumed in a warbled echo:

> *Spinning, spinning,*
> *Spinning, spinning,*
> *Wheel of fate,*
> *Which one...*
> *Sinner from the shadows...*

Fate held her ears. "I don't want to play anymore."
The song continued in an ever-overlapping chaos of sound.

> *Turning, turning,*
> *Turning, turning,*
> *The demon's dance is ending.*
> *Turning, turning,*
> *The spokes are slowing down.*
> *Don't you make a sound.*

She turned to her left and walked down the long dark path. Before she arrived at the end, a tall, slender man in a red suit and white fox mask, which covered the upper half of his face, stepped out from around the bend. Startled, she slowed her step to see if he moved, but the man simply stood there, staring back at her as the clapping echoed through the maze.

His presence made her reconsider her choice, and she turned back to walk in the opposite direction of the stranger. She quickened her pace, frightened of the unknown man. As she moved, the haze cleared enough for her to see the end of the path.

There, a towering Grim loomed in its massive form, its cloaks flowing in the seemingly weightless breeze. The massive skeletal form watched her through hollow eye sockets, a faint glint of light glowing from the darkness of its barren skull. It emitted a hollow garbling and reached out towards Fate.

Her heart stopped as she slid to a halt, petrified.

Again, the chime resounded and a woman called to her, "This way."

Fate caught a flicker of white. She taxed her eyes in the haze until she spied a ghastly pale figure calling to her from a crevice in the hedge. The woman wore a tattered white gown and appeared injured, but she motioned to Fate with bloodied hands as the Grim drifted closer. Long white hair covered her face from view, but in her heart, Fate knew she rested eyes on the Spinner. When the mysterious woman slipped through a hidden opening in the maze, Fate quickly followed, but the woman moved faster and faster, her white gown billowing behind her. Soon, Fate lost sight of the woman and followed the sound of singing. The music brought tears to her eyes and formed a small dark hole in her heart. She slowed to a walk and then finally stopped, feeling overwhelmed with emotion.

The weight of the emotional pain brought her to her knees and she sat, lost in the labyrinth, feeling hopeless. Utter silence hung in the air. She slapped her cheeks, dragged herself to her feet again, and pushed onward, pursuing the distorted sound of clapping and hoping it might lead her back.

As she walked, she ran her hands over the hedge in hopes of keeping touch with reality, but the leaves merely gave way without a sound. She tried to quell her fears, but the labyrinth reminded her of her own reflection—hollow. The entire world had come to a stop.

The mist coiled around her as she wandered lost. A deep instinct warned her to return to the gazebo and wait for help, but she had meandered too far to find her way back, so she continued forward.

Stopping, stopping,
Stopping, stopping,
If you hear her whisper,
She tiptoes through the crowd.
Stopping, stopping,
If you hear her whisper...

The woman's voice called out to her again. "This way."

You are Fated now.

She rounded a corner and stood mere steps away from a crouched blackened form. This creature's presence differed from the Spinner, exuding darkness deeper than any she'd experienced before.

Faint wisps of black smoke rose from its back. The creature's skin looked as dark and as wet as ink as it hunched over on all fours sniffing the air.

It looked up at her with empty sockets.

Fate pressed her hands over her mouth to suppress a scream.

The creature remained crouched in place, as though waiting for her to do something.

She searched for an escape, but saw only the wall of the hedges and the waiting creature. With her gaze locked on the beast, she inched back around the corner, hoping it would leave her be.

Once safely around the corner, she released her breath and turned to flee, but a second shadowy creature blocked her path. She backed herself against the hedge, and pressed into the leaves and branches to conceal herself.

Although it lacked ears, the creature had heard or sensed her, and tilted its head in her direction. Its body creaked and snapped as it crept forward, emitting low clicking sounds from its throat. Hands—more like claws—gripped the soil as it moved forward.

Fate froze and held her breath again. As it drew closer, she bit down on her lip to keep herself from crying out, and leaned so heavily against the hedge that a branch snapped.

The creature's head twisted in her direction and it lurched forward, unhinging its jaw for a bone-chilling screech.

Darkness burst from Fate's chest, lashing out into points. It fiercely thrashed at the shadow creature, defending her as she rolled into a ball.

The sound of the clapping and singing echoed all around her.

The creature shrieked, shattering her surroundings like glass, and the world lost all sense of direction. Darkness consumed her vision and she lost consciousness.

16

EMPTY LIKE ME

Fate snapped her eyes open and white light flooded her vision.

Hero looked down at her, his eyes seeming to glow against his light features. "Are you all right?"

Her heart pounded so hard, she thought it might split open her chest. "What happened?"

"You collapsed."

She forced herself upright and gazed around her. The darkness had faded and the sun shone through light billowing clouds.

Abyssus leaned down, looking rather amused. "Not much for fun, huh?"

She smacked his leg. "It's not funny. My head really hurts."

Lara crossed her arms and rolled her eyes. "I agree. She's not fun in the slightest. You've completely spoiled the game."

Fate sighed, doing her best to maintain her patience, but Lara grated on her last nerve. She knew other girls just as irritating, but no matter how she tried to placate her feelings, Fate simply hated Lara.

"Let's get you up before you ruin your dress." Hero helped her to her feet with ease.

It astonished her how strong he was in spite of his frail appearance. She made a mental note of how often Hero seemed to defy the image he presented, and a little voice in her head told her that not all that appeared before her did so in its truest form. Of all the people she'd ever known, she believed this to be most true of Hero.

She glanced back at the labyrinth, half expecting to see the shadow creature staring back at her, but the beautifully groomed hedges held the air of any fresh spring day, and the invitation of joy and relaxation. Her balance wavered as the strange static hum crept into her ears again.

Hero frowned as he steadied her. "Do you need to sit again?"

She looked him in the eye, wanting to see the subtleties of his reaction. "I had a nightmare. It seemed so real. There was a man in a fox mask, a Grim, and some kind of smoke monster."

His eyes glinted with excitement—just for an instant—and he calmly stated, "You must have hit your head. You're safe now. We'll get you back inside."

Fate groaned. "I'm serious, Hero. It nearly scared the life from me."

Hero removed his gloves and held his hand to her forehead. "You don't seem to be ill."

As he withdrew, she gasped and grasped his wrist before he could put his gloves on again. "Your hands.... What happened?"

"My hands?" He opened it wide then turned it from back to front. A black stain covered it from his fingertips to the center of his palm. He lifted the other hand, revealing that they both contained the black stain. His frown deepened, and he lowered his brow. "Is there something wrong with them?"

She gaped at his hands, remembering how he stared at them when they were in the brothel, and then she looked directly at him, her soul warning that he knew exactly what she spoke of, but that he upheld his façade for Abyssus and Lara. The occasional gleam in his eyes made her uncomfortable, yet there was also something comforting about the way he commanded himself.

She turned to Abyssus and Lara. "You don't see it?"

Abyssus looked down at Hero's hands as Lara shook her head. "See what?"

She released Hero's wrist and opened her own hands, inspecting them, surprised to see they glowed faintly with white dust.

Hero held steady. "What do you see?"

"Nothing." She laughed off her surprise. "I think you may be right about me hitting my head. We should go inside."

As Abyssus and Lara started for the palace, Hero leaned forward, so close their noses almost touched. He looked her dead in the eyes with uncustomary intensity and whispered, "You're a terrible liar."

Her heart jumped into her throat. The heat of her panic radiated through her skin as she momentarily lost herself in his gaze. He caused her both anxiety and exhilaration. For once, she saw another as empty as herself. As their eyes locked, something tugged at her soul. "We're falling behind."

He withdrew, breaking his gaze, and extended his arm to her. "Lady Fate."

She accepted his offer and allowed him to escort her back towards the palace. As they walked, the same specks of white dust that coated the labyrinth stuck on Hero's coat. She questioned the experience... the longer she stared, the clearer she saw the red haze rising from his skin. Tiny particles, like flecks of blood, drifted upward into the air and dissipated.

Miasma?

Far ahead, Abyssus glanced back at the pair with a broad smile. He took Lara by the arm and dragged her into the palace at an accelerated speed.

Fate covered her mouth and stifled a laugh.

Abyssus, although well-intending, often lacked subtlety.

Hero smiled. "You have a nice laugh."

"Thank you."

"You know, when we get inside, there is something I'd like to show you."

She nodded.

While Lara and Abyssus engaged in some banter, Hero kept his gaze ahead on them. He spoke casually, and yet something about it felt threatening. "I know you can see me."

Fate's body jolted as he held onto her arm with a firm grip. There was no way to feign composure, as he most certainly sensed her fear. "Of course I can. What are you saying?"

He stopped his observations and looked at her. The light shone on his eyes in a way that accentuated their color, and a faint white ring appeared around his pupils. "You really are a terrible liar."

She swallowed hard. Any mistake could cost her the freedom she sought. "I thought it was strange... I've known for some time that you were Tainted, but.... I guess I just didn't know that the term *Stained* was literal. I thought they kept you locked in the palace to protect you. Now, I understand that they were trying to protect others *from* you."

He stared down at her, still keeping a firm hold of her arm. "Seems you see quite a lot."

"I suppose you're going to threaten me now?"

He lessened his grip, stepped back, and flashed a soft smile. "It shouldn't be necessary. I should think we have much in common, you and me. You may not be Tainted, but my eyes see something dark in you as well."

She expelled the weight in her lungs. His words rang true no matter how she spun it. They were both empty and, under the current circumstances, they needed each other.

Hero led her to the palace, swept a hand towards the ornate handle on the back door, and opened the way with a coy smile.

Fate checked their surroundings and realized that Lara and Abyssus had entered the palace without them. She lifted the front of her gown and walked passed Hero, glancing at him as she stepped back into the celebration hall.

Abyssus hung over the table of sweets and waved at her upon entry. "You've got to try these."

Lara sat in a chair looking miserable, until she saw Hero. "There you are. Did she twist her ankle or something?"

Hero patted Lara on the shoulder and brought her unimaginable delight. "No, she does need to rest though. So, can I count on you to take care of things down here until I get back?"

Lara's glee faded. "Where are you going?"

He winked at her. "Not to worry, dear friend. I'll return." His words helped her return to a more jovial mood.

She again snarled at Fate after Hero turned away from her, an outward display of loathing to everyone but him. To Fate, this said Lara cared enough about his opinion of her to hide her detestable behavior.

Abyssus leaned against the table with a coquettish grin. "We'll see you when you get back then."

Hero hovered his hand around Fate's back as he led her away from the party, and exchanged a curious look with Abyssus over his shoulder.

Fate looked back to see if her brother paid mind to where they were off to, but he appeared more interested in the baked goods than her safety.

Hero started up the curved stairway. "You seem nervous."

Her eyes darted from the party, to the entryway, to the stairs, and landed on the next floor, which appeared painfully far away as they traversed each carpeted step. "Do I?"

They finally arrived at the top of the stairs. "You do. It's unfortunate, really. We could do quite well together if not for the fear."

She looked at him as plainly as she found possible. "I'm not frightened of you, Hero. I'm confused by you."

His eye twitched, and he scratched his neck. "Please don't act. I will admit you are a wonderful dancer, and your singing is beyond compare, but I must advise you to leave the lying to me. You have no skill at all."

"So, you admit you've lied to me."

"Don't take it personally. I lie to everyone. You must understand, to some degree. After all, I am Tainted and nearly the last of my clan. What would you do in my position?"

He always made sense to her, even if she hated the manner he chose to express himself.

She sighed. "It appears we have more in common than I was willing to admit."

He started walking down the hall at a leisurely pace, which allowed her to move at her own accord. "Indeed."

She followed him, peering at the paintings that lined the walls. Each captured a Rahma, an unusual trait for any palace in Mu save the dismal Macellarius. Image after image revealed the takeover that had happened in Nitor. "Aren't there any of your clan?"

He halted and turned to her with a bitter expression. "Why would my father care about that? He can't stand me."

She froze, unclear how to respond at first. "We really are alike."

He continued walking to the end of the hall and opened the door to a small study.

She stepped inside and admired the built-in bookshelves packed with books. The titles illuminated the depth of Hero's obsession. "Are *all* of these about folklore?"

He smiled as he beheld his collection, and sat down on a red armchair before the fireplace. "They are. If the Council saw this, they would burn every single one."

Fate ran her fingers over the spines, amazed by the lack of dust. They appeared to be old copies of long-banned tales, each title and pattern gilded across the cover. "How are you able to keep all of these without getting in trouble?"

"Honestly, I just use what is available to me. As I've already explained, my father hates me. As a child, he kept me close because I was a convenient tool for him to maintain power. Now that I'm older, we are... strained. So, he stays far away from me and the rooms I choose to occupy. Lara is the only one that comes in here, and she won't say anything."

She folded her arms. "That girl is infatuated with you in an unhealthy way."

He scanned the books in search of something. "We've been friends for many turns now. She doesn't like you because you're a prostitute."

Fury burned in her cheeks. "I work in a brothel but I haven't been auctioned off yet. I'll be out before anything more happens."

He looked at her and narrowed his eyes. "How are you going to accomplish that?"

Lacking answers, she stared at him with every defiant cell in her body. If she answered, she risked telling him her plan to use him. That seemed like a bad way to win over someone's affections.

He returned to his hunt, his gaze moving quickly over each title. His eyes moved so fast that he appeared to fake his search. "You sound jealous."

His audacity staggered her. "You sound arrogant."

"You're not wrong. Ah, here it is." He rose from the chair and went to one of the shelves, removed a large book, and carried it to the small, polished wood table across the room.

Fate moved closer as he leafed through the pages, her attention caught by the immaculate staging of the room. She studied first Hero, who stood at the table, then the large window behind him, and the screen that diffused the window light for the perfect reading setting.

He seemed wise beyond his age, and that gave way to concern. He was an admitted liar and, from what she gathered, a fanatic when it came to controlling his environment.

When her curiosity waned, and her gaze returned to him, she realized he had been waiting for her. "Sorry."

His mouth turned down, and his eyes lacked luster. "If you're too tired...."

She shook her head. "No, I was just admiring your set up. This really is the perfect reading room."

His bottom lip stuck out as he looked around the room, a pout if she knew any better. "It is, isn't it?"

She joined him at the table. "What do you have?"

He flipped the cover closed while keeping his place with his hand, revealing the inscription on the deep blue cover:

The Story of Night and Day

"I think I've heard of this one."

Hero chuckled. "It would be unbelievable if you hadn't. Everyone's heard of it at some point."

"You sound like Lara."

He nudged her with his foot. "Now you're just being mean."

She challenged. "I thought the Council outlawed Undalian folklore."

"They did. I guess we're both rebels."

His pun brought a smile to her face. For all his flaws, she enjoyed spending time with him.

She tossed her hands on her hips. "So, are you going to read it to me or are we just going to look at it?"

He chuckled. "Oh, you want *me* to read it to *you*?"

"Why not? You have a soothing voice."

"I thought the voice thing was your job, Tocsin."

"Did you just call me a name?"

The comment, albeit his own, had apparently triggered his passion for folklore. He stopped leaning on his hand and waved it around to make gestures that suited his descriptions. "It means you use your voice as a weapon. Tocsin could disintegrate a person with their voice."

"Rude. I thought you liked my singing."

He rested his chin on his hand again, and leafed through the book avoiding her gaze. "I do, that's the problem. You tempt me with an unmatchable voice, flawless dance, and the ever-powerful folklore."

"You really are obsessed with folklore."

He flashed his usual mischievous smile, leaned one arm against the table, and placed his free hand against his hip as though to mock her. "Hmm... I don't know... a striking beauty with the Gift of Song?" He scanned her from head to toe. "Sounds like you."

She combatted her embarrassment with an instant retort. "Except, I'm a performer, not some kind of powerful, ethereal being. I barely learned to fence. How in nine hells would I even dream of disintegrating someone with my voice?"

His face soured as he turned back to the book. "You're so serious. Learn to live a little, Miss Fate."

She released one heavy sigh. The fact that he always got his way frustrated her to no end. To make matters worse, she knew this and still let it happen. "Okay, I'll read it, but at least sit down."

"Hmm," he answered in agreement.

As she went to sit, he took the book in one hand and led her, by the waist, to the red armchair. If not for the fact that she had yet to turn around and walk forward, she may have deemed it as courteous or romantic. Instead, he walked her backwards, plopped her down on the cushion, and plunked down next to her.

She stared at him for a long moment.

His behavior so contradicted his feathery appearance that it baffled her. He seemed to lack social cues, and yet understood them well enough to flirt with others.

Unless he doesn't know he's flirting. No, he definitely knows what he's doing.

He pulled half the book onto his lap, waited, and checked to see why she wasn't reading. *"Nein? Oar'ce raos."*

She shook her head hard to break from her thoughts. "What? Don't just start speaking in the Language of Ages out of nowhere. You know I can't understand."

He blinked and shifted his head slightly to one side. "I didn't."

"Funny. Nevermind that. I'll start reading, so be patient." Initially, she believed that the size of the book indicated its length. However, when she opened it, she noted that the pages were thick with vibrant watercolor-style paintings. She ran her hand over the title image, one of space in blue and fuchsia. If every book looked like this, she fully understood why Hero loved them.

She turned to the first part of the story, careful not to bend or dent the page. To her, the book and the images emitted an aura of beauty, love, and sorrow.

Hero watched her without blinking, instead of looking at the book.

She cleared her throat while looking at the two beautifully painted pages, one filled by space and stars, the other by gold and fuchsia clouds. On the dark side, a character with long, ebony hair stared up at the bright half, while a character with long, white hair peered over a cliff, covered by white flowers.

Fate read aloud. "Long, long ago, there were two realms, one of shadow and one of light. In these realms existed two powerful rulers named Luna and Syo." She turned the page again. Covering both pages, another stunning image depicted the Realm of Light and the white-haired ruler amidst a field of glowing flowers, luring her further into the story. "In the Realm of Light lived Syo, who stunned all with a pure inner and outer beauty."

Hero continued watching her in silence.

She flipped to the next pages, where tiny flecks of crystal embedded into the paint showed Luna in the Realm of Shadow, emitting what appeared to be blue fireflies. The fireflies reminded her of stars in the night sky. "In the Realm of Shadow lived Luna, a master of rebirth and the spiritual arts, but lonesome beyond all compare."

She continued to the next image, one of Syo on hands and knees peering down at a violet sea. On the following page, Syo appeared to be falling down a vortex into the Realm of Shadow. "One day, while trying to study a glimmer in the ocean, Syo fell from the cliff Light into the Realm of Shadow."

The next image showed Syo down in the darkness, and Luna running to aid. "Surprised, Luna ran to investigate and aided the injured Syo, until the being of light may return to the upper realm."

She flipped the page to find only a magnificent image of the two rulers conversing beside a body of water, laced by a glowing light.

Fate continued to the next image. Luna and Syo turned away from each other, returning to their respective realms, with the narrow fold between the pages appearing to be the only thing that separated them, though they must be worlds apart. "After returning to their Realms, they continued to think of each other, and a deep longing grew."

Syo ran down a stairway of light, looking back at their realm, and escaped into the darkness. "Although the Universe forbade it, they continued to meet in secret."

The next part of the story showed Luna and Syo lying between the swirls of clouds and space in an embrace. Fate read, her chest feeling heavy. "...and they fell in love."

She swallowed hard as a lump formed in her throat.

A new character entered the story, painted with flowing red hair as bright as an apple. The image showed the character walking in space, on what appeared to be water, as he approached Luna and Syo. After that came an image of him holding them by the hands. "Eventually, one of their peers, the Sage, noticed their deepening relationship and forewarned of the consequences. However, Syo refused to leave Luna down in the darkness."

In the following pages, Syo stood at the edge of the Realm of Light before a golden gate. "As the Sage warned, Syo's meetings with Luna brought the higher powers to seal off their realms."

Parted, Luna and Syo each cried a single tear painted to look like crystal. "As the two lovers were forced apart, Luna grew ill." A moth fluttered through the opposite page. "Luna called to Syo one final time."

The lovers met at the gates, reached through the bars and shared a kiss. "As Luna died, she gave to Syo the remainder of their shared life-force.

A poem filled the last page:

> *And the goddess kissed the sun,*
> *Before taking their plight,*
> *For there was no true love,*
> *Fonder than night.*

Fate blinked several times to force back the tears welling in her eyes. It baffled her how a story could captivate her so thoroughly, filling her with such tremendous longing.

Hero leaned against his hand and studied her. "It moved you."

She swallowed and wet her dried lips before trying to speak. "It did. I understand why you like these stories. They're beautiful."

He agreed as he stood. "Hmm."

"They all seem to tell the same story."

"What do you mean?"

She sniffed, carefully considering her explanation. "*The Sands of Time* and *The Story of Night and Day* almost seem like the same story."

He leaned forward, bobbing his head as he thought. "Hmm. Similar, but not the same. So either it is the same story told by two different parties, or it's two stories with similar meanings."

She leaned back against her chair still feeling moved. "Then it doesn't matter which it is. In the end, it reminds us not to lose sight of what is important."

He gently closed the book, stepped in front of her, and knelt down. "I'm going to bid for you during the auction."

Although she had continued to try to win his favor, she'd never expected to succeed. A knot formed in her throat, rendering her speechless. She made a final attempt to keep herself together but the sudden relief made her silently weep.

He reached out and wiped her tears. "I mean it. I will be there, and I will win. I swear it."

Fate's hands trembled. Her voice caught in her throat and her mouth refused to work, but tears streamed down her cheeks without fail.

He bit his lip with a frown. "I didn't think to ask if you would mind. I'm sorry if I've been rude."

She set her shaking hand on his arm and spoke. "If I must be purchased, there is no one I'd rather trust than you. I hope it is not an inconvenience." Despite the plan to trick him, she had a true fondness for him.

Hero laughed hard, shaking his head. "An inconvenience, she says. Lady Fate, you truly amaze and bewilder me."

As she observed him, she questioned if she still dreamt. Her savior was not at all as she expected, but just as courageous and confident as she had hoped. Still, an underlying fear crept into her mind. "What will you do with me?"

Shock washed over his expression, and he laughed again, and ran his hands over his face. "What will I do? I was thinking I'd marry you but, if you would prefer, we can find some other solution."

She blushed again, and even her neck and chest flared. "Oh, I thought...."

"You thought what?"

An overwhelming panic set in. "Never mind. I should probably get back."

He turned quickly, his gaze following her. "Wait. Never mind what? What did you think?"

She fled the room and hurried down the hall to the stairs with Hero chasing after.

He shouted down to her as she descended. "Are you sure you're all right with it?"

She stopped at the bottom of the staircase and looked up at him still flushed. "I am. More than you know."

He rested against the banister with a sheepish grin. "Good. Then I'll make arrangements."

Fate pressed her lips together, feeling the excitement swell. "I'll wait for you." The butterflies fluttering about her stomach made her want to scream, but she turned to make an appropriate exit.

On her way towards the front door, Abyssus trotted up. "Wait, are you leaving already?"

"I have to get back."

He fidgeted with a frown. "I thought it would be good for you to stay awhile, you know, and get to know Hero better."

Hero called down from the second floor. "Abyssus, come talk with me."

Abyssus cast a sideways glance at Fate and gasped. "Tell me it's good."

Fate pressed her lips together with a smirk. "I have to go, and Hero is waiting for you."

Abyssus pointed at her. "Vixen. I love it!" He kissed her on the cheek and dashed up the stairs to hear the news.

Fate hurried out the door and down the long drive to the gate. She barely managed to acknowledge the guards as she passed through. Her feet struggled to keep pace with her enthusiasm as she sprinted back to the brothel and flew open the screen, slamming it behind her.

The brothel girls watched in amazement as their elder sister squealed like a wild animal and raced through the hall into the sunken hearth room in search of Fortuna.

Fortuna sat, reading by the fire, when Fate entered with a bang. The sound caused her to jerk involuntarily. The madam rested a hand against her chest. "Praise be, child, are you trying to end me?"

Fate rested her hands on her knees, trying to catch her own breath. "Hero...."

Fortuna closed the book and stood, gripping it so tight Fate thought it might burst into flames. "Hero... what?"

Fate nodded, still out of breath.

Fortuna mirrored her actions with wide hopeful eyes. "Hero... what?"

Fate swallowed and let out a frustrated groan. After a brief fanning, she caught her breath and stated, "Hero is going to bid on me."

Fortuna sucked in air, set the book down on a table, and started for the door. "We have much to plan for. Did he state his intentions?"

Fate scurried after her. "Marriage."

Fortuna stopped walking.

Fate only saw her mentor's back from behind, a hush falling over the regal woman. She moved to peek at Fortuna's expression, and pulled back in surprise at her sudden movement.

Fortuna thrust a fist into the air and drew it to her side. "Yes!" As she turned back to Fate, her amber eyes blazed.

Fate's sisters poked their heads out from around the hall and chattered.

Fortuna waved a threatening finger. "Not a word of this to anyone, understood? This is the most important thing that has ever happened. Fate becoming High Queen may save you all. If even one person outside of our own hears about this, that may all be gone."

The young girls replied in unison. "Yes, Madam!"

Fate trusted her sisters, and they trusted her. She had no doubt that they would make it to the auction with her secret intact.

17

BID ME FAREWELL

The day of dread arrived without fail. Every girl in the brothel knew to fear and respect it.

Fate followed Fortuna down the long corridor with her hands folded in front of her, dressed in the fine gown created especially for this day. She twisted her fingers into a knot. Their footsteps sounded hollow against the smooth wood as they crossed the brothel exterior by way of an outdoor walkway.

Fate had always avoided this part of the brothel, giving rise to her anxiety. She wished they were still inside the warmth of the hearth room. She wanted to see her sisters and feel their good wishes for her. A part of her still feared that Neco would buy her, but she'd already decided that if the worst happened, she would murder him before he could fulfill his wishes.

Moonlight cast shadows across the walkway, making the journey seem longer.

Never before had she wanted to disappear into the darkness as much as that moment, but she reminded herself to trust Hero. Again and again, she repeated it in her head, but his being an admitted liar slipped into the back of her mind and jarred her confidence.

Ahead lay the double doors into the private sector of the brothel. Since childhood, she'd dreaded the thought of passing through them. They appeared glorious with their golden carvings and embellishments, but they hid the ugliest part of the brothel. The Auction Room lay beyond those two doors.

The closer they came, the further her heart sank into her churning stomach.

Fortuna hesitated at the doors, resting her hands on the handles. "Are you ready?"

The attendees' voices echoed from the front of the building. Among them, Neco's voice reverberated in her ears clearer than any other. She loathed him and dreaded facing him under these circumstances.

Fortuna looked back at her with confidence. "It'll be all right."

Fate nodded because she chose to believe in Hero's vow, and because hiding from her auction wouldn't prevent it. Time slowed as Fortuna opened the doors, and her life passed before her. She wondered what had become of the time she thought she had. A feeling of helplessness overcame her, and she shuddered.

Fortuna turned and embraced her. "It's going to be all right. You're fine."

Fate felt petrified and sick with anxiety. She spent several long moments gathering her thoughts and courage despite the immense terror now overtaking her. "I know."

They stepped inside, revealing a little stage sheltered by screens. The stage provided enough room for five people to stand shoulder to shoulder.

Voices carried from the other side of the screens, the sound of gathering bidders, no doubt.

Fortuna closed the double doors behind them and whispered, "Trust in Hero. He'll keep his promise. I'm sure of it."

Fate wished she held such certainty. She blew out air, hoping to relieve her anxiety, but her hands shook and her legs felt weak.

Fortuna looked over Fate's outfit, ignoring the tremors in her beloved pupil. She examined every detail before moving Fate to the center of the stage. Once satisfied, she pulled the screen back and exposed Fate to the attendees.

To Fate's horror, they all wore masks. She stood before the concealed participants and awaited the outcome before the auction began.

Only the most privileged and wealthy people participated in the auctions.

That fact made Fate sick to her stomach. They had everything—while so many had nothing—yet they yearned for more. They bought and sold people for their enjoyment or amusement, not once considering the feelings of those they besmirched.

She stared out into the crowd as they whispered and laughed amongst themselves, paying little attention to the person they anticipated bidding on.

More people piled into the room, filling every chair before lining the walls. Their chatter grew into a din. Gradually, the air thickened and the temperature rose from all the bodies in the room, and attendees began fanning themselves.

Fate canvassed the growing crowd. She spied Neco wearing his most prized cloak, clearly wishing to stand out. Even if he tried to hide, the massive Askan guard beside him made him impossible to miss. Each of the people before her worked hard to make themself known in spite of their halfhearted disguises. She recognized many of the brothel's regulars, although she doubted their ability to afford her.

Time seemed to extend into eternity as she stood waiting for the auction to begin.

Her distress eased when she noticed Nigel sitting in the crowd. He wore a well-tailored green suit and mask to match. She wanted to smile but knew better than to betray his trust. He often purchased girls from the auction and felt that if things went wrong, he would try and do the same for her.

She continued to search for Hero, but none of the bidders fit his appearance—too tall, too short, female, dark hair... the list went on and on, and her fright grew with it.

He abandoned me?

The words ran through her brain several times before she shook the feeling and whispered, "He'll be here."

Fortuna moved to Fate's side looking concerned. "We can't wait any longer."

Fate repeated the words to Fortuna, hoping to make them true. "He'll be here."

As the room reached its capacity, two guards shut the doors and the audience fell silent.

Fate swallowed, hoping to ease her nerves, but her hands trembled. All the while, she desperately searched the masked participants for any sign of Hero.

Fortuna stepped up to the edge of the stage and commenced the auction. "We have gathered this moon, on the eve of the seventh sun during the fifty forth eupha, for the auction of Lady Fate of Macellarius. Our Lady has come of age this very day, clean of taint and touch. You will be bidding for the grace and elegance instilled in her by my own hand, as well as other notable Royals of Mu. She holds the knowledge and training befitting a King or Queen, and will bring both honor and pleasure to the winner of tonight's bidding. Know well that she is of Royal blood, and Feh, so we will be raising the minimum bid to five thousand neos to accommodate her worth."

The crowd murmured amongst themselves.

Fortuna continued her speech with a glance at Fate. Her hands were steady but something in her eyes reflected concern. "I will conduct this auction at the pace I see fit. Payment is required upon demand, and we shall finalize the transaction at my discretion. If this does not meet your expectations, you may take your leave now."

She waited as a few people slipped out.

Fate watched, wondering if Fortuna was attempting to buy time, or if the rules were explained so thoroughly at every auction. She tried to keep her mind off the well of terror at the bottom of her soul.

Two of her older sisters walked through the room, handing out paddles to each of the guests. They eased their way through the crowd and made certain they accounted for everyone.

Fortuna waited patiently until they completed their task, and then exchanged a single nod with each girl. "As per etiquette issued by the Council, bidding will end at the count of five. Place your bids in a timely manner. Late bids will not be accepted."

The people whispered to one another as their anticipation built.

Fortuna looked from person to person, her eyes searching just as much as Fate's "We now start the bid at five thousand neos."

Fate stood frozen in place as nearly every paddle in the building went up. Fortuna's words echoed in her ears as all sense of feeling left her body. Only a distant, but deafening, ring persisted. Many masks, cloaks, and paddles lay before her... but not Hero. Darkness stirred within her as hope dwindled, and her pulse quickened.

Fortuna continued. "Seven thousand neos."

Her voice blurred and faded in Fate's ears as the room jumped around before her eyes. She struggled to keep calm and focused as her throat constricted.

They're really selling me. What will happen to me? Hero?

A sense of melancholy enveloped her as the bidding continued.

Fortuna proceeded with caution, her gaze studying each bidder. "Eight thousand neos."

Fate's own thoughts fluttered like butterflies escaping through holes in a net. Nothing but sheer terror remained, until her body relaxed and gave way to a dark and bitter rage. As she stared out at the sea of bidders, a deep-rooted loathing rose within her.

The Spinner's song echoed in her ears.

> *Spinning, spinning wheel of fate,*
> *Which one will you choose?*
> *A sinner from the shadows,*
> *Shall you win or lose?*

A chill filled the air and drew her back to the trance she'd experienced in the maze. Her heartbeat slowed and a deathly calm held her in its embrace.

> *Spinning, spinning wheel of fate,*
> *Which one will you choose?*
> *A sinner from the shadows,*
> *Shall you win or lose?*

For the first time, she saw all of Mu as her enemy, and she wanted to destroy it all. It mattered not who the guilty or innocent were, as long as she could extinguish everything. The bidders seemed small and frail to her, and she found joy in the thought of their demise.

From across the room, through blurred vision, the white-haired woman from the maze stood and watched, her scarlet eyes reflecting the same hatred that stirred within Fate. As she turned her head, a slight jingle arose from tiny bells on her jeweled hair comb. The wisps of her white hair wafted about her head like spider webs caught in the breeze.

> *Turning, turning wheel of fate,*
> *The spokes are slowing down.*
> *Hush, the demon's dance is ending,*

Before the end of the final verse, a distorted and warbled voice called out to her. "Return to me."

Fate gasped as her consciousness returned to the stage. No one seemed to notice or care that she acted strangely. Her eyes turned to Fortuna, who remained fixated on two bidders. "Fifty thousand neos."

The crowd bantered in hushed voices.

Fate's eyes widened as she caught up with lost time.

When did they progress this far?

To no surprise, Neco doggedly pursued his lifelong obsession with possessing her.

The bidding moved at an alarming pace. "Sixty thousand neos... I have seventy... eighty thousand neos."

Fate twisted her clammy fingers as the numbers faded in and out. Her head felt fuzzy and the sounds from the auction, far away.

"One hundred thousand...."

The bidders battled for the prize behind the safety of their masks and the comfort of status. In the crowd rested a sea of strangers and only one ally—Nigel, who remained in the bid with a slight faltering in his hand and his gaze.

Behind Fortuna's still eyes lay a hidden sadness. She locked her sights on Nigel, but the weakness in her intonation expressed the reality that they had reached their limit. "One fifty... two hundred...."

Fate looked back and forth between the two bidders, feeling her future slip away, once again, like sand between her fingers. All the effort they'd put into winning Hero's favor had meant nothing. Her future hung in the balance and she could do nothing to control it. As if that weren't enough, she caught herself shedding a tear. She had trained to hold a façade, and still failed to upkeep it when it mattered most. Anger and sorrow welled up in her soul, and she gritted her teeth, unable to cease her silent weeping.

Fortuna blinked hard, closing her eyes to the reality before her. She knew well how much she and Nigel could wager in this auction. "Two hundred and fifty thousand neos...."

Nigel glanced around as he lowered his paddle.

The room spun in circles and a gentle bell chime resounded in Fate's ears. For an instant, she believed she'd fainted but, instead, everything around her moved ever so slowly. She observed the auction from this suspended state, in awe as particles of dust drifted by at a crawl and sound reverberated in a hollow never-ending loop.

She staggered back in fright as the bidding closed.

The sound of Fortuna's voice faded back in as the present moment returned to its natural speed. "One... two... three...." She grimaced. "Four...."

A man stood up at the back of the room and raised his paddle for the first time.

Fate paused as she realized she hadn't imagined the bidder. Her gaze trailed across the room to Hero, who calmly placed his bid. The fuzziness in her head seemed worse now, as she grappled with her shock, rage, and, ultimately, her relief.

Fortuna let out an irritated laugh and accepted the bid by raising her hand towards him in acknowledgment.

Neco spun around on his chair, cursing the person he could not see was his nephew.

Hero winked at Fate and nodded.

Her lip quivered as she fought back the urge to cry. She recalled her training and held herself together to the best of her ability. The fact that he'd kept his word warmed her soul, even if she hated him for giving her such a terrible fright. Love and hate seemed one and the same with Hero.

Fortuna resumed the auction, assuming a tone of confidence and authority. "Three hundred thousand neos...."

Neco persisted, unwilling to give up the girl he'd coveted for so long. He raised his paddle and motioned to Mortis.

The brooding Aska rose from his seat and strolled to the back of the room.

Fate knew better than to expect a well-mannered man. She remembered how he'd defied even Neco's orders, and feared his bloodlust.

Hero kept his gaze locked on Fate, his face and body remaining calm as he drove the bid higher.

"Four hundred thousand... four-fifty... five hundred thousand...."

Mortis marched closer to Hero as subtly as a mountain of a man could, but the guards saw everything. They stopped him and held him against the back wall, where he leered ineffectively.

"Five hundred and fifty thousand... six hundred... six-fifty...."

Fate relaxed with more distance between them. When her gaze returned to Hero, he stared back at her with a confident smirk.

Fortuna bowed her head forward slightly, emphasizing her words. "Seven hundred and fifty thousand neos...."

Neco's hand shook.

Fate opened and closed her hands, nervously watching a quiet battle unfold. She knew precisely how Neco had acquired the finances to participate in this auction, but she couldn't fathom how Hero had managed the same in such a short amount of time.

The bid reached one million neos, and many of the attendees rose to their feet to witness the momentous occasion.

Fate feared what affect the auction might have on Hero's reputation, but he seemed more relaxed than ever.

Although common for wealthy Nobles to bid on prostitutes, the Council publicly frowned on such things, and often used the act as leverage to disgrace and remove anyone they saw fit to dispel.

She tried again to trust in Hero's confidence, and even managed to form a genuine smile.

Fortuna punched her words as they marked a new record for a bid. "T-two million neos!"

A din rose in the crowd as people watched history in the making.

Neco tossed down his paddle, ranted under his breath, then shot up from his seat and turned fully to look at his opponent. "Who—" As he noticed his nephew in the darkness, he choked back his words.

Hero moved only his eyes to acknowledge Neco, his expression stoic as usual, with a slight glint of mint-colored light in his gaze.

Neco may have wanted to say more, but he just sat back down looking haunted.

Fate checked Mortis, expecting him to do something unlawful in the name of his king, but the Aska just looked off into the distance as though lost inside a dream. Although she wondered why he behaved in such a way, the results of the auction took precedence.

Fortuna and the rest of the audience leaned forward. "Two million neos?" She also glimpsed Neco, using her fingers to count for greater emphasis or, perhaps, out of sheer excitement. "One... two... three... four... five!" She waved her hands out in front of her to cut off the bidding.

The other bidders cheered for the entertainment, seeming to have forgotten that they also participated and bid for Fate as their prize. She found this part familiar, as this often occurred during Fortuna's events. The people loved the madam and the entertainment she provided more than anything.

A woman in all white stood from her seat at the far left side of the room. Her fox mask drew Fate's attention, reminding her of the peculiar man in her nightmarish vision. The woman quickly left, her cloak flowing behind her.

Fortuna closed the auction. "Thank you, everyone, for attending this momentous occasion. We will serve refreshments in the teahouse for any who wish to join."

The crowd murmured about the event, the winner, and his prize. So few Caeles existed in Mu that it left no doubt about *who* had won, only *why*.

Fortuna worked to usher everyone out of the Auction Room, including Neco, who brushed off her hand and marched straight for his guard.

His admonishment did nothing to sway Mortis from his trance, and they soon left altogether.

The auction room gradually emptied, until only Fate and Hero remained. She searched for the proper words to express her feelings.

Hero shifted his weight onto one foot and stared at the doors as Fortuna closed them. "It's better this way. We have so much in common, I think we're better off together."

Fate pressed her lips together and nodded. "I thought you abandoned me. "

Hero squinted one eye and gazed at the ceiling. "Uh, I didn't really have a choice. If I'd bid sooner, I'd never have been able to keep control of you. This way, I can hang it over your head."

She smacked him with a shout and a growl, which sent him into a fit of silent giggles.

Once the laughter subsided, he answered honestly. "But really, I'm sorry I was late. It was unavoidable."

She knew she didn't have the right to ask him the cause of his tardiness, so instead she questioned, "How did you get in when the doors were locked?"

A familiar gleam in his eye prepared her for a lie. This brought her to further suspect that he kept secrets far greater than anyone imagined.

He folded his arms and leaned against the wall, kicking one leg out. "There's a crawl space. I know, not normally the way a Royal enters a room but, what can I say? I'm not a regular guy."

She smirked at his choice of fabricated honesty. It most likely worked on people who chose not to see the real Hero. "I see. Classy. My savior crawled through the muck to rescue me."

He shrugged.

She took the cuff of his sleeve into her hand. "The most amazing part is... he managed to crawl through the filth and grime without getting a single speck of dirt on him. Now *that's* Caeles clean."

He tried to contain his laughter but it forced its way out into an uncontrolled burst, which he quelled with the back of his hand.

His laughter made Fate laugh. "I don't think I've ever seen you laugh, not for real anyway."

Hero's laughter vanished almost completely, and he stared at her with an empty expression.

Fate twisted her mouth and brushed the stray strand of hair from his face. "It's nice."

"What do we do from here?"

The Auction Room's doors opened again and Fortuna entered, exasperated. "Oh, I'm sure there is going to be hell to pay for this stunt. Does your father know about this?"

Hero turned to her scratching his ear. "I can deal with my father. He has little sway in... well... anything."

Fortuna turned to Fate, her face tense and her voice stern. "Not to mention Mortis. Something is wrong there. He's not right."

Fate lowered her brow and probed the madam to further her own suspicions. "What do you mean?"

Hero ran a finger over his lip as he thought. "I know what you mean. The life is gone from him."

A spark of excitement flared in Fortuna's eyes. "You see it too. Praise be, I thought I was going mad."

Fate reached out and took Fortuna's arm. "Wait, do you know him?"

Fortuna wrapped her hand around Fate's forearm and returned her grip with a solid squeeze. "I do... *did*, very long ago. He was always a gentleman. I don't understand what happened. Please, stay away from him. I have a bad feeling."

Fate looked at Hero as he wrestled with whatever thought troubled him. "You should let Fortis know. I'll tell Firmus. We'll need to get Abyssus out of there immediately."

Fortuna released Fate and removed the pipe from her cleavage. "Yes, my brothers should be of some help. They may act foolish but they are not to be underestimated."

Hero smirked and rubbed one eye with a finger. "They are a handful, those two, but, yes, they are probably two of the most skilled warriors in Mu. Together, they should be able to handle just about anything. I'll see what I can do quickly. I'm not concerned about it being sloppy, as long as we can assure his safety."

Fate finally breathed a sigh of relief.

Fortuna clicked her tongue against her upper lip. "We should be able to get him out early tomorrow. Neco has already committed tonight to guests, so he and Mortis both will remain in the brothel. If anything changes, we'll be the first to know."

He tipped his head and smiled at Fate. "You should rest. This has been enough for any day."

She hesitated before accepting his correct assessment.

Fortuna took a drag from her pipe and released a steady stream of smoke as she spoke. "We have paperwork to fill out and two Rahma worlds to shatter. Both Neco and Niteo are going to try for your heads over this."

Hero's smile grew into a wide grin. "I know. It's fantastic, isn't it?"

Fortuna's lips quivered and then she smiled. "Actually, yes, I will take great pleasure in assisting you."

Fate looked between the two. "I guess. I'll say goodbye to my sisters."

Fortuna lifted a finger. "I've already sent word. We have something prepared for this day. Go get some rest. I'm sure they'll send for you once everything is ready. Hero, if you would join me."

Fortuna turned and walked for the door at the back of the auction house.

Hero started to follow but looked back at Fate. "Enjoy the time with your sisters. I'll be back for you in the morning. Much will change for us tomorrow."

She agreed and watched as they exited the building. The stress of the auction subsided and exhaustion crept in.

With one last look around the auction room, she slipped through the same door she'd entered, and ambled down the long hall back to her room. The brothel seemed different now that she was leaving. Everything appeared smaller and more distant than she remembered.

She closed the door to her room, walked to her bed, collapsed onto the soft mattress, and drifted into sleep.

18

A QUEEN'S DUTY

The cool darkness had aided Fate's rest, but a low hum stirred her from the deep slumber. Her eyes fluttered open and she sat up. Darkness loomed around her as far as the eye could see.

At first, she stared into the darkness trying to place her surroundings. A faint chiming caught her ears, and memories of her strange experience in the maze invaded her mind. The droning hum and the high-pitched jingling of the chimes indicated that something ethereal called to her. This time she let it happen. Whether it was a dream or a vision, she embraced it.

Her room spun and all color faded to black.

When her mind cleared, she stood holding her arms close to fight off the frigid air. Even with the chill, this place brought unexpected comfort. All of her senses warned — or *should* warn — her to be afraid, but she experienced only a sense of calm and ease.

She stepped into the darkness and saw long strands of white wispy threads that caught the scarce light. As she moved farther, more threads laced her surroundings, clustering like a massive spider's nest.

As she cast her gaze upon it, she understood. "The Spinner's web."

She reached up and allowed the tears slipping from her eyes to drop onto her fingertips, then inspected them. They twinkled like crystals before sliding off her skin and disappearing into the darkness.

A woman's voice rose in the distance, singing a slow, sad song.

Fate shambled forward, cautious. Her own darkness spun and swirled inside of her, tickling her ribs as it bounced about. Just ahead, she glimpsed the Spinner.

The singing stopped and the woman turned suddenly, then darted into the darkness with her white gown catching air as though underwater.

Fate bolted after her, desperately needing to know how they were connected. Her soul called out, but the Spinner vanished once more into the darkness.

Fate ran until her muscles burned and her legs grew weary. She leaned forward, clutched her knees as she gasped for breath, and stammered, "Wait."

An echoing clap resounded through the empty space.

She shielded her ears and shook her head. "Please stop. I just want to ask a question."

The clapping persisted and the song began:

> *Spinning, spinning,*
> *Spinning, spinning,*
> *Wheel of fate....*

She spun in a circle, trying to pinpoint the origin of the song, but the echoing made it impossible. The singing nagged at her, taunted her. Each echo stirred more negativity, calling to something deep within her, something lost.

> *Turning, turning,*
> *The spokes are slowing down.*
> *Don't you make a sound.*

The claps boomed through the darkness, and Fate's vision blurred just as the white-haired woman darted into her line of sight again.

Fate reached out. "Wait."

The woman moved closer in a blurred haze.

After a final chime, a soft voice whispered, "Return to me."

The words and the sound caused Fate's body to lock up. She could no longer move as she willed, and simply fell to the ground at the white-haired woman's feet. "Please...."

Icy fingers brushed against her cheek. "Wake up."

Fate opened her eyes, and Tori stood looking down at her. Fate blinked hard and rubbed her eyes. "I'm sorry. What did you say?"

Tori smiled and swept away the hair from Fate's face. "Wake up."

Fate sat up, still disoriented. "I was having the strangest dream."

Tori stood agape before looking at Myrna, who raised her brows. Tori sat on the bed and rubbed Fate's arm. "Did you say you were having a dream?"

Fate drew her knees to her chest. "It was so strange. I think I saw the Spinner. She ran away from me. There was singing... it wouldn't stop. I just wanted to ask her a question."

The three girls sat in silence before Fate finally addressed the looks on their faces. "What?"

Myrna scratched her cheek and chewed the inside of her cheek. "Ancients don't dream."

Fate stared into nothingness. Putting the pieces together made her feel small. "I really must be a Doll."

Tori winced as she clutched her own arm. "Dolls don't dream either. This is really unusual."

Fate scanned her room as though the answers were hidden somewhere among the decorative fans. "I don't understand. Who dreams?"

Myrna took a spot on the bed next to Tori. "Rahma, and sometimes Half-Breeds.... It's a Mortal Affliction."

Fate studied her hands, which seemed foreign, like those of a stranger, and fought against an asphyxiating well of doubt and turmoil. "What am I?"

Tori grasped Fate by the shoulders and looked her dead in the eyes. "Free. You are free, Fate. Soon, you'll be High Queen, and it won't matter who or what you are other than free."

Fate nodded. "That's right. I *am* free."

Tori stood and extended a hand towards the door. "Now, go and say goodbye to our sisters so their hearts remain strong."

Myrna stood and rested a hand on Tori's shoulder. "They need your support now, Fate."

Fate leapt from her bed with a sudden gush of motivation. "They're going to get more than that when I'm High Queen. There is much to do. For now, let's bring any peace we can."

Her sisters followed her out of the room and down the hall to the sunken hearth room. Rushing through the brothel with them reminded Fate of when she'd first arrived. She stopped and looked back down the hall at her home, and saw her past self, a despondent and hopeless girl. If she could, she would tell her younger self that everything would be okay.

Tori called softly from ahead. "Fate."

Fate caught up to Tori and Myrna and slowed her gait as she reached the sunken hearth room. Tiny string lights hung aglow from the ceiling, each one a symbol of her sisters and their hope for the future. Their trust in her shone from the small bulbs and candles that lined the walls and stretched out onto the exposed patio. Outside, large lanterns hung from the eaves and lattice, while even bigger lotus lanterns floated on the surface of the pond, casting colorful reflections onto the water.

Fate covered her mouth as she stepped towards the fire pit, taking in the glittering streamers and handmade paper flowers.

Each of her sisters bowed their heads with a warm smile. "For the balance, we stand."

The brothel appeared magical, like one of the stories in Hero's folklore.

"Thank you," she said. "I would not be here if not for all of you."

Myrna heckled. "Neco put you in here, not us."

Fate raised a hand. "I mean, this day... this terrifying, wonderful day. I won't forget our bond or what we've done here. I will make changes. I promise that. It may take some time, but I will find a way."

The group of girls cheered and shouted for the festivities to begin. Several of the elder sisters scurried out of the room and returned with huge trays of food, which they set upon the long tables for the younger girls to feast.

Fate giggled as she watched them, reminded of the fish in the pond, which swarmed the surface whenever they tossed flakes. The scent of those flakes left an impression in her memory, like the sound of laughter or the clatter of pots and pans. She closed her eyes and took in the sights, sounds, and smells of her home.

If nothing else, she hoped to aid in Fortuna's efforts to control trafficking in Mu. As Queen, she wanted to better the lives of everyone, no matter their breed or clan.

She opened her eyes again, a smile planted firmly on her face. Although it may figuratively be the end of this chapter in her life, it felt so vivid that she saw the pages turning. A clicking reverberated in her ears.

Maybe not the pages of a book, but the turn of a wheel.... The Wheel of Fate is spinning. Her smile faded. *Only some of us may emerge victorious.*

Yuzu stepped away from the festivities and knelt down at Fate's side, her hand pressed against Fate's knee. "Sister, you don't want to eat?"

Fate smiled and stroked Yuzu's head. "I do, but I'm happy to see you girls enjoying yourselves."

"Will you still visit us after you're queen?"

"Of course." She removed the bell bracelet from her wrist, placed it on Yuzu, and adjusted the red chord to size. "Take this. Whenever you hear the chime, know that I'm with you and that you're in my thoughts. When I come to see you, I'll know how to find you by the sound."

Yuzu threw her arms around Fate's neck. "Thank you, big sister!

She hugged Yuzu back. "Now run along and eat. I'll be here for the rest of the night if you wish to see me."

Her heart felt at ease, seeing Yuzu so full of life and joy. It told her that, compared to her childhood, she, her sisters, and the Madam had managed to improve the lives of these young girls, even at their own risk or sacrifice. Although her body and eyelids had again grown heavy as the day had worn on, she wished to remain in the joy and relief she witnessed.

Tori took a seat beside her and passed over one of two glasses in her hands. "You've done well. You'll do even better once you're away from this place."

Fate sipped the bitter juice, and puckered her lips at it. "*This place?*"

"This may be our home, but it's a brothel nonetheless, and you're meant for much more. Even if it brings you despair, always remember that whatever may happen, everyone here has faith in you."

She wondered what Tori intended, but understood the meaning behind the words and nodded with a hum of agreement. Soon, everything before her would seem like a dream.

Fate and Tori sat on the floor, ate, and talked until the younger girls fell fast asleep. Once a hush fell over the room, Tori excused herself to clean up and follow Myrna to bed.

Only a handful of sisters remained awake.

Fate fought her fatigue, knowing the older girls normally worked in the late hours, to protect the young from the horrors they endured. She wanted to spend more time with them to show her appreciation for their sacrifices.

One of the elder girls crouched next to Fate. Her loose brown hair swept in soft tussles over her shoulder as she patted Fate's shoulder. "You should rest, little sister."

Fate shook her head. "We don't get this chance, ever. Just a bit longer."

The girl kissed Fate on the forehead. "We're proud of you. We know you'll make great changes."

"Thank you." Fate struggled to keep her heavy eyelids open as her exhaustion grew.

Fortuna, who'd arrived a short time earlier, sat across the fire pit, covered in sleeping girls and smoking her pipe with a subtle smile.

Fate admired the madam's beauty, grace, and strength, as she knew the madam must have taken on a monumental burden when she purchased the brothel. Her actions were that of a true heroine, not of a typical Royal. Fortuna had become Fate's surrogate mother. Although the madam kept secrets, as everyone in Mu seemed to, she worked hard to better the lives of those around her.

Fate nestled in the moment, thinking about what kind of Queen she intended to be. When she removed her personal concerns from it, she realized that she wanted to be like Fortuna. She wanted to be a strong, courageous queen who fought for the rights of her people—someone who stood against tyranny, and who formed strong alliances and a formidable army.

Overall, Fate had learned the true responsibility of a Royal in the brothel, far away from the social circles of the Ancient nobles. Her gaze drifted from Fortuna down to Yuzu, who slept curled up against Fate's lap as she stroked the small girl's hair. Time had passed, teaching Fate valuable lessons in trust.

Not all people who lied were bad, and not all who told the truth were good. Most presented a façade, and even the people who saw the truth behind the veil kept secrets to protect whom and what they cherished. The world held plentiful mysteries, and she set a new goal to discover them.

The time to sleep had arrived, as her eyes defied her with every blink.

Fortuna finally swayed the sleepy girls to their beds before she moved to Fate's side, stating the obvious. "I know it's hard to let go, but you really need to get some sleep. Hand Yuzu to me."

Fate followed the madam's instruction and rose from her spot to return to her room.

Her body grew more sluggish with each step, until she arrived at the most blissful sight conceivable: her bed. She pulled the silk sheets down, climbed inside, and promptly went to sleep.

Hero's voice echoed in her mind. "Fate." He called to her again and again. "Fate... Fate... Fata Miina, *muora.*"

Her eyes rolled open. The ceiling blurred until she found focus in her dreary haze. "What did you say?"

He leaned into view. "Did you drink last night?"

She turned her head to the round window and spied the sun high in the sky. Her memories of the auction and her time with her sisters crawled back one by one. Shortly, the drowsiness faded and she bolted up, cracking her head against Hero's.

He withdrew from the bed, clutching his face with a strangulated sound. "*Kui rasta!*"

Fate decided not to ask what that meant since it sounded bad. "Oh, I'm sorry."

He growled while rubbing his head. "You say that a lot."

"I'm sorry," she said without thinking, and tried to swallow what had already come out.

He rested a hand on his hip. "Did you even pack?"

She jumped from her bed. "Oh!"

"I know. You're sorry." He threw his hands up. "I'll help."

She shook her head in a fluster. "No! Uh, I'll pack. Why don't you have some breakfast? I'll only be a moment."

Skepticism crossed his face, but he took his leave with only a single comment on his way out. "If you take too long, I'll come looking for you."

She pressed her hands to her cheeks, and then smacked them hard. His presence had left her in a state of disarray, and she paced the room in two full circles before collecting herself enough to pack.

Once her head cleared, she quickly gathered her personal items into the suitcase Fortuna had provided for her, closed the lid, and walked to the door, where she took one final look at the room that had been home for nine turns. Just like this, her time at the brothel ended as quickly as it began. Although her heart filled with endless gratitude for her freedom, it also thumped with fear for the future of her sisters.

After calming herself, she stepped into the hallway and closed the door.

Hero leaned against the wall at the end of the hall with several little sisters bouncing around him and giggling.

Fate walked down the hall to meet him, amazed at how people, including herself, felt drawn to such an apathetic person. In all of his detachment, he'd mastered the art of moving people's souls through his actions. She gazed at her future husband thankful for his participation, for if not for Hero, Neco would own her.

Hero stood upright. "Ready?"

The little sisters complained in a chorus of, "Aww...."

He smiled down at them with a wink. "No need to whine. I'll be back for training."

"Yeah!" The girls hugged him and ran off to resume the chores they'd been avoiding to remain in his presence.

Fate watched on after the girls. "You really have a way with people."

A slight sadness crept into his gaze. "It's easy when you're numb to it."

Although tempted, she decided not to press him further on his comment. Her efforts would most likely be lost to a lie.

Fortuna stepped into the hallway. "Everyone is waiting."

Hero moved to Fortuna's side with Fate hurrying after, and the madam led them to the front of the brothel, where all of her sisters waited.

Fate bid them goodbye, doing her best not to cry as they sobbed.

Hero rubbed her back, but his eyes ventured to the passing clouds overhead.

Overcome with the permanence of her departure, she concluded her goodbyes, hurried inside the carriage, sat on the fluffy cushion, and focused on how ridiculous taking a carriage seemed when they could simply walk to the palace.

Hero sat across from her and, as if hearing her thoughts, said, "It's for appearances. Silly, I know, but expected nevertheless."

The coachman closed the door, hopped up to his seat, and started for Nitor Palace. The clopping of horseshoes lasted a short time. As expected, it only took a fleeting moment to arrive at the steps.

The coachman opened the door and Hero helped Fate out of the carriage by the hand. He led her up the steps, looking back with a smile. Whenever he looked pleased, it inevitably led to something negative. "My father is going to be furious."

Fate shot him a fearful glance.

He smiled and kissed her hand. "Not to worry. Remember, I am the heir to the empire. If anything untoward were to happen, it would be to him, not either of us."

Their entrance into the palace brought a new breath of life to Fate. Even though she'd visited Nitor before, it somehow seemed brighter and more refreshing. Everything glistened around her, thanks to Hero's meticulousness, no doubt.

Servants bustled about and waved to her before hurrying off again.

The coachman entered behind them with Fate's suitcase. "I'll take this to your room, Lady."

Fate answered in a weak voice. "Thank you."

Hero squeezed her hand. "You'll adjust, don't worry. Give me a moment. I'll be right back." He loped off into the palace and left Fate to stand in the foyer.

While she waited, she studied the crystal chandelier, once again reminded that everything in Nitor shone so brightly, just like Hero.

Lara strutted in from the hallway and took one look at Fate with a deepening frown. "Oh, it's you."

Fate nodded politely. "Good to see—"

"Sorry, but I'm here to meet with Hero." Lara marched up, ignoring the greeting altogether.

"I'm sure," Fate said, adrenaline and rage causing a rush in her veins. This woman vexed her endlessly.

Lara sighed and placed her hand on her hips. "I don't have time to stand here and keep you company just because you're insecure. You're a big girl. You'll be fine. Now, do you know where he's gone or not?"

Fate skipped over formalities as her fury overflowed. "Why are you so loathsome?"

Lara snapped, "Me? What is it you think you're doing, exactly? I will protect my friends, at *any* cost."

"Protect Hero, you mean."

Lara squared up as if ready for a fight. "That's right."

"From what? Me?"

Lara stuck a finger in Fate's face. "I see right through you, to your black soul. You are the last thing he needs. Do you know what you'll do to him?"

Hero strolled back into the foyer, his gaze passing from Lara to Fate.

Fate crossed her arms, ceasing the argument.

Hero stepped to her side. "Is everything all right?"

She feigned a smile. "Lara was looking for you."

He glanced at Lara.

Lara ran a hand over one of her braids. "I heard there were changes made to the schedule, and I wanted to talk with you about it."

"Ah yes, I made them to accommodate Lady Fate."

Concern draped Lara's face like heavy curtains. "For how long?"

He looked at her plainly. "Until we marry or move to Inoue Palace."

Lara's mouth hung open and her eyes glossed over.

In spite of herself, Fate actually felt sorry for her.

"Very well," Lara responded, and took leave without further argument. Her pace quickened as she neared the corner.

He took Fate's hand. "I'll show you to your room."

Her eyes trailed Lara, her concerns lingering, but Hero's words snapped into her brain with sudden impact. "Did you say *my* room?"

He stopped with a simper. "We aren't married yet. Were you planning on sharing a bed from the beginning?"

She retorted, "No, of course not. I'm just surprised, that's all."

"What? That I'd respect you?"

She averted her eyes. "Well, yes."

He led her up the stairs. "You'll find that many things are different for you now, Lady."

A thud at the door stopped their ascent. As they turned to look, shouting reverberated through the entrance hall.

Abyssus barreled in through the double doors, bounded across the foyer, and started up the stairs.

Before either of them could react, Mortis burst through the doors in chase.

Hero pushed Fate towards the top of the stairs and spun back. "Guards!"

Abyssus took two stairs at a time, but Mortis caught him with ease and threw him against the railing.

Fate moved to the banister in a flash, the momentum nearly throwing her over. "Abyssus!"

Hero leapt down the stairs, grabbed Abyssus by the shirt, and flung both of them over the railing to the ground below just as Mortis swiped the air after them.

Guards rushed the room to defend the pair.

Mortis charged down the stairs with thunderous steps, careened into the guards, and sent them flying.

Hero quickly collected two swords from a block in the hall below and tossed one to Abyssus.

Abyssus warned, "We cannot win this fight."

Hero looked at Abyssus, then to Mortis, and finally back at Abyssus again.

Abyssus shouted, "Something's wrong with him!"

Fate hovered at the top of the stairs, looking for a weapon.

Mortis charged Abyssus again with brute force.

Hero stepped between them, repeatedly stabbing Mortis with his blade until it broke.

With one solid swing, Mortis struck Hero and catapulted him into the opposing wall. A bang echoed through the hall upon impact, and the broken blade clattered to the floor.

Abyssus released coils of darkness, creating a veil between them, and frantically defended against Mortis's overpowering brute strength while cursing under his breath.

Mortis's hand pierced the veil, reaching for his evasive opponent with increased fury each time Abyssus slipped away. Finally, his hand grazed the blade and it spun through the room and straight into a pillar.

A fissure ran up the pillar and across the ceiling above Abyssus's head. He glanced between Mortis and the crumbling part of the hall, taking careful steps away from both threats. "This is it. This is how I die."

Fate's vision turned white with rage and panic as she watched her brother from above. With a surge of adrenaline, she ripped one of the marble statues from its pedestal and hurled it over the balcony. The object fell and crashed down onto Mortis's head.

The beastly man turned and stared at her with empty eyes.

A chill shot up her spine, making her fingers numb. She swallowed hard as he stampeded up the stairs after her.

Abyssus retreated from danger and jolted Fate from her petrification with a shout. "Fate, what are you doing? Run!"

Mortis reached the top of the stairs and launched himself into the hallway, slamming into the wall.

Fate ducked, covered her head, and scrambled out of the way.

Hero and Abyssus raced up the stairs to aid her as she escaped into one of the rooms.

She spun in a frantic circle before fleeing out onto the terrace.

Mortis hit the door so hard that he knocked it from its hinges, then stood panting in the doorway, his eyes fixed on Fate.

Abyssus shouted her name again from the hall, but Mortis left her no time. She lifted her dress and threw her leg over the railing as the massive soldier stormed the terrace. Desperate, she clung to the pillar, trying to ease herself down, but her grip gave way and she fell onto the grass below, rocking her entire body and rattling her teeth. Coughing, she crawled away from the palace, flailing at the ground until she could teeter back to her feet. Her gown tangled around her legs, hindering her movements as she struggled to flee.

The ground shook as Mortis landed firmly on both feet behind her. She need not look to know the man's malice and insurmountable might.

With her bruised and battered limbs, she staggered away from the looming presence at her back.

Just as she felt the heat from his hand, Hero and Abyssus sprang out from both sides and interceded in the attack. Plumes of black smoke blinded Mortis as chunks of ice sprayed from the ground, entrapping him within a prison.

Fate looked back, gasping in her fright. Seeing her brother and Hero relieved her, but only momentarily.

Hero pushed her towards the garden as Mortis's first shot broke through the ice. "Go!"

Fate hesitated, fearful that if she left them now, she might never see them again. She stayed beside them and continued watching, then lit the ground beneath Mortis with an explosion of electricity.

The beast of a man jolted but continued to rage against his restraints.

Hero solidified the prison with a thicker layer of ice, but it did nothing to stop Mortis's rampage. "I can't create a prison strong enough to bind him. We have to do something."

More guards emerged from the palace and surrounded Mortis with spears.

Hero shouted, "Cease your feud."

Mortis growled in a low, vacant tone while lashing his hand from inside the ice prison.

Abyssus shifted his weight and prepared for another assault. "We need more guards."

Hero shot him a look of dismay.

Mortis lurched forward, shattering the entire prison. He grabbed spears from two of the guards and, in a snap, crushed them with his powerful hands.

The rest of the guards attacked, stabbing him many times, but to no avail.

Hero and Abyssus grabbed Fate and ran for the gardens.

The fight ended quickly, as Mortis left a heap of dead or unconscious guards and resumed his pursuit.

Fate looked back at the closing Aska, her breath quickening with her step. "What do we do?"

Hero bolted through the gardens. "The maze!"

Abyssus and Fate followed closely behind him as he zipped around corners, sprinted down passages, and whizzed through the maze. He guided them out the other side, back towards the palace.

In a mighty eruption, Mortis dove through the hedge.

The trio sprinted past the fallen guards, back into the palace, and out the front doors. When they arrived at the gate, the guards lay dead at their post.

Abyssus panted. "Praise be."

Hero murmured, his eyes shifting rapidly from side to side and his brow knotting. "The horses." He dashed across the front lawn and around the side of the palace.

Fate straggled along as her brother tugged her by the hand. The pain in her lungs spread through her body, making her stomach churn. In all her training, she'd never seen Hero move so fast, and she never knew her brother possessed the ability to keep up.

Hero stopped at the edge of the stables, slowing to a walk as he reached up to the door. He remained there, his expression shrinking as he took in some unseen energy. As Fate and Abyssus caught up, Hero, without moving any closer, pushed open the first stall and stared down with a graven expression at the mutilated horse on the ground.

Blood dripped from the beam onto his head, leaving a stain on his white hair.

Abyssus and Fate stood open-mouthed and canvased the rest of the stables.

Once Abyssus realized what had befallen the horses, he covered his sister's eyes. "Don't look."

Fate held her churning stomach and choked back vomit, fighting against the stench and the gore.

"Holly!" Hero bolted from stall to stall, kicking each one open. He turned back to Fate with tears in his eyes. "She's not here."

"Praise be." Fate reached her hand out to him, sharing his relief.

Crates tumbled down from the side of the building and Mortis crashed through them, sending pieces of wood flying in all directions. He lurched forward, his sights set on Abyssus.

Abyssus narrowly dodged him, shoving Fate as he bent back from Mortis's reach.

She fell into the stall beside a horse's corpse, feeling the stab of the bloodied hay against her fingers.

Hero vaulted clear of the attack and landed on the balls of his feet, his stance lowered as he focused onto Mortis. He pulled a small blade sheathed to his thigh, and countered Mortis's next attack, leaving a deep cut across his opponent's hand.

Mortis snarled, ignoring Fate to pursue his new target.

Abyssus pulled her up by the arm as his gaze trailed after Hero. "We need to get out of here!"

Hero snapped back at Abyssus as he swerved away from Mortis's grasp. "No kidding! What exactly would you like me to do?" He took hold of the soldier's arm, wrapped his legs tightly around it, flipped onto his back, and sank the blade into the nape of Mortis's neck over and over. Blood splattered across Hero's face, making him seem deranged.

Fate gaped as Mortis plucked Hero from his shoulders and tossed him across the stable like a toy. She knew at that moment that she looked not at a man, but a monster.

Abyssus charged forward and hurdled, planting both feet solidly to Mortis's back to knock the man over.

Mortis tumbled face-first to the ground, giving the trio a chance to escape.

The force had thrown Abyssus back, but he'd caught himself on one knee, and now darted towards Hero, taking his sister along by the arm. "Go!"

They ran along the stone wall, along the property line, until they hit the hedge.

Abyssus forced his way through the shrubbery into Macellarius, with Hero and Fate at his heels. None of them looked back as they darted across the front lawn of Macellarius palace in a dead sprint. With a slight lead, they bolted for the Eastern Woods.

Fate gasped. "Where are we going?"

Hero and Abyssus answered simultaneously. "The woods."

As they ran, the forest grew denser and darker.

Fate's heart pounded, and her legs wobbled, and she lost sensation in her toes. She persisted in her dash, though, ignoring her body's plea for rest. Exhaustion and anxiety plagued her with dizzy spells. The trees appeared to dance and spin all around her as she blindly followed Abyssus and Hero deeper into the woods.

A flicker of red moved through her vision, and by instinct, she stopped. The spinning ceased, making it possible for her to see Mortis tackle Abyssus to the ground.

Fate shrilled, "Abyssus!"

Hero punted Mortis back and ripped Abyssus onto his feet by one of his belts.

Mortis howled and slammed his fist into the ground before rising again.

Even Hero gaped at the massive Aska. "By all that is."

Mortis shook his head and lunged for Fate.

She moved away but not fast enough. His massive hand closed in on her, giving her only enough time to brace herself for impact.

A loud clang rang out, and Fortis suddenly stood between Mortis and Fate, the side of his blade stuck partially into Mortis's arm.

"What the...?"

Firmus leapt from a nearby log and shouted, "Move!"

Fortis scooped Fate up and evaded the incoming flames. They retreated behind one of the trees, observing the scene from afar in case their attacker pursued again.

Firmus covered Mortis in a thick blue flame, until the monster dropped to the ground.

They watched as he burned.

Fortis turned to Hero. "What in nine hells is going on?"

Firmus shook his head. "I hope you have a good explanation for this. Mortis is a Royal."

Hero gasped for breath and sat hard on the ground. "Yeah? Well, so am I."

Fate coughed and wheezed and collapsed into Fortis's arms, and he gently set her down.

Abyssus threw his hands in the air. "It's a funny thing—"

Mortis jolted from the ground, his body singed by flames and skin melting away from his bone. He grabbed Hero by the arm and lifted him from the ground.

Hero's short blade fell as he struggled to free himself. He tore at Mortis's hand and thrashed until he too fell to the ground. This time, he had been too unprepared, and failed to break the fall.

For a moment, Hero lay motionless on the ground, then rose on his elbows with a grimace.

Mortis collected the blade from the ground and swung.

Fate clenched her eyes shut, but only silence followed. She opened her eyes again to see that a cradle of darkness had blocked the assault, giving Hero the chance to stagger away. She checked

Firmus and Fortis for a reaction, but they were too distracted by considerations of their next move to comment, or perhaps even to notice the flicker of shadow before them.

The ground shook as Mortis lumbered after Hero again.

Only Fate looked at her brother, noticing his extended hand as the trail of darkness dissipated.

Fortis and Firmus whisked past her in pursuit, attempting to reach Mortis before he could close the gap between himself and Hero.

Fate turned her head to follow the faint wisps of darkness, and Abyssus vanished before her eyes. Her gaze trailed to Mortis and the blade in his hand, which he brought down towards Hero.

Abyssus appeared in a flurry of shadows between the two men, his arms spread out to either side.

Fate opened her mouth to shout, but summoned only silence as the blade pierced her brother's chest and burst free from his back. A breath caught in her throat, emitting a choking sound.

Mortis drew back the blade and shoved Abyssus aside, his gaze once more locked on Hero.

Hero stood still, aghast as he was showered with Abyssus's blood, unable to break his gaze from his friend's wounded and collapsing body. His eyes had caught sight of *something*—something that Fate could not see—distracting him from Mortis's advance.

Fate shifted her gaze from Hero and back to the blade impaling her brother. As his body went limp, her heart stopped, fluttered, and then cracked. Her darkness lashed inside of her, fighting to break free from its skin cage. She held her torso, groaning until a strange droning sound left her lips. The droning turned to a shriek that echoed and multiplied in response to her swelling energy, and a pulse of light shot from her body. It poured out in ripples and waves towards Mortis. Branches snapped under the pressure, and rocks floated from the gravel as long, dark tendrils expanded away from her with the billowing darkness.

It consumed her until she saw only black.

19

HAUNTED

Fate opened her eyes, wracked by a stabbing pain. She coughed violently and rolled onto her side, wheezing for air.

A woman in silver armor sat on a wooden chair beside the bed, her posture upright and proper. The stark white hair and mint eyes immediately divulged her clan.

Fate blinked a few times in succession, unsure she really saw the woman correctly. A faint memory of the auction crossed her mind, as the woman had been there as well. So few Caeles existed that Fate deduced this must be Hero's relative.

The woman spoke with an even intonation. "Breathe slowly."

Fate slowed her breathing, in through her nose and out through her mouth, as her mind whirled in scrambled memories of the attack. Reality poured in and spilled through her thoughts like ink in water, and the image of Mortis stabbing Abyssus seared into her mind. She opened her mouth to cry but the sound stuck in her throat. Tears flooded her eyes and ran over her cheeks onto the pillow.

The woman leaned forward and stroked Fate's head. "I am so sorry."

Fate buried her face into the pillow and sobbed. She clenched the sheets and cried until the memories of her brother finally eased the image of his death. She swallowed hard to calm the sorrow and pain in her throat. It rose again as her mind replayed all the times she begged him to be wary of Mortis. Guilt swelled inside her as she wondered why she couldn't get him to heed her warnings.

The white-haired woman placed a gentle hand on Fate's back. "Though you may not wish to hear it, the pain will ease."

Fate shook her head, fearing that the loss of Abyssus had crippled her soul.

"It may not mean much to you now, but Hero is all I have left of my sister, my family... my clan. I understand your pain."

Fate's tears stopped, and she took a hard look at the woman with the fox clan's unmistakable features.

The woman beside her was a Caeles—one of only two left. Her words, although seemingly unbelievable to Fate, must be true, for she knew loss better than most.

Fate wiped her face and forced herself to sit up and acknowledge her caretaker.

The woman reached out and wiped Fate's face. "You have a good heart, Fate. You must not let it break. We all mourn Abyssus—we all loved him—but we must also honor his memory and his beliefs. He believed in truth and in fighting for justice. He died to protect Hero but, as all Ancients do, he shall one day return."

Fate listened, her mind trailing off in memories and then returning to listen. "Where is Hero?"

"Here. Do you want to see him?"

She bit her lip, trying to decide if she wanted to see anyone.

The woman dropped her chin and looked Fate in the eyes. "Do not lose your light. It is a gift few possess."

Fate drew her knees to her chest without responding.

The woman stood and left Fate to her grief.

Fate curled into a ball, replaying Abyssus's death repeatedly in her mind. Waves of sorrow swallowed her and then released her, until finally they lulled her to sleep.

She lay quietly in the darkness for what seemed an eternity. All sound left her ears save a low drone far in the distance. So many tears fell that they stung her cheeks.

A clanking sound stirred her from her thoughts, and light flooded her vision. She clutched her eyes, shielding them from the bitter sting. After a moment, she opened them to see the same white-haired woman sitting beside her bed with a tea tray.

Fate stared at her, not certain if she was real.

The woman poured a cup of tea and carefully stirred in honey. "My name is Chi."

"Fate."

Chi smiled and extended the cup. "Yes, I know. My nephew seems quite fond of you."

Fate pulled herself into an upright position, took the warm cup, and carefully sipped. She deduced Chi to be the woman from the auction, and concluded that she'd most likely provided Hero the money to bid.

Images of Abyssus crossed her mind again and more tears slipped down her cheeks into her tea. She held it in her palms, unable to drink.

Chi leaned forward and again wiped Fate's tears away. "There are no words that can ease this pain. Only time will help. I understand exactly how you feel, and I will care for you through this hardship. From now on, you can consider me family—as your brother did."

Fate looked up into the woman's mint eyes. "You knew my brother?"

Chi nodded. "Very well. Who do you think supplied him with all of his books and goodies?"

Fate let out a halfhearted laugh, reflecting on Abyssus's addiction to sweets.

Chi shifted on her chair to study Fate more closely. Both she and Hero observed in such a scrupulous manner, most evidently a trait of their clan. "Fate, were you dreaming?"

Fate recalled both Myrna and Tori informing her that dreaming was not an everyday occurrence for Ancients. Unsure of how to respond, she hesitated in a pointless attempt to buy time. In truth, her soul felt weak, and her mind lacked the fortitude to come up with a compelling and believable answer.

Chi poured herself tea and sipped it before continuing. "I suspected as much. I do not mean to make you uncomfortable. I am just observant, and it is my job to know the details of everyone who enters the Capital."

Fate blinked hard, her mind like a box of spilled marbles. "The Capital?"

Chi furrowed her brow and tightened her lips. "Yes. Where did you think you were?"

Fate looked aimlessly around the room. "Nex."

Chi set her cup down, stood, and moved the window. She then drew back the curtain and opened the window.

Light spilled onto the floor, accompanied by chiming from the trees. The sound harkened back to her most distant memories. "The Ussan."

"Hmm. You can hear it?"

Fate drifted as though caught in a dream. "I can."

Chi returned to Fate's bedside. "Tell me."

Fate stared into empty space as she desperately tried to reclaim the memory. "The trees hold memories—feelings."

A slight smile formed on Chi's lips. "That is right. How do you know that?"

Fate turned, and they stared at one another for a long, quiet moment. "I'm not sure. I remember... *something*."

Chi set her hand on Fate's knee. "What do you remember?"

The touch sent a tremor over Fate and a bright image flashed before her eyes. She rubbed her forehead and clenched her eyes shut to block it out, but the pain wracked her. A forest of crystal trees crumbled and shattered like glass, showering the land with shards. Another image followed, of a group of people huddled around a fire, including Chi. At Fate's side sat a frail-looking man, who took her by the hand. His face appeared blurry, but she sensed that he smiled as he spoke to her. Finally, an image of a shrine flickered, and she involuntarily jerked her body in response.

She finally replied, "Something sad... something upsetting... something that needed to be corrected."

Darkness seeped from her skin and coated her arms in thick ink, which spilled across the bedsheets and drew the warmth out of the room.

Chi retreated, knocking the chair back.

Fate's hair rose, wrapped in wisps of darkness. It coiled around her and floated upwards towards the ceiling. A cold, dark rage filled her soul, causing her to shudder from the pressure.

"Fate!" Chi clapped her hands together, snapping Fate from her trance.

Fate gripped her head as if it might clear the ringing in her ears.

Chi stepped to Fate's side and placed a gentle hand on her back. "Do not fight. It will only make it worse."

Fate looked up at Chi's severe expression through blurred vision. "What's happening to me?"

Chi winced. "It is difficult to say but all is not what it seems. I would like to get to know you better, Lady Fate, before I come to any conclusions."

Fate lay back on the pillow still gripping her head. "You were there when the Ussan fell."

What little color Chi held in her cheeks vanished, and her gaze fixed straight ahead as if trapped inside her haunting past. "I was."

Fate rolled onto her side. "How did I get here?"

"The High Queen brought everyone here until we could sort out this mess."

"Sort out?"

"Hero and the Ignis boys claim that Mortis murdered your brother."

She snapped to despite the ache in her heart and head. "He did."

"Hmm. Mortis's sister claims that your brother fled a legal duel, illegally involved you and Hero, and unexpectedly drew in Fortis and Firmus. They are holding a hearing on the matter."

Fate shook her head. "He tried to kill us all. How many witnesses does the High Queen need?"

"She is not the one who presses for Mortis—it is the High King. Be clear on this fact. It may well save your life. Our Queen has demanded an investigation but, with Isis involved, it is complicated."

"Isis?"

Chi frowned. "Mortis's sister—also the Queen of Askadel, a fact that will hold much weight in this hearing."

Fate threw her feet over the side of the bed and staggered upright. All thoughts and retorts regarding Mortis and his sister fled her mind as she swayed with dizziness. "What's wrong with me?"

Chi shook her head. "I am not certain. Fate, do you dream often?"

"Why do you keep asking about dreams?"

She pressed a finger to her bottom lip. "Have you ever heard of the Spinner?"

Fate's mind instantly returned to the day she played *Rota Fortunae* in the maze, when the clapping, the singing, and the sound of the Spinner's voice had echoed in her ears.

Chi's ever-calculating eyes studied Fate's every move—an animalistic stare. Her actions only solidified the Caeles traits that she and Hero shared.

Fate shook herself free of the echoes and stabilized herself. In all the chaos, her thoughts trailed back to Hero. "I'd like to talk to Hero."

Chi folded her arms and pursed her lips, as if calculating once again, engaged in a visible internal debate. "Very well. He is in the next room, but I would still appreciate a direct answer from you."

Fate, tired of being pushed around, glared at Chi. "When I have one, I'll let you know."

She pushed her way past Chi and into the hallway of the small cottage, to a front room with a table and, judging by the shadow of a flame, a furnace. At her left, another room's door appeared sealed shut by tiny specs of frost. At first, a warm air wafted in, carrying the aroma of spices, but as she neared the next room, a chill settled in.

Chi leaned out of the doorway and warned, "Be careful. He is in a fragile state. I do not want you injured."

Fate glanced back, initially believing Chi had told a morbidly inappropriate joke. However, the Caeles's facial expression confirmed her sincerity, so Fate nodded once and returned her attention to the closed door in front of her. With a gentle tap, she knocked and waited for an answer.

After a moment of silence, she collected the bulk of her dress into her hands and tried the frozen doorknob. The struggle to open it grew more desperate as the thin layer of ice thickened.

"Hero," she commanded. "Open the door."

He remained silent.

She groaned while twisting the knob with all her might, and threw her shoulder into the door. Tiny particles of ice scattered through the air each time she hit it, until the door burst open and she stumbled inside.

Chi shouted from the other room, "Hey!"

Fate marveled at the thick layer of ice coating the walls, furniture, and floor. Her eyes traced the ever-growing ice as it stretched across the floor towards the hallway. She turned her attention to Hero, who lay at the edge of his bed murmuring to himself.

"Hero, can you hear me?"

No reaction.

She pressed a hand firmly on his back, and a sharp pain pierced her head. Her eyes flooded with light, the room spun, and she hit the floor.

Hero's whispers sounded clearer as her vision faded. "I'm sorry, Abyssus."

Fate opened her eyes in another spinning room, and sat up.

Tall, built-in bookshelves containing scrolls surrounded her. At the base of each shelf stood a heavy, wooden sliding door, its smooth carved ledges thickly coated in white, glowing dust.

She tried to remember a time when she'd seen carvings in such detail, but her fascination with the doors shifted when she noticed a small path made of light leading out into space. The twinkle of stars summoned her with the promise of curiosity fulfilled. Tiny blue orbs rose from the path and floated away, mingling with the starlight. She traced the length of the path far into distance. It hung in the vast openness of space and as though leading to the unknown.

At the edge of the path, not far from where Fate had woken, a white-haired boy sat with his back to her. She knew of only one group of white-haired people in all the world—Caeles.

He kicked his legs over the edge of the path, allowing them to dangle in space and collect particles of the glowing blue ether on his socks and shoes.

Fate so rarely encountered ether that she paused to study the blue light, fascinated by its presence. It suggested something of the shadow realm—something dark existed here. Even if all beings possessed some minuscule amount of it, no one ever saw it quite like this.

She brushed off the faintly glowing white dust that coated her dress, and observed the area. Above her, instead of a ceiling, the night sky twinkled in all its glory. The bookshelves and sliding doors had replaced the walls, and the floor she stood upon seemed nonexistent except for the subtle film of white dust that indicated the translucent surface. Astonished, she stared down at her feet and farther, to a mixture of space and what appeared to be fragments of mirror. The only way in or out of the peculiar room was the path of light.

A distant chiming sound, like the tinkle of a chandelier, echoed throughout the space.

She cautiously approached the boy and crouched down. "Are you, possibly, Hero?"

He turned his head, exposing a black mask that covered his eyes and contained only a small slit for his mouth.

She withdrew, astonished to see the same child from her dream. Once the shock eased, she calmed herself before returning to the child's side. With a clear mind, she realized jumping to conclusions often proved a poor decision. The boy looked Caeles, but that didn't necessarily make him the one Caeles she knew so well. Not to mention, the boy in front of her was just a child, and Hero was grown. Upon closer examination, the boy's aura differed from Hero's too.

The child kicked his legs back and forth over the edge of the path and hummed happily.

She eased next to him, doing her best to not cause alarm for either of them. "Why do you wear a mask?"

"They say I'm Tainted."

Fate tucked a stray hair behind her ear as she studied the boy and the mask. If not for the ominous manner in which the mask obscured his facial features, she'd never have feared the boy. He appeared delicate and soft, like a tiny, white cloud that glowed with ethereal light. "How did you become Tainted?"

Hero's disease consumed so much of her life and her thoughts that she wanted to understand how the Tainted came to be.

The boy shrugged. "I saw something I should not."

"What did you see?"

He tilted his head far to one side and pointed into the darkness below.

She leaned over the edge and peered at the vortex of swirling darkness. "If I look, will I become Tainted too?"

The boy stopped his kicking, sat in a long silence, and then finally laughed.

"Why are you laughing?"

"Mistress, are you not already like me?"

Fate recalled the game of *Rota Fortunae* and the voice she'd heard just before it started. *Safe journeys, Mistress,* the voice had said. She inhaled through her nose, trying to ease her jittery nerves. Little by little, all the dots connected.

She returned her focus to the boy. "Mistress? To whom or what?"

He covered her eyes with his small hands. "That's what you said before."

"I said—"

"Now," he answered gleefully, "you're empty just like me."

The truth rang in his words, leaving her with a sense of dread. Too many times, she'd looked into the mirror at her own emptiness.

The boy continued, still holding his hands over her eyes. "You're also blind, no?"

She took his hands into her own and removed them from her eyes, fearing he might actually be able to blind her. No sooner had she removed his hands than she felt him frowning through the mask.

She quickly changed the subject. "Don't you want to remove the mask?"

The boy sat in uncomfortable silence, his aura churning and wavering as he chose his next words. "You are not Mistress. Who are you?"

"I'm Fate," she said, placing a hand over her chest. "Cruentus Fate. Who are you?"

"I'm nobody." He pulled his knees close and hugged them. "I have to go back."

"Ah, is it the place with all of the scrolls? I'll take you back." She offered her hand.

The masked boy accepted her offer and walked beside her, back towards the bookshelves. As they walked, he kept his head pointed towards the edge of the pathway... towards the darkness below.

Fate followed his line of sight and watched the particles floating up and out from the vortex. As she studied them, something nagged at her, and she wondered if the boy felt the same sense of longing and nostalgia.

They soon reached the door to the scroll room. After opening it, she ushered the boy inside.

His courage did not last long, because he escaped before she took a full step inside.

She trailed him with her eyes until they crossed the form of a pale man with long crimson hair, who sat at a spinning wheel. The stern look on the man's face made her believe the boy had fled to avoid admonishment.

The man spun the wheel without paying mind to Fate or the boy. As he did, his long red hair spilled over his shoulders, streamed down his back, and formed a small pool on the floor. All the while, his bold green eyes remained fixated on the task before him.

"Lost again," he said, pumping the pedal with his foot. He fed web into the wheel and allowed it to coil around the spool.

Fate looked around to confirm that the man had spoken to her.

He continued his task without looking up. "I told you, you must choose wisely to never know regret. If you are here, then you've made a poor choice, and now you're lost."

"Um, who are you?"

"All that matters is what I can do for you. In your times of doubt, rely not on what you feel or think you know, but what you hear."

She stared at the strange man, confused by his lack of logic. "People can say anything they'd like, but their actions reveal their true intentions."

The red-haired man let out a silent laugh and shook his head while continuing his work. "You are still so resistant to your own nature. Perhaps it's just your way." He looked up from his work and gazed at her with loving but sad eyes.

Unsure of how to respond, she walked around the room, allowing her eyes to feast on the plethora of scrolls, most so old they appeared as frail as butterfly's wings. "That boy... he's Tainted."

"Hmm."

"What will you do with him?"

"Do? I shall teach him, because that's what I do. You shall judge him because that's what *you* do."

Her body stiffened, and she frantically tried to back out of the responsibility suddenly thrust upon her. "Me? No, I'm not judging anyone."

"Is that not the Spinner's job? It's your turn to spin the wheel." He stood and motioned to the device. "Which sinners will you choose?"

Fate shook her head. "I won't choose."

The man stared at her with empathetic eyes. "Not choosing *is* a choice."

She slowly stepped to the spinning wheel with dread in her heart. Her body moved onto the seat even as her will resisted. Her hand lifted and, despite her efforts to stop it, spun the wheel. It clicked as it wove the fine silvery web into glowing white dust.

The man leaned over her shoulder and examined her work. "See? You are still a gifted spinner. Now, all you must do is decide which path to follow. Win or lose."

Fate's failed attempt at pulling away from the wheel filled her with a sense of helplessness. "I don't want to."

The man crossed his arms and stared down at her. "But you already have. We all have."

"Wha—"

The solidity of the floor gave way and she fell into space, plummeting deeper and deeper into the darkness below.

Fate jolted with a scream and lurched forward into someone's hands.

"Whoa, easy now."

She turned her head to see the man attached to the voice.

For an instant, she thought he was Abyssus, but she remembered his death and a surge of sorrow filled her soul once more. The man before he bore a remarkable resemblance to her brother, and yet, upon closer examination, seemed not at all like Abyssus save for the Iu coloring and roguish charm. Others might argue at their similarities, but Fate knew Abyssus far too well to confuse anyone for him.

She slumped back onto the bed and stared at the ceiling. "What happened?"

The man rested his back against the chair next to the bed and crossed one leg over the other, the act nearly charming, albeit handled too sloppily to be so. "You don't listen."

"Excuse me?"

He sat forward again, and clarified. "You were warned to be cautious. Hence, you don't listen."

"Are you always this rude to people you don't know?"

He answered with a wide grin and a chuckle. "Absolutely."

"Who are you?"

Chi entered the room carrying a tea tray, and gasped when she saw him. "No."

He turned to her and kicked his feet up.

She kicked them back down as she set the tray down, repeating, "No."

He laughed. "I'm already here."

She pulled him from the chair and shoved him out the door. "No, you are not."

Fate watched the commotion, confused.

The man shouted from the other side of the door. "Chi, don't act like this."

Chi protested. "I said no and I mean it. Come back later."

Fate whispered, "Who is that?"

"Fine," he said. "I'll come back when things have calmed down."

Chi kept a firm grip on the door even after the man had conceded. A large bang ensued, followed by vigorous jiggling of the handle, until he apparently gave up and left. Chi held her position for a long pause before finally returning to the tea.

Fate waited for an explanation while Chi poured two cups and sat beside her. Given that Chi remained silent, Fate took the tea and sipped it, still curious about the bizarre interaction.

Chi took a deep breath and slowly exhaled. "That was Iunu Kyou."

Fate stared at the closed door. "The High Prince?"

"One and the same, unfortunately."

She remembered Abyssus telling her they were Dolls, and that the Grim had made her for the High Prince. "I see."

"You gave me some grief today. I told you that Hero was in a delicate state, and you barged in there like a creature from the Abyss."

Fate rolled the warm cup back and forth between her palms. "I'm sorry."

Chi sighed. "I am just trying to keep you both safe. He told me, you know."

"Told you?"

"That he intends to marry you."

Fate slouched, feeling worse than before. Her actions were not that of someone joining a family. She'd thought only of herself and her own feelings, but many others loved Abyssus as well. She held no ownership of their feelings, and it made her feel guilty that she'd acted as such.

Chi peeked at Fate, then turned her gaze to the ceiling. "I was pleased to hear the news, honestly. You and your brother have always been dear to me."

Fate found the comment curious since she was only meeting Chi for the first time. "How is that?"

"You would not remember, I am sure."

Fate searched her empty memories in the hope she'd find a morsel of recollection. She intended to probe Chi about the subject in the future, but for now her heart weighed too heavy to pursue such matters. "It sounds nice. I wish I could remember it."

Chi nodded. "At least you remember the forest."

"Hmm. Is Hero doing any better?"

"He is, thankfully. You should be able to see him shortly. For now, rest, and I have plenty of books if you would care for something to read. It might be some time before you can go out or home."

"Because of the hearing?"

"Hmm." Chi collected the teacups and tray.

Fate riddled briefly on what to do with her time. Thinking about Abyssus or the hearing might drive her mad. Before Chi left, she asked, "Do you have any books on the Spinner?"

Chi stopped instinctively, her eyes fixated on Fate with a mixture of excitement and caution. "I do." She exited the room and let the door close behind her.

Fate plunked her head back down on the pillow, her whole body feeling the loss of Abyssus. She needed to find a way to make sense of her tragedies. Everything in Euphoria seemed marred and impossible to navigate.

Chi returned with the book in hand and gave it to Fate. "I hope you find what you are looking for."

Her words seemed ominous, but Fate accepted it. "Thank you."

After Chi left, she ran her hand over the worn red cover. The title, which should not have been surprising, sent chills over her skin: *Rota Fortunae*.

She swallowed hard. The Spinner haunted her, so she decided it best to embrace and resolve it. Lara had warned her of such things at the start of the game, but Fate had never considered it an actual possibility.

She nestled into the pillow. "I'll find out what happened to us, Abyssus. I promise."

20

DOT TO DOT

A few days passed and Fate remained in the study, reading any and every book Chi provided on the Spinner or related folklore. She found herself enraptured by the stories, and this newfound addiction led her to wonder how Hero fared during the chaos. Although only a room apart, they kept to themselves, and she finally admitted to herself that she missed his insight and company.

It felt wrong to be parted from him when they both felt so low. They'd helped each other through difficult times, until the worst point of all befell them. The loss of Abyssus had thrown their whole world out of alignment, and now she lacked a way or the strength to offer Hero comfort. In her weakness, she turned to reading as an escape, which only served to fuel her guilt for abandoning Hero in his time of need.

Reading gave her a brief reprieve, but eventually thoughts of Hero and her brother distracted her too much to continue. She sat up from her reading and stretched her back, and a knock came at the door.

Chi entered only a moment later. "They have arrived at a decision."

Fate held her breath.

Chi's frown forewarned of bad news. "They have sided with Mortis. Because Abyssus could not testify, there was none to prove that his death was not the result of a legal duel."

Fate slapped the book shut. "He murdered my brother! What about Fortis and Firmus? Hero? We were all there! They didn't speak with me. Did they talk to any of them?"

Chi hurried to Fate's side, patting the air. "I understand your feelings but we have no way of proving it was murder."

"His dead body!"

Chi pleaded. "I understand more than you know. This is the Council and the High Court—you do not want to storm in there."

Fate stood on the bed, her anger growing with every breath. "Nine hells I don't."

Chi snapped, "Then ruin your chance to become High Queen. I will not stop you... I never could."

Fate fell silent and her legs gave out beneath her. She flopped down, buried her face in the blankets, and screamed into the mattress.

Chi sat on the bed and spoke in a low choked voice. "My sister's Bound, my dear friend, was murdered right here in the Capital just before Hero was born. They searched for his killer but found no one." She gestured to her surroundings. "All of this power and nothing was done."

Fate ceased her fit and looked up at Chi, surprised at her stillness. This woman had endured things far beyond Fate's knowledge—buried things that no one dared speak of. Feeling foolish, she sat up, straightening her dress and hair. "I apologize for my outburst. It was childish."

Chi wrapped an arm around Fate's shoulders and laughed. "Sometimes it is the only thing we can do. Just know that you are not alone, and we will not forget what Mortis did. We will find a way to bring him to justice."

Fate sought to commiserate. Something told her that Chi's and her fates were somehow intertwined. "I heard that something happened to Hero's mother as well."

Chi stared out the open window into the city streets beyond. "It still feels like it just happened."

Fate waited quietly and allowed Chi to work through her memories and emotions. Having just lost her sibling, she knew the scar that it left behind.

Chi pursed her lips as if holding back something painful. "They actually accused Hero. Can you believe that? A child. I know our clan is misunderstood, but a child? The absurdity is too blatant. Tainted or not, a child could not overpower my sister. Irritating as she could be, she was an extraordinary warrior."

"What do you think happened?"

Chi shook her head, her eyes fixed and haunted. "I do not know. It makes no sense."

Fate wrenched her fingers, unable to put all the pieces of the twisted puzzle together. "What should I do now?"

Chi turned to Fate and squeezed her arms. "Move to Nitor Palace. Stay by Hero's side. He is many things, but the most important of all of them is that he is loyal. If you are to be his wife, he will protect you, and I would ask you to do the same for him."

Fate sighed, releasing the tension from her body. She retrieved the book from atop the covers and handed it to Chi. "Thank you for lending me this."

"Did you find what you were looking for?"

Fate noted that Chi had made a similar comment when giving her the book. "What is it you think I'm looking for?"

"Answers. You wanted a book specifically about the Spinner, so I assumed you were looking for something in particular."

"Yes, but it was you who brought up the Spinner when I heard the chiming. Why?"

Chi froze with wide eyes and an open mouth.

Fate pressed. "Does the Spinner have something to do with that sound or the Ussan?"

"Both."

"So, she's real?"

"Depends on who you ask."

"I'm asking you."

The door opened and Hero entered, appearing uncharacteristically haggard and upset. His usual glow had dimmed and deep rings had developed under his eyes. He clenched his teeth so tightly that he seemed to jut his jaw. The temperature dropped and small ice crystals formed on the window.

He spoke in a low scratchy voice. "We are ready to return."

Fate stood instinctively but felt clueless about how to ease Hero's pain when her own still lingered. As much as she loved Abyssus, he'd spent far more time with Hero than with her.

Chi rubbed her palms together and nodded. "I have taken care of everything." She handed Hero the book.

He looked down at the title without expression before turning and exiting.

Fate twisted the ends of her hair in her fingertips to keep her emotions in check. "Thank you for your hospitality." It troubled her to see Hero so upset when, usually, nothing ever affected him.

Chi looked Fate in the eyes, a mien of concern filling her glassy gaze. "If you want to know more about the Spinner, Hero is an expert."

Fate curtsied, left the room, and followed Hero through the small, cozy home. The pot over the fireplace bubbled and saturated the room with the scent of meat and spices. She glanced back at the rounded shelves full of bottles and jars, and made a mental note. Her gut told her that Chi kept as many secrets as Hero.

He kept his head down all the way to the carriage and stepped up.

Fate let herself inside and sat across from him, running her fingers over the wool blanket on the bench. Her thoughts raced with ways to offer him comfort, but he felt like a stranger to her now. By the time the carriage started rolling, the temperature had grown so cold that she had to wrap herself in the blanket.

Anything and everything reminded her of Abyssus. She doubted her ability to provide comfort when her own heart ached so much. Rather than focus on her pain, she worked to distract herself and Hero.

He leaned against his hand and stared out the window, burrowing his face in the bright red knit scarf draped around his shoulders and neck.

With a quivering smile, Fate said, "That's a beautiful scarf."

He looked back at her, his eyes turning red and glossy. His mouth opened and closed in an attempt to muster words but nothing came out.

A feeling of loss came over Fate and the heaviness in her heart grew. Without him saying, she knew why he fought for a response. *He got it from Abyssus.*

After a while, he cleared his throat and asked. "So, you were reading about the Spinner?"

"I started that one but I didn't get very far."

"Hmm." He leafed through the book, wearing a deep frown.

Her words caught in her dry mouth and, before she thought to stop herself, she blurted the first thing that came to mind. "Are you... well?"

He wiped away his tears and glared. "Are you?" Frost crept across the velvet seat beneath him as his gaze pierced her.

She felt the sting of his bitter words, and her focus traveled from his cold stare to the red lace at the hem of her dress, searching for anything to keep her mind off the negativity. Her vision blurred but she kept the tears from falling.

Hero rubbed his face with a rough, tense hand. "I'm sorry. That was...."

Fate looked out the window at the passing trees. She pressed her lips together and controlled her breathing. Her nose no longer passed air, and her throat turned dry, but she did her best to remain poised.

Hero leaned forward and took her warm hand into his icy one. "I really am sorry. I'm not good at this sort of thing. I'm not close to many people."

She finally gained the courage to look at him and confirm that he spoke the truth. As they touched, she felt his pain, more than she'd imagined.

The frost subsided, and Hero's hand gradually warmed.

They sat in silence for the remainder of the trip, and entered the palace worn and heartbroken.

The servants rushed to them, offering their condolences and comforting the pair as best they could.

A short time ago, she'd viewed the palace as gorgeous and bright, full of life and hope for a new future. Now, it was her brother's deathbed.

Hero gripped one of the servant's arms with a weak hand. "Please, show Lady Fate to her room."

The man nodded and escorted Fate up the stairs.

She glanced back at Hero, wishing they could mourn together. His grief left her feeling uneasy. Things were already a mess, and she feared his volatile emotions might lead to more trouble. Abyssus and Hero's friendship finally made sense to her; they were both emotional and headstrong. It may even be the reason she loved them both.

She followed the servant down the long hall to her new room.

He opened the door and revealed the spoiled surprise Hero had prepared for her—a glorious room full of lights and shelves of alphabetized books. A heavy fabric hung over a canopy bed, bearing a red and gold pattern, and each piece of furniture shone with fresh mahogany polish.

The beauty fell to despair, for every fine detail meant little now that Fate's light had faded in death's cold touch.

The servant warily examined her facial expression. "Milady?"

In a meek voice, she responded, "Thank you," and stepped inside, closing the door behind her. She shuffled to the bed and collapsed, her head full of things she didn't want to think about, and her heart full of grief. With little to ease her suffering, she rolled onto her back and stared at the ceiling. Dreams came easier when her life had turned into an endless nightmare.

Her breathing slowed and darkness enveloped her, until nothing from the present remained.

This time, when Fate entered her dream, she felt her surroundings shift into place. A nostalgia swept in, a sensation similar to visiting a childhood home or memory.

The sound of breathing echoed and trailed, then silence returned. She recognized the mats on the floor and the shelves that billowed with scrolls. A soft clicking arose from the spinning wheel at an empty corner.

She first sat upright, then stood and navigated through the open space, noting the lack of dust. The sound of chiming still tickled the air from time to time. Above her, stars twinkled, and beneath her feet, a dark swirling vortex spun as it reached down into endless black.

After strolling around the room once, she decided not to pursue these mysteries. Her instincts told her to find the boy.

She ventured out onto the path of light in search of the small boy, but saw only the path of light and the endless expanse of space before her.

"Are you lost again?"

She turned and faced the boy, pressed her hands against her knees, and bent down. A natural tone of endearment sweetened her voice. "How did you do that?"

He wore a white shirt under a loose black robe, which appeared much too large, enough to suspect it belonged to someone else. "Do what?"

Fate beckoned a response with a poised smile as she gestured back at the room. "I just came from there and it was empty. Were you hiding?"

The boy scratched the mask where his cheek would be. "To call it empty is a gross inaccuracy, no?"

She folded her arms. "I meant... you were not there."

He pointed to the path beneath his feet. "No, I was here."

"You were not. I just walked this way and did not see you."

The boy turned back towards the room and started walking. "See, I told you, you are blind."

Fate caught up to him in a few strides. "What's your name?"

"Leoht."

They strolled into the scroll room and lingered there longer than before. The absence of the red-haired man calmed the boy and allotted Fate time to explore. She moved across the translucent floor and, for the first time, noticed another space behind one of the bookshelves. Curiosity led her to what appeared to be a garden. Two large planets hung just out of reach but illuminated the tufts of grass, flowers, and plants. In awe, she moved into the garden, admiring a blossoming tree with tiny pink flowers. At the base of the tree, the gentle trickle of a creek spilled over small, smooth stones and fed the pond below. The sound of the water engendered memories of the brothel. When she peered into the pond, her wonder grew as the fish here flaunted iridescent scales.

"Is this where you live, Leoht?"

Leoht laughed. "You're silly. No one lives in the Room of Forgotten Memories."

The scrolls lined up on the shelves all looked the same—aged parchments bordered with green cloth and gold inscriptions. She wondered if the inscriptions were names. "Are all of these memories?"

"Sure."

She hung her head. "That's really sad."

He looked up with the blind concaves of the mask directed at her. "Is it? Do you want me to tell you one of yours?"

Fate crouched next to him. "I have a scroll here?"

Leoht shrugged. "Sure, just about everybody does. Yours is about your brother's notebook."

A memory of Abyssus flashed in her mind, one of her visit to the palace and the journal he showed her then. "What about it?"

"He put it in the room Hero made for you, so you won't feel lonely without him."

She stiffened. As reality swooped in, her heart began to race with anticipation. She shook her head. "That can't be one of my memories because it never happened."

Leoht turned away from her and shrugged again. "Grownups never listen. You are just like him."

"Him? That man, the one with the red hair... was he your father?"

He shook his head and scoffed. "Do we look alike?"

"Who is he then?"

"The God of Life, Casluhim."

Fate repeated the name. "Casluhim."

"Hmm. He can be kind of grouchy but he's all right."

"Is that why you were hiding from him?"

The boy cocked his head to the side and puzzled quietly before finally explaining. "I wasn't hiding from him."

"Very well. You weren't hiding from *him*, but you were hiding from *something*."

The boy stopped walking when he reached the center of the scroll room, turned and pointed to a tall thin man with white hair, a red blazer, and a fox mask, who stood by one of the bookshelves.

Fate jumped.

The man vanished, then reappeared before her. He appeared to be the same man she'd seen in the maze.

She lurched backwards with a gasp.

Before she could fall, he gracefully collected her into his arms and spoke in a melodious manner. "I'm sorry. I seem to have startled you." His aura shared similarities to Hero's, but the masked man's presence left a deeper, stronger impression.

This energy made Fate shudder.

The masked man brought her back to her feet and looked deep into her soul with polychromatic eyes. "You look ill, Mistress. Are you feeling well?"

"That's not Mistress," Leoht complained.

The man countered, "My eyes see more than yours, little one."

Fate felt uneasy, and goosebumps ran over her skin. "I'm not quite sure."

The man led her to a chair and sat her down. "Then rest, please. You don't visit often. What can we do to make your stay more comfortable?"

Fate grew increasingly rigid with each word he spoke, and with every casual stroke of his hand to her skin. She withdrew as far as the chair allowed. "Who are you?"

"Me?" The man pointed to himself and looked around as if the room were filled with people. His eyes gleamed with anima, giving them an iridescent glimmer. "Hmm. Call me Solaris."

A jolt shot through Fate. She wondered if all her reading might have affected her dreams. The idea of characters from folklore randomly popping into her head, and taking form, seemed indicative of an ill mind. "I think I'm going mad."

Solaris laughed, dark and cold. "You've been mad for eons—downright furious."

She sorted through the folklore in her head. "Mistress? You think I'm Ulnaire?"

He squatted down next to her. Even with the mask, she sensed his grin. "Only if you consider me Solaris."

She withdrew from his touch. "What does that even mean?"

Leoht sat hard on the floor and sulked. "I'm tired of this. I want to see my father. You told me I could see him if I brought her."

Fate's eyes widened. "You tricked me?"

He flopped onto the floor and flailed his legs in frustration. "Ugh, grownups are so irritating. They never tell the truth."

She turned back to Solaris. "What do you want?"

He reached out with his forefinger and touched the center of her forehead. "For you to wake up."

Fate's eyes flew open and she gazed around the room, finding herself quite alone and thankful for it. She rolled out of the bed, walked to the window, and leaned against the frame. "You really are losing your mind."

A light knock came at the door.

She hurried to it, relieved for any company she might find, opened it, and paused at the sight of Hero.

He turned his foot from side to side while he waited in the hallway with the book in hand. "I wanted to return this to you so you could finish your reading."

She opened the door wider. "Please, come in."

He stepped inside and looked around. "I hope it's to your liking."

She hugged her waist and swayed out of nervousness. "It's lovely. Thank you."

He gave only a slight nod in response.

She floundered for anything to talk about. "I heard you were an expert on the Spinner."

"Hmm."

"Perhaps, if you have time, you might be willing to tell me about her."

He inspected her at length before finally asking, "Is this because of the game?"

She slouched in her own self-defeat. "It's about my dreams."

His eyes grew wide and bright. "So, you *do* dream often. You lied."

"I didn't. I'm dreaming *more* often than before."

He pressed a finger to his lips and pondered aloud. "Hmm. It really could be an Awakening. So, what is it about your dreams that makes you curious about the Spinner?"

She ambled to the bed and sat on the edge. "Well, recently I've been dreaming about a room with huge bookshelves and lots of scrolls... the Room of Forgotten Memories."

Hero sat beside her, scratching his forehead and shooing a few resistant strands of hair from his face. "That could be from the book I gave you though. It's described in *Sands of Time*."

"Was it? I don't remember that."

He waved the book around. "Not to mention, it's in here, for sure."

Fate debated the possibility. "Maybe, but I didn't get very far in that book."

"What else?"

She reflected on her dreams. "I just met Solaris, and he had the most amazing eyes I've ever seen."

"In what way?"

"They were every color you could imagine, and they glowed in the darkness."

"Good, what else?"

She grew more comfortable with Hero's drive to find the underlying cause of her conundrum. "There was a boy. At first, I thought it was you, but then I wasn't so sure, and he told me his name was Leoht."

"Ah, Leoht Miina," Hero said with a nod.

"Does that make sense to you?"

He shrugged. "Of course, it's in all of the folklore. Leoht Miina is a legendary character."

"He was just a boy in my dream."

"Yeah, but I, like many others, happen to believe that Leoht Miina is the Man Who Stood at the Edge of Time."

She shook her head. "I don't understand what that means."

Hero lay back on the bed and stretched his hands towards the ceiling. "Simply put, he was extraordinary—a legend—the future Grandmaster of the Universe."

She pursed her lips, still not following how the information pertained to her dreams. "What does that have to do with the Spinner?"

He sat up. "Nothing. I'm just explaining who you're dreaming about."

She continued. "Solaris—rather, the man who allowed me to consider him Solaris if he could consider me Ulnaire...."

Hero frowned. "Sounds problematic. Solaris isn't a real character like Leoht Miina. He's a compilation of three characters—the Lord of Time, the Lord of Harmony, and the Lord of Chaos. They're all different people, so calling anyone Solaris would be a lie, as would be calling you Ulnaire."

"Even you told me I was like Ulnaire."

He held up a finger. "*Like*, not one and the same."

She blew the air from her puffed cheeks, trying to wrap her head around the information. "None of this makes any sense."

He stretched his legs out in front of him and flexed his ankles. "It does in a twisted sort of way."

"How so?"

"Let's say you're having some kind of Awakening, which is usually the case for Ancients that dream. It means you were someone else before, as we all were."

"Okay...."

"A part of you is trying to tell you something... to *wake you up*, if you will."

She waved her hands in the air. Whenever she felt the dots connect, it filled her with such excitement, she could barely muster words. "Solaris told me to wake up!"

"See?" A flicker of calculation crossed Hero's expression. "Did Leoht seem strange?"

"Strange how?" She ruminated on her interactions with the boy, each as vivid as the dream itself. "He wore a mask and said he was blind."

"Yes, you see, that would be after his father abandoned him."

She bounced to her knees and shouted, "He said he wanted to see his father, and that Solaris lied to him when he said he would take him."

Hero turned to face her, matching her enthusiasm. "All right, then somehow the Spinner is involved — "

"Oh!" She gasped, remembering the red-haired man. "There was another man too! He sat at a spinning wheel, had long red hair, and spoke in riddles. His name was... uh.. Casi... Casu...."

"Casluhim?"

"Yes!"

Hero rested his chin on his hand. "He's the God of Life. That's so weird."

Fate's zest dwindled with his confusion.

He shifted his gaze to the ceiling. "That's a really strange combination of characters — a Messenger, a Lord, and the future Grandmaster."

She chewed the inside of her cheek, anxious about the conclusion Hero might come to. "Is it?"

"Well, yeah. They're all part of different stories, and yet, they come together in your dreams. Have you dreamt of the Spinner herself?"

She sighed. "Not exactly. I think saw her in the maze and in one of my dreams, but someone always calls her away."

"I guess we'll have to slowly put it together with each dream you have. You should write them down when you wake up, so you don't forget anything. I would also read more on the subject. Familiarize yourself with the stories so you'll better understand what you are experiencing."

She reached out and took Hero's hand into hers. "Thank you."

He stared at their intertwined fingers. "I'm glad to help."

She suddenly stood, recalling part of her dream. "The journal."

He looked up at her with childlike curiosity. "Journal?"

She scoured the room. "It may sound crazy, but Leoht told me Abyssus hid a journal in this room."

Hero stood and immediately joined the search. He went to a part of the shelving unit and sifted through the spines of the books. "I'll check here."

They tore apart his fine décor, tossing books from their homes and displacing jewelry boxes, silk sheets, and pens. If they thought a journal might fit someplace, they rummaged that spot until it lay barren.

Just as Fate lost faith in her dream, Hero sprang up from the floor and waved a black leather journal. "I found it!"

In seconds, they proved a part of her dreams true and recovered a remnant of their loved one.

Fate drew her hands over her mouth, her eyes and nose burning with tears. For the first time since Abyssus's death, she gave a genuine smile.

Hero swept his hand over the journal as though he'd uncovered a rare antiquity. He gawked at it, lost for words.

She allowed him a moment to take in their findings and Abyssus's presence, then extended her hand.

He gave her the journal, his expression frozen in the moment he'd found it, full of sorrow and longing.

She gripped it but didn't fully take it for another few seconds. An aura seeped through the pages. After she collected it, she traced it with her fingertips. Her brother's laughter and susurration passed through her ears.

He knew. He knew his fate well enough to leave a part of him behind. So why didn't he stop it?

Memories overcame her—vivid recollections of sitting out on the balcony and leafing through the journal as the garden trees cast down shadows of leaves upon her brother's face.

The rustle of the breeze and the cool spring air still brushed against her, trapping her in the past—a time when he still lived.

She inhaled and expelled the ache in her chest. The memories of Abyssus reminded her of how she'd warned him, and brought back the image of the blade plunging through his torso.

She embraced the journal to absorb her brother's aura, but the pain only grew, until her legs succumbed to the weight and the room filled with her wails.

Hero knelt at her side and brought his arms around her.

Together, they sat on the floor and mourned the most important person in both of their lives.

Fate ran her fingers over the cover. "He left this for a reason. We need to find out why."

He quietly agreed. "Hmm."

She took his hand and squeezed it, thankful to have his company. He alone understood the magnitude of her sorrow. "I'm glad you're with me."

"Me too," he said, his voice still choked with anguish.

She sniffled and wiped her nose.

He nodded towards the journal, urging her to read it. The warmth from his arms and the sensation of his aura soothed her.

She flipped through the pages she knew and found new content to study.

> *"I recently visited the High Queen, Lady Heqet, in the Capital to inquire about the location of the new Hall of Records. Although the Lady herself is restricted, by Council law, to reveal such information, her aide, Akira, has been of great assistance.*
>
> *"He's well-known in the Capital because of his unique appearance—a donned fox mask and polychromatic eyes, strange for a Caeles. Strange for anyone, really. His origins are unknown, but most are too frightened to probe him... probably because he's tainted."*

After reading a snippet, she paused. In just a few words, her world turned inside-out. It told her that not only did her brother go to the Capital without her, but that he kept information from her, and that Hero also had failed to mention this man. "Do you know someone named Akira?"

Hero answered. "Hmm, my cousin."

She held her place with her hand and looked Hero in the eyes. "You've never said anything about him."

"It never came up."

Fate shook her head. "There are only three Caeles in all the world, and it didn't occur to you or Abyssus to tell me?"

"He's a pain. We don't really get along."

She checked the passage again and, without looking up, said, "He's Tainted too?"

"Hmm. The Council already tried blaming the Caeles for the Plague but the Igni were the actual origin, so they had to drop it."

She snarled at the book. "...and has polychromatic eyes."

He shrank. "Yeah...."

She stretched out on the floor and settled in, determined to read the entirety of her brother's journal and uncover what else they had buried. A part of her hurt from the betrayal, but she resolved to understand *why* they'd kept things hidden.

A WHIRLWIND

After spending the rest of the day reading the journal, Fate sat up and stretched her stiff body. It had been some time since she checked on Hero, who now lay asleep on her bed. She gathered her gown and crawled to her feet, flinching as the book thudded to the floor.

He stirred for only an instant before rolling over and returning to a comfortable slumber.

She walked around the bed, set the journal on the side table, and leaned in, noting how peacefully he slept. Looking at him closely reminded her of her dreams and of Leoht Miina.

She brushed the hair from his face with the softest touch possible, wondering if the boy from her dreams shared any resemblance.

Given the recent events, she decided to leave him to his much-needed rest, and snuck out and down the hall in search of food. Her thoughts drifted as she came to a painting of Niteo. She concluded that somewhere in the palace, there must be paintings of the Ancients, who used to reside in Nex. The Rahma lived short lives.

Neco and Niteo were the first Rahma rulers, so there ought to be an explanation.

She wondered aloud. "What happened to you?"

Instinct and hazy memories guided her through the long halls. She knew it well enough since the structure mirrored Macellarius palace. Once she arrived, she peeked inside.

A plump woman worked at a large cutting block in the center of the room. Deep wrinkles formed on her brow, framed by loose strands of long brown hair that she had tied back into a tight bun.

The woman worked methodically, chopping potatoes and placing them into a deep pan. In a flash, she spied Fate and a huge smile stretched across her face. "Oh, Lady Fate, welcome."

Fate responded to the gesture by smiling so hard her cheeks hurt. "Thank you."

The chef stepped to another table and picked up a tray, which contained a freshly baked bread stuffed with spiced meat, and soup. "They tried to tell me that we would not see you until dinner, but I told them that you were not Prince Hero and, petite or not, a woman needs to eat."

Fate approached the tray, her mouth watering even before she smelled the soup. She took the tray handed to her. "Thank you for thinking of me."

The chef squeezed her hands together and leaned back. "Aren't you the sweetest thing ever? I told them you would be like this. No one wants to listen to an old lady, but you know hard work... unlike some of the little snots we have to serve."

Fate laughed. "I can imagine."

"Now, go eat, dear. The dining area is out the door to your left. Let me know if you need anything. It's my pleasure, honestly."

She beamed as she took her tray out of the kitchen to a large table just beyond the entrance hall. The table seemed much too large for one person, as it had at least twenty chairs on each side. She supposed that in Hero's mind, these were for the maids and soldiers, while in Niteo's mind, they were for his royal position-climbing guests. Either way, it made for a lonely meal.

She picked a chair and sat down before the bowl of steaming soup, the scent of which left her speechless. Memories of her childhood flooded in, and after seeing the chef prepare food, so did memories of the brothel and the meals she made with her sisters.

Even more distant, the faded memories of Abyssus tickled her mind. She envisioned him there before her, still a child, prepared to gobble down a cake. It came as a shock that she understood the chef more than she understood her brother and, more so, that she missed her family in the brothel more than her royal life.

The recollection enhanced Fate's eating experienced. She lifted the savory first bite, opened her mouth, and took in the culinary vision. Her mouth watered again in anticipation and... Lara stepped in through the back doors.

Fate's mouth hung open, her meal a mere lick away.

Lara sat across from Fate and clasped her hands together on the table. The way she settled in seemed like the preface to some kind of consultation.

Fate waited in silence for the storm she knew would blow in.

Lara let her words stew in her mouth before spewing her hatred. "You should return to the brothel. You don't belong here."

Fate took a deep breath, doing her best to remember that Lara, although Rahma, technically held a higher social standing than she did. "Lara, like it or not, I'm here to stay. We should do our best to get along."

Lara's knuckles turned white. "Hero is not going to marry some whore."

Fate set her sandwich down. "You're right. He'd be marrying the Princess of Macellarius, bringing the two kingdoms of Nex together for the first time since its creation."

Lara stood, stepped back, and pushed in her chair. "Say what you like to make yourself feel better. We both know what you are and what you aren't. You are not meant for Hero, and we both know it. You may care for him, but not enough not to use him to save yourself. If you were decent, and you truly cared for him as I do, you wouldn't pursue him the way you have. You are so self-absorbed that you probably forgot that his birthday is coming up."

Fate sat quietly staring at Lara, lacking a response as the sting of truth tore at her already wounded soul. The weight of Abyssus's death had consumed everything, even Hero's birthday, which she always remembered.

Lara huffed. "I didn't think so. Stop trying to act like you care about anyone but yourself. Every action and inaction gives you away. You're hollow, like an empty nutshell, and just as hard to crack. Do us all a favor and leave. Go far away from here, and never come back. You'll only bring trouble. Somewhere in that black soul of yours, you know it's the truth."

Fate remained frozen in her seat, her palms sweating — all words lost to her.

The malefic girl spun on her heels and walked away victorious.

Her food somehow lost its luster, and Fate's mood greyed with the room around her. Not even rage dwelled within her after Lara's venomous berating.

SMALL CRIES

Fate sat at the desk in her room, clenching her teeth and rubbing her brow with the heel of her hand. She'd been reading her brother's journal off and on, unable to break from the bad taste in her mouth left by Lara's verbal assault. Even after two days, it still rotted her every thought and made her stomach knot. She debated whether her hatred of the girl rested in her genuine evaluation of Lara's behavior, or irritation from hearing the truth.

Lara's words had cut deep, as Fate still needed a gift for Hero's birthday. She'd worked to become his wife but hadn't taken the time to learn much about him on a truly personal level. Everything she learned ultimately benefitted her in some way. Guilt gnawed at her.

Hero sat across from her, looking up from his studies. "Are you okay?"

Fate half lied. "Yes, just thinking."

He grimaced. "Still can't figure it out?"

She took the escape he provided. "There's a whole chapter here on Spirit Walking. It seemed he knew something about my dreams."

"What did it say exactly?"

She flipped through the pages, skimming them as she summed them up. "It says that Spirit Walking, or dream walking, originated in the Beyond with the Goddess Zipporah, and then there's a brief interlude about a group known as the *Tocsin*, which she created—a group capable of harnessing the power of song as a weapon. They sound a lot like the Tau, but at the same time not really. After that, it goes back to those who can Spirit Walk and how they can be affected, as well as affect other people's dreams."

He sat, aghast at her version of a summary. "Never mind, I'll read it later."

She ignored his complaint. "Of course, my dreams are nothing like that, but it does appear he was looking into it—in great detail, even. I just don't know *how* he knew. I never told him about my dreams."

He used his index finger to flick the corner of the page back and forth. "Well, that's just Abyssus. Do the research and then dig up things that only the Gods knew."

"Why would he keep something like that from me?"

Hero set his own studies down. "It's hard to say. Maybe he thought he was protecting you."

"Maybe." She closed the journal and was in the midst of considering his words when she noticed a tiny number one etched into the corner on the back cover. "There are more."

"What?"

She pointed to the number. "There are more journals."

"We searched the room completely. That's the only one in here."

She rubbed her head. "There must be some kind of indicator as to where to find the next journal. He was too meticulous to leave it like this."

He tapped his teeth with the end of his pen. "True. That journal looks quite old. He was always jotting something down. There's no way he took all of his notes in just one or two of those. There are probably a few of them."

"Hmm." Fate studied the journal's exterior but found nothing unusual other than the number. She exhaled hard in frustration and shook her head.

"Maybe you just need some time to think about it."

"Maybe."

He closed his workbook. "I have some things to attend to. Why don't you go for a walk or go shopping? When was the last time you shopped for yourself?"

She squeezed the journal, not wanting to admit that she hadn't ever shopped for herself and, furthermore, that she felt guilty about her selfish excitement when she should be looking for something special for his birthday.

Hero rested his head against his hand. "You can go to any shop. I've already informed them of our relationship. As the future High Queen, you may have anything you like."

She jerked her head up to look him in the eyes. The words whirled around in her head before she finally asked, "What, exactly, is our relationship?"

"We're to be wed, no?"

"Yes." Fate answered but it felt hollow. Even though she cared for Hero deeply, the thought of sharing a bed with him alarmed her. She swallowed hard and smiled.

He stood and closed his book. "I'll see you later?"

"Hmm." She waved as he exited.

Once he was out of sight, she pressed her hand to her chest, confirming that she felt fright. The sensation baffled her. She'd spent her whole life training to please her partner, and now, at the first hint she may actually have to do so, she felt pure, unbridled terror.

She stood, smacked her cheeks a few times, checked herself in the mirror, and left. The long hall seemed warmer than usual, leading her to wonder if Hero's mood had lightened since Abyssus's death.

When she arrived in the foyer, a coachman stood, waiting. "Prince Hero said you wanted to go into the city."

"Uh, yes, that would be lovely, thank you."

He ushered her out and into the carriage.

After a short ride, the carriage stopped along rows of shops.

Nitor's city life greatly differed from Macellarius and the brothel. The storefronts were cleaner and more inviting, lined by planters of winter flowers. Mannequins decorated the windows, and shopkeepers stood out on the street greeting people as they passed.

The coachman opened the door for Fate. "I'll wait here for you, Lady, until you are ready to return."

She took in the sunlight and the mellow breeze. "Actually, if you don't mind, I'd prefer to walk back to the palace." The reflection of Hero's mood had lightened her mood as well. It had been a long time since the sun shone in Nitor.

"Are you sure, Lady? The bags may be heavy for you."

"I'm certain. Just between us, I'm shopping for Hero's birthday."

"Ooh, that's a hard one, Lady. I wish you well in your search."

"Thank you," she said, seeing the coachman off.

She meandered through the streets and checked from vendor to vendor, trying to find the perfect gift for Hero's birthday. She took comfort in the warm, sunny day, and the kindness and wares of the shops in Nitor, compared to the crime and suffering in Macellarius. Even with things being much better than ever before, she still struggled to find something that matched Hero as a person. She needed something special—something that even Lara wouldn't think of.

Discouraged after spending much of her time looking at commonplace items, she ventured off the city streets and walked along the river's edge, hoping the fresh air would clear her weary head. Hints of snow still clung to the blades of grass as she walked.

A tiny whimper carried through the air, prompting Fate to lift her head. The second time, a pained yip urged her to seek out the poor creature. She tracked the cries to a cluster of rocks and peered inside the cracks.

An ashen puppy whined and cried upon seeing her, its bitsy tail wagging with enthusiasm despite its foot being tightly jammed between two rocks.

She slipped her hands into the rubble, carefully freed the puppy from its trap, and picked it up. "Oh, baby, how long have you been in there?"

It licked her face and neck frantically as she held it close. She warmed it, and then held it away from her to inspect it. "Let's see.... Oh, you're a girl."

Dirt and debris stuck to the puppy's thick fur. Judging by its appearance alone, it seemed to have been out in the wilderness for much of its short life.

She set it down on the grass in front of her, pulled the comb from her hair, and preened the small pup.

Its fur puffed out as she detangled it, emphasizing its stubby legs and little beady eyes. It looked chubbier in its mass of fluff.

She plucked the puppy from the grass. "I know just what to do with you." She placed her comb in her pocket and hurried back towards the palace with the puppy in tow.

The guard at the gate eyed her as she crossed.

One of the guards stated, "Oh, he's going to love that."

Fate grinned. "You think?"

"Absolutely. The King never let him have anything of the sort, but he loves animals."

The second guard added, "Look at how well he treats Holly. He treats that horse like a girlfriend."

Fate teased, "Hey now, should I be jealous?"

The guards laughed.

She quickly made her way through the side door near the kitchen, and peeked in to see if anyone lingered nearby. Once she saw the empty hallway, she rushed inside and slipped, unseen, to her bedroom, where she locked the door behind her.

She took the puppy to her tub and started the water. "Next, we'll get you something to eat."

The puppy wagged its tail and lapped at her hands.

She plopped it into the warm water and scrubbed it free of dirt, exposing vibrant grey — nearly silver — fur. The puppy jumped and yipped with excitement. She shushed it, then pulled her from the water, wrapped her in a towel, and dried her thoroughly before releasing her to run free in the bathroom.

"Not too loud, now. You'll ruin the surprise."

Fate slipped out of the bathroom as the puppy erupted in a fit of yipping and racing about in circles. She shut the door before it could escape. With a smile on her face, she skipped the rest of the way to the stairs and trotted down to the kitchen.

The chef worked at her counter, cutting fat from the evening's share of meat. She looked up, saw Fate, and grinned. "Welcome, Lady. What brings you in this close to dinner?"

"Scraps, if I may."

"Scraps?" The chef raised a brow but collected the cut pieces of fat into a bowl for Fate.

Fate took the bowl. "Thank you."

The chef eyed her with a suspicious grin. "If I didn't know better, I'd say the Lady has found her birthday gift for the prince."

"You always see right through me."

The chef winked. "Five children and you can see through walls and around corners if you want."

Fate laughed and fled the kitchen before the chef exposed any more of her secrets. She scurried down the hall, up the stairs and back into her room, but when she turned to shut the door, she noticed the bathroom door open.

Panic-stricken, she dashed to it, flung it open, and found Hero sitting by the tub coddling the sleeping pup.

He looked up at her. "Shh."

She set the bowl down, took a seat next to him, and scratched the now-puffy little dog on the top of her head. "It was supposed to be a surprise."

A genuine smile crossed his face. "It was. I heard crying, so I came to see what it was and found this baby."

Fate leaned forward on her hand, tipping her head to the side to get a better look at Hero's bliss. "Happy birthday."

Hero stroked the puppy's fur. "I love her."

"What are you going to name her?

"Persephone."

The name rang in Fate's ears like an echo of an echo. Something felt strange about it.

The room again expanded away from her, and gentle chiming again filled her ears. Far in the distance, a voice again called to her. "Return to me."

She clenched her teeth and weathered the storm in her mind until the ringing stopped. "That's an odd name for a puppy."

Hero defended, nuzzling the sleeping puppy with his nose. "Maybe, but it's her name just the same."

She touched the side of her head. Part of the feeling still lingered, not quite pain but something uncomfortable. "Of all the names in the world, why do you think that one suits her most?"

He laughed. "I never said it did. It's just the one I'm going to use.

She gazed at Hero with his new gift. Curiosity, joy, and guilt washed over her and painted her world with new colors. The feeling baffled her because it seemed without origin. She put on a practiced smile and excused herself for some air. "I'll let you two bond."

He paused with his head on Persephone's head and gave Fate some of his attention. The fact that he still paid her mind in this state at least expressed some bond between them, be it that of a courtesan and her patron, or of two friends. "Where are you going?"

"Just to the balcony. I want to go through Abyssus's journal once more and see if I can figure out what he did with the others."

Hero nodded and smiled as he baby-talked his puppy. "We'll stay right here then, until it's time to eat."

Fate exited the bathroom, picked up the journal, and walked out the back door onto the balcony. She sat on the floor and peered out the balusters into the garden. Her hair and the skirt of her gown caught in the breeze as she gazed down at the yard. Nitor felt cheerier than Macellarius, but a dark shadow seemed to hang over all of Nex.

She combed through the book again, hoping to find the hint she'd missed. "What were you trying to say?"

As much as she wished to focus on the journal, the name Persephone kept ringing in the back of her mind. Her ears again filled with distant chimes. "Persephone...."

A white flash blinded her. Shortly after, a sharp pain struck her head, accompanied by the loud ringing and a vacuous scream. Darkness fell all around and the air grew stale and cold. Her heart beat rapidly, flittering and skipping beats.

A low haze poured onto the balcony, marring the edges and making the space feel vast and empty in the darkness. Clicking arose from the mist, and something else lingered in the dark with her, but she struggled to identify its location because of the reverberation. She held her breath, unable to break her gaze from ahead.

A dark, gnarled form crept from the shadows, groaning and ticking. Its thick skin appeared wet and as black as tar, in part due to the darkness, which seeped out in wisps and drifted into the air.

Fate froze, daring not to move, recalling this beast from the maze.

The shadowy creature cocked its head back and freed a bloodcurdling screech. A pulse shot out and knocked her back against the wall.

Jolted, she checked the area for the creature in spite of finding herself in the warmth of sunlight once more. The birds chirped around her. Nothing had changed. Whatever had occurred, it had happened either in her head or in a separate reality.

She reached up and put her hand to her mouth, and noticed that blood stained her fingers. She checked again and discovered it came from her nose. "Uh." She set the journal down and hurried to the bathroom.

Hero looked up from Persephone and spied Fate's bleeding nose. "What happened? You just left."

She held her nose while walking to the sink, and fibbed. "I don't know. It just started bleeding." She wanted to keep the strange occurrences to herself. Explaining a nosebleed proved difficult enough.

He stood. "Let me see."

She rinsed her face with water. "It stopped."

He pursed his lips until they formed a thin line. "We should keep an eye on that."

"It'll be fine. You have Persephone to look after." The visions spooked her enough to lie to his face. "I can take care of myself."

He shot her a sideways glance as he turned and exited the bathroom. "If you say so. I'm going to make Persephone a bed in my room."

She feigned playfulness. "You mean put her in your bed."

He gazed down at the pup with an impish grin. "Maybe."

Seeing Hero interact with the puppy brought Fate a measure of peace. Together, they made something right in the world. She watched as he left her bedroom, and waited until he closed the door to collapse onto the floor and allow her rattled nerves to ease.

Her heart still hurt and her ears still rang. "What's happening to you, Fate?"

She spent the rest of that night searching through Abyssus's journals, trying to make sense of her world before it fell apart. Eventually, her eyes refused to remain open and she fell asleep.

23

STORMY WEATHER

Fate woke the next morning still fatigued and uneasy from her experience the previous day. She stared out the double doors at the rising sun and pondered her state of mind. She'd questioned her sanity on occasion, but this time felt different—a real possibility that she'd gone insane. Whether or not she wanted to accept it, her mind may have snapped under the pressure.

Her door slammed open, and a blonde woman, enveloped in scaled armor, entered looking furious. "You."

Fate sat up, clutching her blankets as the woman shook a finger at her. "Me?"

The woman marched across the room. "What were you thinking?"

Fate strained to recall the woman but came up blank.

The woman spun on her heels and pointed back at the empty doorway. "You gave him a puppy?"

"It's his birthday."

The woman exploded. "He's Tainted! That poor creature. Do you have any idea what you've done?"

Fate gaped at the woman, unable to respond. She hadn't thought of the ramifications of her gift despite the fact that even Hero himself had warned of the Plague's effects. "I mean... Holly... he had a horse, so I thought a dog might be nice."

The woman glared. "Holly is special. That's why he's able to have her."

Fate floundered as this woman made her feel hopeless and helpless. All she'd wanted was to wish Hero a happy birthday and find a proper gift, and yet, apparently, she couldn't even do that right.

The woman stormed back to the door and seethed. "I hope you're happy with the results."

Fate sat dumbstruck as the woman shut the door. The slam caused her to jerk her shoulders, as she stared at the empty room. "Good morning, Fate. I'm sure it's going to be a lovely day." She fretted for some time before finally crawling from her bed to wash and dress.

It took several long internal conversations and encouragement until she gathered the courage to open the door. Not even a speck of dust crossed her path. She stuck her head out and contemplated her next move. The ironclad woman had scared her, but she also wanted to eat. Her stomach growled, protesting against her staying in her room any longer.

She tiptoed down the long hallway, listening for anything that revealed the location of the angry woman. Something about the palace had changed. The servants moved about in silence, whereas they usually laughed and joked. If her suspicions were correct, the eerie quiet was a result of *that* woman.

Fate slunk through the halls to the kitchen. She expected to hear pots and pans, as she would have in the brothel, but it was quiet here too.

The chef looked up from her work. "Lady, I was wondering where you were."

Fate checked the hall behind her. "I was accosted by a shouting woman in my bedroom."

The chef nodded with a grimace. "That would be Lady Isis."

Fate gaped at the chef.

"The Lady Isis is the Queen of Askadel."

Fate shook her head. "Why is the Queen of Askadel in Nex?"

"Oh dear, I thought you knew... she's Mortis's sister."

Fate's heart climbed into her throat. "Mortis's sister?"

The chef raised a brow, astounded by Fate's ignorance. "You really don't know her?"

Fate considered confiding in the chef but remembered that Isis, as Head of Artillery, had been in Nitor far longer than she had.

"By title only," she said.

In truth, she *did* know Isis, but hadn't seen the woman since Abyssus first mentioned her during childhood. During that time,

Hero's act of dangling off the edge of his balcony took precedence.

The chef walked across the kitchen and picked up an already prepared plate of food. "I was expecting you."

Fate, afraid of running into Lara or Isis, ate in the kitchen.

The chef returned to her work and happily prattled with her.

Fate took a bite of delightful food and savored the flavor, pleased to have finally gotten to enjoy the chef's masterpiece, her previous attempt having been ruined by Lara.

The chef glowed with pride. "Glad to see you're enjoying it."

Fate chirped, thankful for any conversation that didn't bring up anything unpleasant. "You make the most wonderful things. It's like a slice of perfection wrapped in a blanket of sunshine and a cool breeze."

The chef chuckled. "The way you make it sound, I'm magic."

"You are to me."

"You are the sweetest."

Fate set her sandwich down and stared at her plate. "You may be the only one who thinks so."

"That's not true. I've heard from much of the staff that you are a true Lady."

She shifted on her seat and twisted the ends of her hair. "Lady Isis yelled at me this morning, and Lara hates me completely."

The chef rejected the idea. "Oh, I think they're both just fiercely protective of our prince. Give it time. They'll warm up. You know women, suspicious at first but best friends later."

Fate thought about the chef's perspective on women. She'd never considered gender an issue, but Ancients differed greatly from Rahma in this context. Fate debated if this differing opinion might actually apply to her circumstances. "I hope you're right. It would be nice to get along with everyone."

She finished her meal, thanked the chef, and left the kitchen without hiding. If there were any possibility of reconciling the conflicts, she wouldn't hide from them.

Lara passed her in the hallway without a word. She sneered and turned her head, but kept any ill thoughts to herself.

Fate turned as she passed, expecting some kind of ridicule or snide comment, but Lara just continued down the hall and out into the garden. "Well, it's an improvement, at least."

She climbed the curved staircase and headed for her room. She no sooner entered than a knock came at the door.

When she opened it, Isis stood, arms crossed, in the hallway.

Fate braced herself for the next round of complaints.

Isis looked down the hall towards the staircase before speaking. "I wanted to apologize."

Fate stood silent, confounded.

Isis continued. "I didn't know who you were. I am truly sorry for your loss. You may not believe me but, if Mortis had been killed in that duel, it would have ended the same."

Fate fumed. "My brother wasn't a fighter. He would never engage in a duel."

Isis stepped back and shook her head as if confused. "Your brother was one of the most skilled combatants in Mu."

Fate fumbled her thoughts and words. "What? Who are you talking about? My brother kept to his books."

"Prince Hero keeps to his, too, but it makes him no less a skillful fighter."

Fate reflected on her brother's constant secrets and Isis's words.

Isis nodded and took a deep breath. "I didn't come here to upset you further. I just wanted you to know that I do not see us as enemies. We have both lost someone dear with Abyssus's passing. I can hardly believe it happened. I'm not making excuses, but something was—*is*—wrong with my brother. Ask anyone of import and they'll tell you he's a gentle soul."

Fate snapped, "He was anything but gentle, and I'm not just talking about that day."

Isis put her hands up. "I know. I think King Neco has done something unspeakable to him. I'm just trying to save my brother."

Fate's mind whirled. She tried to understand Isis's feelings but, in the end, she felt that Isis had enabled Mortis to get away with murdering Abyssus. She relented only for Hero's sake. "Do what you must."

"I do. That's what I was trying to warn you about earlier. I know I can be abrasive, but I do everything in my power to protect those I care for. For now, I wish you the best, and will respect your relationship with our prince. You may one day be my queen. Know that I will aid you whenever possible, and that I hold Council favor should you need assistance."

"Thank you."

Isis gave Fate one final nod before leaving.

Fate lingered in the doorway for a moment and then closed her door, her emotions thrashing in a hurricane of turmoil. She hated Isis for defending her brother's killer, but empathized with her as a sister desperately trying to save her brother. Everyone knew of Neco's treacheries, but she doubted a Rahma could harness the power, intelligence, or skill to overpower an Ancient of Mortis's prowess and status. It all made her sick.

She sat at the table in front of the window. Her brother's journal called to her, the morning light illuminating it as if to shine a spotlight on something she'd overlooked or missed.

The memory of Abyssus's words nagged. *"You'll never learn if you don't try. You don't think these journals wrote themselves, do you? I told you that one day you would thank me for them."*

She responded, even though she knew she was alone. "Yeah, so there must be something important inside, right?"

She brushed the smooth leather with her hand, put the thoughts of Isis behind her, and flipped through the crinkled pages, scanning for something new or buried. The location of the other journals remained a mystery.

After looking for a time, she shoved the journal and it spun across the table. "Come on, Abyssus! Why must you always make things so complicated?" The strain in the palace, and her uncertainty of the future, weighed on her mind. If things stayed as they were, she would never be able to prove that Mortis had murdered her brother, and she'd never learn enough about the Tainted to fully understand them before ruling.

It can't stay like this.

She left the room, her stride brisk and determined. The palace servants greeted her as she passed by, prompting her to bow her head. In her determination, she sought out the study Hero had first brought her to. Since they'd entered from the outside, it took time to navigate. From the entrance hall, she roamed the halls on the left side of the palace, meandered through the sparring hall, and down another long hall until she encountered a small closet and a bedroom door.

Fate squinted at the door to her right. She sensed Lara's presence inside, either from her belongings or from the girl herself. Nevertheless, she wished to avoid confronting anyone that may hinder her search.

She studied the wall to her left, where a tapestry of white flowers hung from the ceiling to the floor.

Was that always there?

These flowers reminded her of something she once studied. "Oh, Moon Drips?" The faint recollection led her to touch the fine artisanship, and she lay a hand over her heart to quell the harrowing sensation rising. With the fabric gathered in her hand, she caught a glimpse of a wood frame beneath, and lifted the tapestry to peek.

Another door hid behind it.

Fate checked her surroundings and tried the handle. *Locked.* She pressed a hand to her chin and ruminated. *What could be inside?* Staring at the locked door did her little good. She wished she had learned to pick locks like her brother, but retreated for now.

A servant girl stopped her as she walked back through the entrance hall. "Lady, would you care for a carriage?"

Fate waved her off. "No, thank you. I need some time to think, but your offer is appreciated."

She continued her trek back into town, through the few patches of melting snow. No one in the community would have information on Ancient history or folklore. In fact, she doubted that anyone in Mu would make such information accessible due to Council Law.

Her mind whirled and helplessness seeped in again, but she refuted it and stamped her foot. "No."

In her times of need, her thoughts returned to the brothel and the only mother she knew. As much as Fortuna kept secrets, she also seemed like one of the only people in her life that taught her about the world she lived in.

Fate admired the polished stone path as she marched towards the brothel. It had been so long since the sun shone that she had forgotten what lie beneath the dense snow. Blotches of greenery peeked out from the dirt and rocks.

Even from a distance, she spied the blossoms in the brothel courtyard, bright red.

Fortuna sat on a bench beneath the tree, smoking her pipe as she read from the usual journal. The way she constantly checked it made it seem like she expected to find something new every time she bared its contents.

Fate felt a bit sorry for her.

The Madam sighed and stared up at the red-blossom tree, appearing weary at best. She turned her attention to Fate as soon as she noticed her pupil. "Back so soon?"

"It's my home, after all," Fate said, twisting the skirt of her gown around her hands.

Fortuna displayed a placid smile, set the journal on the bench, and crossed the yard. She took a long drag off her pipe. "Praise be, child, what are you doing here? I hope it's for a pleasant visit, but your face suggests otherwise."

Fate demanded, "I need a book on Tocsin."

Fortuna clacked the pipe against her teeth. "On what?"

Fate pressed the matter. "A group of people called Tocsin. They use their voices like the Tau... sort of."

After a long pause, Fortuna confessed, "I'm sorry, you've lost me. You know I would help if I could. Sounds like some really old lore. Where did you learn of this group?"

"Abyssus left behind a journal. It was in there."

She sucked on her pipe intermittently as she mulled over the subject. "Hmm. I see. Your brother was always full of surprises, seemed far wiser than his age at times, and like a child at others."

Fate's focus drifted to the fish in the pond, bringing back thoughts of the rainbow-scaled fish from her dream. It hurt to acknowledge that her brother had kept her in the dark. "It seems he had a lot of secrets. Isis apologized to me this morning. She implied that Abyssus wasn't all that he seemed."

Fortuna narrowed her eyes and sucked on her pipe again, puffing out smoke between words. "I'm not entirely certain I like that woman."

Fate searched Fortuna's face for hope. "You think she's lying?"

Fortuna's eyes darted around as she deliberated her answer. "Lying? Maybe. Maybe not. I'm not sure she uses the truth for good. Lying would just be another tier of deception."

Fate lowered her head as memories danced in her mind, but not in a pleasant or forgiving manner. They taunted her with reminders of her ignorance. "I don't know what to think anymore."

Fortuna hid her own sadness with a practiced smile. "Why don't you check our library here? I'm often surprised at the information hiding right under my nose."

Fate nodded and kissed Fortuna on the cheek. "Thank you, Madam. You always make me feel better."

Fortuna patted Fate's back. "It's because I care. If you don't find what you're looking for, let me know and I'll see what I can do."

"Thank you." Fate stepped towards the portico.

Upon entering the hallway, several of her sisters shouted and raced to greet her. A flurry of chatter and hugs came from every direction.

Fate always found herself so caught up in the chaos that she'd missed her opportunities to visit them. It brought back memories of her childhood and the elder sisters that she waited for now. "I'm sorry, I've just been really distracted."

One of her sisters replied cheerily, "Don't worry."

Yuzu held her hand. "We know you can't visit all the time. You are training to be queen."

Fate admitted, "Not yet. I still have many things I need to do before that."

Tori turned the corner and her expression brightened as she spotted Fate. She joined the circle of sisters. "Welcome back. Are things going well?"

Fate knew the Vem's heightened vision would catch any deceit. "As well as can be expected. I'm still new to the palace, so there will be an adjustment period."

Tori calculated her response. "Of course. We're always here to help."

"I'm on my way to the library to see if I can make sense of some of Abyssus's notes."

Tori wrapped her arms around Yuzu. "We need to let big sister finish her studies."

The girls whined and hugged Fate before giving into Tori's request. They waved and hurried back to their chores.

Tori watched them to make certain they followed through, and returned her attention to Fate. "Anything we can do?"

Fate glanced around to see if anyone else approached. "I'm looking for a book on a group called the Tocsin."

Tori's eyes bulged, and she hunched in closer. "Why are you looking for *that*?"

"You know about the Tocsin?"

She pulled Fate into a storage room and closed the door. "Why are you researching Tocsin?"

Fate glanced at the surrounding crates and shelves stacked around her, careful not to bump into anything, but the girls had kept it tidy. "I told you, they were in Abyssus's journal."

Tori chewed her bottom lip. "The Tocsin are in the *Books of Grim*."

Fate shook her head. "I've got the *Teachings of Grim* and it's not in there. I've looked."

Tori sat on a crate. "Not what modern Ancients have written, but the original books. What have you learned so far?"

"That the Goddess Zipporah created them, and that they used sound as both a gift and a weapon."

Tori rested her elbows on her knees and bobbed her head in thought. "It's a bit more complicated than that. Before Zipporah, things like music didn't exist. People followed her and respected her nearly as much as the Grandmaster."

Fate took a seat on a crate opposite Tori. "So, she was pretty important."

"Hmm. The skill she gave started out as a gift, but like many gifts, it turned into a weapon."

Fate leaned closer. These stories told of the beginning of their universe, the very philosophy of their grand Euphoria. She found it troubling that anyone would alter the origins of their universe.

"Something went terribly wrong. Some people believe that there was a war between the Voidsent and the Beyonders. Some believe that the Grim betrayed the Grandmaster and tried to seize control of the Universe. Some feel that the King and Queen of the Void hated anything from the light, and wished for nothing more than to return the world to darkness. Depending on what you read, or who you talk to, there are different stories as to what happened, but ultimately, the stories all agree that the Queen of the Void demolished the Beyond. She destroyed everything and forced the Beyonders into the Mortal Realms. Although there are many versions, you can find parts of the story in just about all folklore, but mostly in *Benevolence of Queen*." As Tori spoke, she stared into nothingness, and a heaviness settled into her body, making the small woman seem even more petite than usual.

Fate studied Tori's expressions and discerned pain but didn't understand it. "I'm beginning to understand why Hero is so fixated on folklore. It isn't just mythology... they're records about our world and how we came to be."

Tori shifted her eyes towards Fate. Her expression remained fixed in horror. "You can't imagine. A divine existence ended in a flash. There are no words to properly describe such a thing."

"But the *Teachings of Grim* and *Benevolence of Queen* did just that, no?"

Tori blinked and pressed her hand to the back of her neck. "In some menial way, I suppose, but I can't say the words expressed an event like that properly."

Fate let out a subtle laugh. "You make it sound like you were there."

Tori's eyes moved from Fate to the door. "If I was, it would be safe to say that I'd be irreparably scarred. Anyone would be."

Fate let Tori's words sink in, questioning the possibility of her sister being alive during the reign of ethereal beings. "You're creeping me out."

Tori shook her head and stood. "Sorry. I've always found this topic rather haunting."

"I see why. I'm just trying to piece together what any of this had to do with me or my brother."

Tori squinted as she touched the door handle. "In what way?"

"Well, Abyssus was trying to find out where we came from — we certainly aren't the real children of Neco. Somehow, his search led him to the Tocsins. We thought someone would have to know the truth."

"Hmm. Someone always does. Be careful, Fate. Sometimes the truth sleeps for a reason. Waking it may bring down the Mortal Realms as quickly as it did the Ethereal Realms."

Fate blinked twice, wrapping her mind around the severity of Tori's warning.

Tori opened the door and exited the small room. "I wish you well in your search. Sorry I couldn't be of more help."

"That's all right." She hollered as Tori hurried away. "Thank you for what you shared."

The entire experience left Fate feeling ill at ease. She rubbed her palms together and considered the information. With a soft exhale, she climbed down from the crate and left the room.

Before she'd taken two steps, she knew which direction to take. Her thoughts raced with vivid recollections of Hero, and she traced back his every movement and word to the moment they'd met.

Folklore... mythology.

The tapestry of the Moon Drip flashed in her mind, followed by the locked door and, finally, the memory of Hero talking to her before they read the *Story of Night and Day*.

Rather than march aimless and bewildered, she needed to return to the source of her curiosity, and to the person with whom her brother spent most of his free time.

As she started her return to Nitor Palace, dark clouds rolled in. A pit formed in her stomach as a chilling wind swept through the brothel courtyard. She stared up at the sky, listening to the droning of a storm above. "Hero."

She rushed back to the palace as quickly as her feet allowed. Her heart beat furiously inside her chest and the contents of her stomach turned to a thick sludge, threatening vomit. She sprinted through the courtyard, threw open the entrance doors, and took a few more steps in past the flustered servants. Hair stuck to her clammy face.

With heavy breaths, she inquired, "What happened?"

One of the servants approached with tears in his eyes. "We can't find the prince."

Fate closed her eyes, rested a hand over her chest, and calmed her frayed nerves. She needed to focus her emotions and energy to properly sense Hero, as she doubted that he'd vanished. Her aura settled and the nervous rattle in her chest dissipated. The energies from the world around her reached in, but she ignored them and waited until she could feel Hero in the midst. As soon as she did, she followed it out to the back garden. Snowflakes spun through the air and a biting chill befell Nitor Palace.

She squinted up at the sky. *I have to find him quickly.*

The garden made her feel small at the worst of times. No matter where she looked, she saw flowers, hedges, décor, and sky. She turned her head in each direction, as dizzy as when she'd played *Rota Fortunae*. Ever since that day, she felt as if trapped in the game.

As she thought of it, she dashed for the labyrinth, calling, "Hero! Answer me."

Her fingers tingled in the cold, and her breath cast out in small puffs of white. She kept running through the sea of leaves until she reached the center of the labyrinth, where the gazebo stood. Nothing. She opened her mouth to shout, and stopped to listen to a hollow screech.

Panicked muttering reached her ears as she struggled to follow the sound. Finally, she found Hero as he knelt down on the ground tearing at the hedge. "Hero?"

He gasped and looked at her, his eyes wide and his pupils hardly more than a speck.

The moment Fate saw his horror, she looked down at his hands and at the branches wrapped around Persephone's tiny body. "Oh, no, no...." She dropped to her knees and helped him fight with the vines entangling the pup's neck.

Persephone whined and kicked.

Hero's short blade lay broken on the ground beside his knee, drawing Fate's attention.

She glimpsed it, and then looked at him as he trembled and continued watching Persephone suffocate in the vine's tight grasp. Fate shivered as she tugged at the vines with one hand and stroked the pup's head with the other.

Hero repeatedly tore at the vines with bleeding hands. He took shallow breaths with sheer terror in his eyes, as new vines uncoiled from the hedge and ensnared more of Persephone.

Fate struggled to loosen the vines around Persephone's neck, hushing her as the pup thrashed and whimpered. She closed her eyes, fighting back her brimming tears. At times like this, she needed to remain composed... like Fortuna. Even if her heart ached, she needed to keep her head.

Persephone stopped crying and her still-warm body offered its last few heartbeats.

Fate gritted her teeth. She couldn't imagine how the Madam managed to bury such terrible feelings when they fought so desperately to escape. The darkness inside her writhed. She kissed Persephone's head and looked back at Hero, who drew back a sharp breath.

His lip quivered and he let out a sudden cry.

Fate embraced him as he sobbed into his hands. When she held him, she realized how much he truly hurt inside and that he masked his pain to protect her. Seeing him in this state hurt more than her own grief. The ever-composed prince trembled in her arms and exposed all his hidden weaknesses. She thought of the deaths of his friends at the Astor Tournament, his bond with Abyssus, and finally the death of his puppy.

How long have you endured?

Hero explained as he sobbed. "I tried... she got stuck... wouldn't cut... I'm so sorry."

Fate hugged his head. "Shh. I know. It's not your fault."

His body shook and he cried harder at her words.

She remembered Isis's words and the Tainted's condition — everything around them seemed doomed to suffer.

It's not your fault... it's mine. I'm so sorry, Hero.

The bizarre way the vines moved gave rise to new concerns. Something unnatural had killed Persephone, and if she didn't find out what and how, Fate fretted that she may be the next to fall.

24

CURIOUS CREATURES

Fate stood inside Nitor Palace and watched the garden from her bedroom upstairs. The sun trickled a warm glow through the window but the dark clouds still menaced the palace with their icy drafts. Although she couldn't see Hero in the maze, she knew of the grim task he performed, and her guilt for giving him Persephone swelled. She pressed her hand to the cold glass, hoping to reconnect with happy times. It seemed the world had grown darker by the day since Abyssus's death.

The circumstances made her wonder about the Tainted. Some believed that the presence of miasma resulted in the attraction of negativity. Others believed that the negative energy the Tainted themselves emitted caused the natural, balanced anima in all things to rot and wither. She wondered if these things were true or if the connections were merely coincidental. Not many of the Tainted existed in Mu, just Hero and....

A knock came that made Fate turn towards the door.

A servant girl popped her head inside. "Sorry to disturb you, Lady, but the Queen requests your presence."

Fate walked to the nervous girl. "Queen?"

"Yes, Lady. The High Queen is downstairs."

Fate wavered, dumbstruck as she processed the girl's words. "*The* High Queen?" She hurried to the mirror before the young maid answered. If she looked a mess for the High Queen, new rumors would circulate, and she felt her presence had already brought too much grief to Hero.

The servant girl opened the door wider to allow Fate to pass.

She rushed down the long hall as gracefully as possible, just in case someone saw her.

As she descended the stairs, Hero led the High Queen and her aide out of the foyer. Her heart sank, knowing that he'd never reached his intended destination, and that he put on airs while mourning the loss of two loved ones.

Her eyes locked on the High Queen's aide and her mouth fell open—white hair, a polished red velvet coat, and a metallic silver fox mask, which covered the upper half of his face.

The man from my dream.

A black cat at his feet reeled its head and pierced her with its cobalt blue eyes, calculating her.

Hero caught sight of Fate, drawing the attention of the High Queen and her aide.

Fate brooded as she stared at the man she'd seen in the maze during *Rota Fortunae*. He stood before her now at the bottom of the stairs, and her skin crawled with goosebumps.

The High Queen glided up the steps, the jewels hanging from her crown swaying and then resting beside her twinkling violet gaze. She gathered Fate's hand in her soft, willowy grasp and greeted her with a pearly grin. "Lady Fate, it's a pleasure to formally make your acquaintance."

Her beauty was rivaled only by her elegance. Long dark hair flowed around her shoulders in silken waves. Her crown and gown both glistened with crystals and gold, a symbol of Inoue, the Capital of Mu.

As striking as the High Queen may be, Fate kept gawping at the masked aide.

He followed Queen Heqet up the steps, all the while keeping a watchful eye on Fate. His lanky frame indicated a general lack of strength, but his aura suggested otherwise. He seemed familiar, but his mask conveniently disguised his identity.

As Queen Heqet twittered happily, the man touched her arm and interrupted. A smooth and deep voice spoke from beyond the mask. "Though you may be High Queen, it is impolite to show up uninvited. Do try and remember that this is your first time meeting."

Queen Heqet brushed off his hand with a small frown. "Don't be a nag, Akira. I may be High Queen, but I don't need to be aloof."

Fate repeated the man's name under her breath. *Akira.*

He gave up his admonishment of the High Queen and rested back against his heels, boring a hole through Fate with his polychromatic eyes.

His presence stirred something inside her. She desperately wanted to understand why but kept herself composed.

Hero squinted subtly at their interaction before shining a pleasant smile at Queen Heqet. "High Queen, we are honored by your visit."

Queen Heqet folded her hands at her middle and bowed her head to him. "It is an honor to see you again as well, Hero. You've grown much since our last meeting."

Fate broke her focus on Akira for a moment to study the High Queen's mannerisms. She wondered if Heqet kept her hands to herself because of Hero's Caeles heritage, as most knew that the clan disliked intimacy, or if she feared him because he was Tainted.

Queen Heqet crossed the room and embraced Fate. "I am so sorry it took this long to visit. We all mourn your brother. He burned so brightly. We will pray for his quick return."

Fate withdrew from the Queen's embrace and stared her in the eyes. "Can we return?"

The Queen hesitated, her eyes shifting from side to side as she deliberated. Her focus returned and she looked Fate dead in the eyes. "This is my fault. If I had been able to protect you and Abyssus, none of this would have happened."

Fate considered the paths set before her. "Am I a Doll?"

Heqet's shoulders drooped as her composure transformed into outward sorrow. "You are. You and Abyssus both."

Fate glanced at Hero, trying to free herself from her guilt, but his disappointed expression only deepened her concern.

The Queen's aide stepped forward with a bow. "We should move this conversation to somewhere more... exclusive."

Hero crossed the foyer and started up the stairs. "Follow me."

Fate noted two servants attempting to conceal themselves as they eavesdropped. She didn't care if everyone knew she was a Doll, as long as *she* heard the truth.

Akira took Fate by the arm and guided her towards the stairs. His hand sent a shock of energy through her body, which made her scalp tingle. His cat hopped to one side, allowing Akira to move freely.

He leaned down, analyzed her with his polychromatic eyes, and once again spoke in a low, smooth, almost melodic manner. "You look like you've seen a ghost."

Fate stared up at him, feeling as though the floor might give way and she'd fall down into the depths of space, as she had in her dream.

He cocked his head to one side and, with the slightest of smirks, said, *"Cer iste ke ramun, Reinka?"*

Static filled Fate's ears. The chimes rang but they sounded someone hollower than usual. A part of her knew precisely what Akira had meant when he posed his question.

Heqet glanced over her shoulder with a scowl. "Don't tease her." She smiled at Fate again. "Not to worry, Fate. He knows that he's eerie, but don't let him fool you—he's a wonderful companion."

Fate looked ahead to Hero, who walked on without response. It took all of her strength not to gawk at the unusual man as she pondered the exact relationship between the High Queen and her aide.

Hero led them to his study and opened the door, his expression concentrated. He kept his gaze lowered, away from Fate.

Akira ushered Fate inside and released her, then took a seat on top of one of the tables. His cat leapt into his arms and coiled into a small black ball on his lap.

Hero frowned. "We have chairs."

Akira shrugged. "I'm tall."

Hero moved toward the window, leaned against one of the pillars beside the door, and crossed his arms. His eyes appeared dark and brooding as he glared at Akira from afar, and this seemed to please the odd man, whose smile showed through the slight opening on his mask.

Heqet sat on a chair across from Fate, her brow in knots, rubbing her temple. The cheery airs she'd exuded had faded away to reveal a stressed woman.

Fate fretted about the tension in the room. She watched Hero for a moment, but couldn't help herself looking at Akira.

The man immediately simpered back at her.

Heqet leaned forward and took Fate's hands into her own again. "I wanted to come sooner."

Fate tried to ignore the pressure from Akira's gaze as she faced the High Queen, but his presence made the air thicken, as if it meant to stifle or strangle her in its grasp. Her arm still felt warm from his touch, and the darkness inside her rumbled, eager to come out of hiding, though she'd never known how to release it even if she wished. As hard as she fought it, her gaze returned to him as he continued to watch her.

Out of nervousness, she looked at Hero again, and couldn't help but notice the tinge of betrayal in his icy stare.

So, this is Hero's cousin. Why don't they get along?

More than anything, she kept thinking about the man from the maze and her dreams. Given that she'd never met Akira, it baffled her that she would dream of someone who matched his peculiar appearance.

Heqet continued speaking despite the tension. "The Council forbade me to interfere in any way once they found out Neco had possession of you. The explanation of how that happened was faulty at best, but there was little we could do once the decision had been made."

Fate felt a certain disgust for the High Queen's excuse. So much so, she managed to escape the dynamic between the two Caeles. "So, you let me rot in a brothel to be fondled by drunk Rahma?"

Heqet pressed her lips into a grim line before speaking again. "I tried. I really did. I begged them not to force my son's choices, but they have their rules."

Fate sat back on the chair, her head rushing furiously. If allowed, she would have thrown a tantrum, but a queen would never behave this way, so she shook her head instead. "So, everything my brother discovered was true. You could have done something."

Akira hopped down from the table, causing Hero to stand upright and his cat to wake from its slumber. The lanky man scanned Hero with a silent chuckle and then crossed to Heqet's side. "Sure, she could have done something... under penalty of death: her death, her husband's death—not much of a loss there—"

Fate gaped aghast at how rudely and freely Akira spoke of the High King.

"—her son's death... both of them, just for good measure."

Hero stated, "You seem to have a negative perception of the Council."

"Don't you?"

"Akira, please," Heqet interrupted, then sighed and rubbed her temple again.

Akira returned to his roost, clearly pleased with his interjection.

His cat leapt to his shoulder, watching the interaction with intelligent eyes.

Fate gripped the arms of her chair. "That still doesn't explain why or how you're here now. You didn't come all this time, so why now?"

Akira stroked his cat's head with his gloved hand. "Abyssus."

Fate silenced herself, suddenly reminded of her brother's gruesome death, and of how no one had come to take them back after Neco stole them away.

Heqet sighed again. "Fate, I understand why you're upset. Believe it or not, I am in a similar bind. My husband is not my natural Bound."

Fate focused hard on Heqet and her words. The tension in her head brought her to rub her forehead, to remove the wrinkles and prevent a headache.

Heqet formed a pained smile. "My Bound was killed during the Fall of the One Hundred. You probably aren't familiar, being so young, but the loss was devastating, not just for me but for all of Thule."

Hero finally joined the others, crossing the room to sit on the arm of Fate's chair.

Heqet continued. "The Grim helped us reform but, in order to save the Ancient society, they created forced bindings."

Fate leaned forward on her chair. "Forced? How do you *force* bindings? I didn't know that was possible."

Akira nodded his head while turning it to one side. "Indeed. It is not an ideal solution. If you force two incompatible souls together, it can bring about strange things."

Rather than simply asking another question, Fate thought about what he might mean, and a feeling of enlightenment swept over her. "Like the Tainted?"

"It's possible."

Heqet glanced at each of them before resuming. "Unfortunately, filling a void with something or *someone* that doesn't belong is only a temporary fix for permanent damage."

Akira chimed in. "Like filling a hole in a pipe with a rock, rather than mending the pipe itself. Even if it works, it may still leak."

"Correct," Heqet said, closing her eyes with a slight nod. "In any case, those of us with forced bindings became known as the Fallen, and we came here to Mu to create a new life. I would like to tell you that our troubles stopped there, but much happened, and I'm afraid the Council has banned, by seal, for any of us to speak of the details. What I *can* tell you is that it resulted in many of the Ancients in Mu lacking a Bound. There were too many losses, and some of the bindings were too unstable to complete. When my sons were born, we thought they would be Bound but, alas, my misfortunes seem never-ending. So, Fate, you were created for Kyou, so that you may both, one day, rule Mu."

Fate shifted on her chair. "So, I was really supposed to be High Queen one day."

Heqet looked at Hero and then back at Fate. "Our universe is a curious place. As fate would have it, you may still take the throne. Your name may have been more appropriate than any of us could have imagined."

Hero readjusted on the arm of the chair. "So, what has brought you here, really?"

Heqet sat up straight, wearing her shame across her face. "We've come, first, with our condolences and an apology for arriving far too late. Second, I want to offer Lady Fate the opportunity stolen from her as a child. If she should so choose, I am willing, and ready, to train her to become the queen she was created to be. Finally, I wanted to discuss a proper binding between the two of you."

At the mention of the binding, Akira frowned and jerked his head away.

Hero set his hand on Fate's shoulder and smiled. Albeit brief, he glimpsed Akira as he said, "I think a binding would be in order, if we are to be married."

Akira's head snapped back as he scowled at the pair, "You're engaged?"

The cat draped its tail around Akira's shoulders and neck, easing the strain that showed in his throat and veins.

Hero replied coolly. "Of course. You don't think I'd move her into the palace for play, do you? We may both be Caeles, but we have very different ideas about how to treat people."

Fate puzzled over their banter. She found it difficult to tell how well they knew each other. She took Hero's hand to show her solidarity with him.

Akira analyzed her hand on Hero's with a deepening frown.

Heqet clapped her hands together with a light pop. "Wonderful! This would be the next step for Hero's promotion and Fate's acclimation. Please allow me to aid in your transitions."

Hero answered with a bow. "Very well."

Fate nodded. "Yes, of course." Her gaze repeatedly wandered to Akira, partly in curiosity and partly in mistrust.

Akira held his cat, appearing more sullen and withdrawn than before, with his ankles and arms tucked in close and his multicolored eyes gleaming through the holes of his mask like two exotic jewels. His cat gently nuzzled his face, keeping a watchful eye on Hero and Fate as Akira pouted. Whatever snide comment he kept under his breath showed in his expression.

Fate pondered the depth of Akira's and Hero's relationship, and feared she'd accidentally interfered with clan laws. Hero had saved her from the brothel, and the last thing she wanted was to cause him any trouble.

Heqet stood and fanned out the skirt of her dress. "I must continue my planned schedule. I know that this meeting was both short and unexpected, but I thank you both for your time, and I look forward to preparing you for the journey ahead."

Akira slipped from the table and strolled towards the door, muttering to himself.

Fate squeezed Hero's hand tightly as she bowed to Queen Heqet. "Thank you for visiting us during your busy schedule."

Heqet beamed and gave a gentle wave. "Of course. One day, this will be your job. The least I can do is prepare you for it. When you are ready, come to the Capital and we'll get you settled. Hero, you will be much closer to your aunt. I'm certain she will be ecstatic to hear the news."

Hero ran his knuckle over the tip of his nose. "Certainly."

Akira sneered and shook his head.

Heqet ignored the sleight. "My husband will have training for *you* as well, I'm sure."

Hero nodded. "Let him know that I look forward to it."

Fate again looked at Akira as he opened the door, and the image of him turning back to her triggered the back part of her mind. She remembered this moment as though it had played a million times in her head. The sound of distant and garbled chanting rattled around in her thoughts.

Akira noticed the way Fate looked at him, and squared to face her. His expression grew dark and menacing, and a cryptic smile stretched across his face, obvious even behind the mask.

Heqet turned to leave and stopped upon noticing Akira. "What is that face?"

Akira stepped forward and pressed a gloved hand to his mask. "I'm not the only one with interesting eyes." He turned after his comment and exited the room without explanation, his cat trailing close behind.

Heqet sighed a final time. "He's an odd sort." She exited the room and followed the palace servants down the hall.

Hero gestured to them to show her out.

Once Heqet moved out of earshot, Fate turned to Hero. "How well do you know Akira?"

Hero scratched behind his ear with a grimace. "I know *of* him. We've had limited interaction, and it's never been pleasant. I'm not sure what to think, though. My mother and aunt never really trusted him."

"What do you mean?"

"He's Caeles but no one knows him. Our clan was always small. We all know each other by scent. It's unusual for us not to recognize one of our own."

"So, they don't know him?"

Hero shook his head. "Not at all. Even more bizarre, my aunt told me that he didn't smell of the Ussan."

Fate fought to follow Hero's meaning. "That's peculiar?"

"How should I explain? Even I smelled of the Ussan, when I was born here in Nex. It's a trait of our clans, Fox Clan and Wolf Clan alike."

"Hmm." Fate puzzled over Akira's strange appearance, attitude, and intentions.

"It seems a shame we can't seem to get along. There are so few of us left."

The High Queen kept Akira close, which should prove his worthiness. Still, the lingering feeling of suspicion made her question that line of reasoning. "So, he's close to the High Queen but not his own clan...."

Hero shrugged. "Don't spend too much time on it. He's a conundrum to everyone."

Fate heard his advice but doubted she was capable of heeding it.

He stepped around her and started for the door. "I still have things to do."

"Hmm," she said with a small nod, knowing he meant Persephone. She wanted to join him but could tell he wished to be alone.

"When you have a moment, I'll show you where I've laid Persephone to rest."

Hearing this left her with overwhelming dread and guilt. Poor little Persephone's death had been swallowed up by the Queen's visit, and she hoped for the chance to make up for her choices. It reminded her that Abyssus's death had also been overshadowed by the trial that followed. "We can go right now."

He shook his head, the corners of his mouth pulling down with a minor quiver. "Not now. Maybe tomorrow."

She hurried to his side. "Whenever you need me."

He nodded and, for the first time, leaned in and kissed her forehead.

She stood in a daze as he left the room, worried that she'd lost her hold on reality. At least she could keep herself busy studying the Caeles, and potentially learning more about the Fall of the One Hundred. Soon, she would be surrounded by people she barely knew. Research gave her a chance to protect her interests and, if all went well, save her sisters.

Early the following morning, Fate left her room, stretched her arms, and made way for the dining hall with a book in tow. Thoughts of the tapestry continuously resurfaced but she couldn't seem the find the right opportunity to ask about it.

Given the events of the previous day, she'd fully expected the snowfall outside the window on her way down the stairs.

Hero sat downstairs in the dark, drinking a cup of tea and staring out at the yard. The grey tone only made him appear more downcast.

Fate crossed the room to stand beside him. "Good morning, Hero." At times like this, she only knew how to press onward. Dwelling on sad things often made things worse and longer-lasting... though she understood his feelings entirely.

Hero moved at half-pace to look at her, his expression somewhat glazed. "Hmm."

"I wanted to ask you about something. Perhaps I'm sticking my nose where it doesn't belong, but nevertheless...."

He tilted his head slightly.

She held the book forward against the skirt of her gown. "What lies behind the Moon Drip tapestry in the left wing hall?"

He glanced around the dining hall and placed his cup down, then looked back up at Fate for a moment. Eventually, he stood and moved close enough that his chin almost touched her shoulder. "Come with me."

She followed him, but found his secrecy curious.

Surely, someone must have noticed it by now. It's not completely inconspicuous.

Hero led her to the study and stood in front of the tapestry, scanning her in a dubious manner. He seemed to suspect something but didn't say what bothered him. Again, he checked his surroundings, removed a key from his pocket, and unlocked the door. He ushered her inside and locked the door again as soon as they entered.

Around them, a two-story study teemed with scrolls and books. A polished desk held peculiar golden tools which, at closer inspection, appeared to be used for astronomy.

Hero tucked his hands back towards the door. "How did you find this place?"

"What do you mean? I just lifted the tapestry. Anyone could find it."

He squinted. *"Nolai."*

'Interesting.'

She recalled the meaning from his previous use and felt comfortable responding. "How so?"

He crossed his arms and circled, inspecting her from all sides and angles.

She opened her hands to each side. "The door is hidden in plain sight. I'm sure any number of people have noticed it by now."

He pressed a finger to his chin and contemplated. "The door is concealed by illusion. Neither Abyssus nor I would attempt to hide something with such little effort. If you truly wish to hide something, you do it correctly."

"Illusion? How?"

"The books in this study are outlawed texts that I've hidden, with help from a trusted ally. You wonder how Abyssus and I know what we do?" Hero waved a hand out to the library. "Here is your answer."

Fate gazed up towards the ceiling at an image of space, painted with the constellations. Everything she sought to know lay within reach. "It's like your own private Hall of Records."

"Correct." He tapped a foot and stared off, his expression concentrated and borderline irritated. "You're welcome to read any of the texts from this library, as long as you keep it, and the books, hidden. I like to keep things organized, so if you want to borrow something, just ask and I'll retrieve it for you."

"Thank you! I'll make sure to use it wisely. The more information I have access to, the more I can learn and assist."

He nodded. "Very well. I trust you won't let me down."

She turned back to the embellished wooden shelves and their plethora of knowledge.

Now... where do I begin?

25

CRYSTALLIZED

Fate remained in her bedroom reading for the rest of the day, learning more about Mu. She discovered the majority of books Hero kept pertained to Undal. The most famous stories told of the Caeles Ruler, Emperor Viro, the sealing of the Spinner, and a pair of warriors known as the Twin Wolves. None of it explained Akira and his strangely colored eyes.

She kept at her research, reminded of Abyssus. Just as he'd said, she wanted to thank him for his constant efforts and diligence towards learning and studying about the world they lived in, and, if needed, to wrench the answers so his sacrifice held value.

She lifted her head to address a knock at her door. "Enter."

The door opened and Lara stood before her, swaying awkwardly from side to side.

Fate stared at her unwelcomed opponent, and rested her hand on the book to keep her place as she awaited the next wave of verbal assaults.

Lara fidgeted and swayed, all the while strangling her arm as if it might escape her body.

Fate finally asked, "Did you need something?"

Lara winced. "I wanted to make amends."

"For what?" She strained against a sneer.

Lara looked around the room and moved back to the doorway. "I was rude to you before. I said some things I shouldn't have."

Fate thought about the girl before her, a Rahma most likely under the influence of miasma poisoning, one who cared deeply about Hero, and braced herself for an undeniable truth. "You were only trying to protect your friend."

Lara nodded. "I know, but you are important to him, and I should have accepted that."

Fate chewed the inside of her cheek, uncomfortable with Lara's confession. She wondered what had brought about the sudden revelation and guilt. "Thank you."

"I'd like to invite you to tea."

"Oh." She looked down at the books on the table.

Lara continued, sounding distressed. "So... we can get to know one another properly. It would be bad if we fought all of the time."

Fate thought about Heqet's recent visit and the implications of declining a fellow Royal in a formal request. When she and Hero became High King and Queen, Lara would take the throne in Nitor. As much as she hated to concede to the hateful girl, etiquette required her to do so. "That sounds nice."

Lara laughed nervously. "I've had the cook prep the water and bring us some caramels."

"Oh, you mean right now?"

She slouched. "I'm sorry. I didn't realize you were busy. I didn't really think this through, I guess."

Fate rose from the table, not wanting to miss this chance to settle their differences. "No, it's fine. I can come back to it later."

"Really? I wouldn't want to inconvenience you."

"It's fine. I think it would be nice for us to get to know one another."

Lara beamed and motioned for Fate to follow her down the long hall.

As they strolled, Fate looked at the pictures hanging on the walls. She usually kept out of the deep parts of the palace, to avoid getting lost. Images of the other kingdoms livened up the walls—lands of trees, seas, and small villages, all of which she one day hoped to visit.

"I haven't been down this way," she said.

Lara looked back as she walked, her brown braids swinging behind her like two tails. "Really? Oh, you'll love it. This wing is much brighter. My room and Lady Isis's rooms are down this way, not to mention the King's."

Fate scolded herself for being ignorant of something right under her nose. If she continued to let a Rahma surpass her in knowledge and talent, she would never make a proper queen. "I guess I've been preoccupied."

"Completely understandable. You just lost your brother, after all. Who wouldn't be?"

She marveled at this side of Lara. Her posture and demeanor seemed like that of a different person from the girl who'd shouted at her in the kitchen. "Thank you. Sometimes I feel like I'm struggling to keep up."

Lara entered a sunroom filled with golden statues and white marble tables. At the far end of the room there stood a stone wall with three cream curtains. Atop a hand-woven rug sat a simple table, covered by a white lace tablecloth and flanked by two big blue chairs.

Fate followed Lara over to the table, admiring the display of small delicacies and a porcelain tea set with hand-painted roses. The pastries stacked on the raised platter reminded her of something Abyssus would have delighted in.

Lara sat on the chair closest to the pastries, then reached out and stole one, licking off the frosting. "I love these things. I've asked the chef to teach me how to make them but she just laughs and says it's her pleasure."

Fate giggled as she picked up a tea bag from a small bowl at the center of the table and dropped it into her cup. "Sounds like her. I don't know how she makes such magnificent things."

"Right!" Lara grabbed a tea bag for herself and plopped it into her cup as she took a larger bite from her goodie.

"What are these? Are they the caramels you mentioned?" Fate leaned forward and collected a small brown square from the plate in front of her.

Lara pointed at the plate, picking up her tea to sip it and clear the food from her mouth before responding. "They are. Those things are to die for, really. You should have more than one, if your figure allows it."

Fate bit into the heavenly morsel, and instantly her mouth watered from the slice of bliss. Her eyes widened and she covered her mouth as she quickly devoured the treat. "You aren't kidding."

"I told you... to die for. She really outdid herself with those."

Fate couldn't resist the morsels. She snatched a second from the plate, and quickly sipped her tea, letting the flavors blend together. She savored the caramel and the moment she shared with Lara. It felt good to finally have something move in a positive direction after her recent traumas. "I'm glad you came to get me."

"Are you?" Lara finished her pastry with a smile.

Fate polished off another caramel and took a quick sip of her tea. "I am. I don't have many friends outside the brothel."

"Do you have *any*?"

Fate thought about it for a moment. "Well, I guess, if you don't count Hero, I have two."

"Really? Who?"

She shrugged with a questioning grin. "Fortis and Firmus?"

Lara stared at her with a flat expression. "The Igni are your only friends. That figures."

"What do you mean?"

She flashed another pleasant smile. "They're sluts and you're a whore."

Fate choked on her tea. She set down her teacup and studied Lara's expression again for a moment, trying to decipher if she'd misheard. Neither girl spoke for an extended time, and as the moments passed, she questioned why she engaged in a tea party with someone who'd hated her so deeply since she first arrived.

The room suddenly felt small, and the heat from Lara's hatred suffocated her.

Lara's smile waned and she returned to her dead stare, as if she was not truly looking at Fate but at something in her own mind.

Fate lowered her gaze to the plate before her and placed her hands on the arms of her chair. "I think maybe I should go."

Lara laughed and kicked her feet playfully. "What? Why? We're having such fun. Do you want a cupcake?"

Fate hesitated, feeling as though she'd imagined Lara's slight.

Lara frowned. "What's wrong?"

Fate shook her head. "Oh... nothing. What were we talking about?"

"Um, friends you have other than me. You said Fortis and Firmus, which makes sense since they Fortuna's brothers."

Fate took another sip of tea, doubting her memory. She eyed Lara, who drank her tea and grabbed another pastry.

Lara took a bite and moaned with glee. "Before, if I ate even one of these things I gained weight."

"What do you mean *before*?"

Lara leapt from her seat and placed a hand on her hip. "Now I can eat these all day and not gain anything."

Fate looked at Lara's figure, noticing her fit curves for the first time. The realization made her take note of the difference in her overall appearance.

Lara seemed to have become more attractive with each passing moment. Upon closer inspection, her hair was no longer brown but auburn. It shone healthily in the light. Her skin shared its glow, and something about her features differed—her lively eyes and the balance of her facial features. She seemed renewed... no, better than before.

Fate had never paid close enough attention to place what precisely had changed about Lara, only to notice that *something* differed. "What's—"

"Happening?" Lara finished her question. "I've bested you. Not that it's an accomplishment to brag about."

The room swayed around Fate in a blur and she braced herself against the table.

Lara cackled. "You really are dumb, you know that?"

Fate stood with a sudden rush of fear. Her skin felt hot and her mouth watered again. The air in the room grew too thin to take a full breath. She placed a hand against her stomach and bent over the table, taking shallow breaths.

Lara followed Fate as she staggered towards the door. "What's wrong, Fate? Not feeling well? That's what happens when a filthy whore thinks she can stroll in and lure my Hero into her ridiculous plot to become High Queen. No one cares about your goals! We only care about Hero!"

Fate clawed at her burning throat as she stumbled onto the floor, coughing and gasping.

Lara antagonized her happily while circling. "I honestly didn't think you would come so easily. I thought, *wow, she's really going to follow me all the way*? And you did."

Fate dragged her failing body across the room, heaved a stomach full of black goo onto the floor, and sobbed.

Lara squatted next to her. "That's disgusting. If you weren't going to die, I'd tell you to clean yourself up."

Fate's vision jumped and swayed, and ringing filled her ears as blackness closed in from all angles. The sound of shrieking filled the room, and her breathing grew labored.

Lara, seemingly unaware of the horrific sound, carefully pulled Fate's hair away from her face. "There we go. I want to see your face."

Rage built inside Fate's heart as the darkness surrounded her. Her last breath burned like fire as she fell into the darkness.

Fate floated in the cold embrace of space and listened to the soft chiming of bells. The small twinkle of starlight glistened all around her as she drifted. "Crystal?"

A woman's voice agreed. "Hmm."

"It sounds nice."

"You're just going to let her kill us like that?"

Fate spoke, her voice breaking into three tones: a whisper, a deep voice, and a high, melodic voice. "No, I am not."

She floated down to a gleam below, and stood on the reflection of space as the unseen crystal chimed around her. In the distance, a large object radiated immense light. As Fate drew closer to it, the chiming intensified. A chrysalis hovered, most evidently the source of the sound. She reached out to it and ran her fingers down the rough surface. The energy made her jittery, even with a small touch.

The chiming sound broke as a crackling filled her ears, and a fissure ran down the front of the chrysalis. She withdrew with a gasp, forced to stop as an icy hand grasped her shoulder.

A man's voice whispered from behind, *"Wake up."*

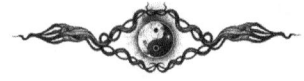

Fate lurched upright, her hair weightlessly swimming through the air. It danced and swayed around her.

Lara jumped and fell onto her back, and scrambled away.

Fate doubled over, spewed more of the black liquid onto the floor, and unleashed a blood-curdling scream. A pulse of energy shot out from under her, striking Lara and the surrounding furniture. The table shook and the chairs splintered as they flew from their places. The tea set shattered with the piercing sound.

Lara receded until she pressed herself against one of the tables. She screamed as a nearby vase exploded, and shielded herself from the spray of glass.

Fate lunged forward onto all fours and twisted her head to the side. Her dark hair, now soaked in black fluid, stretched towards the frantic Lara like a tentacle.

Before Lara could escape, Fate wrapped her in the dense strands of hair and dragged her close. Black smoke rose from the ground.

Lara's terror rushed through Fate's veins in a flood of sheer ecstasy.

Lara cried, "Fate, stop!"

Fate's fury welled up in plumes of black smoke and tendrils. She dragged the thrashing Lara closer, and inspected the pathetic creature flailing in her clutches.

Anima and ether moved through her mortal form, and she growled with displeasure. Memories flashed and faded fast as her pulse quickened, and thick black liquid oozed from her ears, eyes, nose, and mouth.

Hero burst through the doors and shouted, "Fate?"

He slid to a stop and leapt back, slamming into Akira as the odd man appeared in a flash of light and black smoke.

Akira shoved Hero to one side as he bounded to a safe place on top of one of the tables.

Fate twisted her head, taking in the energy each of them emitted.

Lara's muffled cry rang out the moment she saw Hero, but his eyes remained fixed on Fate.

He stretched his hand out towards her without a word, and stepped forward.

Akira bolted between them, slapping Hero's hand back as long dark tendrils of matted wet hair extended from Fate. He snapped, "That is not Fate."

Hero said nothing but pushed Akira aside and focused only on Fate. "Return to me."

Pain coursed through her body unlike any she'd ever known. A mixture of spiritual and emotional agony locked up the flow of her energy, and she let out a wretched and shrill scream. Darkness billowed from the ground beneath her.

Lara thrashed violently as Fate increased the pressure of her grip, choking the life from the helpless girl.

Fate marveled as blood poured from Lara's body... the way darkness did from her own. She listened in the mortal silence to Lara's last garbled breath.

Once the hateful girl died, Fate continued to constrict her until Lara's bones snapped and her chest finally collapsed. She then turned her dark eyes to Hero, and spoke in three separate voices. *"Aula et media. Sa hau muren sosae il acesu aula durul fenne?"*

'I hate this place. Why would anyone want to live somewhere so... quiet?'

Hero gaped at her, giving time for Akira to intervene by stepping between them.

Akira kneeled. *"Ara dia ou'nan."*

'I offer my assistance to you.'

She studied his mask carefully, reminded of something lost. *"Kai setil."*

'Remove your mask.'

"Hau so'er dusom ou." He looked up at her and then stood.

'I would if I could.'

She dropped Lara's lifeless body and hissed, *"Irln ya."*

'I know you.'

"Ye."

'Yes, you do.'

Her power diminished and her body convulsed, forcing her to spew more of the black tar. Small blue orbs of ether rose out of the black smoke and floated past her. She gasped and took a step back, and collapsed onto the floor beside Lara's corpse. Her vision dimmed and she turned to look into Lara's lifeless eyes.

"Sa veir naim? Nuin nohs pa olesa... Anwa som de cai."

'Why do they die? It seems so unfair they cannot come back. She really was quite clever.'

Akira moved closer but froze as pointed tendrils of hair threatened him. He huffed and then retreated, seeming heavy of heart as he glared at Hero.

Hero inched forward, keeping himself low and mindful of his surroundings.

Fate continued her exhausted and weary thoughts. "*Pa onok kun jet ge deinus. Olk ilu ge jyadu reh otwam de rai.*"

'The Grandmaster should not have left them in such a state. It may be the most irresponsible thing he's ever done.'

Black fluid slipped from her eyes, blurring her vision further. Her heart ached with understanding as she slipped into darkness.

The sound of birds chirping awakened Fate. Light stung her eyes, and she winced from the pain. Every bone, muscle, and vein in her body throbbed.

Chi leaned forward on her chair beside the bed. "Don't move. The effects of the poison are going to cause you some discomfort, but it's best if you lie as still as possible. We are extracting it as best we can."

Fate moved her mouth, noticing the stiff ache of her jaw and the dry scratch of her voice. "We?"

Heqet entered and nearly dropped a tea tray at the sight of Fate's open eyes. "Thanks to all that is!"

Fate tried to recall the incident. Her recollection, hazy at best, brought images of Lara inviting her to tea, then the sensation of choking, and finally an image of Hero with his hand stretched out to her. "Hero...."

Chi nodded. "Hmm. He and Akira brought you here. Appears they caught her in the act."

Heqet sat on the edge of the bed and helped Fate with a sip of tepid tea. "Here. Your throat must be dry."

The tea burned as it slid down her raw throat, but soothed her at the same time. Rising tears caused her nose to block and made it difficult to breathe.

Chi stroked Fate's arm. "The pain will subside soon. You are doing well. Most would have died. You are stronger than you seem."

Fate attempted to reclaim her memories, but they dwindled in the fog of her mind. All she grasped at slipped away, leaving her with a feeling of unfulfilled hope and a horrific ache in her bones.

Akira appeared in a corner of the room with glowing eyes. Black wisps of smoke clung to his pants and coat, but soon dissipated. "How is she?"

Fate stared at the queen's escort, questioning his real identity. Something about him left her with a twinge of concern. Without cause, she felt defensive whenever he was near, and he seemed to know it.

Chi replied to Akira's question. "Surprisingly well."

Akira narrowed his eyes. "She is full of surprises, no?"

Heqet smiled down at Fate, taking her hand into her own. "I'm sure she will change Mu in ways no one could ever imagine."

A small smirk formed on Akira's face. "Indeed."

Hero strode in, uncharacteristically frazzled, hair stuck to his sweat-drenched brow. "Fate!" He rushed to her side and pressed his face to her free hand. "I thought we'd lost you."

She wondered if he was truly as upset as he appeared, or if he had been physically active before coming into the room.

Heqet ran her hand over Hero's head. "It's not safe for the two of you in Nex. You should stay at the palace."

Hero nodded. "Anything to keep her safe."

Akira crossed his arms and nodded. "Agreed. It's wise to keep them close. There's no better way to keep an eye on them both."

Questions piled up in Fate's mind. She wondered if her sudden surge of suspicion stemmed from deduction or from miasma-induced paranoia. It seemed Mu was full of liars and manipulators, which left to question who she could truly trust. Her eyes moved from Akira to Hero and back again. Both vied for her trust, and she hesitated to offer it to either.

Hero had won her confidence when he rescued her from the brothel, but he'd clearly kept secrets and admitted lying to everyone, including her.

Akira made her skin tingle and her heart weary, but she felt drawn to him at the same time. The two Caeles were locked in a mystery, and they made her feel insane. She wondered if the memories dancing about in the deep recesses of her mind held the explanation as to why.

For now, she needed to rest and allow her weakened body to recover.

Chi eventually chased everyone but Hero from the room, and then left the pair alone.

Hero stroked Fate's forehead. "Sleep. I'll stay with you until you're well again."

She liked the warmth of his touch, but still felt nothing akin to romantic love. The unique qualities of their relationship bordered on peculiarity, and this stirred fear for the future. She wrestled with her feelings until finally surrendering to sleep.

Fate remained bedridden and dreamless for several days. Each day, her body grew stronger but her mind darkened with concerns, not only for her future, but for the future of Mu. She kept her thoughts to herself in spite of the abundance of visits from doting caretakers.

Hero never ventured too far. He kept by her side as promised and tended to her every need.

She watched him closely, wanting to believe that she could place her trust in him, but something deep inside warned her that she must observe and keep quiet. As she recovered, she decided to place her focus on Abyssus's journals, before the Capital's responsibilities would consume all of her free time.

She tired of lying in bed, pulled the blankets from her body, and dropped her legs over the side of the mattress. Her feet dangled above the floor, tingling from the icy air. It felt nice against her skin, especially after spending so long cooped up.

Hero roused from Chi's chair and stretched. "Welcome back."

Fate observed his delicate appearance with deep consideration. Everything about Hero seemed striking and elegant. Few people ever managed to leave her with a sense of awe. She kept her thoughts to herself, though, and did her best to smile with genuine affection. "Thank you."

"Do you need anything?"

She shook her head.

He stood, straightened his vest and jacket, and stretched his stiff back. "Are you intending to get up?"

She gripped the mattress on each side of her. "I am."

He quickly moved to her side to support her by the waist. "Let me help you."

She leaned on him and stood for the first time since the poisoning. Her body drifted on its own, detached from her mind, and her feet felt as though they might float away.

Hero chuckled, tickling her ear with his breath. "Trust me, I've got you."

She let herself go completely, and he held her with a gentle smile. "See? Where would you like to go?"

Fate considered his offer. "I never got the chance to explore Inoue. We returned to Nex so quickly."

Hero drew his mouth to one side in his usual way. "Fair enough, but we'll need to get you dressed first."

Fate grasped the neck of her sleeping gown. "Good point."

He laughed, and his radiance lit up the room.

She wondered if it was all in her imagination, or if Hero's mood somehow affected the environment for some other reason. She knew that it stormed when he was upset, and froze when he was sad.

She needed answers, and hoped to find them in the Capital.

26

BURIED TRUTHS

The sun cast long, soft beams of light over Inoue as Hero led Fate out of the cottage and down a sloping path to overlook the city.

She held onto him with one hand for stability, and ran her other over the woven silks of the gown Heqet had provided for her. In the Capital, plush clouds passed overhead and rays of sunlight reached down onto rooftops, chasing away the shadows. Aromas of sea salt and spices permeated the cool breeze.

"This is all so different." She gazed out at the massive city, from the small cottages and nearby shops, to the towering silver palace on a hilltop in the distance. The vision before her sprawled out like the tail of a magnificent bird.

After spending so many turns in the grey confines of Nex, Inoue overwhelmed her senses. The buildings gleamed with their smooth white surfaces as flecks of silver in their walls shimmered in the light. Small, tightly-packed white stones formed the streets and walkways, making them seem cleaner than possible, and the city felt brighter for it. Everything she set eyes upon sang of its Ancient heritage.

She turned to the sound of delicate chiming and spied the crystal trees of the Ussan peeking over rooftops in the distance. A lump formed in her throat as the sounds filled not only her ears but her soul.

Hero patted her arm. "Welcome to Inoue."

She hesitated, dumbfounded as people bustled about. This place made her feel small, and the sensation reminded her of something, but she failed to grasp it once again. A hole in her heart cried out and tears slipped from her eyes.

Hero's smile faded. "Do you need to go back inside?"

She shook her head. It seemed silly to cry now, after she'd managed to keep herself composed during some of the worst times of her life. "No, it's just really beautiful."

He wiped her tears. "No need to cry about it."

His intentional rudeness made her laugh aloud.

He too looked out over the city with a sense of wonder. "So, what would you like to see first?"

She shrugged, still lost in the awe-inspiring display. "Everything."

He laughed and led her into the city, careful not to move faster than her injured body allowed. "Why don't we try one thing at a time, and see how we do?"

Each step brought her a new level of excitement, filling her with a rush of energy and exhilaration. Although still recovering from the poison, she felt better than ever before. She took in the crisp ocean air and exhaled her lingering concerns, to give way for a newfound hope.

Hero peeked at her with a placid smile.

Fate caught him out of the corner of her eye. "What?"

"You look happy, that's all."

She admired a cart of pastries as they passed by.

He glanced back. "Do you want one?"

She shook her head. "No, they remind me of Abyssus."

"I'm sorry."

"Don't be. It's a good thing." The experience helped her come to terms with the loss of her brother. She hadn't dealt with her feelings properly, and had even shut Hero out when Persephone died, but looking out at the majesty of Inoue reminded her how important life was. She decided to honor Abyssus by living to the fullest, and by protecting Hero.

"Do you need to sit?"

She squeezed his arm tighter. "Not at all. As long as you're here with me, I would like to look around some more."

He paused, pursed his lips, and blinked hard before nodding his head with a subtle smile. "Anywhere in particular you'd like to go?"

Fate looked out at the crystal trees spread out over the rooftops, and pointed. "I'd like to see the forest."

When her gaze returned to Hero, he looked paler than usual. His eyes locked on the treetops with foreboding. "The Ussan?"

"Hmm." She studied his expression, unable to pinpoint the cause of his discomfort.

"It's loud there."

She fumbled for words. "What do you mean 'loud'?"

His eyes shifted to meet hers. "You can't hear it?"

She listened to the chiming and reflected on her memories from childhood, knowing that he referred to the voices of the forest. Although she could no longer hear them, she hoped that, if they moved closer, the forest would speak to her again. "The chiming?"

He nodded. "If you want to go, I'll take you, but it's too far for you to walk from here, at least until you get stronger. We should catch a carriage."

He guided Fate to a bench, sat her down, and hurried down the street.

No sooner had he vanished into the bustle than Akira leaned down over her shoulder and hummed.

Fate scooted to the far end of the bench. "What do *you* want?"

He took a seat next to her, wearing his usual fitted red suit and a frown. "Rude. I came to check on you."

She masked her surprise and calmed her racing heart, convincing herself that he frightened her rather than exhilarated her. In truth, she found it difficult to distinguish one from the other. Her whole life, feelings drifted just out of reach, making precious any sensation strong enough for her to grasp.

She raised her chin and said, "I'm well, thank you."

He leaned closer to her, curiosity dominating his gaze. "That was quite an episode you had there."

"Yes. I'd like to put it behind me and focus on things to come."

He grinned, looking smug. "I'll bet. It's not every day you crush the life out of the King's ward."

Fate froze, watching his face for signs of deception, but he merely stared contentedly at her, a slight smirk on his lips. "Lara?"

"Oh yes. It was a glorious thing to witness."

She searched her mind but recalled nothing of Lara beyond them sitting together, talking, and sipping tea. "I wouldn't...."

He moved closer, allowing his lips to graze her ear. "You wrenched the life from her."

She jerked away from him and scoured the area for Hero. Many strangers traveled the stone-paved paths to purchase from vendors and chat around the Centre. However, Hero remained out of sight.

Fate stood up and rounded the bench, her legs wobbling like a newborn foal as she tried to put some distance between her and Akira.

He also stood, keeping an ever-watchful eye on every move she made. "What's wrong? It's not like it was an accident. Some part of you must remember."

She shook her head and backed away from him.

He calmly pursued her, taking a step only when she did. The glimmer in his polychromatic eyes made him seem more predator than man. "It *is* in there, isn't it? Can you hear it?"

Her body shuddered under the duress. "Stop."

Rapid footsteps approached.

Fate turned her head and spied Hero sprinting towards them, dodging people as he crossed the Centre.

"Hero," she called weakly.

Akira shook his head. "You think you can trust him? Do you even know who or *what* he is?"

Fate spun to face Akira again, to determine if he spoke the truth.

His gaze stayed unwavering as his resolve. He whispered before Hero arrived, "Soon you'll understand." He disappeared in a whirl of black smoke as Hero reached Fate.

Hero looked behind him to ensure Akira had actually left. "What did he do?"

Fate rested her head on his chest, relieved to have him back. "Nothing. He just frightens me."

He let her rest and regain her composure. "Better?"

"Hmm."

"I think it's best we return home for now. I'll take you tomorrow."

Fate accepted his suggestion as her body trembled, warning of the impending exhaustion.

He walked her to the carriage, and they returned to Chi's cottage.

Chi paced the small yard as they arrived. She yelled at Hero as he helped Fate out. "It is too soon. What were you thinking?"

"I was thinking that we've both spent too much of our lives in cages."

She crossed her arms, red-faced.

Fate looked at Hero and saw her one true ally in the world. He may be odd, difficult, and a liar, but he protected and defended her more than anyone dared, even more so than Fortuna.

He continued. "I am sorry we distressed you, though."

Chi wore her concern as comfortably as she wore her armor. "I was about to call out the guard."

Fate clung to Hero as her strength dwindled. "We're sorry."

Chi walked forward, threw out her arms, and embraced them. "Come inside. I will make some tea." After a heavy sigh, she opened the door and ushered them inside.

Hero walked Fate to the den and set her on one of the chairs as Chi headed for the furnace to prepare tea.

Fate looked around the small room filled with books, and enjoyed the warmth of the fire. Even though she had been there for a time, she only just noticed a station covered with bottles and bowls. "What are those?"

Hero glanced over his shoulder at the work desk. "Chi's medicines. That's how she saved you."

She considered her conversation with Akira and finally asked, "Hero, what happened?"

"What do you mean?"

"In Nex."

He stared at the fire with a locked jaw.

She waited until his silence grew unbearable. "Did I kill Lara?"

He pressed his hands together and sucked in air over his teeth. "You did... in self-defense. She poisoned you."

She grasped at the fleeting memories of her and Lara talking and laughing. "I don't understand."

"I'm not sure what exactly transpired, but it was clear that she put crystal in the caramel. That's why we needed Chi. To be honest, I'm not sure you would have survived if it were not for Chi and Akira."

"Akira?"

"Hmm. He used his flash step to get you here. There's no way I could have done so at that distance. I owe him your life."

She sat back on her chair to mull over the facts. The constant discomfort Akira caused made it difficult to imagine ever placing her trust in him. He set her nerves on end, yet he'd clearly made a great effort to keep her alive and well. "I see."

"Still, there *is* something off about him, so I'd be careful."

Chi entered with a tray. "Be careful of what?"

Hero sat up straight and took a cup of Chi's spice tea. "Of Akira."

"Hmm." She handed Fate a cup, took one for herself, and set the tray down before continuing. "He is an odd sort. I am not sure I fully trust him either. He smells unnatural for a Caeles."

Fate recalled Hero's explanation from earlier. Their view of Akira appeared to be consistent by her calculations. "Why does the Queen keep him around?"

Chi sipped her tea and collected a book from one of the shelves. "They are friends."

Fate raised a brow. "That's all? How did they meet?"

Chi chortled as she moved to the hallway. "That is a very good question for which I have no answer. I will tell you when I find out."

Hero motioned to the book. "You off?"

Chi held the book up. "Not all of us have free time, dear boy. I still have much to learn." She then strolled out of the room, book and tea in hand.

Fate held the hot cup in her hands and watched the steam rise. It baffled her that the Capital ran with such ambiguity, and even more so that the High Queen kept someone Tainted at her side without anyone knowing of his origins or intentions.

Hero patted Fate's knee. "Don't get spoiled."

"I won't," she answered, looking up at the bookshelves.

"She says... eyeing Chi books."

She set her tea down on a small end table and stood to get a better look. With thoughts of death and illness out of her mind, her determination to study returned as strong as ever. She hoped that Chi might have a book on the Tocsin, but most seemed to be books on plants and tonics. Then a thin red book caught her eye, and she pulled it from the shelf, noting that it lacked a title. As she ran her hand over the rough surface, she spotted the number two in the corner.

In disbelief, she clawed it open to see the writing inside. Abyssus's penmanship stretched across the aged pages from top to bottom. As she confirmed it, she released a string of incomprehensible shouts.

Hero jumped to his feet as Chi rushed in from the other room. "What's wrong?"

Fate beamed. "It's Abyssus's. It's his journal."

Chi stared blankly. "I don't follow."

Hero pointed at the shelf. "She found it on your shelf."

Chi stuck out her bottom lip with a pout, reminding Fate much of Hero. "I do not see how. He has not been here in many turns."

Fate held the journal close. "He planned it."

Hero snapped his head around. "What?"

Fate nodded. "He did. He must have known something we didn't. He always kept secrets from me."

Chi tried to comfort her. "Brothers do that sort of thing."

Fate shook her head. "No... he knew something." She looked at the journal, inspecting it more carefully. Inside the cover, she found an inscription of the title, *Lords of Light and Shadow*. Below that, Abyssus had etched a series of odd words. "Perhaps, if we can decipher this...."

Hero lifted his chin and examined the curious text. "The Language of Ages."

Chi shook her head. "I will leave you to it, but stay out of trouble, and Fate, make sure to take your tonic. I left it on the nightstand."

Hero waved. "Thank you."

Fate neglected a proper response to Chi's departure, and spun the book back so she could see the text again. "Is it?"

Hero answered with confidence. "Hmm."

She eyed him. "So, you can tell me what it says?"

"Of course. Here, give it to me."

She handed him the journal, eager to learn its contents.

Hero quickly scanned the journal, reading over the subject matter in half the time a normal Ancient would require.

Fate marveled at his intellect, astonished that so many allowed him to waste away, locked in the palace under Rahma rule.

Once he'd read enough, he looked up. "It's about the Lords of Light and Shadow."

"It said that in the title."

He snickered as though appreciating her challenge. "Apparently, all of them must gather in the Mortal Realm to stop some kind of calamity."

Fate leaned forward. "The Calamity refers to the Spinner, right? So, it's referring to the mythology taught by the Grim."

Hero shook his head. "No, it's presented as fact, and says that if they aren't able to meet... the Mortal Realm will be destroyed."

She leaned on her knees with her elbows. "Mortal Realm as in Mu."

"Yes." He continued as he leafed through the journal. "Mu, Thule...."

"What kind of calamity could she cause?"

He twisted his mouth, as usual, and reviewed more of the journal. After a moment, he closed it again. "It doesn't really specify. All I can say is that there is mention of the Demon of Undal, the Plague, and repeated mention of the Calamity. Now, you're correct about the Spinner being the Calamity, but the Demon of Undal is someone altogether different."

"The Demon of Undal? Who's that?"

"One of the Twin Wolves," he said. "They were real people, a Bound pair, caught up in the collapse of the Three-Tier Balance. As the story goes, one of them was killed and the other became the demon. It's a Caeles tale and a warning to those who cross the clan, more of a scare tactic than anything—hurt a Caeles and the demon will get you."

She ruminated. "That sounds vaguely familiar. I think I read about them, Weren't they revered?"

He trailed off, deep in thought. "Hmm, and very dangerous."

All the mention of folklore as history left Fate feeling uncertain.

Hero tapped his lip and leaned back on the legs of his chair to stare at the ceiling. "According to other books and folklore I've read, the Fates are the actual origin of the Plague and not the Caeles."

"But I only know of two people who are Tainted, and you're both Caeles."

"You're not wrong, but it didn't start with us, so it's plausible that the stories could be accurate."

Fate tried to follow his train of thought. "Do you believe that?"

He sat forward, still pondering. "I do. It makes sense if the stories of Undal were fact. The Three Fates were the keepers of mortality. The Spinner, according to folklore, also decided the fate of the Mortal Realms. So, if you connect the two, the Spinner *must* be one of them. If you add that to the Verna sealing the Spinner, it all makes sense. They needed to stop the spread of the Plague."

"Oh, so the Verna sealed her?"

"Hmm. It was brutal, and I think a lot of people tried to hide it."

Fate ran through the details. "So, they sealed her to stop her from Fating people like in the children's song, But aren't there still two more Fates?"

He showed his gloved hand. "...and there's still a Plague."

She stared down at the books. "So, it didn't work."

"If these tales are real and not myth, as the Council would have us believe—then we can trace the Fates and the Plague back to the destruction of the largest city in Undal, the Ignis Capital of Chien. It would also explain the collapse of the Crystal Empire and, finally, the Fall of the One Hundred."

"The One Hundred?"

He paused and gave her a curious look, as though trying to discern if she really didn't know the answer. "The original clans of Thule—they were all crushed by the Demon of Undal."

"Was the Demon also responsible for Chien and the Crystal Empire?"

"No. There aren't any complete records I am aware of that explain what happened in the Crystal Empire, but the destruction of Chien was caused by the Verna Twins—mainly Verna Noctuae."

Fate leaned closer. "I haven't read anything on the Verna Twins."

"You won't. The Council completely erased them from history."

"Why?"

"Isn't that the question? It all leads back to what happened in the Crystal Empire. Stories say that the Plague originated in the Caeles family, in the heart of Old Ussan, and that they spread the infection to the Verna family. They say that's why they had to seal the Spinner. Still, if you believe the Spinner and the other Fates are the real cause of the Plague, then it begs the question. It still doesn't explain the Verna Twin's widespread rampage. They practically wiped out the continent."

Fate scooted to the edge of her chair. "Why would the Council hide something like that?"

He shrugged. "Trying to contain the Plague, most likely. Not doing a very good job, though."

"Hey, if the Council erased the Verma Twins from history, how do you know about them?"

A curious expression crossed his face. "Look around. I collect illegal books and documents."

Her frustration finally boiled over. "Wouldn't it be better to share these with people? Help bring the truth to light instead of hiding it away?"

"And start another war?"

"Well, it can't remain a secret forever. The Council should have just told everyone what happened."

"Sure, but then someone has to take the blame. They wanted to make sure it wasn't them."

She huffed. "We need to find the rest of the journals. I'm sure Abyssus stumbled onto something."

Hero frowned. "You need to rest."

"I've rested well enough."

He looked down his nose as he held up the journal. "I'll read through this in more detail. You should bathe, take your tonic, and get some sleep. Tomorrow, I'll take you anywhere you want to go. We can go to the Ussan or search for the next journal, but we won't go anywhere if that poison kills you."

Fate sighed at hearing the truth put so plainly. She needed to find the journals, the only connection she had to Abyssus. Finding them would ease the loss of him. She wanted to tell Hero, but knew the information changed little about her condition. She slowly stood and complied with his request.

"Thank you," he said as she returned to her forced recuperation.

She entered the room Chi had prepared for her and flopped on the bed, defying at least one part of his request. She lay there for a brief moment before realizing that her mind had drifted. As sleep crept in, it lured her into the darkness once more.

27

A SONG IN THE TREES

Fate stared at the large bookshelf, which towered endlessly above her. She then looked down, where the floor should be, into the vast darkness of space. Stars twinkled and hummed, singing of her return to the Room of Forgotten Memories.

Sensing a presence, she turned to find the small white-haired boy in the blinding mask. "Leoht?"

The boy tipped his head to one side. "Yes, Mistress."

Fate raised a brow. "That again? I thought you accepted that I'm not your Mistress."

He moved to an end table next to a lamp and played with the white dust that coated the book opened there. "Hmm. Only because you will it so."

She walked to the chair facing the table, and sat down so she could meet him eye to eye. "Are you Hero?"

He hesitated. "I'm Leoht."

"You call me Mistress, but you told Solaris that I wasn't your Mistress."

"You weren't, but now you are."

Fate paused, carefully deliberating her next approach. "It's interesting. You seem to be like Hero, and Solaris could be Akira."

He turned to her, looking up from the table. "Is that how you want to play?"

"The God of Life said the same thing, but I don't want to play at all."

His voice softened and he shifted his head downward. "We all have to play. If we don't, we'll lose."

"What will we lose?"

He hesitated. "Everything."

She inhaled deeply in a poor attempt to maintain her patience. "Who are we playing?"

"The Universe."

She sprang up, tired of the endless riddles. "That's absurd. You can't play a game with the Universe, especially if, when the Universe wins, it's destroyed."

Leoht Miina looked up at her but said nothing.

She continued her rant. "It doesn't make any sense. Why would the Universe play a game like that? Either way, it loses."

He tapped his mask and pondered her question. "True... but in this game, everyone loses, so I guess that isn't really a factor."

A hot wave washed over her and the air strangled her. "Everyone loses?"

"Hmm. It's unfortunate, but it can't be helped."

She shouted, "Why would anyone play?"

He retreated behind the table, distancing himself from her flash of rage. "Because we want to lose less."

She crossed her arms and reviewed the riddle and meager bit of information. Her thoughts raced with passages from Abyssus's journals and Hero's folklore. She pressed her fingertips to her forehead, and sighed. Then a shimmer caught her eye, and she fled her aching thoughts to get a better look.

The silver chain that hung from Leoht's neck glimmered in the low light.

Fate knelt beside him and reached out.

He shielded himself from her advance. "What are you doing?"

She feigned a smile. "It was so shiny, I just wanted to see."

Although the mask covered his face, his glare permeated the metal. She treaded carefully. "Was it a gift?"

He caressed the chain, his touch tender, his eyes soft and distant with longing.

She watched him for the slightest hint that might reveal the source of his turmoil.

A voice spoke from behind her. "Manipulating a child... your degradation knows no bounds, *Reinka*. If I can even call you that now."

She turned to face Solaris, whose thin frame and long limbs seemed to accentuate his ominousness. It made no sense, and yet, she found herself frightened by him. "Akira."

A slight smirk crossed his lips for an instant. In moments, it turned to sinister enjoyment, a smile that expressed uncanny bliss. "Trudging around in dreams and picking on children... I would have thought this beneath you. I am delightfully surprised."

She steadied her racing heart and spoke with tenacity. "You dare call *me* a manipulator."

He raised his chin and studied her, calculating her every move the way she'd calculated Leoht's. His gaze unnerved her, as he appeared to prod at her like a science experiment. "I do, and the worst kind too."

She drew her arms close to her body, defending herself, though she knew it did nothing to block his all-seeing gaze. "What is your connection to Hero?"

He cocked his head to the side. "We are related."

She narrowed her eyes, her determination growing with his obstinacy. "In what way?"

He stepped forward and growled, "By blood. In what way are you related to Abyssus? Tell me that."

She huffed. "He's my brother."

He sang. "Wrong."

Fate quaked as she deliberated the truth. She must not let Akira impede her course of discovery. She locked her knees and balled her hands into fists.

His eyes glimmered and a wide grin stretched across his face. "Oh, now she's serious. What fun."

She pointed at Leoht. "Is he Hero?"

Akira bent at the waist, leaning far to one side. "You tell me. You're the one who thinks she has it all figured out."

Fate bellowed, "Just answer me."

He righted his posture. "I have. You don't listen. You didn't listen to him and you won't listen to me."

"Where is the other man, the one with the red hair." She hoped to get a straight answer from one of them. If she could control her dream, she might find the answers she sought.

Akira put out his blackened hands to show her they were empty. "He's gone. I don't think he'll be back. Knowing him, he's probably upset that you don't listen. He hates to repeat himself. In all fairness, he did warn you."

She squeezed her head with her palms, having never imagined arguing with her own thoughts as she did now. The mess inside her mind made her restless and frustrated. She steadied herself again.

"The necklace...." She glanced over her shoulder at Leoht, who cowered behind a chair shaking his head.

Akira's gaze shot from Fate to Leoht as he hissed, "What necklace?"

Leoht cried, "You're mean. How could you?"

Fate demanded with an outstretched hand, "Let me see it."

Akira advanced to Fate's side. "Yes, Leoht, let us see it."

Leoht clutched his necklace and sat in a ball as if to shield it from them. He clung to it desperately while pleading, "No, he'll take it from me."

She snapped, "Akira, go away."

The tall man squinted one eye, paused for a long time, and then grinned.

Whenever he seemed pleased, Fate's skin crawled. She wondered what thoughts crossed his mind in those moments.

After this brief interlude, he crossed an arm over his chest and made a dramatic bow. "Certainly," he said, and vanished in wisps of black smoke.

Leoht backed away from Fate. "He's lying. He's a liar. He'll take it."

She beckoned to him again with her open hand. "Just show me."

He begged, "I'll tell you where the third journal is if you let me keep it."

Fate hung on her words. She wanted to know both but, ultimately, the journal held more weight. "Where is it?"

He bartered. "You'll leave my necklace alone?"

"Hmm," she affirmed.

"He hid it in a cave below the palace."

"Which palace?"

"The one in Keor."

Fate jolted upright with a heaving gasp. Her heart pounded and her fingers tingled, and it took a moment to process her surroundings. Sun spilled through the window in an intense glare, alerting her to the fact that morning had come. She leapt from the bed, bounded out of the room, and sprinted into the foyer.

Hero and Chi stared at her, wide-eyed.

Fate panted. "Where's Keor?"

Chi held her cup to her lips as if frozen.

Hero pressed his forefingers together and answered calmly. "Keor was the capital before Inoue."

Fate twisted her head to one side in confusion. "*Before?*"

"Hmm. From when Mu was Undal."

Her eyes traced the room as though to uncover answers hidden within. "So, it's in a cave below the palace."

Chi broke her silence. "What are you on about?"

Fate tapped her foot as excitement surged through her body. "The third journal... it's there. We have to go get it!"

Chi's teacup clanged as she set it down. "You do not seem to understand your condition. Your body cannot withstand the crystal you have ingested. Are you trying to die?"

Hero interjected. "Chi has a point. That cave is most likely underwater now."

Fate persisted. "So?"

Chi laughed in frustration. "So? So, it is filled with crystal from the Ussan... more crystal than is in your body right now. That water is deadly, and I will not allow either of you anywhere near there."

Hero picked his cup up and sipped from it as he scanned Chi from the corner of his eye. He wore a curious expression that bordered on dubious, one that reflected calculation and furtiveness.

Chi waved her finger at them. "Stay away from the crystal."

Fate stammered after Chi's blatant refutation. "But... I...."

Chi's intensity grew, making her aura swell and generate crushing pressure. "I do not want to hear it. You will not go near the Ussan or the cave. End of discussion."

Hero observed the argument while calmly sipping his tea.

Fate choked down her words with begrudging silence. She understood Chi's fears completely, as she too remembered fearing when Abyssus meandered in search of answers. This was precisely why she knew she must seek out his journals and unveil the truth he'd left behind.

Hero set his cup down. "I'll take you to the edge of the Ussan instead. It's a lovely sight." He used his usual glazed expression as he stared up at his aunt. "I presume it's acceptable to view the forest as long as we remain within the city's confines. Perhaps, even from the palace."

Chi nodded, the tension leaving her body as she placed her hands on her hips.

Fate frowned at him, completely baffled by his indifference to her plight. More than anything, it felt like a betrayal to Abyssus after his sacrifice.

Chi released an exasperated sigh. "Thank you."

Hero gave her a slight nod and a pleasant smile.

Chi turned to Fate one final time before exiting the room. "It really is for the best. I hope you understand."

Once Chi had left the room, Fate plunked down on the edge of the bench, fuming. She glared at Hero, the heat rising in her cheeks while he sat content and patiently observing. "Traitor."

He grinned. "I'm not sure I appreciate that expression."

She resisted shouting at him. "You could have at least tried to help me."

He raised a brow. "When Chi is set, she's set. Besides, you haven't thought things through carefully." He allowed her a moment to toil through her emotions, and then smiled in a self-assured manner. "Fortunately, I have."

"What do you mean?"

He stood and straightened his vest, and his grin grew wider. "Let's go on our tour and you'll find out."

Fate gathered the skirt of her gown in her hands and wrung it to release some of her frustration. "I'm not entirely sure that I trust you."

"As well you shouldn't."

His comment only left her questioning the situation more. *Are all Caeles difficult by nature?*

Hero shouted down the hall, "Auntie, we'll be back in a bit."

Chi hollered from her reading room, "Stay away from that cave."

"Of course," Hero replied, but shook his head, chuckling.

The weight in Fate's chest lifted as she caught onto his antics. In all her frustration, she nearly forgot who she dealt with. He never did as others wished without a good reason, and always seemed to get his way, even if it meant being underhanded or flat-out dishonest. It reminded her that he bore the Taint. While his craftiness could aid her now, it could also cause great harm.

She followed him out of the cottage to the stone-paved Centre. Her back sweated knowing that she went against Chi's warnings and wishes. It left her feeling more ill than the crystal in her body. Nevertheless, she looked ahead and gathered her resolve to uncover the truth.

As they moved through the city streets, Fate caught glimpses of life in Inoue Com. People bustled about carrying wares like woven baskets, quilts, and lanterns. the whole community exuded a warm light and the aroma of spices and honey, something that made one feel at home. It made her wonder if Rahma could ever learn to live like the Ancients, or if the truth rested in the Council's belief that this newer breed indicated the end of existence. Her place in the Rebellion seemed less stable, the more she learned. She wanted to believe as Fortuna did, that all life deserved its chance, but the facts aligned against her dearest madam.

She admired the skill of the Ancients as she gazed at the way they made simple buildings into works of art. The white, molded stone walls of each home displayed carefully crafted embellishments made of clay, metal, and a variety of colorful stones. Upon closer inspection, she noticed that each one resembled a flora or fauna indigenous to the northern part of Mu.

Hero leaned forward, inspecting her. "Are you still with me?"

She turned, taken aback by the way his hair glowed in the faint sunlight. He emulated the Beyond more than anyone she'd ever known. "Yes, I was just admiring."

He shone a coy smile. "Thank you."

She smacked his arm. "The buildings."

He nodded knowingly. "Impressive, no? They were made by the Fallen."

Fate stole another look at the art around her. Inoue Community seemed to be full of anima, a place full of life and light. It still exuded the traditional touch of Ancient heritage. "The Ancients that fled Thule?"

He made a throaty sound. "Read your folklore properly. They were cast out by the pure bloods."

She pouted, deeming his manner of correcting her distasteful. "You speak as though you were there."

He gave a downward glance. "So, what if I was?"

She shook her head, unwilling to let him win the debate. "Then you'd be taller."

He clutched his chest with a horrified gasp.

She reveled in her success. "Looks like I do study after all."

The chimes of the Ussan caught her ear, drawing her focus away from their playful banter. They sang in a way that demanded her attention. She became entranced in the song, and in her efforts to understand the melancholic way it made her feel.

Hero gazed out at the glowing white forest that peeked out over the rooftops, curiosity again crossing his expression. "You can hear it."

"Hmm." The chords lured her closer. She stopped at the border of the forest and listened to its hollow chimes. Whispers traveled across the terrain, calling her to the Ussan's crystal embrace. She heard it say, "Return to me."

Hero tenderly grabbed her hand to cease her progression. His touch pulled her from her trance for a moment, though the forest kept her hung within a dreamlike state.

He remained composed, gradually pulling her back with a gentle tug. "I thought you wanted Abyssus's journal."

The memory of Abyssus snapped her back into reality. She spun in a circle, regaining her bearings, and stopped when the cool, salty air swept against her cheeks. In the distance, the violet sea ebbed and flowed, and the ocean waves crashed against the shore.

Hero leaned his chin against her shoulder. "That's right. The cave is that way. What an incredible sense of direction you have."

She lingered in the song of the Ussan as it danced over her memories.

The forest whispered again, "Return to me."

Her heart skipped a beat but reality kept her grounded, as Hero again pulled her back. This time, the longing proved too great, and she yanked her arm against his grasp. "Let me go."

He tightened his grip. "You'll be shredded to pieces."

She blinked at him, then glanced back at the forest as the whispers escalated. Something wished for her to enter, and it fought relentlessly to keep her attention. A feeling of loss washed over her.

Hero warned, "Every rock, tree, and blade of grass in the Ussan is made of crystal. Each one cuts more cleanly than the sharpest blade, depositing crystal dust into your bloodstream. If you go in there, you'll die."

Fate tried reasoning with herself and surveyed the area. The surrounding guards watched her, only keeping their distance to respect Hero, each one stiff with alertness, their eyes wide and fixed on her every move.

Hero nodded at them and then led her away. "We are here for the journal. Do your best to stay focused."

She gripped her chest and gave in to his will. "I'm sorry. I'm not sure what I was thinking."

He strolled down the long, broken stone path to the beach, still holding her hand. "You heard the call and thought you would charge in there... as it suggested you could."

"How do you know that?"

He assisted her down the stairs from ahead. "Because I can hear it too, along with many others—most of whom died because of it." As she raised her head to take in the sight of the sunlight against the ocean, he finished his thought. "The forest calls to someone. We can only dare to question whom."

She held back her hair as it brushed against her face in the breeze.

Hero led her down to the smooth, silvery sands. "The sand here is crystal but it's much too fine to harm anyone. It glows during the nightfall. We should come to see it."

Fate breathed in the ocean air and tried to ignore the song of the Ussan. It beckoned her to cast aside her logic and run carefree to her death. She looked down at her sand-covered shoes. "It's awful."

Hero matched her line of sight, clearly surprised by the comment after his invitation. "What, sand in your shoes?"

"No, to hear all of those cries and do nothing."

He exhaled some unknown burden. "Agreed." After clearing his throat, he quickly trotted down the beach.

She watched him for a moment, and then realized that he wasn't stopping. "Hey!"

The instant she started after him, he bolted into a dead sprint.

She growled and raced after him as he laughed.

They rushed through the sand to the cave's closest entrance.

Fate looked up the rocky crags to where the palace rested, its white walls glimmering lavender and pink in the sunlight. Everything looked more colorful from that vantage point. She admired the combination of skill and placement.

"It's beautiful."

Hero trotted to her side. "Hmm. Everything they built was sewn with anima. That's why it takes on that opalescent coloring."

"It's just stunning. Strange as it may be, I feel like I've been here before."

He shrugged. "Maybe you have."

"I'm a Doll." She knew he needed no reminder, but his constant denial of her state of being upset her.

He put his hands in his pockets. "Even a Doll needs a soul."

She glared at him. His persistence grated on her nerves.

He kicked the sand with his bare feet.

She dodged the mess and dusted off the skirt of her gown. "When did you take off your shoes?"

He chuckled. "Ages ago. I don't want sand in them. Nasty stuff."

Fate looked back down the long stretch they had run and tried to place a time when Hero stopped to remove his shoes. She frowned in disbelief. "I don't recall you stopping at any point. I would have taken mine off at the same time."

He shrugged. "I guess you spend too much time in your head to pay attention to what I do. A poor wife, you'll make."

She snapped, "Rude." Although she knew he intended his words for play, something about them made her combative.

"I've heard that before. I'm afraid you'll have to do better."

She jumped at him, and he darted away laughing. She gave chase briefly, but the weight of her legs in the sand grew exhausting.

He approached her and patted her back. "It's been fun, but we really should get that journal before it gets too late. You still grow weak quickly. We need to get back before you collapse or Chi will kill us both."

Fate gestured to the ocean between them and the cave. "How do you propose we do that? There has to be twelve lengths between us and that cave."

Hero removed his coat, folded it, and placed it on a rock. He then followed suit with his vest. "We swim."

She gawked at him. "Chi said the water was full of crystal. How is this any different than the Ussan?"

He placed his hands on his hips and stepped back towards the water. "Because we can't float through the Ussan."

She rapidly stripped off her gown and kicked off her shoes, leaving only her undergarments.

He bit his lip and raised a brow. "I'm not that easy, Lady."

She kicked sand at him. "I can't believe you. I would have never imagined you'd be so facetious."

He stepped into the water with another wide grin. "Now you know."

She charged after him. "You're such a liar."

He waded out deeper into the ocean and said, "I did warn you. You really aren't very good at protecting your assets." He then dove beneath the surface.

Fate froze instinctively when he didn't immediately surface. "Hero?" She looked frantically as she kept herself afloat.

He resurfaced much farther out and shouted back. "Don't dive too deep. There's quite a bit of crystal down there."

She swallowed hard, noticing the light emanating from the underwater crystal. When Hero submerged again, she held her breath and dove under. Much to her amazement, the crystals glowed and twinkled in clusters at the ocean's bottom. She heeded his warning and swam shallow, avoiding contact with the taller shards. The light from the sun above and the glow of the crystals below created a magical shimmer, icy blue, under the water.

Fate held her breath as she took in the sight, until she felt that her chest might burst open, and then resurfaced with a gasp.

Hero stood on the opposite shore, shielding his eyes from the glare. "Don't dally. It's not good for you to stay in the water for too long."

Fate waved her hand to signal that she'd heard him, and continued until she met the shore. As soon as she arrived, she dragged herself out of the water.

He tossed the wet hair from his face. "Tired, huh? You stayed in too long."

She panted and inspected the rippling water. "The crystal did that?"

He offered her a hand as she climbed out. "Hmm. It was draining you of ether."

Shortly, she stood beside him and took a moment to regain her bearings. "I thought crystal restored anima."

He nodded. "It does, but you're a darkness elemental, and crystal *absorbs* ether. That's why the crystal in the caramel poisoned you. They especially like moisture. Hence, they grow best in water."

Fate gradually caught her breath.

Hero continued. "...or, in your case, saliva and blood."

She reflected on the day Lara poisoned her. "I killed her."

He averted his eyes. "You defended yourself."

"She was your friend."

He looked her dead in the eyes. "A friend that poisoned my wife to be."

Fate stroked her wet hair. "Still, I'm sorry."

"We aren't here to trudge up things we cannot change. Let's get Abyssus's journal."

She nodded as he turned to the cave entrance, and started walking blindly after him into the darkness. Long strands of blue moss hung down from the ceiling, appearing much like curtains in the entrance. The walls glimmered with flecks of crystal.

Hero glimpsed at her from over his shoulder. "Watch where you step. There is crystal everywhere."

She looked down and noted the glowing shards that peeked out of the sand. The entire cave twinkled with bits and fragments of crystal. She kept close to Hero, tracing his footsteps with her own. "Why would Abyssus hide his journal in such a dangerous place?"

He studied every inch of the cave with a watchful eye. "Probably thought no one would look here except us. Most likely means he put something important inside."

She examined the dark, murky walls of the cave, and wondered what secrets her brother still kept, even in death. Even if they found all of his journals, she might never truly unveil the truths he'd buried. Her heart ached knowing he'd chosen to place his trust in someone or something else. She considered all she knew about Abyssus and realized that, in the end, she knew very little.

Her gaze ventured back to Hero, and she doubted what she really knew about her husband to be. He remained a puzzle to her—dismal and depressive one moment, and playful the next.

They stopped in a massive cavern that stretched upward towards the palace. A crumbling old staircase clung hopelessly to the wall of the cave.

She traced the stairway up towards the ceiling, noticing that moss held a rusted sconce in place, marking a once great structure. "Is that Inoue Palace?"

Hero paused as if to consider his answer. "It's Keor Palace."

Fate stared back at him, finding herself irritated by his persistence in believing folklore even though, deep down inside, she truly feared it may all be real. "Fine. Either way, it's the Capital's palace."

"Hmm." He moved deeper into the cavern and searched for signs of Abyssus's journal.

Her hesitance to accept Undal as real bordered on irrational. Hero had shown her so many things that proved his theories and, still, she internalized her dismay. As she gazed up at the staircase again, memories of her brother crept into the back of her mind. She felt lost without him. Abyssus was her rock, and she drifted aimlessly without him.

Hero motioned to a pile of rubble. "Fate."

She shook from her thoughts and hurried to the debris as Hero pulled a metal case from under an old broken pillar.

He opened that case and revealed the third journal. The blue cover gleamed in the cave's scarce light.

A quick glint caught her eye as Hero crawled out from beneath the collapsed pillar. She checked for the source of the light as he tucked a silver hourglass back into his damp dress shirt.

Fate stopped breathing as a flurry of emotions and thoughts seized her. She swallowed her feelings to keep her poise, and coolly reached for the journal. Now that she knew of the artifact, she noticed it through the sheer white fabric of his shirt, and it took everything in her not to stare at it.

He grinned as he passed the journal to her. "We'll be back before Chi even questions it."

She locked her gaze, gripping the book to ease her bubbling curiosity. "Leoht?"

Hero cocked his head and squinted. "What about him?"

"He wore an hourglass like the one around your neck," she lied, hoping to trick him into confessing.

He pressed a hand against the necklace, giving her a look of distrust for the first time since they'd met. "It was a gift from my mother."

She persisted. "Are you Leoht Miina?"

He took a step back. "Fate, what's wrong with you? You can't possibly think that he's the only person in existence to ever have an hourglass necklace."

Fate clutched the journal as though her life depended on it. She didn't understand why she needed to know, but she pressed on anyway. "Just tell me the truth."

He kept his distance, and kept his hand over the necklace. "The truth is that this is the only thing I have left that my mother gave me. There was something else, but it's been misplaced, so I'm rather protective of this."

Fate crumbled with his hurt expression. She'd unintentionally allowed her dreams to sway her waking beliefs. "I'm sorry. It's just that you appear much like him."

He shrugged a shoulder with his usual coy smile. "Then he must be handsome."

She answered plainly. "He's a child and he wears a mask."

"Oh, right." He tried to put his hands in his pocket but the fabric stuck from the moisture.

She cast him a sideways glance. "We should get going. If we don't swim back soon, we'll still be wet when we return, and I doubt your aunt will miss that."

"Agreed," he said, starting back through the cave to the water.

As they emerged from the cave, Fate spied someone on the opposite shore but, when she turned her full attention, they had vanished.

She grabbed Hero's arm and pointed. "Someone was there."

Hero checked the stretch of beach on the other side of the water. "Are you sure?"

"Hmm."

"Let's move quickly. Anyone might be after this journal."

The pair dove into the water and hurried home as quickly as possible.

28

MOON DRIP

Fate and Hero exchanged a quiet nod before she rushed into her room, changed out of the salt- and crystal-coated undergarments, and into fresh, clean ones. She shook out her gown and shoes before redressing. Once contented with her appearance and the removal of all traces of their escapade on her bedroom floor, she exited the room with the journal in tow, and returned to the den.

Chi's cottage always emitted a warm glow. It felt like home even though Fate was a guest. Having a moment to herself, Fate sat on the armchair in front of the fire and thought deeply about this, and considered that maybe, rather than the cottage, Chi felt like home.

Hero interrupted after a few minutes, looking pleased.

Fate kicked his foot when he sat down, which only made him giggle. At the sound of another set of footsteps, she tucked the journal into the skirt of her gown. "Isn't Chi going to smell the salt water?"

"Watch."

Chi joined as soon as she noticed their return and eyed the pair. "Welcome back. Hero, why are you laughing?"

He gazed down with a wide grin. "Because my bride to be is flirting."

Fate's eyes grew wide, which only made Hero laugh more.
His lies are endless.

Chi put a hand to her cheek. "No need to be embarrassed. It is good that you two get along so well. I will start some tea."

He tipped his head back to rest against the chair, and whispered, "We really are going to drown if she keeps making so much tea."

Fate chuckled and snagged the journal from the skirt of her gown. As much as she attempted to shake the feeling, she eventually looked up at Hero and revisited her inkling that he was Leoht Miina. She decided not to press the issue further, tucking it away in the corner of her mind. If Hero was Leoht, and Akira was Solaris, then she needed to find the red-haired man to complete the puzzle. With an exhausted sigh, she settled back onto her chair to read.

Chi returned carrying her tray of tea, forcing Fate to once again hide the journal.

Fate and Hero glanced at her, then at each other, and burst into a giggling fit.

Fate held back her laughter as best she could, but tears welled up in her eyes at the effort.

Chi looked between the two of them. "I suppose I will stay in my room tonight. It appears you may need some... personal time." Her comment caused an outburst of laughter, eliciting from Chi a smile, a quick nod of approval, and a quick retreat into her quarters.

It took some time before they got ahold of their amusement.

Fate finally confessed, "I feel bad. She seems like she'll really stay in there all night."

Hero waved her off. "Don't. She wants a Caeles heir. Let her believe what she wants. It's better if she thinks happy thoughts. If she knew the truth, it might make her sad."

Her admiration of him grew each time he displayed such thoughtfulness and insightfulness. She'd been uncertain Hero really understood the platonic nature of their relationship until that moment. "Thank you."

He tipped his head. "For what?"

She ran her finger over the corner of the journal's pages. "Staying by me... protecting me... saving me from a fate worse than death."

He blinked, expressionless. "There are lots of fates worse than death. I only saved you from one. It's not so much." After his statement, he stared off at some distant and unseen place.

She thought of the Ancients who'd experienced an Awakening, and cast a glance at him. At times, Hero struck her as someone from the past, especially when he prattled on about history and the truths about their world.

She sighed despite herself. "Do you think it's sad to live forever?"

He hesitated, and when he finally did respond, he opened his mouth but said nothing. He remained this way until he gave up and closed his mouth again, still silent.

Instead of answering the question, he kicked up his feet and said, "You should get some rest. I'll go through the journals and see what we have."

"I feel like all I do these days is sleep."

"True, but then you dream."

She turned her head towards him, surprised by his words. "You think I should?"

He leaned towards her and slipped the journal from her grasp, smiling. "It did help us find two of the journals."

"It scares me."

He gazed into her eyes and ran his fingers across her cheek. "Then we'll take this journey together."

Fate placed her hands on her lap. After all this time, she wanted to place all her faith in him and pursue their efforts to reveal the truth, whatever it may be. "Promise?"

He said nothing again.

She waited for him to respond.

He leaned forward and kissed her. His anima coursed over her lips. The kiss seemed unusual, different from the clients at the brothel, and not at all like the love stories she'd read.

He withdrew, remaining mere inches from her face, with one hand against the arm of the chair. "It's a deal."

Her face ran hot again.

He smirked. "The hot-cold thing?"

The room spun, and she held no spirit for joking. "What was that?"

"A pact."

She stood and touched her lips. "What did you do?"

He adjusted his posture, his face riddled with an apology. A smidge of panic rose in his intonation and his gaze as he answered, "I made a promise. I wanted your trust."

"Oh," she said, uncertain of whether she believed him.

"I'm sorry. I should have asked."

She shook her head. "It's all right. I think I'm just overly tired. You're right. I should get some rest."

He looked down at the floor. "I'm sorry."

Fate dwelled on the awkwardness of the moment. Everything she and Hero had fought for hinged upon their union and their ability to work together, with the help of Abyssus's journals. All her training had led to this, so it made no sense to destroy it all over a simple kiss when she had faced far worse in the brothel.

As a reply, she kissed his cheek. "Don't be sorry. I think it's sweet, and I do trust you."

He kept his thoughts to himself, though he let show a meek expression with flushed cheeks and a weak smile.

"Really, it was a wonderful day," she continued as she made her way to the hall.

He waved slightly. "Then I'll see you in the morning."

She flashed a bright smile. "Yes. Let's hope my dreams bring us news, and we have as grand a day tomorrow."

He continued watching as she rounded the corner.

She hurried down the hall and into her room, closed the door, and leaned against it, cringing. For all her training, the real thing still put her on edge. Something about the sincerity made it more difficult to grapple with. She wrestled with her guilt before crossing the room and changing into her sleep gown. The warmth of the covers welcomed her to bed and encouraged new dreams and discoveries.

Her body, heavy with fatigue, dropped onto the mattress.

She fell through it into a warm, crystal-clear pool of water—a dream. She swam by the long roots of the water plants, floating on the surface, and brightly-colored fish examined her as they perused.

She took in the magnificent sight until her lungs burned, and then surfaced. She paddled her arms, keeping herself afloat as she gazed up at the sky. It appeared no more than a large reflective sheet with a semi-translucent quality, allowing her to see beyond the thin veil into an impressive display of stars. She steadily swam to the shore, strained against the weight of her clothing, and finally pulled herself from the water.

A grand opalescent building sat just beyond a field of glowing white flowers. The delicate-looking walls almost defied logic. They appeared no more durable than bubbles, but as the breeze blew, the structure remained steadfast.

She moved towards the field as the breeze carried a flurry of petals into the air. "Moon drip."

A man's voice rang out clear as a bell. "Don't go that way!" Behind her, Akira stood holding his cat.

Instant frustration brewed inside her. "Akira...."

The cat leapt to the ground and ran into the building.

"I mean it," he said.

"Why not?"

He stepped forward and spoke softly. "You'll regret it, like before."

"You're saying I've been here before?"

He paused. "You don't remember?"

She treaded lightly, feeling as though both Akira and Hero pushed her towards something she couldn't yet comprehend. She glanced at the building, wondering if it was wise to continue. "Where did your cat go?"

Akira turned to the building. "Bes goes where he pleases, as all cats do."

"Your pet... that's his name? Bes?"

"Besil, yes, and he's many things, but he is not my pet."

She pressed him further. "And Leoht is what exactly?"

Akira sneered. "Problemsome."

She hesitated. "Th.... That's not a word."

"Tells you how loathsome he can be."

Although it was not the answer she'd hoped for, it at least gave her some insight into their dynamic. "You seemed unhappy about the necklace."

He crossed his arms defensively. "As I said, problemsome. Why are you here, *Reinka*?"

"You've called me that a few times now. What does it mean?"

He swayed towards her, squinting, his movements somehow assertive compared to his previous, withdrawn body language. "Perhaps you should study more and prod less."

She strolled towards the water.

He followed at a short distance. "Where are you going?"

She turned sharply. "Why are you worried about me leaving this spot?"

His polychromatic eyes reflected his displeasure, and he squinted harder than before.

She bolted, racing as fast as she could towards the field of flowers.

He appeared before her in a cloud of black smoke and blocked her way. "Don't."

She leaned around him to get a peek. "What's over there?"

"Tragedy." He sounded genuinely sad, and his tone ceased her persistence.

She gazed up at him, mesmerized by his colorful aura, which appeared like luminescent strings wafting around him in all hues. His presence seemed familiar, comfortable even.

He reached out and stroked her cheek. "I'm sorry things have turned out like this for us. I will do my best to fix it."

Her heart wavered at his gesture, but her lingering fear made her withdraw. "I—"

"It's all right, *Reinka*."

A gust of wind blew the surroundings and Akira away, leaving her in the darkness of space. The sound of water dripping broke her concentration, and she shifted her feet to discover she stood in shallow water. Ahead of her, the shadow of a large tree rose from the water, its limbs appearing eerily like arms and legs.

Again, a man spoke to her. "You should not be here."

The God of Life stood beside her. His black robe, sewn with intricate green flowers, slipped down his back, alongside his long red hair, and into the water below. The colors melted together at his feet and swam away as fish.

Her body remained fixed in the presence of such magnificence, unsure of how to approach any topic with the fascinating person. "Are you the God of Life, Casluhim?"

He remained engrossed with the tree. "It doesn't matter who anyone is. Once she decides to follow a path, not even fate can stop her."

The sound of chimes filled the air, drawing Fate's attention. "Who?"

He clenched his eyes shut. "It's too late."

Several dark forms materialized nearby.

She looked more closely, noting their incredible size and skeletal nature, shrouded in black capes that floated about them and gave off wisps of black smoke. "Grim."

"Hmm," Casluhim agreed. His body appeared heavy and his face tense.

The weight of whatever burden he carried filled the air, suffocating her. She gasped and reached out to him.

The sound of the chiming intensified and more Grim arrived.

The tree writhed and hollow screams sprang from its limbs, sending a ripple across the water. A bright blue ring of flame dissolved into large moths, which took flight. The moths scattered — hundreds, maybe thousands — each shimmering with ether as they fluttered and disappeared into the stars.

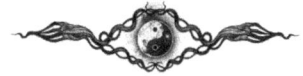

Fate sat up in her bed, sucked in air, and coughed long and hard.

Hero opened the door and inspected her from afar. "Are you all right?"

She fell back onto her pillow, still amazed by the vision. "I dreamt about Casluhim."

He sat on the bed and rubbed his face. "And that made you cough?"

She sat back up. "At first, I was in a pond near some building and a field of white flowers. I remember they were called Moon Drips... like the tapestry in the palace."

He yawned. "Those are only found in the Beyond."

"Akira was there... or Solaris... and he stopped me from going to the field."

He squinted and made a sour face. "The Goddess Zipporah was killed in a place like that."

She pouted. "I would have thought it had something to do with the Spinner, since Solaris was there."

Hero shook his head and shrugged, stealing her pillow and then lying back onto her bed.

She balled-up her blanket to rest her head, and then rolled onto her side. "But then, I was in space. The ground was water and there was this big ominous tree made of bodies."

He drifted closer to sleep and mumbled, "The Tree of Hellfire."

"And that's when I saw Casluhim and the Grim. It was amazing, but I couldn't hold my breath any longer." She glanced down at Hero and sighed.

He slept comfortably beside her.

"Right. I'll tell you about it tomorrow." She snuggled against his side, grateful to have someone to tell. Without Hero, she'd be all alone.

Thanks to his warmth, she slipped back into a dreamless sleep.

29

THE FIRST SEAL

A subtle creaking sound urged Fate to consciousness. She opened her eyes and found Hero shirtless beside her in bed, his warm, bare flesh pressed against her face. The echo of a murmuring heart reverberated in her ears, an irregularity. As she came to, she spotted Chi in the doorway with a coy smirk. Fate sat up and clutched the blankets, looking around to understand how she'd ended up in this predicament.

Chi scrunched her nose. "I did not mean to wake you."

The blood left Fate's face as she looked at Chi's gleeful expression.

Hero scratched his head as he roused from his slumber, and threw an arm around Fate. "It's all right. We need to get up anyway."

Chi cleared her throat. "Of course. I will go make some tea." She hastily made her escape and closed the door.

The second she left the room, Fate cracked Hero open-palmed against the chest.

"Ow," he complained while rubbing the pink handprint.

She admonished him. "Are you ready to produce an heir?"

He put his arms behind his head and lay back on the pillow. "Always."

She growled and withdrew from the sheets. "Did you find anything important in Abyssus's journals?"

He sat up and shed his playful façade. "Actually, yes. Abyssus was very thorough. I am impressed he gathered so much considering...."

She stared at him and waited, though she already knew what he intended to say.

He stared back, having realized the open wound too late. "...Mortis."

She bit her lip and nodded, her cheeks burning furiously at the thought of her brother's murder and the injustice that followed. "Of course."

He moved forward on his stomach. "He seems to have pieced together most of the folklore."

"What do you mean?"

Hero ruffled his hair. "It appears he focused most of his attention on a group of waking Ancients."

Fate rubbed her eye as she gradually abandoned her lethargy. "So, he was looking for some really old souls."

He bobbed his head rather than fully nodding. "Exactly. He was working with a group, trying to raise the Lords of Light and Shadow."

She pressed a hand to her chin and concentrated. "Why would he do that? Secret groups... illegal folklore?"

A light tapping arose at the door, and Chi spoke, her voice ringing of irritation. "You have a visitor."

They always seemed to have visitors and at the most inopportune moments.

She looked at Hero.

He shrugged with a pout and whispered, "Kyou?"

She plucked her robe from one of the chairs and quickly wrapped herself in it.

He sifted a white knit sweater from the closet, tossed it on, and waited for her before calling out. "Come in."

When the door opened, Fortis popped his head in. He glanced between the two, frowning. "Oh, this all looks entirely too innocent."

Hero chuckled. "Disappointed?"

Fortis entered and sat on the bed next to Hero. "Very."

Fate checked to ensure she'd properly tied her robe. "I never thought I would have so many people invested in my sleeping habits."

Fortis smirked. "Lies. Vicious lies. Remember, I know where you came from."

Fate smacked his arm. Occasionally, Igni's crude humor surprised her.

Fortis laughed and rubbed the spot as he taunted Hero. "Abusive too. Do you have to pay extra for that?"

They laughed at her expense, pausing only when Kyou stepped into the doorway. For once, he appeared sullen. He looked between Fortis and Hero before jeering, "Eh, what are you doing with my son?"

Fortis crossed one leg over another and leaned back with a grin. "Trying to get him to misbehave, to no avail."

A wide mischievous grin spread over Kyou's lips. He threw himself onto the bed, crushing Hero, and tackled Fortis, laughing.

Fate watched the spectacle, trying to comprehend the dynamic. She knew Fortis well, but knew not of the bond between Kyou and Hero, or how they might have formed such a deep connection.

Kyou jumped from the bed as he noticed her staring, and straightened his sleek coat. "Sorry, Lady, it has been some time since we were all together last."

Fate continued her study. "Don't mind me. I'm just observing."

Fortis covered his face and laughed into his hands. He stretched out his foot and tapped Kyou on the behind. "Voyeur."

Kyou floundered and fidgeted with his cuff. "Lady Fate, I don't believe we have formally met."

Fate scrutinized the sad excuse for a First Prince. Everything finally made sense, her entire existence attributed to this mess of a man. "I know. You're Iunu Kyou, the man I was supposed to marry."

Kyou grimaced. "Hmm."

Her eyes moved from Kyou's face to Fortis's foot, which remained on Kyou's behind. "But," she said, "you prefer the company of men."

Kyou flinched and put up a hand in protest. "First, I don't marry children." He then waved a hand towards Fortis. "And second, I prefer the company of this person, if I'm being honest."

Hero pulled himself up to rest on his knees. He gave Kyou his full attention, listening with clear admiration as the man spoke.

Fortis bowed. "Thank you. It feels good to be acknowledged."

Fate pursed her lips and ran her hand over her mouth. "Lovers or Bound?" The entire interaction perplexed and intrigued her. Everything from the dynamic between Kyou and Fortis, to the outward admiration Hero displayed, or even Fate's own connection to the First Prince.

Kyou and Fortis replied in unison. "Both."

Chi leaned against the doorframe with her arms crossed. "Fate, do not spend too much time dwelling on it. The kingdom is a mess, and these two will be of little help unless you find yourself in battle."

Kyou shrugged. "Ow. That's so true."

Fortis nodded. "I'm afraid so. Neither of us cares for politics."

Kyou smirked. "We're much better at other things."

Chi cracked Kyou against the back of the head. "Enough of that. I will not have you two corrupting them."

Fortis cocked his head in Hero's direction and scanned him from head to toe. "What is there to corrupt?"

Kyou complained while fixing his long hair, "Hero is already Tainted."

Chi pointed to each of them. "Not the way you two are. I want an heir. Do you hear me?"

Fortis put his hands in the air. "We wouldn't stop that. There are too few Caeles as it is. Honestly, Chi, you know we're just playing."

Chi scowled. "That is my concern. You two are always playing. When will you start taking things seriously?"

The light faded from Kyou's eyes and his smile slipped away. "Don't mistake playful banter for a lack of concern, my dear Chi."

His tone sent a quake through Fate's body. She glanced at Fortis, who also appeared equally as intense. Their shared expression made it clear that they hid tremendous power behind the masks of clowns. The glint of fire in Fortis's eyes drew her curiosity, but she knew that this was not the time to investigate him further.

"Good." Chi retreated with a huff, her eyes moving towards the sword she'd left propped up against the wall across the room. "These are my kits, and I will not have them mistreated or misinformed."

Kyou turned to her and spoke with sincerity. "They are ours, as well, and we will treat them as such."

Fortis nodded, confirming Kyou's statement.

Chi turned back to Kyou, reached out, and stroked his face. "I am counting on you, sweet boy."

Fate fanned herself, suddenly aware of the underlying tension in the room and the shift of the conversation. These people joked but they carried some invisible weight as well.

Fortis clapped his hands together and jested, "We've made the lady all a fluster. We should make our exit and allow her to dress."

Chi backed out of the doorway and let Fortis pass.

Kyou smirked with a sideways glance at Hero as he backed up. "Unless our dear Hero would like to stay and help her dress... and undress... and dress...."

Hero jumped from the bed and shoved Kyou the rest of the way out. He and Kyou murmured at the doorway in the Language of Ages, playfully hitting each other until Kyou finally left.

When Hero returned, he rolled his eyes. "They are always like this."

Fate found his interactions with the First Prince curious. "I gathered.... Hero?"

He looked her in the eye.

"What exactly is your relationship to Kyou for him to call you son?"

Hero grimaced. "Kyou made more of an effort to father me than Niteo. He started calling me son when I was about seven or so."

Fate smiled and nodded. "I see. Thank you for explaining."

"Of course. I'll see you in a bit." He closed the bedroom door behind him.

Fate moved to the small wardrobe and pulled a new outfit from the hanger. She also collected free undergarments from the drawer and quickly changed, not wanting to miss a moment of interaction.

Kyou differed from her expectations. It fascinated her that he and Fortis were secretly Bound. This, at least, explained the High Queen's involvement with the Rebellion and how she and Fortuna had bonded.

She caught sight of an unusual book beside her bed, and scanned the room to make certain she was alone. Her blood rushed as she gazed at the distinctive journal, recognizing it before she reached it.

The black cover beckoned to her.

She turned the book over but, unlike the other journals, it lacked a number. She leafed through it, checking the pages for Abyssus's penmanship and, sure enough, his scrawl appeared.

"How?" She checked the room again to see if anyone was hiding in the shadows.

Just as Abyssus had said, something strange stirred within Mu, something deeper than the squabble between factions. Abyssus had known it and it got him killed.

Now, she took up the mantle, tracing the words with her finger as she skimmed the notes.

A burst of laughter erupted from outside her room.

She looked up for only an instant, her heart pounding. She wanted to read through the journal before anyone knew about it. She depended on Hero for the Language of Ages, but had concerns about whether he revealed all that the journal told. Fortunately, this journal had been written in common tongue.

In a passage marked *Seals*, about halfway down the page, Hero's name appeared. She knelt behind the bed and used the light coming through the curtain to read.

> *Field Research: Caeles Hero.*
>
> *It's difficult to make a record of Caeles Elaine's death, given that Fate and I were raised on that very day. Although I understand the core of the situation, I can only speculate about the truth. One thing that's clear to me is that it served as an excuse to place seals on her son, Caeles Hero.*
>
> *These seals seem to focus solely on his abilities as a crystal elemental, and on his memories of the murder itself. He is more than capable in all other ways, aside from the effects of the Taint. Most of the Rebellion members seem to believe that his stain derives from his mother's death, but I know otherwise. If this were true, it would have explained his sociopathic tendencies. However, I'm more inclined to believe that both the Taint and his personality flaws stem from much further back, and that the perpetrator of the crimes knows too. I may even speculate that the block on his memories pertains to an Awakening, rather than to the murder, but this is just theorizing.*
>
> *The Council placed three seals upon him in total – one to stop his ability to use crystal, another to block his*

memories, and a third to kill him if the other two seals break. At least, this is what I've been told. I have no way to prove these facts other than my trust in the person who shared these details.

If these things turn out to be false, I may then question my confidant.

Fate reread the passage, wrestling with its meaning. After all that Hero had gone through for her, she felt obligated to help him in any way possible.

She quietly tucked the journal between the mattresses and stood.

The door cracked open, and Hero poked his head in. "Everything all right?"

She smiled, gently patted the bedspread, and approached him. At last, she regained her poise learned at the brothel, and used it to protect her study time. The visit from Kyou and Fortis allowed her time away from Hero, leaving her to fully investigate the meaning behind her brother's journals and notes.

"Yes," she said. "I think I'm just still sluggish from all the dreaming."

"Understandable. I wanted to make sure. You still haven't recovered fully and I didn't want to risk it."

She wrapped her arm around his as they walked down the short hall. "It's good to know that you care."

They arrived in the den with all eyes on them.

Fortis beamed. "You two make me smile."

Hero looked at Fate, seemingly contented to keep their secret.

She watched as he laughed and talked with the group, and wondered if he knew about the seals placed on him. Her darkness churned and twisted about inside her as more questions rose to mind. Did Chi know about the seals? How about Fortis and Kyou? They all behaved so jovially despite the reality of Mu's plight. Anyone and everyone could still be lying.

Hero leaned in. "Are you not feeling well?"

She stared at him long and hard, desperately wanting to free him of the fate forced upon him, but managed only a weak smile. "Not very."

He turned to the group. "If you'll excuse me for a moment, my bride is not feeling well. I'm going to take her to rest."

Chi hurried to Fate and pressed a hand to her head to check her temperature, and nodded. "Take as much time as you need."

"Thank you," Fate replied, continuing her lie. She needed more time alone with the journal, and thought the group might keep Hero occupied long enough for her to find out how to break the seals without causing him any harm.

He tucked her into bed and returned to his guests, as she'd planned.

She pulled the journal from its hiding place the moment he closed the door, and spent the remainder of the morning reading it.

Before midday, she completed her task, crawled from the bed, and returned it to its spot between the mattresses.

The cottage lay quiet as she exited the room. She stopped and listened for a pause before continuing.

Chi rounded the corner and practically shouted, "Praise be, child, you startled me."

"Sorry." Fate hid her disappointment. There was little chance that Chi would leave her be to conduct her research.

"Don't be. I will make some tea."

Before Fate could stop her, Chi strolled off to make another batch of honey tea. She returned to the den and looked at the books on the shelf, in search of anything that pertained to seals. Time ticked by too quickly and, before she could complete her search, Chi returned with a tray in hand.

Fate sat on one of the chairs across from Chi and accepted the cup offered to her. "Thank you."

"It is good the boys are out. It will give me chance to speak with you." Chi leaned back on her chair to observe Fate. The Caeles stare exuded an air of calculation and deep contemplation, as if they inherently perceived details unseen to the natural eye.

Fate remembered this discomfort from the many times Hero had observed her. This knowledge helped her remain calmer on the outside, especially when she meant to hide her displeasure. "Oh, what did you want to discuss?"

Chi sipped her tea. "A few things, actually. First, your binding ceremony. We must get that underway. You two cannot continue to share a bed until we have completed it."

Fate nearly choked on the tea in her mouth. "It's not—"

Chi waved her hand. "There is no need to explain. I was young once too. I simply want to secure your positions legally so the Council cannot complain."

Fate nodded without interrupting.

Chi nodded once. "Very good. Next, I would like to speak of Hero's condition. I was grateful to hear you were already aware of it and still chose to marry."

"I honestly don't understand how his condition would have a bearing on our relationship."

She leaned forward. "I would like to agree but I cannot. It is imperative that you understand what you are agreeing to. When we perform the Binding Ritual, we shall spiritually connect you and Hero. In essence, you will become Tainted."

Fate had run through the possibilities many times in her mind, but had somehow never rested on that conclusion. Her soul shrank, hearing Chi state it so plainly. "I understand."

Chi raised a brow. "Do you? I have been watching you."

Fate swallowed, took a deep breath, and set her cup down in fear she might drop it due to her sweating palms. "And what have you found?"

"You are strong, Miss Fate, I will give you that. My concern lies with your dreams. If you are, which I believe you to be, a Spirit Walker, you may be the only person in all of Mu who can help my Hero."

Fate listened, surprised by Chi's sudden confession. She debated whether Chi fully understood the severity of Hero's condition. If she knew of the seals, then she'd asked for an abnormally dangerous favor, so Fate surmised that Chi only knew of the Taint. That left only a handful of people that could be responsible for the seals placed on Hero.

She maintained no concerns over Chi's loyalty. "Of course. I'll help any way I can."

Chi nodded. "I am so thankful for you. Hero is the last true Caeles that will have a Bound."

Fate eased her nerves and collected her cup, a courtesy she paid to Chi, mostly. "Why didn't you form a binding?" After a short pause, she said, "I'm sorry. That was rude of me to ask."

Chi put up a hand and took another sip of her tea. "No, it is all right. I am unable to produce offspring, so whether or not I have a Bound is irrelevant. No, Hero is our last hope."

Fate twisted her head toward the window and checked the midday sun. "What about Akira?"

Chi pointed a finger, still holding her cup. "Good question. There is something not right about him."

"Many have said the same of Mortis. Do you think it's the same?"

Chi looked as if haunted by some passing thought, and stared ahead at some unseen place like a startled animal. "No. Mortis seems like little more than a shell of the man we used to know. I am not sure what dark force is ailing him, but it is unnatural."

"But you think Akira's condition is natural."

Chi flinched and sucked in air over her teeth. "Not exactly. He is not a natural Caeles... he may not be Caeles at all, but he seems more alive than Mortis. I just do not know what he is after. Moreover, I do not like the way he looks at or talks to Hero. It feels as if he is planning something untoward."

Fate sat forward. "You think he intends Hero harm?"

Before Chi could answer, Kyou entered, leading Fortis and Hero in a bluster of noise and laughter.

Kyou glanced between Fate and Chi. "Oh no. Never leave two women alone to discuss things. We've made a grave mistake, men."

Fortis mockingly gasped. "Chi, what have you done?"

Hero slunk out from behind them and distanced himself from the potential fallout.

Chi squinted in a manner not unlike Akira had when he'd expressed displeasure. "Lucky for you, I am in a good mood."

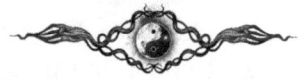

Time moved quickly for the small group. It didn't take long for nightfall to wash over Inoue, and for Chi to bid Kyou and Fortis goodnight.

Fate and Hero remained behind, and Fate reclined on her chair, more at home in Chi's cottage than most places, save the brothel. Passages of Abyssus's journal raced through her thoughts. She watched the fire dance, hoping to ease her troubled mind, and time passed with little sense or measure.

Chi leaned forward and rested a hand on Fate's knee. "You should rest."

Fate sat up, her body stiff after being still for a while.

Chi tipped her head toward Hero, who had fallen asleep on one of the chairs after partaking in one of Fortis's elixirs. "Watch out for the Igni concoctions or you will wind up like that."

"Duly noted." She pulled against the arms of the chair and heaved herself from the cushion. "Should I get him to bed?"

Chi folded her arms and looked over Hero, expressing both adoration and vexation. "How? He looks compact but weighs as much as a house. Leave him. He will be fine. This is not the first time."

Fate took the blanket slung over the back of the chairs, covered Hero, and whispered, "Goodnight."

She followed Chi down the hall, stopping at her door. "Goodnight."

Chi offered a slight nod. "Sleep well."

Once in her room, Fate stripped down to her undergarments on her way to bed. Without bothering to pick up or change, she crawled into her sheets to sleep. Her body sank into the mattress, and sleep took her in a wave of darkness.

The sound of chimes echoed across the sleeping city as Fate faced the Ussan's glowing crystal trees, which stood amidst an eerie haze. An icy gale stung her skin. Before her stretched a frosted stone path that led between the trees. Hero's warning repeated in the back of her mind, and she remained firmly in place, not wanting to venture to her own death. An attack of shivers fell over her and, clutching her arms, she searched the area for shelter.

A white fennec fox with vibrant mint eyes trotted up one of the roads, passed Fate, and stood on the stone path, looking back at her.

Instinct led her to follow the small creature beyond the forest's border and into the unknown. It gave her a reason to flee logic and hurtle blindly towards her death in pursuit of the truth, no matter what may await her.

The fox spun in a small circle and whined, then resumed farther down the path.

She took another step, paused to look back at the safe grounds, and bounded deeper into the forest and its razor-sharp branches.

The fox led her in deeper and deeper, until the chill broke from the air and the haze cleared.

She stood among the towering crystal trees, deep in the forest, each one chiming and gleaming in the moonlight. Her heart swelled with a flurry of emotions as her ears filled with the whispers of the trees. This was what she'd hoped to find — her own memories resided in the Ussan, and she wished to claim them.

She glanced around at the iridescent sheen cast by every rock, plant, and tree. The Ussan overflowed with life, as much as any person. "Anima?"

The fox howled to her from beside a figure on the ground.

Blood pooled from beneath a woman lying in the snow, her crystallized gown torn and stained. She lay lifeless, entangled in her own long dark hair, like a web.

Fate staggered back against the sight, and bumped into a tree. Shock numbed her mind, but she gathered herself and said, "Is that me?"

The fox whined and leapt through an opening in the trees.

"No," Fate said, dismayed. She remembered enough from the folklore and Abyssus's journals to know that Nuvem Fati had met her end in the Ussan. Still, their resemblance unsettled her.

She crept forward to inspect the body. "What happened to you?"

As she looked closer, a glint from two tiny bells caught her eye, and she reached out towards a jeweled hair comb sticking out from the tangled, bloody mess of hair. The chimes sounded in her ears again, and she blinked hard to block out blinding images of the white-haired woman. She hesitated to touch the comb, allowing her hand to merely hover over it.

Is this the woman from the maze? A ghost?

After some deliberation, she stretched out her fingers again to grasp the comb.

The fox yelled from a short distance ahead, pulling her attention away from the tragedy.

Fate reluctantly left Fati in search of the agitated animal. She crawled through numerous spikes of crystal grass and dodged the long, spindly branches of the crystal trees. She heeded Hero's warning with extreme caution.

At the base of a massive tree, the fox whined beside a deep, dark hole.

After a slight hesitation, she peered inside.

Leoht slept in the shadows, curled up into a tiny ball.

She crawled in as far as she was able, and reached for him, but couldn't fit far enough inside to pull him from the burrow. "Leoht?"

The small boy stirred from his rest. "Mistress?"

"No, it's Fate."

He pulled himself onto his hands and knees and crawled out from his hiding place.

She rested her hands on his head. "I'm here."

"I'm lost."

When she stared face-to-face with his grisly mask, she found it easy to understand how the small boy might become lost. "Funny, you've always found *me*."

"Mistress, you smell very nice. That's why I can find you."

Fate chuckled at the strange comment, but quickly realized he referred to the smell of her spirit. She feared he actually smelled Fati—though that could not be pleasant—but was unaware of her death. "Come with me. I'll get you out of here."

He stretched his arms up towards her.

She shook her head. "I'm not going to carry you."

He didn't respond.

Although the mask hid his face, she gleaned that he pouted. "You should learn survival skills while you're young."

"I'm lonely," he said, tilting his head in a way that reminded her of Hero.

"Are you trying to be cute?"

"I really cannot be held?"

"You *do* know that I am Fate, no?"

He kicked the thin layer of snow with his shoe. "I know, but you're also the Spinner. You left for a long time, and that's why I'm lonely."

A chill shot down Fate's spine. The Ussan's chimes shrilled in her ears again as she thought of the body only a short walk from where they stood. Even if he couldn't see the slain lady, Fate didn't want this boy to experience the frozen corpse of his beloved Mistress.

She leaned down and scooped him into her arms. For now, it seemed best to fill Fati's role. "I'm sorry I left."

He hugged her tightly and stuffed his cold mask against her warm neck. "It's all right, Mistress. I forgive you."

They followed the fox back through the woods.

Fate boosted Leoht up on her hip. "Does your mask come off?"

"I've never tried — well, not all the way."

"Do you know what happens if you do take it off?"

He took a lock of her hair into his hand and coiled it around his fingers. "No, but when I try, it hurts me."

She set the boy down and crouched, taking in his presence and his appearance. Thoughts of the folklore and of Hero crossed her mind whenever she looked at him. Somehow, even Abyssus came to mind. A part of her soul ached at seeing this small child suffer the touch of a seal, particularly when she saw little possibility that he'd committed a crime worthy of sealing him.

"Would you like me to remove it?"

He nodded once and waited for her.

She blew warm breath over her cold fingers, took hold of the edges of the mask, and slowly lifted it, watching for any sign of discomfort or miasma.

"I'm sorry," she said. "Is it painful?"

The mask clung to the child by some invisible force. He groaned and raised his hands towards his head. "Take it off. I don't like it!"

She pulled it farther from his face. "It's almost off. Be strong."

She tugged hard at the mask and, with a sudden jolt, it broke free. Both Fate and Leoht fell backward onto the cold, hard snow.

Fate opened her palms to the sky, gawping. The mask crumbled in her grasp and left naught but soot, which danced upon the wind for only a second before disappearing. Ahead of her, Leoht Miina rubbed his newly exposed skin as he slouched before her in a daze. She had imagined he'd look like Hero, but he appeared more delicate, with a warmer complexion and eyes that shined like iridescent crystals.

"Does it feel any better?"

He surveyed his surroundings with wide eyes. "I feel... lighter."

She stood and wiped her blackened hands against her dress, but even after wiping them, they remained stained. She frowned with growing concern.

Leoht stood and tapped his head. "I remember now. Mistress told me to hurry and choose a path. If I don't listen, bad things will happen."

Fate continued wiping her hands. "Choose a path? Do you know what that means?"

He shook his head.

She looked around the clearing, distracted by the large tree that stood front and center. It evoked memories of her dream regarding the Tree of Hellfire, as Hero had called it. She thought about the arm-like branches. "Do you know why I went away?"

Leoht frowned. "I'm sorry, Mistress."

She sighed. "I have to get you out of here."

A man's voice interrupted. "I wouldn't do that."

She trailed the sound to the fox sitting nearby. "You can talk?"

"Of course. This is just a vision. It's my purpose. I've been put here to guide you."

"To where?"

"Here. The first seal has been broken and, for that, I commend you, but I will leave you with a warning."

Fate grasped Leoht's tiny hand. "Why was he sealed?"

The fox continued his message. "Any further recklessness may result in negative consequences. Since you seem to lack a voice of reason, allow me to set you straight."

Fate held Leoht's head close to her side. "Why does Akira come to mind when I look at you? I suppose it's because you're an articulate fox. It's a nice pun."

The fox's icy eyes gleamed. "I am but one of many mysteries here. Tread lightly. When you awaken, I suggest you watch carefully for unexpected changes. When one seal breaks, it often leads to another. If the third seal breaks, Leoht may die."

Fate's heartstrings jerked. For her, this confirmed the correlation between Hero and Leoht Miina. Never mind whether Hero himself knew—they must be one and the same. "How will I know?"

"Crystal," the fox answered, turning its attention deeper into the forest. "Now, I'm afraid our time has passed."

30

ONE AND THE SAME

The following morning, Fate rose from bed and quietly went to the den to peek at Hero.

He still slept comfortably on the chair, snuggled in the blanket she'd given him.

She tiptoed back to her room, closed the door, and returned to lie back in her bed and allow herself to dose until the sun came up.

Sometime later, the sound of chirping birds woke her. This time, she felt rejuvenated.

Chi knocked at the door with the promise of morning tea.

Fate obliged since she felt so light and airy. Once dressed, she hurried out to the den and woke Hero. "You can't sleep all day."

Chi entered with her tea tray. "You most certainly cannot. We have a Binding Ritual to complete."

Fate spun fast, her dress fanning out around her feet. "Today?"

Chi frowned. "Why not? The temple is finally available."

"Okay," Fate said, still shaking Hero.

Hero stretched and rubbed his eyes, and acted as if waking, but answered in a way that showed he'd been listening. "Why not? Auntie needs an heir."

Chi winked. "That is the spirit!"

Fate shook her head at him and took a seat on the chair beside his. She waited until Chi left the room once more before asking, "How are you feeling?"

He sat forward, smacking his dry mouth. "How are *you* feeling?"

She shed the concerns the fox had left with her. "Good, actually. Thanks for asking."

He made his usual pouting expression. "So, I'd better clean up."

Chi returned and pointed at Fate while speaking to Hero. "You had better be at least as pretty as her."

Hero looked Chi in the eyes with a frown and a squint before leaving to dress.

Chi laughed. "He thinks that he is the only one with a sense of humor."

Fate ran a hand over her hair. "I didn't dress for something so important."

"You look fine. We just need to bind you to Hero."

Fate blinked. "Are all bindings so devoid of depth?"

Chi pressed her tongue to her teeth. "Having a Bound is the most incredible thing a person can experience when it is natural. Unfortunately, each turn, fewer Ancients get to experience such a meaningful connection. The Half-Breeds and Rahma will never experience it."

"So, this is strictly a formal thing?"

Chi scooted to the edge of her chair and took Fate's hand. "It is what you make of it. The Council will have their closure, and you and Hero will have each other. Nothing else matters."

Fate nodded, trying to understand why she felt as she did. She held no secret passion for Hero. She cared for him, as she had her brother, but the concept of being pawned off from one person to the next made her feel dirty.

Hero returned dressed in an elegant suit, hand-stitched and embroidered in the Capital colors—white and gold.

Fate stood. "I really should put on something more appropriate."

He crossed the room and spun her by the hand. "You look fine. This is a private affair. No need to go out of your way."

Chi stood. "He is right. You will have many reasons to fuss in the future, but do not fret this."

Kyou poked his head in through the open front door.

Chi sneered. "You never learned to knock."

He opened the door farther without paying her comment any mind. "Should I gather everyone?"

She nodded back. "Hmm."

Fate looked at her soon-to-be in-law, and gulped down the increasing pressure. "Now?"

Hero squeezed her hand. "It's all right. I'll be with you."

She looked at each person, wanting to trust them, but her darkness writhed in her gut with a complaint.

Kyou smiled faintly. "I'll go on ahead. See you all shortly."

Fate rubbed the fingers of her free hand together over and over.

Hero squeezed her other hand, harder now. "It's time."

Chi led them out of the cottage and to the waiting carriage.

An eternity seemed to pass as the carriage hobbled through the city streets to the palace gates.

Fate observed in silence as Chi instructed the guards to open the gates. Now, more than ever, the Capital Palace made her feel small. It emitted a brilliant light from every wall and structure that led up to the main stairway, where High King Khnum and High Queen Heqet waited.

The coachman opened the carriage door and let Chi out first.

She held her blade to her side as she stepped down, and spoke with the palace guards. With a final look back at Fate and Hero, she disappeared up the stairway and in through the entrance doors.

Fate stepped down after Hero, her body rigid and trembling. She glanced at him for comfort, finding him composed as usual.

He pressed his hands together and frowned as he watched her. "You don't have to do this."

She gathered the skirt of her gown and looked ahead at the High Queen. "We'll move forward... together."

Hero smiled after a brief pause. "Your tenacity is charming."

She teased, "Most people just tell me I'm pretty."

He leaned over and scanned her with a wry smile. "How incredibly shallow. Besides, everyone knows that I'm far prettier."

She smacked him as she laughed and stepped forward, keeping her voice lowered as they made way for the Capital Royals. "I am happy that it's you."

"What is?"

"The person I'm forming a pact with—I'm glad it's you. Of all the people I've met since childhood, you seem the one most worth trusting."

He squinted. "What do you mean?"

"Our pact. You asked me to trust in you, and that's what I'm going to do."

His eyes glossed. After a hard swallow, he whispered, "Thank you."

The guards opened the double massive doors before they arrived, and the High Queen and King entered first. Fate and Hero trailed behind, beneath the crystal chandelier, to the left wing, and through a glass corridor.

At the end of the Left Wing, a pale woman with dark hair met them, and led them through the palace into a temple.

Fate's mouth fell open as she stepped through the door. Large curved beams stretched from the floor and met at the ceiling, creating a near-perfect teardrop shape. Sunlight trickled through the stained glass and spilled onto the floor in a kaleidoscope of colors. Live plants sprung from the floor and climbed the support pillars until they burst into flowers.

Kyou and Fortis stood at the far end of the temple near a raised, filigreed wooden platform.

Kyou rushed up to Hero and greeted him with an embrace. "My most precious son!"

Fate stepped out of the way and glanced at Chi as an armed soldier rounded the corner followed by a group of palace guards.

Fate still found it curious that Kyou referred to Hero as his son even though it was clear they shared no relation. Neither of them had spoken of their relationship, and it intrigued her how such a sense of kinship had come to be.

Akira barked from the platform, drawing everyone's attention. "Are we planning on attending the ritual today?"

Fate gaped at him, unnerved by how he seemingly appeared out of thin air. She looked at Chi, then Hero and Kyou, comforted that they remained calm and jovial in spite of Akira's outward irritation.

When her gaze returned to Akira, he simply bowed his head, keeping his eyes locked on her, and spoke in a calm, collected tone. "*Reinka.*"

Kyou led Hero up to the platform.

Fate slowed her gait to make certain she arrived at the platform after everyone else. She kept a vigilant eye on Akira. A part of her felt for his predicament; dealing with people who refused to listen must grow tiresome.

The scent of smoke and ash wafted from him as he passed by.

She leaned towards him and whispered, "Were you around someone who smokes?"

He looked down at her but refrained from answering. Miasma seeped from his very core as his polychromatic eyes moved from person to person with a frown.

Fate, the last to enter, bowed at the High King and Queen soon after entering the room.

High Queen Heqet's spirit dulled in her husband's presence, and formality set in. "Welcome to Inoue Palace. Before we begin, there are some announcements we would like to make."

Khnum stepped forward, comfortable with his interruption. "I've met with the Council. Due to your recent activities and behaviors, they have set forth some rules."

Fate's regard for Heqet diminished. When she beheld the noble queen, she did so with scrutiny and distrust. However, the sense of betrayal shortly vanished, as Heqet blinked hard, emanating deep remorse.

By instinct, Fate also looked at Hero, who seemed to expect the undercut.

Finally, she glanced back at Akira as he held his cat, looking bored.

"Foremost, Hero must, under Council supervision, complete a list of approved studies as the future successor. This means that after your pact is formed, he and Kyou will join a Council-ordained representative on a mandatory journey through Mu."

Fate drew back a breath. "Pardon."

Khnum paused in disbelief, then continued. "Secondly, Lady Fate will study the appropriate duties and etiquette of a High Queen, which is, apparently, desperately needed. Her High Queen will supervise said training, to the pleasure of the Council without fail."

Hero interjected calmly. "This is all very sudden. When are we expected to leave, and for how long?"

Heqet looked out from behind a scowling Khnum. "The tour will last approximately three turns, and the representative will arrive this evening."

Fate staggered back. "Three turns?"

Khnum crossed his arms. "This conversation has drawn on too long. It is of your own making. If you wish to proceed, I suggest you do so with haste."

Hero stepped forward and bowed his head. "It would be an honor to train. I accept."

Khnum's eyes shifted to Fate.

Her mouth hung open, unable to find the necessary words. She watched Hero as he nodded at her, urging for her to proceed. After a strangled breath, she squeaked out an answer. "I accept."

Everyone's attention turned to Akira.

The moody man tapped his foot while he waited. Once he realized that the debate had ended, he set his cat down and conjured a cloud of black smoke that swirled and materialized into a scythe. "Hero and Fate, step forward."

Fate followed the directive, keeping a terrified eye on Hero.

He took her hand and eased her tension with a gentle squeeze and a smile.

Akira reached forward and thrust his hand through Hero's chest, withdrawing what appeared to be a micro-thin, glowing blue thread. The way he managed to reach inside indicated that he possessed the ability to move through objects, as he did no harm to Hero during this transaction. He seemed like a ghost.

Fate gasped, at first in shock, and then in relief. *Anima.*

Akira shifted his eyes to Fate.

She braced herself as his hand burst through her chest. A delicate thread stretched out from her torso, glowing in a bright golden light.

Akira took the ends of each thread of anima and held them together. "To complete this binding, you must form a pact." He glowered as he glanced between the pair. "You must make a promise of souls."

Hero stepped towards Fate and took her by the arms. His aura swelled and radiated through her, producing a resonance between them. "No matter what may come between us, I will return to your side...." He donned a confident but calm smile. "...at the speed of sound."

Fate stared into his eyes. They may not be lovers, but they provided each other the only hope of returning balance to their collapsed empire. It struck a chord of familiarity within her soul. "And I promise to never give up, no matter the circumstance."

Akira scowled as he fused the ends together. "Your binding can now be completed."

Hero leaned towards Fate and pressed his lips to hers, allowing their energies to flow together.

A spark between them caused Fate to withdraw, holding her lip. The pain stemmed deep down, as though she had done something wrong.

Heqet moved to Fate's side. "I am so delighted to officially welcome you both into the palace."

Fate allowed the High Queen to shake her hand. Everything in her life reminded her of a play that she acted out just to please others. The Binding Ritual had left a sinking feeling in her stomach, as though she'd just signed away her life in the worst possible way. She reminded herself that worse things could have happened, if Hero hadn't appeared at the auction.

Even so, she choked back tears as she watched the sun set against the ocean.

This is for the best, isn't it?

As night fell over the palace, Fate strolled through a darkened wing while peeking up at the waning moon. It formed a perfect grin and laughed at her. Despite all of her effort, her troubles waited just ahead, but now she was far from her sisters.

Hero had gone with the Council's representative. The Queen and Akira attended to personal affairs, and even Kyou and Fortis had left shortly after the ceremony.

She wound up alone, sitting against one of the decorative windows as the moonlight cast light onto her back, staring at her shadow.

Her world had spun around again, and she'd looped back into a cage, this time disguised as a grand palace.

She gazed out the window at the Ussan as it glowed against the night sky. The thought of how her morning had started left her with a deep hole in her gut.

The moon loomed over the glowing crystal trees, making them shimmer.

She leaned her head against the cool glass, thinking about the *Story of Night and Day*. If only she and Hero were so close. Inoue Capital made her feel lost again. As before, she began life in a new place, without really settling into the last place. Since Abyssus's death, Hero had remained her only consistency, so she grappled with the fact that he too had left, and would not return to her for three turns.

At least Inoue bore some familiarity, albeit it in some deep part of her consciousness. She presumed that it derived from the Ussan and its resonating trees. Rather than dwell, she decided to leave the hall and go to study — the only real reprieve from her turmoil.

Queen Heqet had given her a gorgeous room on the first floor, before the hall to the Council's Wing. She opened the gold-trimmed door and stepped inside. The amount of space not only came across as daunting, but unnecessary. No single person could possibly utilize the entire area. It comprised a lounge, a study, and a bed big enough for three or four adults. Nonetheless, she accepted the comfort of the bed and threw herself onto it.

Fate missed Abyssus, Fortuna, her sisters, Hero's folklore, and, contrary to what she'd believed earlier that day, Chi's tea. Even the foolish Kyou seemed wise to her now — he had the common sense to escape the caged life of a Royal. Even if her gut warned of these truths, she knew deep down that she must persist, not for herself but for those who placed their trust in her.

Her eyes grew heavy as the night wore on.

The chiming of the Ussan persisted as she lay back on the bed. Soon, the ringing transformed into whispers, and she strained to understand their meaning. The voices grew into a din, but the words never became comprehensible.

She tried to lift her arm but it remained pinned to her side. Again, she attempted to pry herself from the bed, unable to see what restricted her movement. Panic set in. Unable to move her head, her eyes darted around the room trying to ascertain the unseen force that held her captive.

In the glow of the moonlight, she caught sight of the sheen of the webs that restrained her. The long sticky strands pulled tighter, causing her to sink into the mattress. The pressure squeezed the air from her lungs, forcing her to suck in short, tiny breaths.

The bed gave way, and Fate fell through it and the floor, landing in a pool of water. She surfaced, gasping for air, and choked as she slapped the water, still tugging against the webs as they dragged her under.

After violently thrashing, she broke free and swam to the surface, then to the shore, where she collapsed onto the sand.

The chiming surrounded her as she lay there, still panting. Eventually, she looked up through her soaking wet hair towards a massive tunnel encased in a glowing web that stretched farther than the eye could see.

Fate staggered to her feet, still coughing and trembling, and stumbled forward. While taking in her surroundings, she dared not make a sound. Something had made the web, and she thought it best to leave it undisturbed. Her darkness throbbed, heavy in her chest, warning of impending change.

Crystal shards stuck out from the blackened soil along the edges of the tunnel, encased in a shroud of the incandescent web. Each thick strand of web glistened as it stretched from the ground to far above.

Fate knew she must keep moving.

The Dreamscape called to her in whispers. "This way."

Her teeth chattered as she traveled into the tunnel. She hugged herself, wishing for a trickle of sunlight to warm her.

Ahead, something moved in the darkness. White hair or fur gleamed in the low light but remained concealed in the shadows.

Fate's heart skipped a beat, fearing whatever creature had made its nest in this place.

The white-haired woman from the labyrinth stepped into a sliver of light, and approached from the darkened tunnel.

Fate halted and stood frozen as the woman treaded closer, the woman she now knew for certain was the Spinner.

The Spinner moved with purpose, her white gown billowing around her. In a flash of gold and white smoke, the Spinner was instantly upon her, holding Fate's face in her hands and staring at her deeply with luminous crimson eyes, her touch as cold as ice and her skin just as white. Tiny glowing specks of ash drifted upward from her body.

"What have you done?" the Spinner asked.

Fate shook, her mouth open wide as she recognized her own face gazing back at her. She broke free and staggered away.

The Spinner kept her eyes fixed on Fate as she tugged on one of the strands of web within reach. A pulse of blue light ran up the web and produced a ringing sound.

Fate jolted backward, terrified that the Spinner had called forth some monstrous creature. She needed to discover the meaning of her dream, and escape before she wound up trapped.

"Why do you look like me?" she asked.

The Spinner twisted her head from one side to the other and then back again. She took a jagged step towards Fate, but did not answer, and then turned back to the tunnel as though she had heard something.

A lump formed in Fate's throat as hollow shrieks echoed down the tunnel. She instantly recognized the sound of the shadow creatures.

The Spinner turned back to her with tears in her eyes. "The children are crying."

A chill coursed through Fate as the image of the shadow creatures flashed through her mind, but she persisted despite this fear. "Why are they crying?"

The Spinner vanished and reappeared inches from Fate's face. Her silver hair floated around Fate, suspended by an unperceivable energy. "It's our fault."

Fate stumbled backward. "Our?"

"Yes. We did not play the game."

Fate's body shook uncontrollably as her darkness raged inside, causing horrific cramping. She doubled over in agony and grunted.

The Spinner knelt down, stretched her arm forward, and with a clicking sound rising from her throat, crawled towards Fate with her bones snapping and popping.

Fate sobbed, terrified that the shadow creatures would emerge from the tunnel at any moment. She dragged herself away from the Spinner, her stomach retaliating fiercely. A surge of bile hit her throat and she lunged forward, vomiting up a mass of black fluid. It splattered the Spinner's gown and crept upward, turning the white fabric into shining black tar.

Fate's body quaked, and she took in sharp painful breaths as the slick black substance engulfed the Spinner.

The Spinner twisted and writhed as the substance reached her mouth. She wheezed and choked as the fluid drowned her. She dropped to her knees, and then lurched forward, spewing dark liquid in a mass of tangled black hair. A long metal spike erupted from her throat, wrapped in the hair, and clanged on the ground. She convulsed as black seeped from her eyes.

Fate shook her head, unable to blink or scream.

The Spinner's fingers tore at the ground, and her bones cracked as she struggled against a second spike. Garbled cries emanated from her throat and the spike fell from her mouth.

Fate watched, unable to feel her own body, as the Spinner squeezed blackened soil in her fingers and released a booming scream that echoed throughout the tunnel and chamber.

Ether oozed from the Spinner's torso and dispersed in glowing blue tufts as she wailed, "Why?"

Fate shook her head, back-pedaling into the water.

The Spinner looked up with black eyes and wept. "I am Nuvem Fati, am I not?"

Fate recognized her own mantra, and trembled before her own mutilated image with wide unblinking eyes. "It can't be."

Fati twisted her head to the side and gazed upon Fate with the same hollow stare that Fate used herself when looking into the mirror. "We are the Spinner, are we not?"

Fate retreated deeper into the water, gripping her head. "Wake up, Fate."

Fati stood and followed Fate into the pool, spreading the darkness. "We cannot hide from ourselves. What happened... should not have. We must make it right."

Fate swam backwards into a tangle of web. Dense shiny strands wrapped around her and stuck fast. She thrashed against them but her movement only tightened their hold. The web pulled her in towards the shore and the Spinner. She wrestled against the web as it cut into her skin, turning the water around her red with her blood.

Fati waited, arms open, her eyes locked on Fate. "We must continue our duty or the world will fall to chaos."

Fate tore at the webs, screaming.

Fati waved her hands in the air, rapidly moving her fingers. "But chaos... why not chaos?" The webs drew Fate into Fati's embrace. Fati stroked Fate's hair with a motherly caress. "Chaos is not so bad to us, no? We need all three Fates if we are truly to have a chance."

Fate shuddered in heaving breaths through stinging tears, still fighting and straining against the webs and thick tar-like substance now coating them both. "Please, let me go."

Fati looked down at the web and then back at Fate. "I can't. We were Fated long ago. We are the Spinner, not the Spider."

Fate inhaled a harsh rugged breath. "Persephone...."

A shadowy tear slipped from the Spinner's eye as she took Fate's face into one of her blackened hands. "That's right." She leaned forward, pressed her mouth to Fate's, and spewed the thick black fluid, ether, and darkness within.

Fate opened her eyes and stared at the ceiling, a sense of calm washing over her. Everything became clear, and she understood the steps she needed to take. She drew in a deep, clear breath, and reflected on the knowledge she once held as Fati. Her own truth, buried deep inside for ages, had finally been freed, along with the knowledge of what had come before her imprisonment. Her memories crept in, as did the pain of her betrayal.

She frowned. "Everything that has happened, is happening, will happen again."

Her soul ached with the knowledge that her wounds were too great, and she no longer held the power to win the game. Even now, she felt her anima waver, warning of yet another forced slumber, and it set aflame an unquenchable fury inside her. She sat up and crawled from the bed, and crossed the room to the window.

From the window, she exited to the balcony, and to a narrow ladder that led up to the rooftop. The moon hung overhead, so large she felt she could reach out and touch it. "Together, we could make this right."

She looked far into the distance, out over the twin kingdoms of Nex, disgusted. Then, she turned her attention to the streets below. The Ancients she once knew had fallen from grace, and before her now sat a cesspool of lies and depravity. Her slumber had lasted too long. She traced the vast expanse of trees from the eastern and western woods that lay to the south, and even farther to the distant sands of Tir Na Nog. There, she'd find her future.

As she gazed towards the desert land, she thought of the Lords of Light and Shadow. If Euphoria could be cleansed, it would take all of them. They were once so close to uniting, but this cursed land had required a more careful hand than expected.

She maintained only a few certainties among the never-ending variables. First, Neco would die by her hand for his insult. She'd make it slow and painful, just as he deserved. Second, she must protect Hero at any cost, even if it wounded her soul. Lastly, she would hunt down the person responsible for her death and restore the balance.

She turned her sight upward and gazed at the clouds drifting by, and watched as the moonlight playfully hid and let trickles of light cast shadows on the city below. When she'd still slumbered, things had felt distant and bland. After her Awakening, everything seemed unreasonably harsh, leaving a bitter taste in her mouth. Time ticked by too slowly for comfort. Every moment she wasted meant an opportunity lost forever.

She gritted her teeth, refusing to give in to her new vulnerability. The opportunity to make a decision with her full strength had already passed her by. As Casluhim had warned, she must choose her path wisely and play her role well.

It's always easier to see the roads that should have been taken, than to know what judgment to use at the next crossroads.

She no longer questioned his wisdom.

"Cas, how right you were. If only I had listened sooner."

Now that she'd decided to play the game, she intended to play brutally.

---WE HOPE YOU ENJOYED THE STORY---

This is only the beginning.
Be sure to check out the rest of the
"Grims' Truth" series, several books of which
are already available, and many more of which
are coming. Indeed, the current publishing plan
calls for 60 books in the series. We know... wow!

Also, please continue for the Reference Guide,
Book Club Guide, Interview with the Authors,
and more back-of-the-book extras.

THE SPINNER'S WEB
REFERENCE GUIDE

NOTE: All reference guides apply only to the book in which they are included. You can find a full version of these guides at **www.GrimsTruth.com**.

Terminology

TAINTED/STAINED: A condition caused by a spiritual fracture. The term *Tainted* or *Stained* comes from a dark soot-like mark that appears on those who suffer from this ailment. The Council has deemed them *illegal*, by the notion that the Tainted are responsible for spreading spiritual blood called *miasma*, and causing the Plague.

MIASMA: Sometimes referred to as *negative energy*, miasma is actually spiritual blood that causes pain and ailments including: hysteria, paranoia, violent impulses, and delusions to anyone in its presence for extended periods.

SEALS/BRANDS: Spiritual restraints that come in the form of accessories, ink, or burns on the skin. There are so many forms of seals that the temples keep books on them.

Folklore & History

THE BOOK OF BEGINNINGS: The oldest scripture responsible for shaping Ancient society. Like the Book of Ages, the stories are written as folklore. However, since no one knows the authors of these books, there are many who doubt their authenticity.

THE BOOK OF AGES: The second scripture of Ancient society and beliefs. The stories here are more prevalent in Ancient culture and viewed as common knowledge, but rarely referenced due to their fantastical viewpoints and questionable authenticity.

THE TEACHINGS OF GRIM: A collection of passages, proverbs, and teachings by the Grim. Many consider them warnings, but for the studious followers, it is pure wisdom for any who can read the Language of Ages.

ROTA FORTUNAE: A tale from the Book of Ages about a young girl, Fati, and the God who adopts her. She is said to be from the lower realm, and her Soul's Purpose is to decide the fate of the Mortal Realms. However, she is given the opportunity to choose her path, and thus change the way history unfolds. It is closely related, and mirrors, the Story of Space & Time. It also has two endings. This story turned out to be the basis for a children's game.

THE STORY OF SPACE & TIME: A story about a boy called Leoht (Mi'Nih), who is abandoned by his father and taken in by the red-haired God, Casluhim. Unlike many other tales from the Book of Ages, Leoht chooses more than one path and gift.

THE MAN WHO STOOD AT THE EDGE OF TIME: Many people talk about this tale, but all they really say is that it's about a man who broke the Mirror of Space and Time, and then traveled to the Edge of Time.

SANDS OF TIME: A fictional novel written about Bound lovers named Solaris and Ulnaire. They say that the characters were modeled after various personas in folklore. It seems to be an encrypted message about the Lords of Light and Shadow.

Main Characters
By order of appearance and importance....

*CRUENTUS FATE: The main character of *The Spinner's Web*. She grew up in the brothel after being sold by her father, the King of Macellarius, Cruentus Neco. The members of the Rebellion call her the Spinner, after a character from folklore in the Book of Ages. Supposedly, she is a Doll, intended to become the High Queen's successor.

ABYSSUS: The Prince of Macellarius. He is Fate's brother, who left behind a series of journals to help her understand the web of chaos unfolding in Mu. Although he is gone, many still remember him by the remnants of him scattered around the Empire.

CAELES HERO: The Prince of Nitor. He is Tainted and often tries to avoid the eyes of the Council. After winning the Astor Tournament, he earned the title of Future High King of Mu. Despite his skill and status, few hold him with high regard.

The Royals

CAELES ELAINE: The late Queen of Nitor. She passed away when Hero was young. There are rumors that she was murdered, and her son was framed, but no one knows the truth because he was sealed after the incident.

CRUENTUS NECO: The King of Macellarius. After losing Fate to the murder of Prince Abyssus, Neco spends his days wallowing in his failure. No one speaks of his condition. In fact, most people try to pretend he doesn't exist... except, perhaps, Fate.

CRUENTUS NITEO: The King of Nitor. He is often seen with the High King of Mu, attempting to win his place amongst the Royals of the Capital. Since his son, Hero, was a child, Niteo cared only about his position as the King of Nitor and protecting his status, no matter what the cost.

IUNU KYOU: The First Prince of Inoue, also known as the Wayward Prince. He and Fate were initially supposed to be wed, but even Kyou opposed this idea. His intentions are often unclear, but he does appear to have a close bond with Hero.

IUNU HEQET: The High Queen of Mu. She spends most of her time battling against her husband and the other members of the Council.

IUNU KHNUM: The High King of Mu. He's a Council follower as well as a Fallen. Khnum speaks very little, mostly observing wherever he goes, and he has a strong belief in restoring full power to purebred Ancients.

The Guards

IGNIS FIRMUS: Abyssus' former guard. After the death of his closest friend, he moved to the Capital and received assistance from Akira. He spends a majority of his time working between kingdoms and assisting his brother, Fortis, on assignments.

IGNIS FORTIS: Niteo's guard. In spite of his position, Fortis has taken to wandering away from the King of Nitor out of spite. His Ancient blood and Royal background prevent Niteo from changing his decisions; therefore, Fortis does as he pleases and has even gained the title of the Royal Philanderer.

SHINKA MORTIS: Neco's guard. He speaks very little and has an uncanny ability to survive even the most brutal attacks. Most people try to avoid him.

CAELES CHI: The High Queen's guard. She is also Hero's aunt, but rarely has the time or opportunity to meet with him. When she isn't guarding the High Queen, she is directing the Capital's soldiers and studying the Ussan.

Brothel

IGNIS FORTUNA: One of the leaders of the Rebellion. Fortuna spent many turns protecting and teaching Fate during her stay in Mu. Her inconspicuous nature and striking appearance deter many from her real strategy and ability to turn the tides in the Rebellion's favor.

SHAI MYRNA: One of Fate's sisters from the brothel. She left with Nigel after the auction, and rumor has it she assumed an important role with the Rebellion. Her ability to remain hidden fascinates many, especially the few people who see her working.

AEROS TORI: Fate's closest sister. Although she initially picked fights with Fate, they grew closer than any of their other sisters.

Other

AMANA NIGEL: The Madam's Lover. He is a valued member of the Rebellion that often appears in the Madam's stead to relay messages to Fate. His role and capabilities are hidden so well, no one even questions his presence when he arrives.

CRUENTUS LARA: Hero's childhood friend and the King's Ward. She has a strange, obsessive fixation with Hero. In the past, she often tormented Fate, and fired an onslaught of slurs in an attempt to separate her from Hero.

EA'ANAT ISIS: The Head of Artillery in Nitor, the Queen of Askadel, and a devout council member. Her relationship with the Royals is vague. She is often seen with Niteo and bears an air of familiarity whenever she speaks to Hero.

RA AKI: The High Queen's Aide who received the title of *The Queen's Dog*. He is also Tainted, and often avoided by those with keen spiritual prowess. No one is really sure why he meanders about the Capital.

BESIL: Akira's black cat. He has the most peculiar blue eyes, and seems to be the only being capable of calming Akira's moods.

Groups

THE COUNCIL: A group of Ancient Elders responsible for upholding the preservation of Ancient clans and traditions. The citizens of Mu live by Council laws and scriptures. The Council believes that maintaining old tradition and preserving purebred Ancients is their most essential task; therefore, they have outlawed the Tainted and Half-Breeds.

THE REBELLION: The Ancient uprising against Council law. The members of the Rebellion are inconspicuous about their participation, and work in the shadows to return balance to the world they live in.

THE WATCHERS: Ethereal beings from the Beyond. They are responsible for upholding the Grandmaster's laws and are capable of both sealing and erasing souls for their various misdemeanors.

THE GRIM: A group of Ancients who present themselves in the forms of large skeletal beings. The majority believes they have transcended beyond a physical form, but supposedly, they just disguise themselves by wearing a uniform. They always speak in terms of *we*, so as not to disclose their identity.

DOLLS: The *Children of Grim*. Dolls are old Ancients' souls who have returned in the form of a vessel. Currently, the Grim are the only Puppeteers left in existence, as Puppeteering has been outlawed by the Council.

Breeds

ANCIENT: Often referred to as the supreme beings by lesser breeds, yet disregarded by superior beings. Each clan inhibits different elemental capabilities and strengths, and all of them display strong genetic traits that are reflected in their physical appearance. They can live tens of thousands of years, and some even live out multiple lives with a special mate called their Bound.

HALF-BREED: A being that is part of two genetic strains. The Ancients refuse to acknowledge them as true Ancients because they do not have pure blood, but most of them still have elemental capabilities. They live longer than the Rahma but not quite as long as pure blood Ancients.

RAHMA: A lesser group of beings that only live hundreds of years by the Ancients' influence. They are incapable of manipulating elements and possess no special endowments, except that they live longer than Human Beings. They experienced an influx of population when the Age of the Ancients started to come to an end. Although they worshipped the Ancients to a certain degree, many Rahma believed they were greater, and were detested by the higher breeds.

HUMANS: The weakest of the breeds. They did not come into being until long after the Rise of the Rahma had come to an end.

Ancient Clans

FEH – Electricity: The Feh are smaller than other clans, but make up for their lack of stature with tremendous force. Although they have a wide variety of physical traits, all Feh are tiny — the tallest being no larger than a juvenile Ancient. Due to their curious and intelligent nature, the Feh found many uses for their element, and made Nysa one of the most beautiful and sought after kingdoms in the Empire.

GRIM – Darkness: Although they were one of the original clans, the Grim took their leave of the Mortal Realm, and chose to exist in the darkness of the Abyss instead of share a place beside the Ancients and the Rahma, but their reason for doing this is not clear. The large skeletal beings appear to aid in the growth of the mortals, and yet remain separated from them. In spite of this, the clan is at odds with the Mortal Realm and the Council alike, and no one is privy to knowing why and how they operate Niall.

-Sub. REAPERS – Darkness: Reapers are an unusual group of former Ancients, turned rogue, who work with the Grim for unknown purposes. They are able to fold space-time at will, which makes it possible for them to appear and disappear from mortal events on a whim. This creates an uncomfortable situation for the Ancients, the Rahma, and the Council, but that's exactly how the Reapers like it. They are identified by their cloaks of darkness and soul-sealed animal masks. The most frightening forms of Reapers carry weapons crafted from darkness, and are marked by "the Hand of Death."

VEM – Air – RARE: Vem are marked by their delicate frame, pale skin, dark hair, and vibrant blue eyes. They have innate spiritual manipulation capabilities, and are one of the only clans able to Puppeteer. They are shy by nature and thus usually keep to themselves unless they develop a deep emotional bond—which they will keep until death.

RA – Time – LOST: Very little is known about this clan. Their disappearance from the Mortal Realm is one the great Ancient mysteries. They may have left of their own accord, much like the Grim, or some unfortunate events may have driven them to extinction. The only certainty is that they were the sole masters of time. They could stop and even reverse time at will. This fact makes it unclear as to how a clan like this could vanish without a trace, if not by their own choice.

IU – Body: All Iu carry the same traits—they are delicate but tall with pale skin, black hair, and violet eyes. They are seldom aggressive but, if angered, their wrath is much like a dance with death. They are one of the masters of the "Flash-Step"—a movement so quick that the eye cannot follow.

-Sub. IUNU – Body: There is little evolution between the Iu and the Iunu. They are one of the purest sub clans. It is more a shift in clan temperament than an actual sub categorization. After the Verna Conflict, the Iu were all but lost except the Iunu branch family. They upheld the formalities and policies of the Iu clan as a whole.

CAELES – Ice – LOST: This rare and unusual clan rose in Undal with the rise of the Crystal Empire. They were reclusive and hostile towards outsiders, and were the only clan able to withstand the Igni assault during the Verna Conflict. Their Empire rose up out of the Ussan suddenly, and collapsed just as quickly, leaving them nearly one of the lost clans. The Caeles are broken into two factions—the Wolf Clan and the Fox Clan. If not for the cleverness of the Fox Clan, the Caeles would have been lost altogether.

---Wolf Clan are the leaders of the Caeles. They are tall, strong, and agile, marked with silvery hair and an abnormal grey tone to their skin without actually being grey. They have a variety of eye colors, including gray, silver, icy blue, and pale yellow. Their battle prowess makes them a terrifying foe, because if you see one Caeles, there is most certainly a pack nearby.

---Fox Clan are known for being compact and stealthy. They are petite in stature, much like the Feh, but much stronger and faster. Like the Wolf Clan, they travel in packs and are quite capable of taking down much stronger foes. Fox Clan is, above all else, highly intelligent. They are so pale they are considered the albino of the breeds. With icy skin, mint eyes, and white hair, it is hard to believe they are so skilled at disappearing into their surroundings, but they are deadly masters of stealth and cunning. Beware of what you don't see, because it can kill you.

NIS – Fire: The Nis are emotionally and sexually charged Ancients, that appear much larger in stature but remain lean and agile. They are easily recognized by their dark hair, tanned skin, freckles, and amber eyes.

-Sub. Ignis – Fire: The Ignis carry the appearance of the Nis but hold a special trait known as "The Cat's Eye". This trait gives them the ability to see more than most, such as sensing spiritual change and seeing across vast expanses without aid. In fact, these qualities are what brought the Igni into great power during the age of Undal. Even though the clan nearly met their end with the cataclysmic fall of Chien, their drive for sex and an innate need to immediately find their Bound, they recovered from the collapse and ended up being one of the strongest clans.

KA – Mind: Flaming red hair, intense green eyes, and sandy skin are the mark of the Ka. Their spirit burns much like their appearance. They are emotionally charged and passionate about everything they do.

-Sub. ASKA – Illusion: Aska carry the appearance of all Ka but they more volatile by nature. The passion of the Ka is always apparent; however, the Aska often turn to malice. Their feelings can drive them to commit personal acts of vengeance and/or spite. Their gift for strategy makes them formidable foes, so it is best to keep them from exploring deviant resolves.

SI – Spirit: A clan with the power over the spirit and will. They are notorious for their unique connection to the Universe and the Grandmaster as well as their ability to Spirit Walk. They are dark-skinned and often covered by brands that reflect their spiritual beliefs. Many believe that the clan went into hiding and so they have not been categorized as 'lost'.

Locations

In order of placement on the map....

MU: An empire of twelve kingdoms where mortal beings live, both Ancient and Rahma. A majority of the kingdoms are Ancient ruled despite the massive decline in their population. They encourage the union of Bound with the intention of bringing power back to their breed, but have faced difficulty in their endeavor. The Empire is vastly divided by the powers of the Rebellion and the Council.

INOUE CAPITAL: The Capital of Mu is a grand city that overlooks the sea. It is home to the largest population of Ancients in the Empire and some of the grandest celebrations. The Queen hosts regular parties, auctions, and events to bring the people together. It is also the political center for Mu, often called the Utopia of Mu for its magnificent view of the Ussan and its preservation of old tradition.

INOUE COMMUNITY: The community on the opposite side of the Centre between the Capital Palace and the beaches below. The people of Inoue live roof to roof on the slope, adhering to old tradition and gathering for celebrations held by the Royal Family living at the top of the slope. In spite of their spacious region, they prefer to remain close together, as a reminder to cherish their neighbors and their families. Children from this community gather in the Centre to listen to folklore told by the Elders.

USSAN: Rumored to be the only remainder of the once magnificent crystal empire. The forest is guarded by Capital guards at all times, because it is so dangerous, but many people from all around the Empire try to visit the Capital for a chance to see it up close. The citizens of Inoue say that the forest sings and chimes. In some cases, they say that if you listen closely, you can hear it whispering.

NEX: A once luxurious region tarnished by the Plague and Rahma rule. The two sides of the kingdom, Nex and Macellarius, were divided upon the coronation of the Cruentus Twins, Neco and Niteo. It is the smallest and coldest kingdom in all of Mu, and is often neglected by the higher powers due to its Rahma rulers. Even so, it is considered important because it is the only kingdom standing between the Capital and the rest of the Empire.

NYSA: Home of the Feh, it's in the heart of Mu. Although they are few in numbers, they still hold a great deal of power and influence in Mu. With their intelligence and fantastic ability to manipulate their element, the Feh have created one of the most beautiful and peaceful kingdoms in all of Mu. Their King Askelon is a diplomat who is respected by all factions.

THULE: An island where Ancients still thrive. The Council is located here in the Grand Acropolis. It is the largest concentration of pure blood Ancients, and the city rivals the population of all of Mu.

UNDAL: Often referred to as the Old World. Most people believe that it's a mythological world or theorist's tale about the world before Mu. However, there are a select few who believe in its origins and study its history and scriptures.

BOOK CLUB GUIDE

1. Miasma plays a large role in the plot. At this point, what is your understanding of the effects it has on others?

2. How do you think Fate's visions in the Dreamscape pertain to her real life?

3. The Rebellion and the Council have diametrically opposed views on religion and politics. Based on their current arguments, which side do you believe is the most fair? If neither, discuss the reasons why.

4. What reasoning might the Madam Fortuna have had for not training Fate to fight before her meeting Hero?

5. According to the story thus far, the Spinner symbolizes the fate of mortals. What do you think the relevance of this is to the plot?

6. How might the story of the original Spinner foreshadow the current tale?

7. The books of "Grims' Truth" carry many hints in symbolism and subtleties throughout the story. Discuss some of the details that were the most distinct, and what hints they might hold.

8. The story suggests that the Tainted are responsible for the deaths of hundreds, if not thousands, of people throughout Mu. What might be the Rebellion's reasoning behind focusing on the perpetrator of the murders instead of the Tainted?

9. Shadow creatures appear at numerous points in the story. What do you think they are, and do you think they're more than apparitions?

10. There is outward tension between Akira and Hero. Akira accuses Hero of being something other than what he appears to be. There are also several inconsistencies in Hero's stories, and he's an admitted liar, but Fate still chooses him in the end. Why do you think this is, and do you think it's a mistake?

INTERVIEW WITH THE AUTHORS

Q. If you had to give up either snacks and drinks, or music, during writing sessions, which would you find more difficult to say goodbye to?

YIN A. Music. I *cannot* write without music.
YANG A. That's tough. I don't know... can I eat the music?

Q. What is the funniest typo you've ever written?

YIN A. I was supposed to write, "Derek stands in shock and then runs to catch up with Christian." What I actually wrote was, "Derek stands in shock as the runs catch up with Christian."
YANG A. I kept screenshots of our funniest typos but they're on my old laptop, so I'll have to share them on our social media some time. The only one I remember at the moment is 'tress,' which I always type instead of trees.

Q. Do you feel like it's most important to have: A) Strong Characters; B) Mind-Blowing Plot Twists, or; C) Epic Settings?

YIN A. In short, yes.
YANG A. I guess if I *had* to choose, I would say strong characters because, personally, I can sit through just about anything if I'm attached to the characters.

Q. What is your most unusual writing quirk?

YIN A. I will listen to the same song on repeat to evoke a particular emotion while I'm writing a scene.

YANG A. I act out dialogue and scenes while doing daily activities, so I'm essentially having a conversation with myself.

Q. When writing a series, how do you keep things fresh, for both your readers and yourself?

YIN A. I like to keep the plot moving forward. I'm not fond of long lulls in stories.

YANG A. I choose different inspirations during each manuscript, and then capitalize on moments of impact to create emotional triggers. Like Yin said, long lulls are not exciting. It's best to keep moving forward.

Q. What is your writing process like?

YIN A. I outline my stories backward, and then insert significant moments in the 'right' spots before I begin the writing process. There's more, but it's complicated and obsessive.

YANG A. I agree with Yin here. I also outline the story backward and then break the book into three parts, add impact points, and nail where the beginning and the end connect.

Q. What's the strangest thing you had to do to create this story?

BOTH A. We had to pull out a massive corkboard and a bunch of index cards, write down every book, arc, and main character, organize the story by historical events, and then put them in the release order. We strategized carefully so we could keep the story interesting, because it's a long series and we didn't want to lose readers along the way.

Q. Which scene, character, or plotline changed the most from first draft to published book?

BOTH A: Book 1, hands down. (**Publisher's Insert:** Originally published as *Rota Fortunae*, and now republished as *The Spinner's Web*.)

YIN A. We wanted people to be able to look back from book 60 and think: *Wow, that's a completely different story than when I read it the first time.*

YANG A. To implement every single element and utilize it to the maximum effect, we honestly had to rewrite that same book over and over and over.

Q. Were there scenes you ended up cutting that you wish you could have kept? Describe them and the decision-making process.

YIN A. I'm not going to lose them. I'm going to find a way to put them in there. People need to know!

YANG A. Uh, well, during the rewrite of Book 1, we had to strategically pick and choose timelines, so initially the story for book 1 comprised all of arc 1 and you were able to see Fate's downward spiral in a different light. However, I'm very happy with where we ended up.

Q. What special support people (critique partners, writing group, beta readers, editor, agent, author's assistant) do you rely on? How do they help you?

BOTH A. We have incredible beta readers who all have vastly different perspectives. Talking with them during the editing process gives us insight into how readers perceive the story, and what we can improve on before it goes to publication.

Our amazing editor, Lane Diamond... we're so fortunate and grateful to have him polish and perfect the writing and details. He's truly talented.

Our cover artist, Cindy Fan, who captures the nuances in our complicated story and brings life and feeling to the series through the imagery. She's such a huge inspiration to us both.

Last but not least, Evolved Publishing for being so patient with us during Yin's Stage 4 Cancer treatments, and for always believing in us, guiding us, and backing us as we embark on this insane journey... and also for seeing what others did not.

Q. Which scene in The Spinner's Web was most difficult to write? Why?

YIN A. The opening... it was *a lot*. The auction was a close second. I was so stressed for her.

YANG A. It's between the performance and the auction. Both of these scenes survived every rewrite, no matter how much the whole manuscript changed. These scenes were always in the story and both were essential to the plot, which resulted in many revisions.

WHAT'S NEXT?

As you may be aware, Isu Yin & Fae Yang have outlined for us a 60-book plan for the "Grims' Truth" series, so.... yeah... wow!

Needless to say, they're quite busy working on the next books to come. Please stay tuned to developments and plans by subscribing to their newsletter at the link below.

www.GrimsTruth.com

ACKNOWLEDGEMENTS

We have always dreamed and hoped for the day when we could begin telling this beast of a story. Isu, being the elder, first began this journey during her early childhood, then Fae picked it up during *her* early childhood. The struggle has been surreal, so there we'd like to thank those who have supported us along the way.

Thank you Sheila, Charles, & Samuel Dreiling for encouraging us, especially during the early stages of the series. It really meant the world to have close supporters with whom we can share the joy of our milestone.

Thank you Esther Beltran for teaching Yang better grammar. Otherwise, I'm sure our editor would've been at a complete loss.

We also owe a tremendous thank you to our early beta readers: Koemi Li, Anna Maria Gamboa, Mai Vee Vang, Nikki Richards, & Maddy Little for giving us feedback. It makes all the difference in the world to have multiple sets of eyes.

Our street team, ARX, has been so incredibly encouraging, supportive, and helpful we can't even begin to describe.

Thank you Kel Ho, for receiving one of the first editions of the first book and offering words of encouragement, kindness, and support to Fae during such a crucial time. If not for your support, she wouldn't have gained the courage to move forward.

We are extremely proud to be a part of Evolved Publishing and couldn't imagine being anywhere else. The team is wonderful, helpful, and talented.

On that note, we'd like to thank our editor, Lane Diamond, for wearing so many hats within Evolved and doing such a fantastic job of it. We feel truly blessed to have such a wonderful editor. Thank you for your patience, wisdom, and consideration.

Through Evolved, we've also had the opportunity to work with Cindy Fan, Briana Hertzog, and Dale Pease, who've been absolutely wonderful during the design process for cover art and interior elements. We couldn't be more honored to work with you three on this project and appreciate the time, effort, and suggestions made to the final product.

Last but not least, thank you to everyone who has considered reading our book series. We look forward to embarking on this journey with our readers and followers. It's going to be a long haul, but we hope you enjoy it.

ABOUT THE AUTHORS

For as long as we can remember, we have been either plagued or blessed with dreams of the vast universe we call Euphoria. The fascination and devotion we share for these dreams, and all the people inside them, has driven our artistic visions for decades.

We have studied photography, linguistics, graphic art, video editing, traditional art, and literature, all with the intent of sharing this massive story and vision. Though many obstacles may lie ahead, we look forward to embarking on this journey with whomever may find a vested interest in our work.

For more, please visit Isu Yin & Fae Yang online at:
Author Website: www.GrimsTruth.com
Publisher Website: www.EvolvedPub.com
Goodreads: Fae Yang
Twitter: @DollsOfGrim
Facebook: www.facebook.com/DollsOfGrim/
Instagram: GrimsTruth

MORE FROM
EVOLVED PUBLISHING

We offer great books across multiple genres, featuring high-quality editing (which we believe is second-to-none) and fantastic covers.

As a hybrid small press, your support as loyal readers is so important to us, and we have strived, with tireless dedication and sheer determination, to deliver on the promise of our motto:

QUALITY IS PRIORITY #1!

Please check out all of our great books,
which you can find at this link:

www.EvolvedPub.com/Catalog/

Thank you!

CPSIA information can be obtained
at www.ICGtesting.com
Printed in the USA
BVHW042334100522
636631BV00007BA/348